THE
LAST
DAYS
OF JOY

ANNE TIERNAN

REVIEW

First published in Great Britain in 2023 by Headline Review
An imprint of HEADLINE PUBLISHING GROUP

This paperback edition published in 2024 by Headline Review

1

Cataloguing in Publication Data is available from the British Library

ISBN 978 1 4722 9963 5

Typeset in 10.57/16.77pt Sabon LT Pro by Jouve (UK), Milton Keynes

Printed and bound in Great Britain by Clays Ltd, Elcograf S.p.A.

MIX
Paper | Supporting
responsible forestry
FSC® C104740

HEADLINE PUBLISHING GROUP
An Hachette UK Company
Carmelite House
50 Victoria Embankment
London EC4Y 0DZ

www.headline.co.uk
www.hachette.co.uk

'Moving, funny, sharp, and beautifully written . . . Absolutely stunning . . . I laughed and cried my way through and can't wait to read the next Anne Tiernan'
Andrea Mara

'Smart and highly perceptive, this is a writer who is not afraid to tell it as it is. *The Last Days of Joy* is a brave and profoundly honest book, written with dark humour'
Kathleen MacMahon

'Ate this book up. A really engaging, raw, page turner of a novel about family, dysfunction and how the past always catches up with you'
Sinéad Moriarty

'You will fall in love with every one of the Tobin family'
Edel Coffey

'Authentic, deeply moving and full of hope, this book broke my heart a little'
Jacqueline Bublitz

'Moving between the past and the present with a storyteller's natural instinct for when to reveal, and when to withhold, this is an honest, acutely perceptive exploration of the fractious bonds of family – the love that can hold us together, the secrets with the power to tear us apart'
Noelle McCarthy

'A page turner, portraying the madness and messiness of family life. This novel is full of humanity, its cast of characters all at the centre of tragedy, but coupled with Tiernan's deliciously dark humour and sharp observations on modern life – it works brilliantly. I loved it!'
Elaine Feeney

'With intelligence and depth, Anne Tiernan wraps the reader into the warp and weft of the Tobins' secrets, troubles, and joys. An absorbing novel, beautifully written'
Nuala O'Connor

For my siblings, Tom, Niamh and Brian

JOY

In the end it was the birds.

When I woke, I had a moment of forgetting, the sweet unknowing between my dreams and consciousness where I could be anyone. But reality – my own self – lurked just beyond awareness. Like something sinister scratching at the edges, demanding to be admitted, until the revelation, *Yes, there you are, Joy. The same person as yesterday.*

And today, the birds punctured the oblivion with such optimism, I knew I'd had enough. They sounded so welcoming of another day and I begrudged them this. What's worse, even after thirty years here I couldn't tell you the names of the birds I hear. Daddy would be disappointed. Daddy with his love for nature detailed in the battered green notebook that held all the secrets of the universe. *They know enough who know how to learn, Joy,* he used to say. Well, I'm sorry Daddy, somewhere along the way I've grown incurious. *I am every dead thing.*

I know well though the call of the cooing wood pigeon, that soundtrack of hazy Irish summer mornings as a girl. There was a melancholic edge to its song and a stillness to the mornings then. *Soft day, thank God.* The New Zealand light is brash; it intensifies beauty, but it also highlights darkness. It struck me then, in a removed kind of a way, that I would never again hear the wood pigeon. Or see a crow. There's a creature I never thought I'd miss. Not until about a year after I'd moved here and noticed its absence. I could live in this place for another thirty years and still be making comparisons. It's the diaspora's lot: a foot in each place forever. Of two homes, and yet none. I worry I've caused that dichotomy in the children too, uprooting them so young. Motherhood is all second guessing and guilt.

Now, almost midnight, sitting at the kitchen table, I feel a grainy wetness across my hand. Donne. He looks up at me, exposing his grey muzzle and eyes milky with cataracts and it occurs to me, for all the planning of the last few weeks, I haven't thought this through. Donne, like all his breed, is a slave to his appetite and the temptation of a meal might be too hard for him to resist. I imagine the lurid tabloid story: 'Granny Eaten by Own Labrador!' I find this macabre headline almost funny, though I'm not sure if I can trust my emotions. So, although he won't like it, I lead him outside to his kennel and tie him up.

'There you go, old fella, I'm doing you a favour. You'll make a more appealing pet this way.' I cuddle his bearish head and hear a little whimper. I don't know if it's coming from him or me.

Going inside again, I check the note I taped on the back door for Frances, who comes every Saturday morning like clockwork.

Such a good girl. She's been my rock, but I never deserved her. Or any of them.

Franny, please, <u>please</u> don't come in. It'll be an awful mess and we all know how much you hate a mess! Just call 111 and ask for the police. I hope you all understand. I have felt only between lives forever anyway. Love Mum x

It is brief, but as I wrote it I realised there was too much to say and no earthly way of saying it. I hope what I'm about to do will convey an apology, a willingness to do penance.

I sit at the table and pick up the gun. I have taken it from its hiding place, my little train case under the bed, and handled it like this every day since it arrived. Holding it has given me unexpected comfort. I never imagined I would hold a gun, let alone enjoy doing so, but there you go, life has the capacity to surprise to the end. I've come to think of it less as a weapon and more as a switch, capable of turning off the pain. Quick and certain.

It is a beauty though, with its silver barrel and lacquered brown handle, like something you'd see in an old western. Even the name of it is like something from the Wild West, SMITH & WESSON engraved on the side. I think Daddy, for all his gentleness, would have appreciated it. I lift it to my face, inhale the resiny odour and am immediately transported to a well-worn memory. The two of us in the old cinema in Rathmines, watching a John Wayne film, *The Searchers,* with that lovely Natalie Wood. I was a slip of a thing and mainly interested in the paper bag of lemon bonbons and bullseyes on my lap. A whole quarter to myself! My arid 67-year-old mouth fizzes at the thought of them. I'm not sure if I was ever a happy child but the memory of watching that film is wrapped in a feeling as close to happiness as I can imagine. I think of Livvy, and hope she'll carry a warm memory or two of watching films with her gran. That's as much as you can wish for after you're gone; that you're a fond fleeting thought for someone every now and then.

I think it will be okay to pour myself a small vodka from the bottle perched on the sideboard; just enough to calm the shake in my hand but not enough that there is any doubt or gossip. Not like *that* time . . . the little boy . . . I take six bullets from the box stashed in the drawer and load the gun just as I have practised over the last few days. I watched YouTube videos to learn how to do it. You can learn anything from the internet these days. The children might be a bit impressed by that.

Careful to keep the gun pointed away from me and my finger off the trigger, I move over to the kitchen chair that I have placed away from the walls and on top of the old groundsheet Conor left behind after he painted the sitting room. How I loved having him all to myself then. I never told him that though. I'd make excuses to skulk around the room, taking in the wonder of him, his broad shoulders and back hunched over as he coated the skirting, his dark hair curling on his tanned neck. And me like a harpy, asking him how much longer he'd be, mithering him to get a move on as I needed the room back, when the truth was I could have watched him forever. I just wanted to be near him but didn't know how to do it in any way that felt natural. I envy the easy, generous way other mothers love. Mine always seems to express itself wrongly, as though it gets lost in translation, tainted on the way out by faulty wiring. I often think the worst part of me is motherhood.

Enough. I place the gun to my head and close my eyes, and even now that damned day comes unbidden again. Always, always. Like a film I've watched dozens of times and can't turn off, the scenes play out with a grim reliability. First, the before moments, abscessed on my brain, winding me with their clarity. I am driving my blue Hillman Hunter to pick Conor and Frances up from school because it's raining, and little Frances hates getting wet. Sinead is a toddler sitting in the back. I am singing to Sinead. *Dance for your daddy my little lassie.* She is clapping and laughing. Such a delightful baby! She loves the bit about the fishy on the dishy and lisps along.

Go back, Joy, go back, they'll be grand, doesn't Franny love to walk home with her big brother? He minds her, always has her hand. Sure a drop of rain never killed anyone.

But the scene plays on. And we are turning into the road leading to the school. And all roads lead here, to this moment. No, a drop of rain never killed anyone. But I did.

Enough now.

FRANCES

Frances is having a moment, a familiar one. That split second when she realises, with a grim acceptance, that she is about to be involved in something unpleasant. In these moments time has a way of expanding, making it possible to have several conflicting thoughts running concurrently. It had happened often as a child turning in to the cul-de-sac where she lived, holding her breath, squeezing her eyes shut then opening them as she exhaled forcefully and noted the clues the exterior of their little weatherboard house gave her as to their mother's condition that day.

The catalyst for this particular moment is waking to the sound of her phone ringing sometime in the wee hours of a Saturday morning in early February. A moment between seeing the caller ID and ending the 'Ave Satani' ringtone (the theme tune from *The Omen* – Harry's little joke) by choosing Accept. Her thoughts encompass every emotion from *I must change that stupid ringtone* to *Would it really be so awful if she did die?*

Compounding her inner tumult is a gnawing sense of shame at what precisely the ringing has woken her up *from*. She has been reluctantly ejected from an erotic dream involving Andy, an old boyfriend with whom she has recently reconnected on Facebook. The dream was so graphic. Almost disturbing in its lucidity. She hadn't even realised that she knew such degradations existed. It's as though her subconscious has its own Pornhub subscription. Dreams involving inappropriate sex with inappropriate partners have become more frequent. This is odd, given her libido has never been so low.

This is the punishment, she thinks. And wonders, given her very secular upbringing, if Catholic guilt is held in some kind of recessive gene.

'What's up, Mum?'

She says it quietly, though she need not worry about waking Harry. Years of feigning sleep through their daughter's frequent night waking has meant that he has acquired an almost supernatural ability to slumber through any manner of things – earthquakes, tsunami sirens, loudly mating cats, crazy mothers. Livvy is now fourteen so the night waking has long since ceased to be an issue, but Harry's superpower continues. It infuriates and amazes Frances in equal measure. Glancing at his slack, pillow-distorted features, she wonders why children are more beautiful when they sleep and adults uglier, and thinks maybe she doesn't feel too guilty about her dream after all.

In any event, a midnight phone call is not such an unusual occurrence as to require any special attention from Harry.

He had also slept through a fifteen-minute vodka-laden call two weeks ago, the purpose of which Frances couldn't fathom and during which Joy had threatened (amongst other things) to leave Frances's inheritance to a charity for exploited Sherpas, and, inexplicably, to tell Harry about some minor teenage transgression from almost thirty years prior. When this failed to move her elder daughter, she switched to a different strategy of proclaiming regret at being a terrible parent. Flashes of drunken self-awareness with promises of therapy and AA meetings. Then the tears. The self-pity was always the hardest to stomach. It was Frances's cue to end the call.

'Please tell me what I've done to deserve such coldness, Franny?' Joy had wept. Frances imagined her in some kind of hokey melodrama from the 1950s, a black-and-white with Bette Davis or Joan Crawford.

'Frankly, we'd be here till next week. Good night, Mother.' And she lay awake for hours, furious at the world. Particularly at her mother, who, she speculated, would fall immediately into a deep sleep and not make mention of the call again, either because it was lost in the vodka-soaked recesses of her mind or because of her enormous capacity for self-denial. Frances couldn't decide which was worse. When she'd complained, bleary-eyed, the next morning, Harry suggested turning her phone off at night. Frances protested that she needed it as an alarm clock. Harry suggested getting an old-fashioned radio alarm. Frances sighed and wished Harry would just commiserate with her on her dreadful luck in parentage rather than try to fix the immediate and much more trivial issue.

Now there is a nervous clearing of throat on the other end.

'No, Frances dear, it's Sue Preston. I've got some terrible news . . . Have you got someone there with you?'

Harry makes a snuffling sound, then shifts position but continues to sleep blissfully.

Frances looks at him darkly. 'Sort of.'

She tries hard to follow the convoluted narrative, but between Sue's discomfort at being the bearer of bad news and her own confusion at hearing her mother's elderly neighbour in the middle of the night, much is lost. But the general gist involves Sue's insomnia ('a terrible affliction of old age'), her mother's distressed dog ('Joy would never let Donne suffer'), an inappropriately lit-up house ('Power bills are exorbitant these days, you know'), a gunshot ('an unmistakeable sound'), and a spare key under a planter ('Rocket, lock it. That's how I remember').

The denouement is the discovery of Joy on the kitchen floor with a large wound to her head ('but alive dear, somehow alive').

It seems Sue's instincts as a former nurse had kicked in and her quick ministrations to Joy kept her alive till the ambulance arrived. This has just departed, and Sue is still in the house waiting for the police to arrive. She thought it better to ring Frances herself rather than have them break the news. 'You're first on her list by the phone, you know!' Said as though this is something Frances should take comfort from.

After hanging up, Frances sits in bed, surprised by the involuntary eruption of shaking over her entire body. So, this is it.

She's really done it. Well, almost. Frances realises that shocked as she is, there's a kind of inevitability to this moment. It's as though she's been waiting for it her whole life.

She knows there is much to do. Husband to wake, siblings to corral, arrangements to be made. But for now she feels incapable of any of it.

CONOR

Jet lag always gives Conor a seedy feeling, akin to a hangover. He doesn't drink enough to ever be hungover, so he thinks that maybe it's his body compensating, finding another method to flagellate. It seems to him that much of the ageing process involves novel ways for his physiology to betray him. He thinks he might easily descend into some nihilistic pit were it not for the partially sheet-covered figure beside him.

Lara. Everything about her soothes him. Her looks: tonal, almost monochromatic, with her brown hair, tanned skin and ochre eyes. And her easy temperament. Open, inquisitive, *yielding.* Conor has a vague feeling that admiring this in a woman borders on misogyny. Certainly, his mother and sisters would deride him for it. Lord knows he grew up surrounded by bolshie women. But Jesus, Lara is just *happy.* The jaded indifference that afflicts so many of his friends is absent. Maybe it's her youth. Or simply that she didn't grow up in an environment where you were always expecting bad things to happen.

He picks up his phone. Already a slew of new emails needing attention in the few hours since arriving back in Auckland from London. *Two* voice messages from Frances. His sister is the only person he knows who still leaves them. Who has the time to listen? Even his mother sends texts. But Franny hates communicating via any method that allows for ambiguity. And even when she does send a text, it is laborious, in grammatically perfect long hand. He will call her later.

Right now, he needs to capitalise on a meeting with a billionaire Kiwi expat whom he is sure is close to signing up. Conor is proud of his baby. He founded his not-for-profit TheOneForAll – a sort of one-stop shop for donating money – five years ago, at just the right moment. He had sensed a shift in zeitgeist. The affluent feeling that had to give back or at least be *seen* to be giving back. How else could they justify their wealth when so many had so little? Every self-respecting billionaire has a side hustle in philanthropy these days. Charity is big business. And young people no longer blindly hero-worship sportspeople, musicians or, God help us, influencers, unless they are *philanthropic* sportspeople, musicians or, God help us, influencers.

He's witnessed a kind of puritanism developing amongst today's youth. Now it's all about the environment, the poor, the sick, the disenfranchised. The latest endangered species (but only if it is a photogenic one). Baby Boomers were happy for their rock idols to be a bit badass and their film stars to be impossibly aloof and glamorous. Gen X would have admired their favourite stars for merely highlighting social injustice. Or releasing a single or organising a concert for famine victims. However, Conor has recognised that this new generation needs them to put their money where their mouths are. Everyone needs to have a cause. Everyone needs to get political – especially when making an acceptance speech for yet another incestuous and vacuous showbiz award. And if you can't live up to the high moral standards expected, then expect to be cancelled.

Convincing the rich to donate 1 per cent of their earnings – gross or net, Conor isn't too pedantic; there could be tax benefits for both depending on the jurisdiction – to deserving charities is getting easier. Donors don't have to think for themselves about who to donate to but still feel the smug glow of beneficence. These days, giving has become confusing. There are far too many charities, often with overlapping mission statements, not to mention all the Give-a-Little and GoFundMe causes. TheOneForAll simplifies things for a generation with too many choices.

And on a personal level, his abandonment of an unfulfilling fifteen-year corporate law career in favour of philanthropy has been revelatory. He was born for this. He only entered Law in the first place because that's what you did back in the nineties if you were academically gifted and didn't want to be a doctor. Sometimes it seems to Conor that his talents are better suited to a generation later than his own. A generation that doesn't feel bound to formal qualifications and lifelong careers. A generation that values innovation and creative thinking over a steady pensionable job with statutory sick leave. Where good looks and a witty and canny handle on social media can earn you more than years of study. Law, with its strict adherence to exactness, had been strangulating. And at first the world of philanthropy set him free. But lately he's felt a shift, as though it's not quite enough anymore. A nagging feeling that a glittering career, no matter in what industry, can't fill him up the way it once did. Maybe it's why the sleeping figure in the bed beside him has come to mean so much.

Now, he must choose a photo to upload that will appeal to the charity's many followers and the ego of his ex-pat billionaire, Cam. He has already received his permission to acknowledge the meeting. Such is TheOneForAll's reach, even a hint of an association with it has the power to increase interest in a company or a person. And if donating to a charity generates more exposure and thus more revenue, it's a win-win for everyone involved. Donating money is just another form of self-promotion.

He decides on a shot taken by his PA of the two of them sitting on a bench in Hyde Park, wrapped up in puffer jackets and beanies against the London winter. There is a clearly visible brown paper bag to the side, carrying the logo of one of Cam's sustainable, organic, zero-waste and completely recyclable food outlets. Leaning against the back of the bench are a couple of Santander Cycles. The two men look deep in conversation and oblivious to the camera. They are leaning forward with their upper torsos turned towards each other, faces close. Conor's hand is resting on Cam's shoulder. He thinks for a moment and then captions it. *How **we** do business lunch.*

Now for the heart wrencher. He uploads another shot, taken by an intern, at the specialist children's hospital in Auckland they donate funds to. It's of a little girl, bald, sitting in a hospital bed, holding her Beads of Courage necklace in one hand and giving a thumbs up to the camera with the other. Nothing can trump a sick child for generating compassion. And likes. He captions the photo *Aroha (Love), from Katie.*

There is a loud yawn from the bed.

'What god-awful hour is it?'

'Hey babe, five a.m., sorry if I woke you.'

'Shit, do you ever sleep?' Lara moves to the end of the bed to sit beside him. 'What are you doing?' She burrows in against his shoulder.

He shows her what he has uploaded.

'Nice. The first one will appeal to your gay hipster donors. Throw a kitten in and you'll have nailed your basic bitch base too.'

'Basic bitch?'

'You know the type. Likes scented candles and Starbucks frappuccinos. Has inspirational art around the house proclaiming Live! Laugh! Love! Favourite movie is *Love Actually.*'

Conor likes *Love Actually*, actually, and makes a mental note to never mention this fact to her. 'Ah, I see . . . into which one though?'

She cocks her head to the side. 'Hmmm . . . it'd work equally well in both.'

'You're terrible, Muriel.' He throws away the phone and wrestles her back on to the pillows.

'Muriel? Is that an ex?'

'*Muriel's Wedding*?'

'What?'

'Never mind. Archaic film reference. I forget sometimes you were only born in the nineties.' Immediately he regrets referring to their age difference.

The phone starts to ring. Conor looks at it, grimaces, but ignores it.

'Aren't you going to answer that?'

'It's just my sister with some drama involving Mum. Frances only ever rings to offload about her latest drunken shenanigans. I've too much on to get involved now.'

Lara reaches out from under him, picks up his phone and presses Accept. She hands it to him. 'Speak,' she mouths.

Conor rolls his eyes at her but sits up and puts the phone to his ear. Lara stays lying down and watches his naked back as he listens to his sister. As the one-sided conversation progresses it seems to Lara as though he is shrinking. His spine compresses and his broad shoulders curve inwards. He says nothing, starts to shake. She realises, with a voyeuristic thrill, that the great Conor Tobin, celebrity charity boss, media darling, New Zealand's Most Eligible Bachelor 2018, is sobbing like a baby.

SINEAD

Despite it being only five degrees outside and not much more in the draughty studio above a shoe shop on Dublin's Wicklow Street, Sinead gets up to turn off the radiator that suddenly feels as though it is directing its hellish heat solely at her. She wants to open the sash window too, but from previous experience knows that its age and size require a greater energy than she could possibly muster.

Also, the seven participants in her express yoga class are already giving her funny looks.

'Won't take us long to warm up!' she says.

She sees a regular attendee, Carina, side-eye her best friend Joanne. Or perhaps it is Joanne side-eyeing Carina. She finds it hard to differentiate between the two, with their asymmetric blonde bobs and matchy-matchy lululemon gear. Their frequent asides to each other during practice are irritating and disruptive.

And Sinead knows the type well. The type who replaced the biscuits in your lunch box with a note saying, *We're staging an intervention Sinead, it's for your own good!* Or the type who left a Valentine's card in your bag from the most popular boy in the class and cackled hysterically when you read it, flushing, allowing yourself to believe, for just the briefest of moments, that it was genuine.

'Let's start in Sukhasana. Now . . . I want you to earth yourself to the ground . . . then align your head over your heart . . . and your heart over your centre of gravity. Close your eyes and start to focus your awareness inwards on this alignment. Now . . . start to deepen your breath.'

Sinead feels breathless just saying this. Her own awareness is focussed solely on her lungs, which feel as though they are about to combust with each exaggerated inhalation. She goes to take a swig from her water bottle and is crushed to find it empty. She can't remember drinking any of it. Sweet Jesus, she'd sell her soul for a drop. Perhaps taking *two* of those little yellow pills this morning wasn't such a good move. But the results *are* astounding. Over half a stone in one week with no deprivation at all. She's been able to eat as much as she likes. Unlike speed, which deadened her appetite and left her with an aching jaw, or MDMA, where the horrible comedown negated all the previous euphoria, these little golden wonders magically burn the fat away without any of the paranoia and self-loathing. Well, no more than usual, anyway. She hadn't questioned Brad – the shredded Aussie powerlifter at her gym – too intensely about the chemistry involved. He emphasised that it was a short-term thing though. She thinks with results like this she could handle a week every couple of months. But maybe next time she wouldn't teach any yoga.

'I want you to let go. Let go of the outside world and all its stresses. Let go of your own resentments and frustrations. Embrace the here and now. Embrace yourself. Love yourself. Lose yourself . . .' Eminem's song starts in her mind. She tries to refocus, shakes her head to dislodge the song, and a bead of sweat falls from the end of her nose to the wooden floor. She hopes Carina/Joanne haven't seen it. Or the spreading stains under her arms. Perhaps she can manipulate the poses so she can guide an entire class without raising her arms above her head.

And just like that she is thirteen again, in Tauranga High School, puce and sticky after PE, trying to get changed back into her uniform without exposing any of her body.

What's red and white and round all over? Sinead after a game of netball!

Sinead jokes became quite the craze for that first year in high school. She had been burdened not only with the fat gene, but also with a moniker that made her an anomaly in a New Zealand school full of Kims, Kates, Beccas and Nickis. She had been hopeful that a certain Irish ingenue with the same name and a hugely popular international ballad in 1990 would go some way towards making her appear a bit cooler. Instead, that shaven-headed waif only served to throw Sinead's lumpen frizzy-haired appearance into sharp relief.

She wonders if part of the reason she moved back to Ireland in her twenties was to escape the tyranny of her name. Here she can embrace it fully, call herself Tóibín as well, which sounds much more literary than plain old Tobin.

'I want you to tune in to your breath and take note of any sensations you are feeling.' She lets out a long breath herself. A sulphurous odour attacks her nostrils. Jesus, is that smell coming from her? Citrus yellow urine she could handle, but stinking shit breath too?

The latest cartilage piercing in her ear is pulsing hard. When she'd gone into the shop on Parliament Street last week, she'd asked the multi-pierced, heavily tattooed young woman working there which part of the ear was the most painful to pierce. The woman pointed to a spike in her own ear that seemed to skewer a couple of improbable places at once and said, 'This. The Snug.'

That was a misnomer if ever she'd heard one. It looked as far from *snug* as she could imagine. But Sinead said anyway, 'Okay, hit me.'

The young woman simply shrugged, bored, as though used to masochistic women requesting torture. Now though, with each outrageous throb, Sinead wishes she'd been attended to by someone a teeny bit more judgemental.

She catches Carina/Joanne eyeing each other again. What is she doing with her life? Teaching yoga to the kind of women who bullied her in school. She needs to concentrate on her interrupted writing career – if one could call ten years an interruption. More an abruption. For a few months in her late twenties she was quite the young sensation. (Sensations are only ever young.) Her book, *Motherload*, a four-hundred-page barely disguised autobiography, was published to critical acclaim in Ireland and the UK. 'A perfect balance of truth and beauty.' 'Brave, raw, honest, vital.' 'A heart-breaking exploration of alcoholism and childhood trauma', and so on. It made several award shortlists and there had even been talk of an arthouse-type film. Sales were more modest than the reviews, however, some readers finding the litany of pain quite relentless. (The Goodreads comments went along the lines of 'Makes *Angela's Ashes* read like a light-hearted comedy.') With the world in recession, people were looking for escapism rather than a misery memoir. However, it was still deemed a literary success, underwhelming sales notwithstanding. The manuscript had originally been auctioned amongst six interested houses. Sinead had been swayed by the one that offered the biggest advance – a well-publicised six-figure sum – but more importantly in her mind, a two-book deal, which gave her a sense of validation.

And that was her first mistake. She wrote the first one without the weight of expectation, never imagining she'd finish it, let alone find a publisher. But the second book weighed heavily before she'd set down a word. It was something before it was anything. It existed – pre-existence – as a clause in a contract; a clause with a roman numeral and a date (now overdue by about eight years) and a word count (90,000–100,000). Knowing that people would read it gagged her. She became utterly self-conscious of every word. Whereas the first book fell out of her because it felt private, the second became dammed within her because she knew it would be public. What would she even write about? She had mined her own life so thoroughly for the first that she felt she had nothing left to say. And she was discovering she did not have enough of an imagination to write a complete fiction, to imagine someone else's life, get inside their head. Her own could be so overwhelming. Although her first agent had deserted her along the way, and a second, who had stuck around for a couple of years before realising she was a lost cause, her publisher, Maggie remained loyal. Though this was probably borne out of necessity, given she knew the large advance had been squandered a long time ago and that cancelling the contract would not recoup any of the money. Maggie still professed to believe that a second book would eventuate. But Sinead suspected Maggie knew deep down that this was the greatest fiction of all.

'Eh . . . Sinead?'

She feels disoriented, then realises she is bent forward with her forehead resting on the cool wooden floor. How long has she been like this?

'Are you all right? It's just that we haven't, like, moved out of our Sukhasana yet. And it's been, like, ages. It *is* meant to be an express class, isn't it?' Carina/Joanne says.

She somehow manages to grind out the rest of the class. She can't afford to lose this job too. She had been humiliatingly ousted from her position at the iconic four-level bookshop on Dawson Street. They'd been delighted to hire her at first; usually their staff tended to be aspiring writers. To employ a writer with a well-regarded novel already published had felt like quite the coup. However, things soured when her manager walked in on Sinead in a storeroom one Saturday morning, where she sat behind a stack of boxes with a newly published novel by a mercurial debutante in one hand, the other down the front of her jeans.

In fairness, she was very hungover. And these millennial writers wrote sex scenes in such coolly observed yet titillating detail.

When everyone has gone, and after placing her face under the cold tap in the bathroom for several minutes, she packs up her things. She sees a missed call on her phone from Frances. Conversations with her sister have the effect of making her feel guilty for leaving her in New Zealand to cope with their mother. Conor is hopeless in this regard. (Sons usually are.) Or worse, like a feckless loser with nothing to show for her forty years on the planet apart from a briefly celebrated book and a permanent credit card debt. Frances, her older sister, with her willowy frame and pretty name. Frances with her big spotless house and its alphabetically ordered quinoa- and chickpea-filled pantry, artfully placed cashmere throws and Diptyque candles. Frances with her obliging, wine-pouring husband and bright, beautiful, swim champion daughter. Frances with her committees and dinner parties and coffees with the girls after high-intensity spin class. Frances with her self-control and her certainty in the authenticity of her ordered life.

She forces herself to listen to the message.

And just like that, Sinead feels cold.

JOY

I'm back now in the fields behind the two-up two-down terraced house in Rathfarnham where I grew up. I feel like I'm weightless. Pouring and flailing down the steep slope in the middle of the meadow, my legs feeling disconnected from my body, like they belong to someone else entirely. It's my favourite game. You have to close your eyes as you run so you don't see the insects you dislodge from the long grass that is thick with dandelions and daisies and blue speedwell, and you don't know exactly when the dip is coming up. King Kong's Belly, we call this dip. If you run fast enough you can easily get back up the other side. But too fast, you'll fall flat on your face.

(. . . I can hear strange birds. An odd clacking sound. A bit like a wren. It takes on a rhythm. Whoosh-click. Whoosh-click. But I realise now it's not a bird's call at all, not the clucking of the secretive wren. Too mechanical, man-made, for that. And there's a beeping now too, layered on top of it . . .)

The best part is that first step down the dip, because it's always such a surprise that it's there, even though you've done it a thousand times before. I'm laughing and laughing and this time I've judged it right and I won't fall. I open my eyes when I reach the bottom to see a little boy about my age standing at the top on the other side. And it stops me dead. He looks cross, like he doesn't want me to go up there. He's holding out his arm and saying No. And I'm not sure why he is cross with me, but I think he has something to do with a car and a school. So, I close my eyes again.

(. . . And now there are voices. I try to ask who's speaking but there's something hard and unyielding in my throat . . .)

I hear Mother calling me inside. She's using her serious voice and telling me how dangerous it is. That I will die. I am too old, too weak. But that's silly. I'm only seven. I know I'm seven because it's my birthday today and last night I sat on Daddy's knee and he told me to say goodbye to six. That I would never ever be six again. That made me a tiny bit sad, even though I was excited about being seven too. And then we both pretend-cried at saying goodbye to six. And this made Mother angry for some reason and she told us to stop playing silly games.

Come in now Joy, let's play a game, Mother is calling. And I go to her and I'm so happy because Mother never wants to play with me. I ask her if we can play Conkers because I love that even though she says it's unladylike. But she says no, it's a game called Vice Versa. I've never heard of it, but she says it's very simple. I just have to pretend to be her, and she will pretend to be me. This sounds so thrilling and I give a clap.

And it's so much fun at first because Mother starts doing cartwheels shouting, Look at me, I'm Joy, look at me! And I can't quite believe Mother is doing cartwheels and I think I might burst with excitement. And now I pretend to be her and I take one of her Player's and pretend to smoke it and say, I need to lie down I have a headache.

But I think I shouldn't have said that because now Mother is angry and she pulls the cigarette from my mouth and puts her face close to mine and says in a lispy, peevish voice, Look at me, Daddy, look at me, I'm so special and you love me the best. Not silly Mummy.

Suddenly the game stops being fun and Mother sends me to my room. And I'm locked in here listening to the strange clacking beeping bird and lots of voices outside the door, but I can't open my eyes to see who's talking even though I desperately want to. The voices are hushed but I think I can hear them saying that I deserve to be here.

I'm so scared and alone. I want to get out, but I know I shouldn't. I know I can't.

FRANCES

Almost twelve hours have passed since Sue's phone call and she is sitting by her mother's bed in the ICU. There is a partially pulled curtain, but apart from that the bed is in full view of the staff and other patients and their family members.

Frances feels conscious of her every move. The other visitors are holding their loved ones' hands or stroking their faces. Talking to them in hushed, comforting tones. Does it look odd that she is not touching her mother? But Joy disliked physical contact anyway. An awkward half-hug with a pat on the back signifying her desire for the embrace to end was as much as you could hope for.

The doctors and nurses here talk constantly to the patients even though most of them appear deeply unconscious. 'I'm just going to roll you over on your side now, Mr Blake.' 'Time for your wash, Mrs Tamahori.' All spoken in upbeat tones. Frances takes her mother's hand in hers, thinks how little they touched ordinarily. She hasn't looked at Joy's hand in a long time. Why would she? It surprises her how similar her own is. Bloated veins yet scrawny at the same time. Sun-scarred witch's hands. Another defilement of age.

Harry has just left to pick up Donne then go home to Livvy. Frances would have preferred to put her mother's labrador in a kennel. She doesn't like to admit that she is not a dog person. Give her a self-centred, self-sufficient cat any day. But admitting your aversion to dogs – that you don't want to share your nice clean human home with a smelly, moulting, genitalia-licking, arse-sniffing wolf descendent – is a bit like saying you hate David Attenborough or think yoga is overrated. It marks you out as a not terribly enlightened person. Mean-spirited, even. But her mother adores that big oaf of a dog, and it might be somewhat of a salve for Livvy, who has always railed against the injustice of not being allowed her own.

They had discussed whether or not Harry should bring Livvy back to the hospital. He felt he should, given her fondness for her grandmother. (Something no-one else can quite fathom. Joy certainly holds her in much higher regard than her own children. 'Livvy is my reward for not murdering you, Frances,' Joy would joke. A truth told in jest, Frances suspects.) Frances had argued that was precisely why they shouldn't bring her. The woman in the bed holds only a vague resemblance to her mother anyway. Part of her skull was removed during surgery, her eyes are swollen shut, her mouth lolling open. A series of tubes and lines run from various orifices and veins, connected to bags of liquid or clicking, beeping machines.

'Let her remember her the way she was,' Frances said.

'Just fucked up on the inside, then,' Harry replied.

This almost made her laugh. They agreed to bring Livvy in tomorrow. Should Joy survive the night.

Harry had been great though. He asked all the right questions and responded intelligently to the answers. Frances, on the other hand, felt like a half-wit enveloped in a thick fog of ignorance as the various doctors and surgeons spoke to them. How are you supposed to take this kind of information in? Or make decisions?

She managed to glean this fact though: things are bleak. Due to the catastrophic injuries – frankly it is a miracle she didn't die straight away – her mother's death is likely imminent. Should she manage to survive these initial injuries, she will probably die from an infection. Best-case scenario (for whom, though?) she will spend the rest of her days in a vegetative state.

The dedicated nurse assigned to her mother, Bridget, is back. She has been hovering quietly and efficiently now for hours. She checks the various appendages and machines and writes something down on a chart at the end of the bed. There is an aura of great calm about her. It amazes Frances that you could work somewhere like this, surrounded by disease and trauma and death, and appear so unfazed by it all.

'You can talk to her if you like,' Bridget says.

'Is there any point?'

'I think there is some level of awareness, no matter what the doctors say. Sometimes they take a more clinical than holistic view. Anyway, it might be comforting. For you, that is.'

Frances doubts that. But she says, 'Okay, I'll try.' She hopes Bridget levitates off soon, so she won't have to actually do it. Thankfully she does – almost, Frances thinks, like an angel in baggy blue scrubs.

She hears a notification come through on her phone. Her heart glitches when she sees it's a message from Andy, her ex-boyfriend.

Hey there, in Tauranga next week for business, fancy a quick coffee? ☕

She'd been surprised a few weeks back to get a friend request from him. He is someone she hasn't thought much about since university. She'd finished with him and moved on quickly. Broke his heart a little, perhaps – something she has to admit gives her a guilty thrill, now that her heart-breaking days are behind her. But seeing his profile has stirred up feelings of nostalgia, even a little regret, though Frances isn't sure if that is for Andy or for her old self. He married the girl he started seeing after her, settled in Auckland, and, Frances also has to admit, has aged well. In that unfair way men do. They have private messaged each other on a few occasions, nothing too incriminating, maybe a slight *frisson* of flirtation. She had made the mistake of confessing the correspondence to her friend Lauren as they sat poolside watching their daughters' after-school swim squad training a few days ago. She received a message while they were talking.

Lauren had eyeballed her. 'Is Harry sexting you or something?' she asked.

'Don't be ridiculous. The only text messages we send each other are reminders to leave the bins out or to pick up some toilet paper from the supermarket.'

'Well, something's made you look all coy and blush like a schoolgirl.'

'It's nothing. Just a text from my old boyfriend, Andy.'

'Show me.' Lauren held her hand out.

'No!'

'Well then, I'm just going to assume the worst, that something is going on, spread vicious rumours, and it'll cause ructions within the highly cut-throat and judgemental Swim Mom community. Donna will be appalled. You know how those catty bitches work.'

'Yes, indeed I do,' said Frances, 'because you're one of them. Here, you'll see it's harmless.'

She handed her phone to Lauren, who read it out loud in a lascivious tone. 'Guess what song has just come on the radio? Made me think of you. Boy with crown on his head emoji. Winking face emoji.' Lauren raised her eyebrows. 'Well, what song is he talking about?'

'Oh, I think he just means a Prince song we both used to like.'

'*Just* a Prince song? Oh my God, he so wants to fuck you.'

'Jesus, Lauren!' she hissed, then looked around to make sure no-one had overheard. Lauren had no filter. This could be both exhilarating and mortifying. Especially in the echoey and claustrophobic environs of an aquatic centre.

'You don't remind someone of a song that has special meaning for both of you unless you want to fuck them again. You *especially* don't mention a song by that absolute horndog Prince, who would make the alphabet song sound obscene.'

Frances grabbed her phone back. 'Your mind is in the gutter, Lauren. I'm sorry I told you now. I would never cheat on Harry.'

'Hmm. No, you're too straight to have a physical affair. But you're definitely the type to have an emotional one. At the very least it's a micro-cheat.'

'You're just making up words now.'

'Would you show that message to Harry?'

When Frances hesitated, Lauren said triumphantly, 'See? There you go. A micro-cheat!'

'Ridiculous.'

'Do you want to know what surprises me the most, though?'

'Not really, no.'

'That you'd contemplate sex with a man who uses emojis so freely.'

'Why? Not that I am, obviously.'

'It's deeply unsexy.'

'And you're deeply annoying, Lauren.'

Now, Frances rereads the message about coffee. The tone is so casual, without preamble or justification. Presumptuous. As though suggesting meeting up with an ex you haven't seen in twenty years is the most unremarkable thing in the world. You wouldn't send a text like that if you had an ulterior motive, would you? Maybe she's overthinking this. Maybe it's just coffee. Maybe she's the only one thinking about sex. Having X-rated dreams. She puts her phone away and closes her eyes, concentrates on the whoosh-click of the ventilator. Its rhythm is soothing.

'Hey, sis.'

She opens her eyes to see Conor. She stands, and he grabs her in a tight embrace that almost takes her breath away.

He has always done that. He has always been needy. She pats his back three times and frees herself.

Conor takes in his mother's appearance. 'Jesus, she's a mess. I spoke to a doctor on the way through. It's not looking too good.' Conor's face is grey, his normal high colouring drained completely. She wonders if she appears the same. 'Have you been with her all night?'

'Yes, since she came out of surgery.'

'Thanks.'

It seems to Frances such a strange thing to say. As though she's just been waiting here until he can take over. Instead of being the one who has looked after their mother for years.

'I can't quite take this in,' he says.

'I know, I can hardly bear to look at her,' Frances says. 'It's shocking. But also . . . kind of not . . .'

'Yeah, but a gun, Franny? It's so violent. I mean, what the hell? Who even has a gun? I had always thought that if she, you know, did it, it would be pills washed down with a litre of vodka. How did she even get one?'

'I don't know. The police have been asking too. They have to investigate this sort of thing, obviously. Apparently you can order these things from the internet these days.' She lowers her voice. 'Like, you know, the dark web and such.'

Conor holds up his hands theatrically, a look of incredulity on his face. Frances thinks he should have pursued an acting career. He certainly enjoys the limelight.

'The woman couldn't pay a bill online and you think she was able to negotiate the dark web to procure a gun illegally?'

Frances wants to ask him how the fuck he would know anything about their mother's bill-paying habits – bills she could only afford to pay through her and Harry's generosity. Or how she managed her gardening, or her housework, or her grocery shopping or visiting her doctor. Or taking her smelly fucking dog to the fucking vet. But she politely says none of these things.

He continues. 'And how the hell can someone shoot themselves point blank in the head and not die? Only Mum could manage that.'

'Maybe she googled that on the dark web too.'

'Okay, Frances.' He says it sarcastically.

'Apparently 5 per cent of people don't die after being shot in the head. I read it on WebMD.' She adds pointedly, 'I've had a lot of time to kill.' When he doesn't say anything she carries on. 'And when Harry spoke to the neurologist she said something about the gun being pointed backwards from the front of her head. Makes it more survivable. Something to do with the bullet only passing through one hemisphere. Sue stopped a lot of the blood loss, too. I don't know. Harry can explain it better. I'm unable to make sense of much at the moment.'

'Had she been drinking?'

'They said there wasn't a lot of alcohol in her system. Which surprised me. Makes it worse, somehow, like even more deliberate. If that's possible. Jesus though, what a clusterfuck.'

Bridget appears again and Frances hopes she hasn't overheard her. Profanities seem to be dropping from her spontaneously. Like she's losing control of the language centre in her brain.

Conor sits down on the bed and touches the bit of his mother's cheek not obscured by the spaghetti junction of tubes and tape. Frances thinks she has seen this tender pose before, maybe on his Instagram feed, ministering to some sick child or commiserating with some bereaved mother.

'I've organised Sinead to come over, booked her flight.' When he doesn't respond she adds, sulkily, 'Just in case, you know, you were wondering.'

'Sinead, sorry, of course. I hadn't thought. Good ... well done. When does she get here?'

'Tomorrow morning. I thought you could pick her up from the airport?'

'Sure,' he says absently, as though he has no idea of what he has even agreed to. He always makes her feel as though he has more important things on his mind than the logistics of family. As though things that preoccupy her mind and time are petty considerations.

'Great, brilliant.' She can't keep the irritated tone out of her voice but he doesn't seem to notice.

He knits his eyebrows together. 'Do you have any good memories of Mum?' he says, apropos of nothing.

Frances is surprised at the question. 'I mean, mostly when I think about her, I think of a lack. An absence. Both physically and emotionally. But there are a couple of memories I cling to that are different.'

'Such as?'

'Well, one time back in Ireland, I was very little, maybe five or six? We had just learnt how to knit in school, and we had to make a woollen scarf in our own time as homework. I hated it; you know me, not a creative bone in my body. Anyway, I left the knitting in my schoolbag and when I got up the next morning she had finished the whole thing. I was so happy.' Frances smiles to herself. 'It was bright red,' she adds. Her smile fades when she sees Conor looking underwhelmed.

'Look, it's not exactly *The Waltons,* but it's something.'

'Sure.'

'And you know, she is good with Livvy. I guess I see a more maternal side to her when they're together. Like she finds it easier to be loving with her. Maybe because she's a bit removed? Not responsible for her.'

'So, I should've had a kid then, that would have helped?'

Frances eyes him sidelong. 'From your social media posts, it looks like you've adopted one already.'

'What do you mean?'

'The child with the long brown hair.'

'Lara? She's in her twenties!'

Frances raises her eyebrows. 'I see. So you're only twice her age, then.'

He sighs. 'Don't be such a dick, Franny.'

They sit in silence for some time. Frances can't tell how long. The ICU operates in an alternative time zone. Seconds are measured in the clacking rhythm of the ventilators and beeping of the heart monitor; minutes in the ministrations of Bridget or the nurse who later relieves her; hours by one of the doctors checking vital signs.

Conor is restless, continually checking his phone or peering through a gap in the venetian blinds of the window nearest their mother's bed. His head has always been elsewhere. The window overlooks the staff carpark. Frances had checked it out earlier, desperate to get some respite from the green-tinged hue of the ward that makes even the healthy look sick. Looking out, she had been overwhelmed with a desire to just be a person who worked here. A person who could leave when their shift finished, exchanging pleasantries with colleagues as they got into their cars. Then home to normal families with normal stresses such as having to cook dinner or yell at the kids to do their homework or tidy their rooms. Normal families whose matriarch didn't shoot herself in the head.

She used to get the same feeling of envy leaving school every day, as she walked slowly out the gates amidst the whirligig of children and schoolbags. Not knowing what she faced. Frances always held her breath as she turned the corner into their cul-de-sac, closed her eyes for just a second to delay looking at their little white weatherboard house. *Please let the milk be in, please let the milk be in.* Milk in and curtains open meant at least her mother had at some stage got out of bed that day. Milk still out and curtains drawn: God knows. And when she was older, coming home on a dark evening after netball practice or a film with friends, she'd hope for the opposite, for the curtains to be pulled, lights to be on. It seems as though she spent much of her childhood on edge, watchful, looking for clues.

Conor has started to pace. His restlessness is getting on her nerves. As though being here is an imposition on his time.

She'd almost prefer to be here by herself. She's used to being the only one anyway.

'Look, why don't you go and get something to eat. You must be tired after all the travelling. I can let you know if there's any change.'

He looks almost relieved. 'You sure?'

Frances thought he might put up a bit more resistance. Even just for appearances' sake. But she gives a curt nod.

'Okay, well, I might head out, just for a little while. There are some loose ends with a client I need to tie up. And I've got Lara down here with me, I dropped her off at the hotel. I might just check on her.'

She turns back to her mother. 'Whatever,' she says.

As he leaves, he gets a few sidelong looks. A visitor at another patient's bedside says, 'Hi, Conor,' as though he knows him. A young female doctor smiles shyly at him. He smiles back. For a moment Frances worries that he might be asked for a selfie. He'd agree to it, too. #keepingspiritsupinICU. She wonders how he can stand it, being public property like that. But it seems to her that he is more alive when he is in public. As though he feeds off the recognition. Feeds off the likes on his social media. He's always needed external validation. Always surrounded himself with people who tell him he's wonderful. Even as a child.

She knows she has been hostile. It's a pattern of behaviour she finds herself slipping into more frequently. And not just with Conor. Resolving to be nice, the kind of nice she is after two glasses of Pinot Noir – only ever two, although it's amazing how blasted you can get if you drink them quickly enough – only to be overcome with resentment in the moment and feel guilty about it later.

She retrieves her phone from her handbag. There is a text from Sinead.

Made it to Dubai. Upgraded to Business☺ Sweet. Be with you soon.

What must it be like to live your life like Sinead? No commitments or pressure. Play the talented but impoverished writer, knowing others will always bail you out if needed. She didn't even follow through on her publishing contract and it appears as though there have been no consequences. Frances hates to think of that first novel. She still smarts at the description of the uptight sister who makes Mary Bennet look effervescent. Sinead had her publisher in Ireland send her an early copy with a little hand-written note, as though it were a gift. They rowed about it the first time Sinead came back to New Zealand after its publication. Sinead claimed she was being oversensitive; it was a work of fiction, after all. Then when this didn't appease Frances, she went on the defensive, claiming it was her *duty* as a writer to hold a mirror up to the world. Duty indeed. As though writing a novel was somehow necessary. Frances said, 'Well, it didn't need to be one of those hideous magnifying mirrors men use for shaving.' Sinead became furious then. 'Well, if people don't want to be represented badly then they shouldn't bloody well act so badly!' They'd never spoken of it again.

She wonders what Harry and Livvy are doing. Since their daughter started on the tumultuous path of adolescence Harry has been so much better able to cope with her. Livvy is moving farther away from her despite Frances's best efforts to stay close.

Harry tells her not to take it so personally. But how can she not? Motherhood *is* so personal.

Frances had resolved from the moment she discarded her packet of contraceptive pills to excel at it. It would be simple. Just be the antithesis of Joy. She had quit alcohol, loaded up on folic acid, stopped running, started antenatal yoga. Once Livvy was born she started out breastfeeding on demand, only to become concerned that she was raising a child ruined by instant gratification. So she adopted the Gina Ford strict scheduling method – all the rage amongst middle-class mothers then – only to become terrified that she was raising a child with an insecure attachment, so switched back again. Joy was aghast at Frances's neuroticism over feeding. 'Just give the child a bottle, for goodness' sake, stop making a rod for your back.' Which of course only incentivised Frances more. She breastfed Livvy till she was almost three, much to Joy's horror, who was of an Irish generation that considered breastfeeding as almost shameful, done only if you couldn't afford formula. Once Livvy ventured beyond the safety of the house, Frances, still desperate to hold on, volunteered for everything: the kindergarten petting zoo trips, the reading recovery help in primary school, the gala fundraising days, the sausage sizzles, hosting the end of year get-togethers, the PTA roles. She set up parent group emails, then later organised WhatsApp groups for all the extracurricular activities, the dancing, the horse riding, the drama classes. And when Livvy showed great interest in, and talent at, swimming, she never once missed dropping her to early squad training, sitting poolside at five a.m., her eyes red with fatigue and the slight sting of the chlorine that hung like a malign vapour in the air. Never missed a swim competition either, the moist claustrophobic atmosphere cloying on her skin and in her lungs, the screams of encouragement or criticism from the parents next to her cloying in her ears.

She takes out her phone again. She thinks of the Prince song Andy was alluding to. She'd lost her virginity to him on the old brown velour sofa in his studio apartment while the *Parade* album played on his CD player. Afterwards he'd leaned on his elbow and looking down at her said, 'You're something else, Frances Tobin,' and she recalls having an overwhelming sense of gratitude in that moment. More than that, a strong sense of autonomy, of being able to control things for the first time in her life. Here she was, an independent person, living away from home, free of all the uncertainty that entailed, free of being at the mercy and whim of others, free from their appetites, able to act upon her own, choosing to lose her virginity to this person, choosing to be here having sex with someone who found her attractive and interesting. The album became synonymous with that sense of liberation, and from then on if a song from it played at parties or nightclubs she always danced to it, provocatively if she was near Andy, to remind him. It was a delicious little secret.

She types a message.

Hi Andy, that's great. I would love to meet up.

After a slight hesitation she adds,

X

CONOR

Once in the car Conor slumps forward and places his head on the cool of the steering wheel. He is so relieved to be out of there. That smell. And Frances is even pricklier than normal. Understandably. But Conor wishes that sometimes she could just let her guard down, be a little less *rigid*. He finds it so hard to relax around her. So hard to connect. It shouldn't be. Not after everything they've been through. Borne witness to.

The viscous odour of the hospital still on his nose dislodges a memory. All three of them are walking home from school. He is holding Sinead's hand. It is not long after they left their pebbledash and brick semi-detached house on the estate in Navan in the early eighties, so he can't be more than about ten. Eight-year-old Frances is skipping a few paces ahead with her new friend Amy. They are holding hands and singing a song. Amy is coming back to theirs for dinner to celebrate the start of the summer holidays and Frances is so excited, she is fizzing. He remembers it as a period of relative calm at home, the distance from Ireland freeing. Their mother had received a substantial inheritance after the death of her own mother, who had married into money after Joy's father had died, and she used it to flee to the other side of the world. The small white weatherboard ex-state bungalow she bought on a quiet cul-de-sac in a coastal city was so different from the claustrophobic inland town they had come from, where everyone knew your business. They could be a completely new and anonymous family here. She even got herself a part-time job in the local supermarket. Conor remembers her polyester blue-check work uniform that she used to complain made her skin itch madly. This new sense of purpose meant she wasn't spending weeks at a time in bed anymore. And with no sign of that smell, that distinctive almost-sweet odour that came from her bedroom in Ireland sometimes, a smell a bit like the ICU. He couldn't name it as a child, but now he recognises it as metabolised alcohol.

Frances and Amy have their hair in pigtails. Conor notices how perfectly even Amy's are, with a tanned parting running down the back that looks as though it's been drawn on by a ruler. Frances's parting is off-centre, snow-white and crooked. One pigtail noticeably thicker and higher than the other, as though she did it herself. Most likely she did. They are singing a tune as they skip, *Jingle Bells, Batman Smells,* and laughing, Frances amazed, as they all are, by the novelty of Christmas in summertime. As they turn the corner into their cul-de-sac, Conor gets a sinking feeling in the pit of his stomach. He sees that all the curtains are drawn on their little house and he hopes it is just because it is such a hot day. But as they get closer he sees their cat Fitz yowling furiously to be let in, and there is no way Joy would leave him like that if she was up. She always worried he would go off and kill the birds. Once Fitz left a mauled fantail as an offering by the back door and Joy was so furious, she swiped at him. Conor had never seen her be rough with an animal like that before.

Frances hasn't noticed anything amiss though, too absorbed in her funny song and her new friend.

Conor lets go of Sinead's hand and starts to quicken his pace. Maybe he can divert them, bring them to the park, he has some money, maybe even get them fish and chips. But it is too late now, they are already in the house. And as he runs in he can hear little Frances say, 'Oh, I'm so sorry, Amy. She must have a tummy bug. Mammy, Mammy?'

And he sees her then, lying on her stomach on the couch, her head hanging off the edge and a pool of vomit on the carpet. Frances is on her knees using a tea towel to try to scoop up the mess and Amy is standing frozen to the spot, a look of confusion on her face. Amy, who probably has a mother who is predictable and assumes that all mothers are the same. Amy, whose house is most likely a place of sanctuary, where when you arrive home you expect a smell of dinner on the stove or cookies baking. Not the bitter stench of puke. He feels so bad for Frances that he is afraid to look at her. And so they both do what they have to do. Conor offering to bring the distressed Amy home and at the same time placating Joy, who keeps slurring 'Sorry'; though she can't mean it because the incident will never be mentioned again. And Frances trying her best to clean up the mess with the manky tea towel but rubbing the stains deeper into the carpet. And they do it without making eye contact with each other, as though witnessing the other's shame would compound their own.

His phone pings. It's a message from his friend Dave.

Mate, saw the news online about your mum. Really sorry, let me know if you need anything

Conor's stomach lurches. He opens the *Stuff* website. It's the first story that appears.

Celebrity Charity Boss's Mum in Suspected Suicide Attempt.

How did it get out there so quickly? Vultures. In accordance with the law there is no mention in the article of the method, but all the other details are alarmingly correct. Was it his mother's neighbour, or someone at the hospital, even? He is used to publicity, of course. Courts it. It's a necessary tool to generate donations. There is a direct correlation between the column inches he occupies and the charity's bank balance. But up until now it has been benign. A fawning profile about him or praise for the charity's work. Maybe some gossip column speculation about his love life. There had been mention in a couple of the profiles about Joy's alcoholism – thanks to Sinead's book – but that has actually served him well. *Gutsy kid from a dysfunctional background makes good* kind of thing. Kiwis love that. But this feels different to him. It's the association with suicide, a slight inference of blame. Suicide taints perception. It taints those close to it.

When he gets to the new waterfront hotel his PA has booked him into, Lara is in the lobby talking on her phone. She hangs up when she sees him.

'Just my tutor.' She smiles at him. Immediately he feels better. 'What's happening?'

'It's not looking good. They'll run more tests but they don't think there's any brain function. My feeling is they'll wait for Sinead to arrive, then talk about taking her off life support.'

'I'm so sorry.' She hugs him. Then, 'Is there anyone else you need to contact? Like your dad, say?'

Conor is taken aback. In all this, his father hasn't crossed his mind. His father rarely crosses his mind. He gave up that right years ago.

'That prick? We haven't heard from him since he abandoned us back in Ireland.'

'Sorry, it's just you've never spoken about him. I shouldn't have brought it up. Insensitive of me.'

'No . . . no . . . *I'm* sorry for snapping. There's no story there, really. He just couldn't handle my mother's shit, ran off and we haven't heard anything from him since. Good riddance and all that.' He gives a *what can you do* sort of shrug then regrets it, aware that he might seem clinical, detached even. But to him, his father leaving, although dishonourable, was somehow inevitable. He often feels as though he should be angrier about it. But he can't make himself feel what he can't feel.

'I'm so grateful you're here, babe.' He cups her face in his hands.

She removes them and says lightly, 'Where else would I be? Apart, of course, from idly enjoying my summer holidays. Eating avocado on sourdough while bemoaning my generation's inability to ever get on the property ladder. You know, entitled millennial style?' Lara is doing a postgrad in media and communication and Conor suspects she is far more driven than she lets on.

'True,' Conor laughs, relieved he hasn't upset her.

'And on a different topic, may I commend you on an excellent choice of hotel, Mr Tobin. I do believe we are in the penthouse suite. Must cost an absolute fortune!'

Conor laughs again. She makes him feel so *light*. 'You're all I need, Lara,' he says.

'Look, seriously though, I'm here to help you, so if there's anything I can take care of while you're at the hospital. Any admin or general donkey work?' They met when she started volunteering at TheOneForAll at the start of her summer holidays from university. Though she resigned once their relationship started.

'Actually, now that you mention it, Kylie has sent through a ton of emails, all end of year stuff, I'm guessing. If I give you my laptop, would you mind going through them and letting me know if there are any unexploded bombs there? Even a dying mother isn't enough to get her off my back.' Kylie is the organisation's CFO and a real bloodhound. Not one to be disarmed with some light banter and a smile.

'My pleasure,' says Lara.

—

The following morning Conor is waiting at the airport for Sinead's flight to arrive. He has just come from the hospital where he has spent the night, eventually persuading an exhausted Frances to go home and get some rest.

The provincial airport is so small you can see passengers alighting from their aircraft and walking across the tarmac without moving from the multipurpose café/arrival/departure/check-in area. Scanning the passengers, he is at first sure she has missed the flight. Typical Sinead. Then he sees her bringing up the rear of the line that is trotting across the tarmac and through the automatic doors. Her hair has been shaved close to her head, which draws attention to her newly gaunt face. He finds it confronting. In his imagination, she is always ringleted and chubby. As she approaches though, he sees that her eyes still stand out against the black kohl that has ringed them since she was a teenager. Conor wonders if it is ever removed. Or if it has become part of her, like a strange genetic mutation, a foreign body that over the years becomes absorbed into the host.

They hug tightly. She smells strange, almost sulphurous. He holds her back at arm's length to get a good look at her and says, 'You look like you need a decent meal. And some hair dye.'

'Sorry I don't conform to your ideal standard of womanhood, Conor. You've got a few greys yourself, you know.' She ruffles his hair and gives that close-mouthed lopsided grin he remembers. She doesn't take much seriously. He notices that even the dimple that normally pops up on the right side of her face when she smiles looks less substantial. 'I've just lost a bit of weight from teaching yoga.'

Conor raises his eyebrows in surprise. 'True? A yoga teacher? That's very . . . zen?'

'I know, I always thought yoga was just for smug fuckers. Even the word itself sounds smug. Yoga, yoga, yoga.' She sounds almost manic. 'Anyway, it's just a way to make ends meet while I wait for inspiration to strike.' She makes air quotes around the word *inspiration*.

'Still struggling with the difficult second album, then?' The first book had really set the cat amongst the pigeons. If he's honest, he hadn't been too upset; didn't actually recognise himself in the character of the insecure and self-absorbed brother, but Frances had been furious at the portrayal of the buttoned-down sister. Joy refused to read it. There was a horrible confrontation between Joy and Sinead during which she called her daughter a 'treacherous parasite'. But Sinead's use of the word inspiration worries him. Hopefully she won't exploit what's happened – he has so much more to lose now.

Sinead gives a dismissive grunt. 'Let's not go there. Just fill me in on the Mater situation.'

'Let's collect your luggage first.' Conor waves his arm in the direction of the lone baggage carousel. 'We can talk properly in the car.'

'This is it.' She turns to show him the undersized canvas pack on her back.

To Conor it looks like it could hold no more than one change of clothes. He hopes there is also a bottle of deodorant in there somewhere.

'Okaaay . . . I can see you're not intending on a lengthy visit then.'

'I didn't think too much about it to be honest, just grabbed a couple of things and left.' Then she adds, 'Sure, no doubt Frances will have organised my shit for me.'

They both smile.

Conor leads her out to the carpark. 'Nice wheels!' She lets out a long whistle when she sees the Porsche SUV.

Conor shrugs. 'Oh. Yeah, I guess. It's just a company rental. Easier that way.' He likes the impersonal nature of leased cars. The untainted smell. No opportunity to acquire a history.

They get in. Sinead spies the number plate of the mid-range sedan parked in front of them. *6SFULL*. 'Jesus. I'd forgotten about the scourge of the personalised number plate in this country.' Then she turns the aircon on full blast. 'I'd also forgotten how hot and humid it gets here.'

Conor notes the outside temperature on the gauge. It reads only nineteen degrees. 'So I think you should prepare yourself for how she looks. She's a mess. I still can't get my head round the whole gun thing, you know? To the head? It's so brutal. One of the consultants told me it's very rare for a woman to shoot herself. And if they do, it's often in the stomach.'

'How very Freudian.' She leans back against the rest. 'Though it makes sense to me that she'd do it in the head. I mean she was never maternal, so the whole womb symbolism stuff wouldn't apply.' She looks out the window. The buildings near the airport are utilitarian, ugly. Conor imagines she is mentally criticising them. Comparing them unfavourably with the Georgian buildings and cobbled streets she's come from. Then she says, as though debating with herself, 'But then again, maybe shooting yourself in the stomach is the perfect way of rejecting motherhood.'

Conor suddenly feels impatient with her. 'This isn't some dramatised incident in a book, Sinead. She tried to end her own life. When you see her, you'll get it.' He sees his mother's face again, barely human, the distortion, the discolouration. Squeezes his eyes tight for a second.

She says nothing for a while. Just continues to stare out the window. He remembers how she could withdraw sometimes.

'I dunno. It actually feels kind of fictional to me. I feel detached. Like the way I feel watching a sad news story. Sure, it's upsetting and awful and tragic in a general sense. I can *empathise*. But on a personal level? Nothing. Worse than nothing. I think I'm a bit *relieved*. I guess that makes me sound terrible.'

There's no point in arguing with her. It'll be all too real for her soon. 'It's probably just shock.'

'No. It's not. I never felt loved by her. Maybe it was different for you and Frances. By the time I came along she'd used up any maternal inclination she ever had. It's worst for the youngest, you know? You guys left. And it was just me. And she blamed me for her unhappiness. I always felt it. She'd even say as much when she was drunk. And then of course the whole book fiasco. She told me once that she wished she'd never had kids. Imagine! Actually admitting that out loud to your child.' She rests her head back and closes her eyes. 'What a motherfuckin' shitshow.'

He doesn't disagree. It was never going to end well for their mother. Who is he to say what someone should be feeling anyway, when he can't for the life of him conjure up a happy reminiscence of his own? They all have their own narrative. All experienced things differently. And Sinead did get the worst of her, it's true. Before the accident things weren't so bad. He thinks of Sinead as a toddler, her confused and tear-streaked face peering out the window of the Hillman Hunter, waiting for someone to come get her. Joy saying, 'It was the baby, I was just seeing to the baby.'

So instead, he says, 'You sound like a fishwife. You and Franny both.'

She laughs. 'Franny? That's new. She never used to swear. Well, I must have gone native again. The Irish curse like there's no tomorrow, use fuckin' as an adjective to colour every sentence. I found it jarring at first but now I hardly notice. I quite like it, actually. Though it probably sounds more lyrical without my Kiwi twang.'

'Mum hated swearing. Remember she'd go batshit if we did?' He feels conscious of having used the past tense.

'Yeah, funny how she had high standards of parenting in *that* regard.' She puts on an American accent. 'Couldn't show affection to her kids, but sure liked 'em to speak proper!'

They are silent for a while. Then Conor says, 'It seems strange that she would do it now, though. Like, you'd imagine by your sixties you'd have learnt to live with your demons. Suicide seems like a younger person's decision.' He is thinking of how long ago it all was. The accident at the school, their father leaving. Why now?

'Maybe she was waiting for us to be proper grown-ups before she checked out. You know, get our shit together and stuff. Then she thought, Fuck this for a game of tiddlywinks, Sinead's just turned forty and she's still a mess, could be waiting forever for that bitch to sort herself out. So she cut her losses. Me turning forty was the catalyst.'

He shakes his head at her. 'Sometimes, Sinead, I can't believe the stuff that comes out of your mouth.'

When they reach the hospital they walk through the main entrance and a man on his way out turns to stare at them. Conor feels uneasy. There is something about this man, a jolt of familiarity. He racks his brain but can't place him. After the online article yesterday, he worries it's a journalist. Maybe that's where he's seen him before. Reporting at some fundraiser for the charity. Or maybe even interviewing him for a profile in a weekend supplement.

Frances and Harry are standing with one of the doctors in the corridor outside the ICU as they get out of the lift. Frances has her head bowed; Harry has his arm around her shoulder. When she sees them her face crumples.

'Thank God,' she says. 'We have decisions to make.'

SINEAD

Sinead quickly realises that in fact, it is the medical team who are making the decisions, and the one to withdraw life support has already been made. Discussing it with the family is moot. Their mother's brain has been, to quote the neurologist, 'entirely and irreversibly destroyed with no chance of recovery'. Prolonging her life artificially is deemed pointless. (And costly, Sinead thinks. And given her mother's obvious wish to die, cruel.)

Everyone agrees, then. Even Joy.

Sinead wonders what would happen if one of them objected. Hysterically insisted on their mother's sentience. Protracted lawsuits and bitter family divisions. She looks at Conor and knows he would be annoyed with her for thinking that way. He'd accuse her of dramatising things again. Ever looking to be the saviour, he had earlier suggested organ donation. Surprisingly, their mother is not too old. Rather, too Irish. The doctor explained that anyone who had spent time in Britain or Ireland was ineligible because of Creutzfeldt-Jakob disease. Sinead had to keep her eyes averted from her siblings so as not to betray the hysteria that threatened. *Mad Cow Disease. Of course.*

The doctor explained the process of life support withdrawal in detail and with great tact. A series of steps would be taken, with the ventilator the last to be withdrawn. Due to the catastrophic injury to their mother's brain stem, death would probably occur quickly. The opioid dose would be such that their mother would be in no pain. (Sinead's interest was piqued at the mention of opioids. Perhaps they could all do with a little?)

The nurse, Bridget, intrigues her. She's kind, yet almost impenetrable. Maybe you'd have to be. She wonders about inserting a similar character in her new book. Because she has started it. Really started it this time. On the plane. She has made false beginnings before, of course, even getting as far as submitting a few thousand words to Maggie. Maggie had been unimpressed, though politely so. Used gracious lines such as 'Let's just park that idea for now, shall we, darling?' Mind you, Sinead can't even bear to read her own debut now. (God, can she even say debut? Doesn't that imply a follow-up?) Compared to the new breed of Irish writers, the language feels overdone, the style too formal and verbose. As though she is trying to impress her English teacher with her 'What I Did on My Summer Holiday' essay. How do they do it, those young authors? Make such compelling stories with such muted prose. It's another reason why she's found the second book such a millstone. The fear of comparison. Her writing is turgid next to theirs.

But this latest attempt feels different. An image had come to her, so vivid she could almost touch it, of Joy sitting in her old blue dressing gown at her kitchen table, with the Christmas serviette folded under the bockety leg to keep it from wobbling, the old clock on the shelf beside the radio ticking, the dull hum from the ancient fridge in the corner, the radiator clacking on and off intermittently. All so ordinary. Apart from the gun and bullets laid out in a neat row before her. She wouldn't tell the others what she was writing about. They'd accuse her of cannibalising their lives again. But wasn't that what all writing involved? She leaned into it so much it cocooned her with its richness. She barely looked up from her laptop on the journey apart from the occasional toilet break, where she was surprised again at the odd colour of her urine. The other side-effects of the pills have worn off. She'll lay off them for a couple of weeks now. Or at least until the weight starts to pile on again.

Bridget had asked if they would like the hospital chaplain to be present. Families found it a comfort, apparently. Her siblings ended up squabbling over it, as was their way. Conor thought it was a good idea, but Frances claimed their mother, singularly secular, would have hated it. Conor gave in but asked if the time could be changed.

'Why, do you want to livestream it?' Frances said.

'Jesus, Franny.'

Sinead didn't express any opinion. What did it matter anyway?

So here they are at the allotted time, two days since the suicide attempt, gathered round Joy's bed, which has been moved to a private room within the ICU, waiting for the doctors to come. Sinead notices the deft and tactful touches that have been made. Bed rails lowered to allow easier contact; equipment moved to create space; unnecessary alarms and monitors turned off; comfortable chairs and tissues provided.

She studies her mother's face. It is a face both strange and familiar to her. Recognisable yet unfathomable. It strikes her that you only get to know a small bit of your mother. Probably not even the best part.

Bridget explains again the process, the steps leading up to the disconnection of the ventilator, and reassures them that any changes in skin colour and breathing are normal. Earlier she had suggested that they could perhaps bring photos to share as they said goodbye. Frances has duly obliged. She has somehow managed to dig up a few old ones that give the impression of a functional family. Sinead can't ever remember having photos taken when they were children. Not for them the cheesy, wall-hung family portraits with dubious hair and clothes in drab last-century shades of mustard and brown.

One of the photographs captures Sinead's attention more than the others. It shows the four of them, before they left Ireland, in front of a boxy blue car. The car is shiny, new. Sinead is a baby in her mother's arms. Conor and Frances are standing holding hands. Conor is leaning against the car, a wide, proud grin on his face, while Frances is standing erect and serious. Her mother is in her usual recalcitrant photo pose. Head down, gaze averted. It must have been their father who took it. One of his last paternal acts before absconding. Did he know then that he was going to leave? Was the photo taken as a sort of memento?

But it is the car itself that troubles Sinead. It seems to her to possess a malevolence at odds with its shiny, boastful optimism. She is quite transfixed by it.

Bridget interrupts her thoughts.

'The doctors will be here soon to begin the process. Is everyone here that needs to be?'

Harry, Frances and Livvy are at one side of the bed, Conor and Sinead at the other. Frances says, almost apologetically, 'This is it.'

'Perhaps we should wait a minute in case our dear old da decides to make a last-minute dash to be at her side,' says Sinead. She is rewarded with an ironic chuckle from Harry, but Frances throws them a warning look.

Bridget says, 'It's just that a man has been asking after your mother. Slight accent, Irish too, maybe? I thought perhaps he was a relative.'

Conor looks up, brow furrowed. 'We've no relatives here. Do you think he's a journalist? Did he say anything about me?'

Bridget says, 'Yes, he mentioned you all but he seemed nice, concerned.'

'That's how the devious bastards work. I hope you didn't tell him anything?'

'No,' says Bridget, 'but I don't think . . .' Her voice trails off as though she thinks better of it. 'Anyway, before the doctors arrive you might like to share some memories or funny stories?'

There is a tense silence before Harry says, 'Joy, I would just like to say, you made the worst lasagne I have ever, ever tasted. It was truly magnificent in its sauceless, dry, cardboard texture.'

It is true. Joy's hatred for cooking was evident in the food she served. The tension is broken, and they laugh quietly.

Livvy says, 'I liked hanging out with you, Gran. Remember that time you took me shoplifting when I was eight? It was the best fun I'd ever had.'

Frances's head shoots up. 'Excuse me?'

Livvy looks at her mother, almost defiantly Sinead thinks, and says, 'It was one time you got her over to babysit me. She said you must have been really desperate to do that. You'd put a lock on the drinks cabinet, and she thought you'd even hidden her wallet. She was pretty annoyed about it. So, we took your car and went to the supermarket. She got me to keep lookout while she put a bottle of wine in her handbag. Then we went to the confectionery aisle, and she put a big bag of lemon bonbons in there too. She called you a sugar Nazi. Said that like all your generation you had this stupid belief that sugar made kids hyper, when actually it was just over-attentive parenting. I was nervous as we were leaving but she winked at me and we walked straight out of there, past the checkout operators and everything. She said no-one paid much attention to kids and none at all to women over the age of fifty. She told me to wreak havoc while I was young. Have lots of lovers. We sat up late watching a western together and ate all the lollies.' She pauses then, as though remembering something else. 'She left the bottle of wine unopened on the kitchen island.'

Frances closes her eyes. 'Oh my God. And I remember that bottle of wine, too. I thought you'd been careless, Harry! And left it out by mistake.' She takes her mother's hand. 'You're infuriating, Mother, even fully incapacitated.' But her tone is gentle.

The photograph of the car has dislodged a memory in Sinead's head. 'You sang songs to me, Mum. Silly songs. I think . . . I think I liked it.' She can't speak now, feels a constricting in her throat. She looks to Conor to say something and save her. It is his turn. But Conor's head is bowed. He looks pained. He refuses to speak.

There is a gentle knock and two doctors enter the room.

'Are you all ready?'

They are gathered around now, all touching Joy. Sinead studies her family's drawn faces. She wonders why she feels at such a remove from the enormity of what is happening. Perhaps there is something dead within herself that makes her feel this disconnect. The doctors unobtrusively do their thing. Sinead is surprised at some spasms of her mother's arm. She thinks she hears the rub of her leg against the hospital linen. She looks to Bridget for reassurance that this is normal, but Bridget, as usual, is unperturbed. Their mother's eyes open briefly, and Sinead imagines she sees a flash of sentience there but dismisses it as fanciful.

Their mother emits a peculiar sound midway between a snore and a cough. She appears to be gurgling.

'What's happening?' asks Livvy, looking distressed.

The doctor reassures her but checks Joy's mouth and after consulting with her colleague pulls out the tube. Bridget wraps it quickly in a towel.

A few more loud breaths. With each one Sinead holds her own, her heart thumping. But the breaths keep coming and become more regular, settled even. The final breath never eventuates.

Joy has refused to die as scheduled.

JOY

People keep telling me I must look after Mother now. That she will need me to be mature and responsible. That at thirteen I'm almost a woman. And Granny Elsie keeps telling me I must touch Daddy, kiss his forehead and make a cross on it the way she does, because soon they'll close the coffin and take him from the house.

And even though I don't want to so badly, I approach the coffin and place my hand on the side of his face. But then I see it's not Daddy in the casket but a little boy. A little boy with dark brown hair and straight black eyebrows. It's the same little boy that I saw standing at the side of King Kong's Belly. And I get such a fright from the feel of his skin. It's like rubber ice and my hand jolts back as though it has a life of its own.

But I can feel all these eyes on me. People standing around me. Watching to see what I do. I don't want to embarrass Mother in front of Daddy's sisters who are gathered like sentinels about the coffin. She doesn't like his family, who are true west of

Ireland people from Mayo and to Mother's mind unsophisticated and old-fashioned. Culchies, she calls them. And already there is tension between them because Mother wanted Daddy to lie in the chapel of rest, but the sisters and Granny Elsie were insistent that he be waked at home. And I heard Mother say to one of her friends that they better not start their keening nonsense. Or the superstitious kicking over of chairs that is supposed to stop the dead coming back in once they take the coffin out.

I look again, closely this time, and now I see it is Daddy in there. But I'm still surprised at how he looks. Not just how unlike himself he is but also how few marks there are on him. The bottom of the casket is closed over so I start to imagine that the train has cut him in half and if I were to lift the lid, there would just be a bloody stump where his legs used to be.

. . . What is happening? I can't breathe. I can't breathe and I can feel the vomit rise in my throat . . .

I'm in bed now, and I can still hear the voices drifting up the stairs. And they are at times keening and at times laughing softly. I think I should go down and help stand guard, but I can't move. And sleep is fitful because every time I drift off I can see Daddy's bloodied legless body. And I hope they do kick the chairs over when they take the coffin away because I don't want Daddy's disfigured body haunting me. And I feel such anger at him because how could he do this even though Granny Elsie and the sisters keep saying it was an accident, that he just didn't hear the train.

But Daddy could tell the difference between a chaffinch and a greenfinch call at a hundred yards, so I know this is not true.

And Mother says it was no accident either and that Daddy's family are just afraid the priest won't let him be buried in the graveyard if they think it was suicide. Catholic nonsense, she says. Druids, she says, scornfully.

And after Mother's had some of the gin that she keeps in the kitchen press, she gets all twisted and says she knew that he was unhappy. That he hated his life with us. All he wanted was to go back out west and be the master in a little hick school and spend his spare time jotting down the birds he spots in his battered notebook. But he couldn't, she says. Because we trapped him. You and I, Joy. We trapped him here. We did this.

And it feels to me now that I am in the casket. It is softer than I expected, and rather than feeling scared, I feel safe here. I don't want to get out. I turn my head and see the little boy is here again, too. He opens his eyes and they are green. Like moss. A fat tear slides down his cheek. I reach out and touch it and say I am sorry because I understand it's my fault he's in here. And I want to make it better but I'm not sure how.

FRANCES

She has spent the morning in a state of anxiety, unable to eat or apply herself to any of the tasks that have already accumulated in the week or so since her mother's *incident*.

This is how they have come to refer to it. *Accident* is misleading for an act so deliberate. *Failed suicide attempt* is too much of a mouthful, and as Livvy had pointed out, insensitive, because it makes it seem as though death is some kind of glamorous outcome. She had been on the phone with one of her friends yesterday talking about what had happened. After she hung up Livvy confronted her angrily and said, 'Mum, you can't say *committed suicide* anymore. It's not a crime, you know!' Which she'd never thought about before, but this is all new territory they are navigating. They are learning that when suicide is involved, they need to protect the people they discuss it with. Cushion the shock of the word. Of the act. 'So how exactly did your mother end up in a coma?' 'Oh here, have a cup of sweet tea and please sit down before I tell you.' And the fact is, shame is an integral emotion when it comes to suicide. You're tarnished by your association with it. It's why some people would rather a court ruled that their loved one died by some autoerotic mishap than by hanging themselves. Or crashed their speeding car accidentally into a power pole on a straight piece of road. As Sinead said, 'People with happy families don't kill themselves.' Frances objected to that, said it was patently wrong. Still, it gnawed, an unpalatable grain of truth in it.

There are emails relating to PTA business to attend to. Dozens of unread 'Swim Moms' WhatsApp messages relating to the upcoming inter-school competition that is taking place in a couple of weeks. It's the most important one of the year as it's the qualifier for the Nationals. God, how she regrets setting up that WhatsApp group. Half will be bitching about the poor harassed coach, Josh, because he placed their little darling third in the relay event when *actually, Sammy is more suited to first*. There will be loads of unnecessary thumbs up or annoying laughing face emojis apropos of nothing. And then the passive aggressive comments about Livvy's performance. *Gosh, didn't Livvy swim well today, what are you feeding her, hun? Steroids?* Or *Livvy's a total shoo-in for all the individual events, might as well have Ella give up now!* Lauren told her that along with the concern for Frances's *situation* when she was at the squad trainings that Frances missed (for the first time ever), she also picked up on a poolside undercurrent of glee. The possibility that the favourite might, due to *awful, just awful, tragedy!*, underperform for once.

Well, no matter what distractions are happening, Frances will make sure that doesn't happen.

And so, she has spent the morning pacing, changing her outfit, straightening her hair into submission. She has even watched a YouTube tutorial of a girl doing her makeup. Livvy had walked in while she was watching it and said, 'What's the point of you watching that?' as though Frances was beyond any sort of improvement. Livvy had come straight from their pool, goggle indentations around her eyes, wet strands of hair stuck to the side of her face, but still looking radiantly lovely. Frances looked at Livvy, then at her own tired reflection in the makeup mirror beside her and thought, You're right. What *is* the point? Having a teenage daughter is a constant reminder of everything you've lost.

Frances could see that Sinead was taken aback when she had declared she was not going to the hospital today. Frances doesn't care. Let someone else sit in that airless room, startling every time Joy jerks an arm or grunts. Let someone else make small talk with the nurses. Let someone else put the flowers in fresh water or go get the coffees. Or nod gravely when the doctor on duty gives their unwaveringly pessimistic opinion on the futility of the situation. *I know it's hopeless, just tell my brother that.* When Joy had continued to breathe by herself, Conor had insisted that she be moved to her own room within the hospital, her feeding tube reinserted, before he fucked off to San Francisco on some vitally important business. So, just for today, let someone else take over the role of reliable, boring old mug.

Harry seems to be enjoying having Sinead stay. The two of them sit up each evening drinking red wine, even the occasional whiskey. It's like they're a couple of students again.

'More wine for Mademoiselle?' Harry would say, showing the bottle to Sinead like a sommelier.

'Why, thank you, Monsieur, you read my mind!'

'Mademoiselle is pushing it a bit,' Frances would mutter. Furious with both of them and their jokey attitude towards alcohol.

Frances would have her one glass – maybe two – of Pinot Noir with dinner. For the flavonoids. Or resveratrol. Something beneficial, anyway. On these nights, Frances retires at her normal time and leaves Harry and Sinead to it. Lying in bed, hearing the muffled conversation and frequent laughter, she would wonder what they could possibly talk about so late into the night. She doubts Harry's work as a partner in a liquidating firm would excite Sinead too much. Too straight. And what more can be said about Sinead's abandoned writing career?

Now, she looks around the vegan hipster café she'd never normally frequent. She is politely early, possibly overdressed, definitely too made-up. She feels ridiculous, conspicuous, a square peg in this round hole full of man-bunned, bearded baristas and dewy-skinned, tattooed, multi-pierced, harem-panted waitresses. She should go home, go to the hospital, resume normal service.

Then Andy walks in. He spots her immediately. *Of course, I stick out like a sore thumb.* He smiles at her. *Christ, he always had gorgeous teeth.* They have a moment of awkwardness where he goes to kiss her cheek and she lunges forward clumsily for a hug, but Frances quickly finds herself relaxing. Funny how little he has changed. He looks older, obviously, but he is still himself. Full of self-belief and a confidence that is attractive and disconcerting at the same time. All the mannerisms she remembers are there. The way he leans forward, his chin resting on his hand, to listen. The way he pinches the top of his nose and squeezes his eyes shut when he recounts something embarrassing. (Or with Andy, probably *faux* embarrassing – real humiliation is not an emotion he would be too familiar with.) We don't fundamentally change; the exterior just disintegrates.

After some small talk he says, 'So, I read about your mother.'

She is relieved, in a way, that he has brought it up. So she doesn't have to. 'Of course you did. That's just one of the many perks of having a well-known brother.'

'How is she doing?'

'The doctors are giving no chance of recovery. She's breathing on her own, the base parts of her brain are working, but the doctors say there's no cognitive or higher functioning. Conor's still insisting her feeding tube stays in, though. There's no talking any sense to him at the moment.'

'Do you mind me asking how she did it?'

People normally don't ask this. After the shock of hearing it was attempted suicide they tend to get awkward and clam up. Or spout some meaningless platitude. One Swim Mom, Donna, pulled out the old *I've always thought suicide was so selfish!* line. No, Frances wanted to yell at her, it was probably the most selfless thing she's ever done. It was her life that was full of self-ishness. But instead she nodded politely, seething inside.

'Tried to kill herself?' Frances feels a little reckless. 'Shot herself in the head, actually.'

75

Andy doesn't recoil. He is a little like Teflon, deflecting any great sincerity or emotion, and she is grateful, in this moment, for this. He puffs his cheeks and lets out an exaggerated breath. She remembers this mannerism too.

'Wow. She sounds, uhh . . . single-minded?'

Frances smiles at his choice of words. 'Yes. A very singular woman indeed.'

'You know you never let me meet her. I always felt like you were ashamed of me.' But he says this smiling, with the absolute confidence of someone who knows it couldn't possibly be true.

And it comes flooding back. All those years of cutting off friends or boyfriends at the door. Of being ashamed of the state of the house, or the state of her mother. She became adept at keeping her life compartmentalised. She was like an overzealous prison censor, intercepting any communication from the school in case it required their mother's attendance. *Keep your head down, Frances, play by the rules, stay out of trouble, get good grades.* Forging apology notes from her mother to the school about her inability to attend parent–teacher meetings. Being the only one who never invited friends to sleepovers. She stopped getting invites herself after a while because of the lack of reciprocation. Of course, there were times when their mother could have attended the school or been sober in front of her friends, but Frances wouldn't take that chance – that she would fuck it all up. Because Joy often managed to, somehow. One year Frances told a group of her school friends that her mother was dying of cancer just so they would stop asking about her birthday party. And there were times she wished it were true.

'You wouldn't even let me into the house the night of your graduation ball! Mind you, the state of me, I'm not surprised.' Again, it is said without sincerity. She knows he would have spent longer than her getting ready. Would have had his parents buy him a bespoke tux, rather than hiring an ill-fitting one. Sometimes Frances wondered if Andy was attracted to her because of her orderliness. The way she fit nicely between the straight lines. Made herself agreeable at all times. She, because of her own self-control, was the ultimate in low maintenance. He would have liked that she was always careful of her appearance. Kept herself thin, well-groomed and manicured. 'Makes the best of herself,' she can hear Joy say. A backhanded compliment if ever there was one.

Frances changes the subject, not wanting to dwell anymore on her past shame. 'So, how are things for you? The business? Cathy and the kids? You've three, right?' She feels queasy that she has brought his family up. Mentioned his wife by name as though there is no agenda. As though she isn't wearing sexy underwear.

'Oh, business is great. That's part of the reason I'm here actually, looking to branch out.' Andy holds the franchise on one of the busiest supermarkets in Auckland. A licence to print money these days, apparently. 'Me and Cath on the other hand, well, you know, we're having a few issues.'

She is annoyed at him for saying this. It's one step away from 'But my wife doesn't understand me.' It's so clichéd, it cheapens everything. But it's her fault for asking. She half-listens as he talks about his children. As he boastfully complains about exorbitant private-school fees. About the early-morning starts associated with rowing champion daughters. Humblebrags about the pressure of having a perfectionist, overachieving son. She sees her own bourgeois concerns reflected back at her and it depresses the shit out of her.

So, as he talks, she zones out and wonders if she could sleep with him again. Be naked with him. Because the truth of it is, she is not here to rekindle a friendship. She had been thinking about the sex. Though the thought of someone besides Harry seeing her naked terrifies her. She barely allows Harry to. She struggles to see herself as desirable or even sexual anymore. It feels at odds with her role as mother. And though she takes care of herself, no amount of spin classes can mitigate against twenty years of gravity. From his social media posts, she knows he is something of a gym bunny. And teetotal. If he drives a red sportscar she will have to walk out.

But! Those glorious days when she had left home to study in Auckland. Those endless days in bed with him. How free she was then, living away for the first time from the oppressiveness of her mother's addiction. Those university years when you get to reinvent yourself. She is nostalgic for the girl she was back then. It's hard to reconcile this version of herself with the person she has become. It's as though she has become less herself. Maybe it starts in those claustrophobic early years of motherhood, at home all day, just her and the baby. With no-one else to talk to, she ended up conversing with Livvy like some kind of simpleton, referring to herself in the third person all the time. *Mama will do this, Mama will do that,* so it's like some kind of disassociation occurs. She feels like a Russian doll. As though several variants of herself exist within this tidy outer shell.

'And you? Still doing all that science-y stuff?' Andy is asking. After she graduated with her Bachelor of Science, she had worked in the university laboratory as a technician. She'd loved it. The minutiae of her daily work, the recording, the detailing, the organising. For over a year she was responsible for monitoring containers of tiny bacteria. She barely remembers why now, something to do with farming runoff, but back then it consumed her. Each morning she would rush to the lab to check on her 'babies' with all the fervour of a proud new mother.

'No, I gave it up once I had Livvy so I could concentrate on her.'

'And you moved back here to Tauranga? That surprises me. I thought you hated it.'

'Doesn't everyone hate where they grew up? My mother needed me. And Harry was offered a better job. It made sense. At the time.'

She is tired now of making sense.

'And now? What do you do?'

Frances sighs. 'Now I . . . pick stuff up, drop people off, wipe the kitchen bench. I find things for people. A lot. You could call me a to-do list.'

He laughs. 'You were always so hard on yourself, Frances.'

'Yeah well, I always accepted I was never destined to change the world.'

Andy grimaces, like the idea of it nauseates him. 'It amazes me that anyone could ever think they could make a difference. Or want to.'

Frances thinks of Conor. 'I suppose.'

'And just the one kid?'

'Yep. Just the one!' She tries to sound unapologetic. People assume there is some sad story behind only children. Some tale of unexplained infertility. Multiple miscarriages, years of trying, maybe even failed IVF. Because how could you not provide siblings for your lonely, spoilt and egocentric offspring? In the early days, Harry talked about having lots of children. He'd come from a large family himself, had a mother who carried it off effortlessly. But one child was all she was capable of, and maybe, given the state of her relationship with Livvy, not even that. She imagines Livvy's reaction to her meeting Andy like this. Knowing disgust, she thinks. For a fourteen-year-old she has the most remarkable perception. Frances remembers looking into her smudgy newborn face when the obstetrician placed her on her breast, and instantly recognising her daughter. 'Ahhh . . . she's been here before, Harry,' she'd said. He'd laughed and cried and said, 'Oh, but yes, she's always been here, this one.' One minute in and he already couldn't imagine a world without her in it.

Andy leans back in the chair, clasps his hands behind his head, closes his eyes. 'God though, Frances. Families, kids. I mean, I sometimes have to pinch myself that I'm this age, that I'm responsible for other human beings. Why didn't we realise how amazing it was to be twenty? Make the most of every second? What I wouldn't give to go back. Just for a day. Revel in my twenty-year-old body. My lack of responsibility. I'd wreak havoc.' He opens his eyes, grins at her. 'What do you say, Frances? Would you come with me?'

He is so sure of himself, so confident. It almost dazzles her. The way he is looking at her, so brazen, she feels naked.

She would like to be naked.

She can feel herself flushing, but she meets his eye.

'Do I get to be twenty too?' The words seem to be coming from someone else. A different type of person entirely. A person who might, given half the chance, get on her knees now in front of him under the table. She did this once, at a party, in the tatty kitchen of a shared student house, while everyone got high in the living room, the plastic tablecloth shielding her from view when one of his friends walked in to ask him if he had a cigarette. 'Not now, mate, come back later, I'm busy,' he said, not missing a beat.

'If you want. But I'd take you whatever way you come.'

She tries to think of a response but finds she is too flustered. Andy lets the words hang there for a few moments, then stands.

'Look, sorry, but I've got to get going or I'll be late for this meeting.'

'Oh,' she says. 'Oh, okay.' As they walk to the door Frances wonders if she has misinterpreted things. He makes no mention of meeting again. She's the one with the agenda. Foolish, naïve Frances who put on her best underwear. Just in case.

They reach her car first. She steps off the kerb to go to the driver's side and Andy grasps her hand, and as he pulls her in for a hug, says, 'You've always been the one I've wondered about, Franny.' She is too startled to respond and instead just watches him as he walks a little farther down the street to his own car.

On a whim, she takes a detour to the beach on her way home. She sits on a rotting, washed-up tree trunk, ants scurrying through its dank crevices. The blackness of the trunk is so at odds with the golden sand that it triggers a memory of a different beach, long ago, on the other side of the world.

She closes her eyes and remembers the grey, gravelly sand, extending to the grey-green water of the Irish Sea, which melds with the overcast sky at the horizon. It is cold and the three of them are wrapped up in duffel coats, sitting on the red and green tartan rug that lived in the boot of the car. They are eating flaccid jam sandwiches – white bread, as always. Joy is a distant figure standing by the sea's edge. Frances is anxious because her mother has been down there for a long time, unmoving. Sinead is still a toddler and is beginning to whinge. She needs a nap so Frances tells Conor to keep an eye on her while she goes to get their mother. She starts off at a good pace, marching towards Joy, but the closer she gets the less sure of herself she is.

'Mammy?' Her heart is pounding in her chest.

Her mother doesn't turn to look at her, stays rooted to the spot, staring towards the horizon. Frances is unsure what to do and is about to go and get Conor to help, when Joy says, 'I could just keep going now. Just walk out there.' She waves her hand over the expanse of water. 'But I don't think the mermaids will sing to *me*, either.'

Frances doesn't understand. She often feels like this around her mother, confused and uncertain.

'Mermaids aren't real, are they, Mammy?'

Her mother turns then, as if only now aware she is not alone. 'It's a poem.' She sighs. 'You're such a prosaic little thing, Frances, aren't you?'

Frances doesn't understand what this means either, but from her mother's tone she doesn't think it is something to be proud of. Serious, cautious, careful. And now prosaic. Another word to add to the list Joy uses when talking about Frances. Her mother turns and strides back towards the others. Frances must run to keep up.

Now, the memory is interrupted by the laughter of a group of young Brazilians, who seem to take over this beach in the summertime. They are boisterous and loud and give off a vibe of such nonchalant sensuality that Frances feels quite mesmerised. These glorious girls with their voluptuous behinds flaunted in tiny thong bikini bottoms, and beautiful shirtless boys diving athletically as they throw a frisbee to each other. She imagines herself at their age. Remembers a late summer's day at Takapuna beach with Andy twenty years ago. They'd skipped their lectures. Frances had felt torn, but it was only the beginning of term, and they headed there with a box of wine and swam in the ocean and later, when the sun went down, they made love behind the surf club and were almost caught by a man walking his dog. She wants to be that girl again. The girl who skipped class and drank cheap boxed wine without snobbery and had risky sex. This is the version of herself she wants to return to.

The frisbee lands a couple of metres from her feet. One of the boys comes to retrieve it. He looks at her and grins. He has startling green eyes, almost unreal, and smooth golden skin.

Frances smiles shyly, then looks down as he runs back to his friends, embarrassed by his beauty. Shocked by her own desire. He can't be much more than eighteen. The unfiltered New Zealand sun is especially prickly today and she realises she has forgotten to put on sunscreen. She can feel the freckles forming on her nose and forearms and curses her ill-suited Celtic complexion. She kicks off her jandals, traces with her finger the stark Y-shape they have left on her brown end-of-summer feet. The nude nail polish on her big toe is chipped. She digs the offending digit into the sand so she won't have to look at it.

You're the one I've always wondered about, Franny. Well, what the fuck is she supposed to do with that nugget of information? She peels off her clothes, leaving them in a neat pile on the tree trunk. The tide is way out and the sea gives off a turquoise haze.

This is for you, Mammy. And then Frances McEvitt, in her very best, matching silk underwear, runs and hurls herself into the blue Pacific Ocean. As she does, she fancies she hears a cheer from her mother. Then she realises it is, in fact, coming from the Brazilians.

CONOR

Conor is sitting at the bar of his hotel in San Francisco. Normally he is happy to let Angie organise his accommodation, staying in whatever five-star hotel she deems fit. But here he insists on staying in the same place, a small boutique hotel, the King George, not far from Union Square. It has a quaint, shabby-chic air, with a Union Jack flying proudly out front in the stiff breeze coming off the bay. There is a red telephone box in the lobby. The patterned Axminster carpets are slightly worn, the furniture red and mustard velvet, the bathrooms tiled in black and white mosaic.

He had loved America, or at least the idea of the place, long before he'd ever set foot in it. As a young man, while his friends were listening to Britpop or grunge, he was drawn to the music of the great American singer-songwriters: Dylan, Simon & Garfunkel, Springsteen, Taylor. He found himself yearning with nostalgia for something he'd never experienced; a time before he'd existed, a country he'd never visited. Back then, he had a romantic impression of the place from the music. Notions of wide-open freeways, adventurous journeys on Greyhound buses, free-spirited hobos on freight trains, misunderstood boys in pick-up trucks, winsome girls in country fairs. It seemed a place of possibility. A place of escape. A place where love was epic, its demise torturous. Even humdrum, blue-collared lives held the promise of something grander. There was a nobility to their lives, those boxers, prostitutes, steel workers, smalltown kids. Even in misery they seemed poetic, and far removed from the prosaic lyrics of his friends' preferred music. Or the ordinary unhappiness of his own life.

When he finally boarded a plane for the place years later, Neil Diamond's 'America' played in his head for the entire journey, like some sort of optimistic opening number for a musical, a prelude to the adventure ahead. But as it had done for others before him, America disappointed, so far removed as it was from the wistfulness and lyricism of the music he loved. And he came to realise anyway that it wasn't just one vast country but a million different countries set into one vast and changing landscape.

Though as a young man he was duped by the seductive mythology of the Californian dream – The Beach Boys version – as an adult he enjoys San Francisco in all its gritty, grubby reality. And tonight, especially after the last week, it's suiting his mood. Maybe it's the unhinged edge to the place. Everywhere you look there is unabashed craziness on show. Workmen shouting from vans at jaywalking pedestrians. The homeless rummaging through bins. Schizophrenics talking to themselves, to strangers, hurling abuse. Alcoholics with signs proclaiming 'Not gonna lie.

I need money for beer.' Veterans in wheelchairs, their stumps uncovered. Drug addicts asking passers-by for smokes. Smokers giving them one, unperturbed.

He knows leaving New Zealand and his mother looks bad. Frances had been scathing when he'd told her he needed to make a quick trip on some pressing business.

'Oh sure, fine. I mean it's not like there's anything of any great consequence going on here.'

'Come on, Franny. It's just for two nights. Mum's stable for now, anyway. And there's an opportunity I can't let pass me by.'

It was half true. He has a good lead on securing a large donor, but it could easily have waited. This past week sitting by Joy's bed, feeling helpless, in the oppressive atmosphere of the hospital, and under the weight of Frances's glowering disapproval, has made him desperate to escape. It might be different if Lara were around to soothe him. But he hasn't heard from her in four days since she returned to Auckland from Tauranga. He's sent dozens of texts, left several voice messages. No response. He'd imagined that getting on a plane and changing continents might ease his obsessive thoughts. Instead it's made things worse, compounding the distance between them, making it literal as well as figurative. No doubt getting a glimpse into his royally fucked-up family is a turn-off for her. But she was so empathetic and interested at first. She came to the hospital, and helped him with some end-of-year admin. She even went back to his apartment in Auckland to check on things there. He can't make sense of it. Initially she had made all the play for him. Of course, she is gorgeous, but he wouldn't entertain the idea of getting involved with an intern, his position too important. Until he did. After they slept together for the first time, Conor expressed unease at the situation and Lara suggested quitting. He didn't question how easily she'd relinquished a sought-after internship. It seemed to fit with his own intense feelings for her.

So how has it got to here? Where he is insecure and she is dictating the tempo? It is so different from how his previous relationships have played out. He goes over their last few interactions, searching for clues. A moment when he sensed her devotion turning to indifference. Having a mother who blew the top of her skull off could have been that tipping point, but Conor doesn't think it is that. She seems intrigued by his family.

He is finding the banter at the hotel bar a welcome distraction. The staff here know him well. They are mostly Latino and African American, friendly and teasing. They get a kick out of his accent and expressions. 'Sweet as, bro!' they say when he asks how they've been. He plays up the role of laidback Kiwi, hamming up his accent and colloquialisms. He eats a burger and washes it down with a couple of glasses of Californian Chardonnay. He is not much of a drinker, but by imbibing the local beverage of the place he is visiting, he feels he is being more authentic (despite the fact that the locals mainly drink the imported stuff). He is reluctant to leave his perch and head to his room when the staff start wiping down surfaces and cashing up the register.

His preferred suite faces the street. It is past midnight but the level of noise from outside is barely diminished; no double glazing here. Charles, a lanky African American with a patch over his left eye, is playing his 'drum kit' across the street. It comprises a frying pan, a couple of metal bowls of differing sizes and a variety of plastic kitchen implements erected with rubber bands and tea towels on a lamp post. He will be told to move on by the cops but will come back again tomorrow. Conor enjoys the cacophony. He usually finds it easy to sleep here, the outside noise a distraction from the looping refrain in his head.

He scans his Twitter and Instagram feeds, which he has neglected in the last few days. Notes with satisfaction the responses to his recent post about Katie, the little leukaemia patient. He needs to post something new but feels uninspired. It hasn't been the most Insta-worthy of days. He's come to do some fundraising and has spent most of the day giving presentations in boardrooms. Tomorrow will be better, though. Angie has arranged for him to pick up a convertible and he'll spend a couple of hours driving the coast road to Monterey, where the target of his, a young Silicon Valley entrepreneur, has invited him to hang out at his clifftop holiday home.

He tries Lara's phone again. This time it doesn't even ring, going straight through to voicemail. He sends another text.

Miss you, is everything ok with us? Call me when you can x

He should check on the latest from the hospital. Frances will know, but when he tries her number it rings out. Restless in his own company and knowing sleep is some way off, he heads back down to the lobby. The hotel bar is unattended now so he heads out to the street. Charles is still playing his drum kit. It is cold and he wishes he'd worn more clothes. San Francisco always surprises him this way. There is a 24-hour diner on the corner and an Irish bar, Rosie O'Grady's, next to it. Though he's had a couple of glasses of wine already – usually his limit – he chooses the bar.

There is only one other patron when he enters, a construction worker, covered in dust, sitting up at the bar with his hard hat and high-vis vest on the stool beside him. Conor claims a stool a couple of seats away. The barman, scrolling on his phone, looks up.

'What can I get you?' He has an Irish accent. His name tag says Donal.

Conor scans the liquor bottles behind the bar.

'Jameson please, Donal. Neat. Make it a large one.'

Donal pours the drink. Conor knocks it back, having to overcome his gag reflex as he does so. 'Again, please.'

Donal shrugs and pours. Conor sinks the second one while Donal watches him. 'Bad day?'

'Just some girlfriend troubles.'

Donal nods his head. 'The worst kind, all right. Another?'

Conor nods. He wonders what she is doing. If she is thinking of him. He wonders if he's imagined the last few months between them. Have they even existed, the two of them?

'Can I show you something?'

'Sure.'

He shows Donal the screen saver on his phone. It's a photo of Lara taken in the corporate suite of Eden Park, a charity cricket game on in the background. He had called her name and she is turning towards him, her head dipped, so that her face is all big eyes peeping out from silky hair. She doesn't like posing for photos, so he usually has to catch her unawares. It seems strange to him that someone so beautiful and young could dislike having their image captured. Especially when it seems to him as though the rest of her generation act as though there is a camera pointed at them at all times.

Donal lets out a whistle. 'She's a total babe, all right. I can see why you're hitting the sauce.'

The construction worker calls for another beer and Donal moves away.

Conor's phone rings. It's Sinead, and he tries to hide the disappointment when he answers.

'Hey, sis. How's it all going there?'

'Oh, you know, the usual fun and frolics. Leaving the country was an excellent decision on your part.'

'I had no choice, Sinead. I had important business to attend to. Anyway, where's Frances? She's been ignoring my calls.'

'That's not like her. She's just around. How's San Fran?'

'Dirty, overpriced, cold. Full of crazies. Bit like Dublin, actually. You'd love it. And how's Mommy dearest?'

'Great! Sitting up and getting the staff to run out to the off-licence for her.'

'Jesus, Sinead!'

'Just messing around, Misery Guts. No change. I spent most of the day there yesterday. The consultant reckons she can be moved to the private hospital soon. I guess they're keen to free up some resources. Maybe the move will finish her off. Mightn't be the worst thing to happen.'

'Christ, Sinead. You're a liability.'

'Relax, Conor, I'm only saying what we're all thinking. And while I'm at it, why are you doing this? I mean, she's a lost cause. Are you really going to spend potentially hundreds of thousands of dollars to keep her half-alive? The woman wanted to die in the first place. It seems unnecessarily cruel.'

'Well, it seems even more cruel to starve her to death, which is essentially what the hospital is suggesting. Look, her heart is beating strongly and she's breathing. Maybe there's a reason for that.'

'She's probably just fucking with us. Anyway, something weird happened yesterday at the hospital.'

'What was that?'

'So I was in her room and this guy walked in and he saw me and was about to say something, but then got all tongue-tied and left again. In civvies, so I'm pretty sure not a doctor. It was just, I don't know, something about him. Like he was entering with a purpose but then saw me and decided to go.'

'Jesus, shit. Did he have dark hair, our age?'

'Yeah, yeah I think so.'

'It'll be that journalist. I think I passed him the other day as he left. He wrote a piece about me. Well, about Mum attempting suicide. What is the situation with security in that place? Seriously, the sooner we get her out of there the better.'

He feels his voice rising. He looks in the mirror behind the liquor bottles and notices the construction guy staring at him.

'I'm sure the hospital has more pressing demands on its funds than securing the room of a comatose old lady. Even if she is *your* mother.'

'That's not what I meant. It's these scumbags who want to make a story out of personal tragedy. They'll do anything to get more clicks.'

'Well, he didn't look like some hard-nosed paparazzo.'

'How can you tell that from catching a glimpse of him?' He is irritated with her reasoning. As though she imagines a fictional hack like Lou Grant.

He hears her sigh.

'Okay, well, that's the latest update from the Tobin enclosure of the seventh circle of hell. You sound all riled up now so I'm going to go. But y'all hurry back now, y'hear?'

'Okay, see you soon.'

'Bye.'

'Fucking pricks,' he says to himself when he hangs up. He sees in the mirror that the construction guy still has his head turned in his direction. Conor looks directly at him, sees a slight smirk on his face.

'Something interest you here, mate? Or do you always listen in on other people's conversations?'

'Hard not to listen when you're shooting your mouth off in that dumb accent of yours. Mate.'

Conor sits up straight and pulls his shoulders back.

Donal, who has been drying a glass, puts it down. 'Hey now, lads. Settle down. No need for any aggro. We're all just trying to have a quiet drink here.'

'Hard to do when Crocodile Dundee here is broadcasting his bullshit problems all over the bar.'

Conor stands. 'Well, Donal, maybe you'd better tell Bob the Builder here he needs to mind his own business,' he says.

The construction guy stands too and pushes his stool back. Despite Conor's height, he towers over him.

'I'm not surprised you're having girlfriend troubles, you whiny little pussy. She's probably out getting fucked by a real man.'

Conor lunges for him but Donal sticks out his arm and blocks him. 'Cut it out, Johnny,' he says, looking at the construction guy, who is smirking. Then to Conor. 'I think it might be time for you to leave.' He is leaning over the bar with his hand on Conor's arm, preventing him from moving. Conor gets a grip on himself, steps back.

Johnny laughs and sits down. 'Pussy,' he says, then takes a swig of beer.

Donal lets go of Conor's arm and walks around the bar. Conor throws a fifty from the wad of dollars in his wallet on the counter and moves towards the exit, Donal following him.

At the door Donal says, 'Listen, man, what's the matter with you? Picking fights with a fella twice your size. Have you got a death wish or something?'

'I don't know. I'm sorry. I don't know what got into me.'

'No woman is worth getting killed for.'

Conor says nothing. Once outside he stands in the doorway for a moment under the buzzing green neon sign. He closes his eyes and takes a deep breath, tries to slow his heart down. It feels like it might free itself from his chest. The adrenalin subsides and he becomes aware of the nauseous sensation in his guts from the whiskey. He opens his eyes and sees Charles is untying his drum kit from the lamp post. Conor crosses over. He opens his wallet, goes to pull out another fifty, then changes his mind and gives it all to Charles.

Charles looks at the wad of notes in his hand before looking at Conor, bemused. 'Woah. You sure, man? There must a few hundred dollars here.'

Conor nods.

'Thanks, man. Appreciate it.' He has taken off his eye patch and beanie. The whole left side of his face is one massive indentation. Forehead, eye and cheekbone all gone. Conor thinks of Joy.

'No worries.' Conor makes to go, then turns back and says, 'Hey, mate, hope you don't mind me asking, but what happened to your face?' It occurs to him that he may have survived a gunshot to the head.

Charles gives a wry laugh. 'Cancer, man. Started out as a tiny lesion but because I'd no insurance it got huge, and well, here I am with half a face. Told me I wouldn't last five years. That was ten years ago. I'm a goddamn marvel.'

'True? That's amazing. Look, I hope I haven't offended you.'

Charles shrugs. 'Hey, it's cool, man. It's more offensive when people pretend not to notice. Charitable guy like you? I know you're coming from a good place.'

Charles's compliment weighs heavy on Conor's shoulders and he feels a dense emptiness inside that threatens to overwhelm him. He takes out his phone as he crosses the road, checks it. Still nothing. He doesn't see or hear a large delivery truck pulling into the loading bay outside the hotel. It narrowly misses him. The driver sticks his head out the window and yells, 'Hey, man! Helen Keller would have noticed this motherfucker. You trying to get killed?'

Conor raises his hands in a gesture of apology, then steps into the revolving door of the hotel.

SINEAD

She sits on a stool at Frances's marble-topped kitchen island and opens her laptop with a fizzy enthusiasm. Two nights ago, she sent what she had written on the plane to Maggie and she's excited for her response. A spiky ray of sun from the skylight overhead is hitting the keyboard. She waggles her fingers in it, waiting for the app to open. Goldfingers indeed!

Her stomach flutters when she sees an email with an attachment from Maggie. She opens it eagerly.

Darling Sinead,

I'm not entirely sure if you meant to send this to me at this stage? It's such a departure from your debut, and as you know we are under an obligation to keep the second book within the same genre/style so as not to alienate fans of the first. I like the idea of the woman sitting at the table contemplating her life, but to be honest, Sinead, the language and style just don't feel real to me. It feels confused. The stream of consciousness technique that you've used, it's almost as though you're trying to ape another writer, and it doesn't quite come off. What we all loved about the first was that we heard your voice. Distinctive and authentically you. I don't get a sense of the woman's desperation and state of mind because I think any real feeling is clouded behind a subterfuge of overly stylised language and overcooked metaphors. Does that make sense? I hope I'm not being too harsh. I just think you need to trust yourself more, Sinead, and let your own voice shine through. That's what made the first so utterly compelling.

Best,

Maggie

She feels sick. But surely Maggie has it wrong. She opens the attachment she sent to her and reads the first paragraph. It is filled with tenuous and tortured firearm metaphors. Poisonous projectiles, empty chambers, spent cartridges, misfired bullets, smoking guns, point blanks, hollow shells, emotional triggers . . .

Oh God, it's so bad she can't read any more. She slams her laptop shut and thumps her forehead onto the marble. It hurts and the pain is a welcome distraction. When the throbbing stops she sits up and checks the time on the oversized clock on the wall. Ten a.m. A bit early for a drink, but Frances is not here to judge. Remembering the bottle of Pinot Gris she opened last night, she goes to the fridge. She takes the bottle by the neck and gulps the remaining liquid down.

She puts back the empty bottle, knowing this will infuriate Frances, and sees a casserole dish with the leftovers of last night's dinner.

When it is all gone there is a hunger still, so she takes down the biscuit tin that Frances keeps tucked in a corner at the back of the high cupboard, but no matter how many she eats, they can't satiate her.

She is not a writer. She is a person who wrote one book. Ten years ago. Isn't that what they say? Everyone has a book in them? She wrote her one book and now it's time to move on. She could ask Frances for a loan, and pay back the advance. She could stop pretending she is a writer. But she imagines herself asking Frances for the money. It would be so humiliating. Frances, with her perfect, ordered life, who would never allow things to get so out of control. Who had been so contemptuous of the book in the first place. Maybe Conor? He'd be less judgemental. But how could she ever pay him back? She can hardly make ends meet as it is. And owing her family money might be more of a millstone than owing it to her publisher.

Sinead washes and puts away the dish and stuffs the empty biscuit wrappings in the bottom of the rubbish bin. She thinks about putting her laptop in there too. Pushing it and its miserable content under the other garbage. And she thinks, if it were big enough, she should crawl in there with it. Then she and her pathetic words and her shame could be tied up and thrown in the back of a truck and chopped and crushed and spewed out in a stinking landfill in an ugly, hidden part of the city.

She imagines the sensation of being compacted by the truck's metal jaws. She longs for it.

But she doesn't throw her laptop in the bin, instead shoving it into her backpack. A glint of silver in the corner catches her eye. She pulls out a folded-over square of aluminium foil. Inside are three of her little yellow pills.

Just one more time. Just a couple to burn off the biscuits.

It doesn't take long for that terrible heat to begin. She stands at the large Belfast sink and places her head under the tap, alternating between drinking and directing the water onto the back of her neck.

And a memory from school drenches her and she is at the water fountain, trying to calm down her puce complexion after a game of netball. A game where of course she has justified the reluctance from both captains to have her on their team. And she can hear giggling from behind, but she will not turn round and have them laugh at her scarlet face. So she stays there drinking and drinking and then, 'Hey, Sinead, you know whales are mammals, right? They need to come up for air once in a while.'

And she is frozen there, wondering which is preferable, death by drowning or by shame.

'Sinead?'

She turns. It's Livvy. How long has she been there?

'Oh, hi. No school today?'

'Teacher only day. Are you all right? You look a bit red.'

'Just, you know, readjusting to the New Zealand summer.'

'Maybe it's the menopause.' Deadpan.

'Jesus, Livvy, I'm not quite there yet!'

Her niece shrugs, as though forty may as well be ninety.

'Mum and I are going to the hospital this afternoon. Are you coming with us?'

Sinead imagines the airless room with its oppressive smell, her mother's heavy presence, the weight of the interactions with the staff.

'No, I'd better do some writing. I've done nothing for the ten days since I got here.' She wipes her forehead with her sleeve.

Livvy raises an eyebrow. It is an expression inherited directly from her grandmother. There is a frankness to her look that Sinead finds a little terrifying. She wonders if all children are like this, unwilling to conceal their thoughts beneath a mask of social expectation. No wonder Frances only had the one. It must be confronting to live with. It is not helping Sinead's paranoia.

Sinead notes the swim bag over Livvy's shoulder. 'More training today?'

Livvy pulls a face. 'Yeah, just sorting my gear. I think Mum wants me to go after we've seen Gran. Make up for the sessions I've missed.'

'And I take it you don't want to?'

'Doesn't seem to matter too much to anyone what I want.'

'You like it though, swimming?'

Livvy shrugs. 'I used to. Anyway, I thought I might start reading a book to Gran. Maybe something she read when she was young. I thought it might comfort her. I know everyone says she's not really there, but I think sometimes she can sense things. Have you any ideas?'

Sinead knows immediately. 'I think I do.'

Welcoming the distraction from her steaming innards, she walks over to the bespoke bookshelves that line one whole wall of the sitting room. There are hundreds of books, despite neither Harry nor Frances being big readers. Mostly hardback, they are collated by size and colour, so much so that they look fake. Sinead had looked through the titles yesterday out of interest. Many of them, she suspects, purchased en masse, perhaps by an interior designer. She had been amused and frustrated to find titles such as *How to Restore Ford Tractors* and *Swedish Carving Techniques*. And they are amongst the least obscure.

But in the deep red section – next to the brighter red section – of Frances's pseudo library, she had come across a copy of *Little Women* that had belonged to her mother. When she asked Frances how it got there, Frances said Joy had given her the book a few weeks ago. Sinead thinks it a bit odd. She wonders if it was a kind of bequeathing. Had her mother already decided?

'Maybe she meant it as your inheritance, Franny.'

'Wow, an old book and a stinky, decrepit dog. Aren't I blessed?'

'It could've been worse. You could have inherited her addictive personality.'

The pages were yellowed with age and smelled deliciously musty. There was an inscription inside:

To my Little Woman, my Pride and Joy. On attaining the age of 12. Your loving Father. March, 1962.

Sinead had squeezed her eyes shut and inhaled the woody scent of the pages, and as she did she remembered her mother saying how much she loved that book. At the time Sinead thought it strange. It seemed too sweet a novel to tally with her impression of her mother. She wonders now if Joy yearned for the warmth of Mrs March and her brood. She never spoke much about her upbringing, but Sinead sensed she'd had a lonely childhood.

Now, she hands the little book to Livvy. 'This would be perfect. Have you read it?'

Livvy brings the book to her face and breathes in the fusty odour. A kindred spirit. 'No, but I've heard of it. I think I might have seen the movie.'

'Well, it's a little old-fashioned, not an undead character in sight, but the story is lovely.'

'Sweet, thanks. I'm looking forward to reading it to her.' Livvy makes to leave the room, then stops. 'She's not gone yet, you know. Gran. I don't care what they say.'

Sinead doesn't know how to respond. Her mother has been gone from her for her whole life anyway, gunshot to the head or not.

When Livvy leaves, Sinead stares up at the rows of neatly arranged books. Her head spins, thinking about the number of pages within each book, the number of words on each page. All those ideas. All those ideas that the authors were able to translate onto paper. She slides the black steel ladder attached to an inbuilt rail across to one side. She climbs up to the highest rung, tells herself to not look down; the pills and the wine have made her dizzy. She runs her hand across the light grey section. Her hand stops and lingers at the smallest book, and she pulls it out. *Return to High Country* by R.M. Farnham. She has never heard of the book or the author. She opens to a random page, reads it, finds it intriguing. A conversation between a husband and wife. The sentences are taut and straightforward, the language spare, the dialogue convincing. She goes to the copyright page and sees it was published in 1964 by a New Zealand press she has never heard of. She reads the epigraph. 'What has been will be again . . . There is nothing new under the sun.' She climbs down, sits on the hard floor and begins at page one.

She quickly becomes engrossed. It tells the story of Freddy and Martha, a young married couple in the 1950s on a South Island sheep station owned by Freddy's parents. It tells of their struggles with the elements and sometimes hostile environment, Freddy's rejection of his father's traditional farming methods and the tension that causes. It describes Martha's unspoken pain at her inability to conceive and the weight of expectations upon her, particularly from her mother-in-law – a character one suspects has dark burdens of her own. It is an old story, nothing original or new, yet so tender and beautifully told. As she reads she sees all the elements her own writing lacks. The subtle yet powerful undercurrent of menace. The clarity, the authentic dialogue, the humanity of it. It makes her profoundly sad.

After reading the first few chapters, she goes outside to the swimming pool, desperate to relieve the intensifying heat from the pills. The midday sun bites her arms and the back of her neck. The cicadas are in full voice, and she imagines a hundred proboscises piercing her eardrums, rupturing them, and the insects crawling around her head. Her whole body starts to itch. She dangles her legs in the deep end, where the pergola behind her is still providing a bit of shade from the sun, and imagines diving down to the bottom and being cocooned in the blessed cool water.

She curses her inability to swim. They never had swimming lessons, a rite of passage for every other Kiwi child in a country where being able to swim is as integral as being able to walk. ('New Zealand's an island, of course we all know how to swim!' a teacher once said. 'Yeah? So's Ireland,' said Sinead, and was given a hundred lines on not answering back.) Frances and Conor somehow learnt despite their mother's indifference, Frances through a dogged determination to not stand out, and Conor, to whom everything came easily anyway, simply by spending summers hanging out at friends' swimming pools. Sinead's high school devoted a few weeks to swimming lessons each year, but by that stage she was so overcome by shame at her lack of skill and her obscene body that she forged notes from Joy excusing her. It was always on the basis of some near-drowning incident from her past, a lie that Sinead was proud of inventing. Who was going to argue with post-traumatic stress disorder? Everyone had watched *The Deer Hunter*.

Sinead always wished she could have been schooled in Ireland, where she imagined a lack of physical prowess would not have been held in such low esteem. Sure, she would still have been the fat girl, but maybe her quick one-liners and ability to write insightful essays on Anglo-Irish literature could have saved her from being the most unpopular one. She is not outdoorsy enough for New Zealand. She is more suited to Ireland, with its cool weather and indoor cultural pursuits. With her stupid name and treacherous pale skin. Her pathetic literary aspirations.

She longs now for the cool feel of her sheets in her little rented flat on Stamer Street, or the high-ceilinged, draughty yoga studio on Wicklow Street. She will tell Frances she needs to get home. Her mother could stay half-alive for months yet. And it is not like she needs to be here, even if Joy were to die. She has no need to grieve for her mother. She has been grieving all her life.

The tease of the water on her lower legs is not enough. She lowers herself in, holding on to the side. The water laps around her neck but it is still not enough. Her whole head is on fire. She puts her face under the water, keeping her eyes open. All is silent, peaceful now apart from the purring of the filters. It sounds like her mother's hospital room.

The pale cement on the pool's bottom is shot through with blue sparkles. They wink at her, inviting her. She imagines the relief of letting go, slipping under, the cold water first in her nostrils, easing down her throat, then in her fiery lungs, before mixing with her blood and being pumped around her body, like an engine's cooling fluid. She wonders if she'd stay on the pool's bottom or float on the surface, her black dress billowing around her like a macabre waterlily.

She thinks then of Livvy reading her wholesome book – where spinster aunts are austere and unfeeling, not deranged lunatics – and looking out her bedroom window to see her waterlily aunt.

Little Women. Isn't that just the old story of finding love and your place in the world? She pulls herself out.

She goes inside, dripping water on to the polished concrete floor. Frances would not be happy, but the wet clothes are like a salve to her burning skin, and she does not want to remove them. She sees the little grey book lying on the floor in front of the shelves where she left it. She thinks of Freddy and Martha, and how their love for each other is under threat from outside forces. Nothing original there. Nothing groundbreaking either in the conflict between the generations; a theme as old as time. Or the tensions surrounding motherhood. There are no new stories. Just retellings. She looks at all the other books on the shelf. They will all be variations on one theme or another. Told in different voices. What was it she learnt about in that creative writing course she did? The seven basic plots? Freddy and Martha's story could be transplanted anywhere. Ned and Connie on a little farm in the Irish midlands in the 1950s. All the elements of the original story would translate well. The sense of claustrophobia, the generational tension. She picks up the little book, takes her laptop from her bag, sits up at the kitchen island once again. She googles the title and the author. Comes up blank. She opens the book at page one and starts to type. Her hands are shaking but soon the rhythmic clicking of the keys under her fingers and the black script appearing rapidly on the screen soothe her. She just needs some inspiration to get started. That's all.

JOY

Our house was never a noisy one, but it is even more silent of late, since Daddy died a few months ago. Mother avoids me. When I walk into a room she walks out. She looks at me as though I repulse her. Like there is something in me she'd rather not see.

I like to spend as much time as possible at my friend Deirdre's house. She has six brothers, and the house is messy and chaotic and full of life. Sometimes I just sit there in the middle of them not saying anything, not wanting to draw attention to myself, hoping Deirdre will forget I'm there and just let me be, soaking up all the rough and tumble. I even like it when they fight each other, those wild boys, fists and tempers flying.

Deirdre says she'd give anything to be an only child, but I think she only says that to make me feel better. She never comes to my house anyway. I think Mrs Cassidy won't let her, not since Daddy's accident. And I don't feel as welcome in Deirdre's house since it happened. She's never said anything but sometimes I *catch Mrs Cassidy looking at me with a puzzled frown on her face. Deirdre never likes being around Mother either; maybe she senses her disapproval. Mother thinks big families are common. I think Daddy wanted more children, but I overheard her once telling him she wasn't going to be one of those Catholic martyrs, lying back and thinking of Ireland, popping out another child every year like clockwork. Just to appease the damn priest.*

The only time Mother seeks me out is when Mr Reilly, who owns the bar and grocery shop down the road, comes over. He has bulging eyes and a small mean mouth that always glistens with spit. But I think she wants to impress him somehow, so she speaks kindly to me when he is there. I don't know why because I see no kindness in him. He looks at my chest rather than my eyes when he speaks to me. Asking questions, always questions. So, do you have a young fella, Missy? And once when Mother was out of the room: Has anyone kissed you yet, Missy? I bet you'd like it, Missy. He draws out the s sound and reminds me of a lizard, or a snake. It makes me feel sick.

Today Mother went berserk at me. She accused me of wearing a dress that was too tight, that I was too fat for, just to get him to look at me. Wasn't it enough for you to take all your father's attention, now you want Mr Reilly ogling your diddies? I couldn't believe she had used that word, it sounded so silly coming from her mouth, so I had to stifle a giggle. Then she got so angry she slapped my face and sent me to my room.

And I'm here now in my bedroom and there's a knock on the door, and I'm worried that it's Mr Reilly. I think about jumping out the window, but I'm afraid of getting hurt so I hide in the wardrobe and hold my breath, scared that it will give me away. Then the wardrobe door opens with a long, slow creak, and I squeeze my eyes shut. There's a hand on my arm, but it's a gentle touch, and I open my eyes and see it's not Mr Reilly at all but that wee boy with dark hair. Come out, he beckons me, his hand outstretched. Come out now, you'll be grand. And I feel safe, so I take his hand. But I regret it because he's tricked me, and Mother is standing behind him and her eyes are narrowed and she's telling me how bad I am, how useless I am. I am crying but Mother carries on shouting until Mr Reilly comes into the room. And he starts to console me, sits on the bed and pulls me onto his knee.

It doesn't feel anything like comfort.

Mother and the boy make to go, and I call after them. Please don't leave me! But she slams the door shut and I am alone with the lizard man.

FRANCES

Frances is half-listening to Livvy reading *Little Women* aloud to Joy. She is surprised to find she's enjoying it. Could she be so content with such little material comfort? Stitching and mending and scrimping and tending. Maybe if you strip life back like that, contentment is found in simpler things. She can't imagine Mrs March having the time to ponder extra-marital affairs or feeling bitter about the number of stockings she'd darned that day. And even if she did have a minute, she was off ministering to consumptive neighbours and such.

Or. Maybe she was secretly resentful of the lot of them: her useless husband who lost all their money, her blossoming adolescent daughters highlighting her own wilting. Maybe she'd secretly yearned to do something meaningful with her life, like fight for women's suffrage, and felt deep regret that she'd missed her chance and must now cheerlead for her daughters' aspirations.

Frances doesn't say it to Livvy, but she thinks this reading aloud is a waste of time. Even if by some slim chance Joy were aware of her surroundings, surely hearing someone read to you would be beyond frustrating. There you are, desperately trying to reach out and give people a signal that you are not brain-dead after all, and all they can do is drone on about the domestic drudgery of a family living in nineteenth-century Massachusetts.

Her phone pings with a message. It's from Lauren.

Want me to get Josh to call u later with some conditioning for Livvy to do at home?

Frances types a reply.

No need thanks. We will make training later.

She watches the three undulating dots in the bubble.

Impressive commitment! Not even a comatose mother can stop the dream machine of Frances and Livvy!

She types again.

Well we only get one shot at this.

Three dots.

That's what your mother thought!

Frances types again.

Too much, Lauren. Even for you!

She puts her phone away. She thinks about Andy. She has been thinking about him constantly for the last few days and it makes her feel guilty that her mother has not been taking centre stage in her thoughts. Funny how a violent suicide attempt has now just become another part of her life. Just as her mother's alcoholism did when she was a child. Go to school, come home, pick your mother up from the floor and put her to bed. Then do your homework, make dinner. Go to sleep. A body can get used to anything, even to being hanged. She doesn't know where she heard that expression, but it has stayed with her. Her mother's hospitalisation has become just another knot in the rope.

She hasn't heard from him since the café, four long days ago. She feels they are engaged in a dance, where he is taking the lead. It is teenage stuff, this constant checking and rechecking of her messages. The lustful daydreams. Even Livvy would be above it. And yet it is the most alive she's felt in a long time. She seems to be in a constant state of arousal. She wonders if he is thinking about her right now and it gives her a thrill to think that their illicit thoughts might be coinciding. That they might be making love virtually. She leans back in her chair. Good old Marmee has told her girls she is visiting a family with scarlet fever; perhaps she is really having it off with rich old Mr Laurence next door. Frankly, he sounds a lot more charismatic than her own deadbeat husband.

Frances looks at her phone to check the time. She interrupts her daughter's reading. 'We should get going to training, Livvy. You've missed a couple of sessions with everything that's happened and the inter-school is the week after next.'

Livvy sighs. 'I think this is more important than stupid training.'

'Stupid training? We've worked all year for this comp.'

'*We've* worked all year?'

'You know what I mean.'

'Yeah, I do all right,' Livvy says, meaningfully. She resumes her reading.

'Livvy!'

'I would rather be here with Gran. You can't force me to go.'

Frances tries a different strategy. 'Well, Lauren posted Scarlett's latest times online. She's shaved a whole second off her butterfly. You might struggle to still beat her.'

Livvy looks directly at her, challenging her, and shrugs. 'And literally the only people who give a shit about that are you and Lauren.'

'Livvy, don't swear!' Frances feels utterly powerless. When do children come to understand this? When do they realise that the power imbalance can be so easily subverted? That, in fact, it is all an illusion anyway? She imagined she had a couple more years at least. 'Look, I know you may not feel like training now, but you'll be happy you did. Think of getting a place in Nationals. How great that will feel.'

'For who?' Livvy looks back down at the book.

'Livvy!'

The door opens and Harry walks in.

'Why aren't you at work?' Frances asks. She always hates it when Harry arrives early and unannounced.

'Just thought I'd come see my favourite girls.' He kisses the top of Livvy's head and goes for Frances's mouth, but she drops her chin so he brushes the top of her forehead instead. He then goes to his mother-in-law's side, leans down, and with one hand resting on her shoulder, gently kisses her cheek.

'How's my favourite mother-in-law today, then?'

'Jesus, Harry, you'd never dare to do that if she was conscious. She'd intercept with a right hook before you got anywhere near her.'

If Harry is aware of her irritation he chooses not to show it. 'I know! Imagine the fun we could have with her now. Hey, we could get a priest in to say a few prayers over her bedside. I reckon that would be enough to rouse her.'

'Or what about getting a troupe of interpretative dancers in? Remember that time we took her to see that fundraiser for my school?' Livvy is laughing fondly at the memory. Frances has no such fond memories of that incident. She had been wary when she picked her mother up that evening and smelled gin on her breath. One too many and her mother would tip from a childlike playfulness into a jaded scornfulness. You never knew till it was too late which drunk you'd get. Joy tutted and commented loudly throughout the whole performance, which was done without music. Frances sat through it clenched with anxiety. When it was over Joy stood up and proclaimed loudly, 'Well, that's two hours of my life I'll never get back!' Everyone turned to look at them, the other members of the PTA who had organised it looking furious, and Frances felt so ashamed. On the car journey home, Harry and Livvy told her to loosen up, it wasn't that bad, kind of funny, in fact. But they just didn't get it. They just couldn't get it.

Now they are making more ludicrous suggestions and cracking up at their own hilarity. Frances can't listen any longer.

She stands up and pushes back her chair aggressively. 'She can't bloody well hear anything anyway.' She might be shouting now, she's not sure. 'I wish you'd both stop being so ridiculous. Look!' She walks to her mother's side, leans over her and enunciates deliberately, 'You're brain-dead, aren't you, Mother?

A complete vegetable. You've blown out the few remaining brain cells that weren't already destroyed by the booze.'

'Rude.' Livvy slams *Little Women* shut. Harry gives his daughter a look Frances recognises. The *I know she's being unreasonable but just bear with* look.

'Time for me to get out of here. I'm going to the cafeteria.' Livvy stomps to the door.

'But what about your training . . .' Frances calls, but the door has already been slammed.

Harry says, 'That was a bit rough, Franny. This is traumatic for her. She loves her gran, you know that.'

'Yeah, well, she's got no idea. No idea at all.'

'I know. But aren't you glad of that, Franny?' He looks at her plaintively, but she refuses to catch his eye. 'Just give her a break.'

Frances shrugs. 'Whatever.' She is aware of how childish she is being, but it's as though she is not in control of what she's doing anymore. The resentment is fuelling itself.

Harry says, 'Anyway, the main reason I came here was to check if Sinead was with you.'

At her sister's name Frances can feel herself bristle. 'Why?'

'It's just that I went home before I came here. There was no sign of Sinead apart from her wet dress on the guest bathroom floor. It smelled like chlorine. Like she'd been in the pool with it on. Then in the kitchen I found this on the bench.' He holds out his hand – melodramatically, Frances thinks – and there is a bright yellow capsule in it.

'What is it?' Frances finds herself irritated by Harry's amateur sleuthing; smelling wet clothes for goodness' sake, and discovering mysterious pills. Why did Sinead always do this? Have people run around after her, worrying about her, second guessing her actions.

'Well, I'm not sure, but I googled yellow pills and found one that looks like this. It's a fat-burning drug used by gym bunnies and weightlifters. And some of the things I've noticed about her on this visit would seem to fit with that. Like the fact that she's so thin, and when she first arrived she was sweating heavily and smelled like sulphur. If it's this one particular diet pill I read about, it's extremely dangerous. It contains something called DNP, which is apparently used as a pesticide and in explosives. It can do all sorts of horrible things. Cause hallucinations, organ failure, blindness.'

'Well, she's a big girl, Harry. If she wants to jump into pools fully clothed and take drugs to lose weight, then all power to her. Personally, I'm sick of looking out for her. It's been the same my whole life.'

'But I thought you miss her when she's in Ireland?'

'To be honest, I'm beginning to learn that you can miss someone and still be glad they're not in your life.' She looks in her mother's direction when she says it.

'But she could die from this shit. She's not strong like you, she's much more vulnerable. She's your little sister, Franny.' Harry looks perplexed. 'And she can't even swim!'

The irritation tips into anger. 'My little sister? She's forty years old, for Christ's sake. You know what, Harry? Maybe you should have married *Sinead*, if you're so bloody concerned about her wellbeing. You could spend your time looking after her and I'm sure she'd never give you shit about leaving your dirty laundry on the floor or drinking too much.'

Harry looks at her steadily. 'I'm going to leave now, Franny. I know you're under a lot of strain at the moment, so I'll forgive your histrionics.'

Histrionics? She can't let him have the last word.

'No, *I'm* going to leave, Harry. You can stay here with your beloved mother-in-law. The one who didn't make my life a complete misery, by the way!'

Her car provides refuge. She thinks with shame of how she's made Livvy feel about the book. But she just can't seem to find the right tone with her daughter anymore. She watches the group of young doctors gathered around the mobile coffee truck parked across the road from the hospital. Some of them look barely older than Livvy. They are laughing. They look full of confidence. Assured that their lives are purposeful. That their choices have been sound. *That's probably as good as it's ever going to be, folks.*

A buzz from her bag. It's a message from Andy.

Was going through some of my things at my parents' house. Came across this. Remember? ☺

He has scanned a photo of her sitting with his parents at his twenty-first birthday celebration. Andy had taken the photo, and she is looking straight at the camera, her face flushed. Her gaze is flirtatious, provocative even. She can't believe she ever owned skin or eyes that luminous.

And yes, she remembers. They had just rejoined his family after going into the utility room on the pretext of finding the camera. Andy had pressed her against the juddering old top loader, which was on its spin cycle, hitched up her dress and pounded into her in rhythm, shuddering to a halt the same time as the machine.

God, the sex. They had so much of it. She *wanted* so much of it. It felt so vital. Now it was just another chore to add to her to-do list. Another thing to feel guilty about not doing more often. Or more spontaneously. Or more kinkily. She and her other married mum friends discuss the amount of sex they have with their husbands, all relieved to find they aren't the only ones whose libido has all but disappeared over the years. ('How many times a week for you and Mark, Lauren?' she asked her friend once. 'Can I give you the answer as a fraction?' Lauren replied.)

It's not that she doesn't enjoy sex with Harry; it's more that she doesn't crave it beforehand. Dreads it, slightly. She always feels good afterwards though, uncoiled, a generosity coursing through her as she lies draped over him like a satisfied cat. She's always found it very easy to orgasm with him, too. She remarked on that years ago, at the start, and he said it was probably because she was all raw nerves, sensitive. He said it with affection.

'Like a giant clitoris, you mean?' she said, and they used to laugh about that, a private joke for years. It feels like they haven't laughed about it in a long time.

But despite the post-coital satisfaction, she can't help feeling a sense of relief, too. Job done, thanks very much, see you same time next weekend. For a moment she feels profoundly sad looking at the photo and all the loss it represents.

Fuck this shit.

She phones Andy. He picks up, sounds surprised. 'Frances?' Without preamble she launches in.

'So, what's this all about then, Andy? Some mid-life crisis? Are you feeling vulnerable because you're getting older, and you think screwing an ex from your youth will make you feel young again? Doesn't your wife understand you, or is it your kids are getting older and don't need you as much anymore? Is this just some clichéd middle-aged desperation, Andy? Because you know, I've got my own shit going on right now. I could do without your misplaced attention. If it's really me, if it's really real, then let's do this. Otherwise just buy yourself a sports car.'

Silence. Then she hears Andy laughing.

'Frances, you crack me up. Good job you're not on speakerphone. I'm back in Tauranga next week. And yes, just so there's no confusion, it's *you*, Frances. It always has been.'

After she hangs up, Frances stays sitting in the car. There is a steady stream of people entering and leaving through the automatic doors. Hospital staff, visitors, relatives of patients, discharged patients, couriers. All here with a purpose. Some having the worst day of their lives. Some having just another day that will melt into all the others, until one day they will yearn for the ordinariness of it again.

She calls Sinead. The anger has subsided, and worry takes over.

Sinead answers quickly. There is loud music playing in the background, as though she's in a bar. Her voice sounds thick, her enunciation deliberate. She sounds like their mother.

'Franny, I've done something dumb. I . . . Maggie . . . Oh shit . . .' Her voice trails off.

'What are you talking about, Sinead? Where are you?'

'Just in town, catching up with old school friends for a drink.'

Frances recalls the miserable time Sinead had in school. 'What friends? I thought you hated everyone.'

'Man, can you please stop trying to control everything, Frances? Can't I just have a drink without you giving me the third degree? Jesus.'

'Fine.' Frances goes to hang up. Then:

'Franny?' Sinead's voice is small now. She sounds like a child. 'Why did she hate me so much?'

Frances thinks she is talking about one of the school friends. 'Who?'

'Mum. She resented me, I always felt it. My weight disgusted her. I was a disappointment to her. A literal big fat disappointment.'

'She didn't hate you, Sinead. She was sick. The way she was, it wasn't our fault.' Maybe her one therapy session hadn't been a waste of time after all. 'Let me come get you.'

And Sinead is weeping now. You can try to keep it inside you, but it'll always find a way to come out.

CONOR

Conor is back in his apartment in Ponsonby, packing a few things before heading to Tauranga again. As he opens the door his heart sinks and he realises he has still been hoping to find Lara here. Instead, he is disappointed with that hint of stale air that comes from the place being unoccupied for a few days. No musky scent from the expensive French candles she likes to light, or aroma from the Thai food she likes to cook. Not even a trace of the perfume she wears. Something with notes of sandalwood that she had once offered to him.

'Try this, it's unisex. It's fashionable to be androgynous now.'

He had laughed. 'We did that back in the nineties with some Calvin Klein scent, you know. You kids think you invent everything.'

There he went, pointing out the age difference again. It must have turned her off.

He lies down on the king-sized bed and inhales the pillow to maybe catch a scent of her there. But Sharon, his efficient cleaner, must have been in because all he can smell is the fake lavender aroma from the detergent.

He falls into a sweaty sleep and is woken an hour later, disoriented, by the sound of his phone ringing.

'Lara?' He is croaky with jet lag.

'It's Angie. Look, have you seen the *Stuff* website?'

He is disappointed to hear his PA's voice. 'No.'

'Okay, you need to have a read. Then call me back. Don't take calls from numbers you don't know. And don't worry, it'll be fine. We'll sort it. I've already spoken to Raewyn. It's all bullshit, probably libellous.' The mention of the charity's lawyer makes his stomach clench.

He doesn't have to search for long. The story appears at the top of his newsfeed, the most read story of the last hour.

Is TheOneForAll Boss Really Just AllforHimself?

CEO treats charity as 'personal piggybank'

Under the subtitle there are two photos, side by side. The first is of a smiling Conor, one might say self-satisfied-looking, sitting between two glamorous women at a table covered by a crisp white cloth, in front of expensive-looking wood panels and an oversized display of pink blooms. There is a champagne bucket on the table with a couple of bottles adorned with the distinctive Dom Pérignon label.

He tries to place the women and the restaurant, then remembers Megan, the wife of his ex-pat billionaire Cam. They had gone to dinner one night in The Connaught restaurant when he was in London. The other woman is Cam's sister. He can't even remember the photo being taken. The second photo is the one he uploaded to social media of him and Cam eating from a brown paper bag on a bench in Hyde Park. Without even reading the text, the inference of hypocrisy is clear.

He scrolls through the story, blood rushing in his head so he is unable to take in all the details. And there are a lot of them.

Only an estimated 60 per cent of the total donations going to intended recipients. Inflated salaries, with his CEO salary of six hundred thousand dollars the most obnoxious. Luxury hotels, convertible car rentals, Michelin-starred restaurants, business-class flights. Lavish staff parties. Week-long conferences at upmarket Pacific Island resorts classed as team-building exercises. Vast sums spent on consultants with no real value. An organisation filled with people from commercial rather than charity backgrounds. At its heart, a charity being run more like a company than a not-for-profit.

And the most sickening blow. Inappropriate 'relationships' with interns. As though there were several.

There are a few lines at the end relating to his mother's suicide attempt. Juxtaposed with details of an organisation built on excess – one that appears to exist only for the gratification of its boss – they have the effect of making Conor appear deeply unstable, with a monstrous ego that is the product of some mental disturbance. A type of mania.

There is bile rising from his gut. He goes back to the top of the story, but there is no by-line.

Who could do this to him? His mind jumps immediately to the journalist hanging around the hospital. And it meant he had a contact within the organisation. Or worse, and he feels nauseous, could it be someone in his family? He replays his interactions with close staff and family, searching for clues. He rules out Kylie, the accountant. Too straight. Anyway, she'd be implicating herself for financial mismanagement. Angie? No, alluded to in the piece for having an inflated remittance.

What about Harry, who up until last year had been the board treasurer? He'd stepped down, citing other work commitments, but maybe there was another reason. He was affable and kind, true, but did you ever know anyone? And Frances had been a bit strange lately, not herself – beyond a reasonable explanation due to the stress of their mother's plight. The hostility from her recently had been palpable. But she'd never risk implicating Harry in any scandal, even if only to protect Livvy.

Sinead was a loose cannon. And as they had all learnt, had form in this regard. Always shooting her mouth off. Liable to talk to anyone and give them information, especially after a few drinks. She never took anything seriously, might even think it was all a bit of a joke.

His head hurts from running through the possibilities. Who else could know all this? Lara . . . but there's no way. No. He'd give anything to have her here now, to put his head in her lap, let her smooth his hair – his halo of curls, she calls it – tell him it is going to be all right.

There is an incoming call from the chair of the board, Trevor. He wants to reject it but knows Trevor will pursue him doggedly.

'I suppose you know why I'm ringing, Conor?'

'I'll find out who did this, Trevor. I'll get to the bottom of it.'

There is a long pause. Trevor is one of those people who is comfortable with pauses, who uses them strategically in the hope that the other person will fill the silence, or capitulate, or incriminate themselves, depending on his requirements. Conor has never trusted people who can do that. He remembers Trevor telling him that he spent a few years as a school principal. He thinks of his old principal in high school, Mr Turner, who was just as intimidating. Conor doesn't fall into the trap.

'Conor, the issue is not who wrote this. I mean, who cares? It's just journalists doing what they do. The issue is the truth of it. The facts. Is any of it true? And whether it's true or not, how will this reflect on us?'

Conor hasn't given much thought to the specifics of the allegations, being too preoccupied with the source of them. He falters.

'Well . . . the salary is true, but you all knew that. It's in line with other charities our size. And you know how much money I bring in, Trevor. And I don't know the specifics of the contributions, but we are a large charity with lots of overheads. You know I place a high importance on team building and morale. And as for the business-class flights and luxury accommodation, well, you know we have to show up ready, not tired and dishevelled. I need to be fit for the purpose of building philanthropic relationships and—'

Trevor interrupts with impatience. 'But the girl, Conor, the girl, that's what will really hurt you. The rest we can try to obfuscate; after all, it's not illegal, but shagging an intern?

In this climate? We'll have all those MeToo, feminazi lesbians on our back. For fuck's sake, Conor, it'll turn into a circus.'

'Jesus, Trevor, she's a grown woman. It's totally consensual. And she resigned as soon as we started a relationship.'

'It doesn't matter if it's consensual. Or if she pursued you or even if she was the one who forced you into it. It'll all be represented as a power imbalance issue. You know how these things go, Conor. You've been around the block. The poor young intern starstruck into taking her clothes off and shagging her boss.' He sighs. 'I'm going to convene an extraordinary meeting. I would advise you to have a long, hard think about your position. Think about what's best for the organisation. Remember it's bigger than any one person.'

Conor wonders if Trevor used that line when suggesting a student be expelled from his school.

'I haven't done anything wrong, Trevor.'

'Think about it, Conor, and maybe prepare a statement while you're at it.' He hangs up.

The shock turns to anger. Fuck Trevor. Fuck the board. Power imbalance? That's ironic. He isn't going to take this. Prepare a contrite and humble statement exonerating them and assuming the blame himself? It was his idea, his charity, he founded it, did all the donkey work in the early days. He was the one who got the big glamorous donors on board. What did Trevor and the board contribute? Fuck all, that's what. Meeting up once a month to congratulate themselves on the large donations coming in. Sitting round in a circle-jerk of ego stroking.

Trevor, using his position on the board of such a successful not-for-profit to leverage his way in the corporate world. He doesn't remember Trevor being shy of availing himself of any hospitality that was going. He'd attended the conference in Fiji last year. Contributed a large amount to the considerable bar tab. Downing cocktails in those ridiculous Hawaiian shirts and leering at all the female employees.

Hypocritical prick.

His phone is ringing off the hook now, none of the calls from Lara. None of them from his family either, ringing to support him. He switches it off. He needs space to think.

He will travel to Tauranga as planned, ask Lara to join him. They can hide out in a hotel there. She will testify that their relationship only commenced once she'd resigned her position. He will confront the journalist if he is still sniffing around the hospital. He will contact the rest of the board before their meeting. He is confident of their support ahead of that old dinosaur Trevor. *He* is the one who needs to resign. Perhaps Conor will get Angie and some of the other women to lay out some testimonials about Trevor's lecherous behaviour. It will be fine. People like *him*, not Trevor, and that will work in his favour.

On the flight down he thinks back to when he was sixteen. Egged on by his large group of friends, he'd taken one of the bull's eyes that was in the science-room fridge, waiting for dissection in biology class. He had sneaked into the office of the principal Mr Turner and placed it in his lunch box, on top of the ham sandwich there. The original plan had been to place it in the top drawer so he'd get a fright on opening it, but something about the neatly packed box on the desk irked him – a reminder, maybe, of what he lacked – so he chose that at the last minute.

Mr Turner was furious. At a specially convened assembly he threatened schoolwide detention unless the culprit owned up or was given up by other pupils. Despite this, no-one did. Conor didn't worry too much about getting in trouble. Any punishment the school could mete out would not outweigh the feeling of validation the prank gave him. He sat in that assembly basking in the warm glow of his peers' loyalty. A school newsletter was posted to each home, outlining the incident and the school's concern at such a monstrous display of disregard. It urged all parents to speak to their children and remind them of the need to respect authority.

When Joy read the letter, Conor saw her scowl, and was half-afraid she might guess it was him or just lash out regardless. It was the unpredictability that got you. Instead, she laughed. 'Respect those in authority? Ha. What a joke.' And she scrunched up the letter and threw it in the bin.

At the time, he was conflicted about his mother's reaction. His friends would think it was cool, but to him it felt like neglect. He'd have welcomed a lecture on morals and compassion for others, like he imagined his friends were receiving. But now, sitting on the plane as it descends over the golden sweep of the Bay of Plenty coastline, he glimpses the city centre and estimates the position of the hospital. He thinks about Joy there, hooked up to machines, tangled in tubes, her skull half obliterated, her brain like mush but her heart strong, beating on. Fighting. For what, he doesn't know, but he is ready for a fight too.

SINEAD

The man sitting beside her at the bar is droning on about some grievance with a work colleague. Sinead doubts he even has a job. Who else but failed writers or the unemployed would be drinking in this hovel on a Wednesday afternoon?

His hands are large, fat-fingered. They are the kind of hands she hates in a man. They are stupid hands. His stupid hands are pulling the label from his beer bottle and letting the shreds fall to the wooden floor. She would like to say, Would you do that at home? But he probably does, so she says nothing; just nods along with his bullshit.

The way he looks at her, he thinks she's fair game. Why else would you be here on your own on a blazing-hot Wednesday? The rest of the city is busy or at least indolent in the sunshine. But here they are, the dregs, the wasters – the writer who can't write and the sausage-digited bore. There is an indentation on his left ring finger. Has he taken off a wedding ring before he came out, or have his fingers become too fat for it? She can't decide which would be worse.

She looks at his profile as he talks. He was good-looking once, she can tell. A beautiful brown-skinned boy. But his features look defeated now. Like he's had a disappointing life. *Welcome to the club, fella.*

Her phone buzzes. She picks it up. It's a message from Maggie. She is half-afraid to open it. She has sent her what she wrote this morning – the first couple of chapters of Ned and Connie's story – apologising for the previous manuscript, the drivel she wrote on the plane, claiming it was sent in error. ('Just a little experimental piece never intended for the light of day!') Now, she has a queasy feeling in the pit of her stomach. It's the same feeling she gets with a hangover. A sense of having done something shameful and self-sabotaging. The Fear, her friends at home call it. Perhaps Maggie has recognised the book. Perhaps it's not an anonymous little novel at all.

Darling girl! Have stayed up half the night reading what you've sent me. Love, love, love!! So glad the other thing was sent in error! I wasn't sure what on earth it was supposed to be! Going to bed now, it's 3.00 a.m.! Be in touch again later when I've sent it round the team x

A hint of redemption. The slightest glimmer of hope. Obviously she isn't going to copy it verbatim. That would be plagiarism. No, there's lots of scope for making it her own. Making it an Irish story. And anyway, maybe she can keep on sending excerpts but delay the final developmental edits. Pull out of it at the last minute. That will give her enough time to compose something of her own in the meantime. She feels giddy thinking of the reprieve.

The man is looking expectantly at her now and she realises she has missed a question. She puts her phone down and looks at him.

'Sorry?'

'I just asked what you did for a living?'

'Oh.' She wonders if she can say writer anymore. 'I teach yoga, actually.' She doesn't know why she said 'actually'.

Anyway, she has made the wrong choice. A big leering grin spreads across his face.

'True? So you're nice and bendy, then.' He puts a creepy emphasis on the word 'bendy'.

If she had a dollar for every time a man responded with that line. She needs to leave. But he has just put another beer in front of her and she is still savagely thirsty.

'Yeah, I'm super-flexible. Check this out.'

Sinead slips off her stool and lies on her back on the floor. The man is looking bemused, the barman less so. Sinead has not warmed to this barman. He has that surly air of superiority. As though he is doing you a huge favour by serving you. Sinead finds herself being ignored at bars in Dublin quite a lot as she gets older. For a while it wasn't like that. For a while she never had to buy her own drinks.

Lying prone on the floor, she bends her legs and places her hands down flat next to her shoulders before pushing herself up into a high backbend. The barman is telling her to get up, this isn't a gym, but she ignores him. She starts to walk like a crab and Fat Fingers is laughing now. She looks ridiculous but doesn't care. She likes the upside-down perspective and the rush of blood to her head. She thinks of a line from T.S. Eliot's 'Prufrock' about a pair of ragged claws scuttling across the seabed.

She is drunk, walking like a crab in a dingy bar in Tauranga on a Wednesday afternoon, thinking about a dead American poet, and she can feel the hysteria bubbling. She discovers it is very difficult to laugh when your diaphragm is arched towards the ceiling, and she collapses in an inelegant heap. If Frances saw her now!

She lies unmoving for a moment. The room is spinning. Fat Fingers is calling her a 'hard case' – a Kiwi colloquialism she has never quite got. The barman is threatening to throw her out, even if it means losing half his clientele for the afternoon. She stands up, feels a bit woozy and plonks herself down on her stool again.

The man leans in close and says, 'You know what? You'd be halfway pretty if you grew your hair.'

Sinead puts her mouth to his ear and says quietly, 'And do *you* know what? You're completely irredeemable, you fat-fingered fuck.'

First shock, then anger pinches his doughy features. He stands up and looks down threateningly at her.

Then everything goes black.

JOY

I am numb, disconnected from my body and yet acutely, gloriously aware. I am free of myself but am also the self I think I always should have been. Each mouthful softens me. If only I could be this person all the time. I like her. She is funny and flirtatious. Her thoughts are generous and wholesome, as though the gin is coursing through her veins then coating every synapse and rewiring it, disinfecting it, till only a clean translucence remains.

Billy is here beside me in the snug, laughing, enjoying my coquettishness. He gets a kick out of how much I can drink. I am voracious. I touch his arm a lot, and he enjoys it, responds to it, touches me back. And I welcome his touch; well, at least it doesn't disgust me. And I realise I have been starved of this kind of touch. The only kind I receive now is perfunctory and clinical.

. . . We'll move you on your side now, Mrs Tobin, to ease the pressure points on your back. Let's rotate your hips now, Mrs Tobin, to stop them seizing up . . .

I don't know who they mean when they say that. The only Mrs Tobin I know is Billy's mother.

Anyway, Billy's come back from somewhere. Not sure where but I know he's been gone a long time. And I should be angry with him, but I can't feel anger now. I don't love him though. I know that. He is a money man, with no curiosity in his soul, but he is good company, undemanding and uncomplicated. I've had enough of complicated. Mostly he is an escape. From home, from Mother. From him, Mr Reilly. From myself. I wonder if I should hold out for a grand sort of love. But I don't know if I believe in that. I think of Daddy and Mother, how it must have started out as something all-consuming, something big enough for her to defy her family, to marry down, and has ended up as something hard and small and mean.

We are in Neary's pub in Dublin. I asked Billy if we could come here for my twenty-second birthday because I heard a group of wild women came to this place without any men and demanded to be served pints of porter. And when they were refused, they drank the brandies they were allowed to order and then off they marched without paying for them.

How I wish I could have been with them. My life is so insular, it would feel good to fight against something that isn't myself. Billy thinks it's all nonsense, this women's lib stuff. Brassers he calls them, but it intrigues me. I think Daddy would have approved. Mother too, if only she'd let herself feel enthusiasm for anything. I know she'd approve of these women fighting to get French letters, taking the train up the North and bringing them back. Don't have children, Joy, they'll ruin your life, she says.

I'll end up marrying Billy though, and no doubt he'll want to have children, which scares me. I'm not sure if I would be very good at it. But once I marry him I'll have to leave my job in the bank anyway, so what else would I do?

And for some reason there are children here now in Neary's, which is strange because they aren't usually allowed at this time of night. There are three of them, huddled together, no adult in sight. A cherubic little girl with Shirley Temple curls. She is sad though, with a kind of fathomless pain that I understand, an emptiness that longs to be filled. And that little dark-haired boy again with the serious straight eyebrows. He is sitting with an older boy who looks just like him. I give them a smile and a wave, and the little girl and the younger boy turn away from me.

But the bigger boy smiles back, and he is holding out his hand. He is trying to show me something. And I feel like it's important, but my eyes have lost a bit of focus and I can't see what it is. After a while he gives up and turns away too. And I wish I hadn't let myself get drunk. Why have I done it? Debased myself again.

I turn to Billy but he has disappeared. I want another drink so I ask the barman, but he refuses to serve me without a man here. I can feel the mood of the place darkening. I am getting disapproving looks from the other people in the bar. The whispering and pointing has started. No-one will look me in the eye. I am a pariah. You've outstayed your welcome, now go, they're saying. I try to tell them, explain how it's not my fault, but they won't listen. I feel so ashamed, like I have ruined the happy ambience of the place.

How could I have thought I was the kind of person who could laugh in a bar, or order pints for the sisterhood, or make children like me, or even hold on to a man I never wanted in the first place?

And oh God, the hangover has started already; my heart is racing and my head, my head. I try to touch it but I am paralytic. I can only jerk ineffectively. It's like one of those dreams where you can't move or call out, you can feel your eyes roll back in your head with the effort and there is a hideous creature sitting on your chest, suffocating you.

Everyone averts their eyes and their ears and says, Ignore her, she's not there, she's not really there, she's just a drunk, her mind is gone. The drink has solidified now into a glass coffin enclosing me and I am ossified here. I can't smash it, can't reach out and touch them, show them who I am. You've made your bed, now you can lie in it, just like my grandmother used to say to Mother, filthy at her for marrying beneath them. Marrying a man who was gone in the head.

I often think being gone in the head wouldn't be the worst thing.

FRANCES

What kind of family ends up with two members admitted to hospital in the space of a couple of weeks? And both times the damage self-inflicted?

The staff must think they're all crazy. Bridget, the ICU nurse, had done a double take when Frances walked into A&E behind the stretcher. She had glanced at the person in it, *which one is it this time?* Smiled kindly at her. Made as though she was going to stop and talk, but Frances hurried past, giving a *what can you do* shrug as she did. She is embarrassed by that gesture now. Was it nonchalant? As though she was just bumping into her at the supermarket or school drop-off?

She has not told Harry she is back here with Sinead. He would rush straight in. There would be no 'I told you so', simply concern, but the thought of his kindness is unbearable. Anyway, Conor is on his way. He phoned from the airport and didn't seem overly shocked when she had told him he needed to come to A&E to see Sinead rather than his mother. Maddeningly, he didn't even ask why.

Sinead has been stabilised and is out of danger. The doctor had said she would probably wake soon, so Frances is waiting. This doctor was horrified when Frances told her Harry's suspicion about the drugs Sinead might be on. 'I think she just wanted to lose a bit of weight,' Frances said, lamely. She then felt chastised as she was lectured on the dangers. The doctor proceeded to question Frances closely about Sinead's state of mind, her drinking, signs of depression or possible suicidal tendencies. The general gist was that she, Frances, ought to have taken better care of her sister. 'I'm not her fucking mother,' she politely did not yell at this slip of a girl, who probably had no idea about anything beyond case studies in a textbook. '*She's* lying comatose upstairs with a gaping hole in her head.' She just kept her mouth shut and nodded remorsefully.

Looking at Sinead's wan face, her heart swells with a kind of maternal care. Poor Sinead. She always felt herself to be motherless, which is the same as being it, really.

She had been a charming baby, Frances remembers. Always quick to smile – revealing that solitary dimple – and raise her chubby arms for a cuddle. *I wuv you,* she'd say to just about anyone who showed her attention.

'Hey, sis.'

Conor is standing at the curtain.

'Hey, yourself.'

He looks at Sinead, exhales heavily. Her eyes are fluttering and a low moan escapes her. Her head moves from side to side as though she is agitated.

'What has she done to herself this time?'

Frances is just about to explain when Sinead sits bolt upright in the bed and says, 'He hit me, didn't he? That fat-fingered fucker hit me!'

'Sinead, thank goodness you're awake. But what are you talking about? Who hit you?' Frances says.

Sinead falls back against the pillows. 'This guy, in a pub. He whacked me.'

Frances is baffled. 'Are you talking about Elijah? No, you've got it all wrong. He was helping you. I walked in to see you collapse on the floor. Elijah was worried. He wanted to come here with you, but I told him not to.'

'Oh . . . then what . . . ?' Sinead's voice trails off.

'What have you done to yourself, Sinead?' Conor sits down on the bed.

'I just had a few too many beers, I think. And on such a hot day. I was probably a bit dehydrated.'

'Just throwing it out there, but the lethal fat-burning pills you're taking probably didn't help either,' Frances says.

'The which?' Conor asks.

'Little Miss Breaking Bad here has apparently been taking a substance originally used in explosives. Surprisingly, it doesn't mix too well with alcohol. Or the human body.'

'Shit. That's all I need. Who else knows about it?' Conor says.

'Well, there's us, Harry super-sleuth, the staff here. Oh, and her drug dealer, obviously.' Frances pauses. 'What's that got to do with anything, anyway? Are you worried about your reputation?'

'So you haven't seen any news websites?'

'Funnily enough, I've been a bit too busy dealing with self-destructive family members to have time for a spot of leisurely web surfing.'

'Really, Frances? Because every time I see you you're checking your phone, so I thought maybe you'd have an idea of what was going on in the outside world. Although, come to think of it, you're probably just checking Pinterest for home décor inspo.' The aggression in his tone is surprising. He's always been so unruffled.

'You patronising asshole, Conor.' Frances thinks about storming out but doesn't have the energy for two dramatic exits in one day.

He looks contrite, runs his hands through his hair. 'I'm sorry, Franny, I didn't mean it. It's just there's been a bit of a shitstorm in the media about the charity and my handling of it. Libellous bullshit that I can deal with, but it's put me under a bit of pressure. Hey, you haven't spoken to anyone about me, have you?'

'Of course not. I'm not the one who likes to air their dirty laundry in public.' She looks meaningfully at their sister.

Conor turns to Sinead, raises his eyebrows.

She holds up her hands. 'Jesus, of course not. By the way, does anyone care about me here and the fact that I, you know, almost died?'

Conor smiles. 'Fair call, little sis.'

—

Later that evening Frances is driving her siblings back to her home. Conor has been persuaded to stay with them. She had asked, expecting him to decline as he normally did, and was surprised when he agreed.

Sinead has been discharged with a stack of pamphlets relating to substance abuse, depression and eating disorders.

'But what about the ones on sex addiction and gambling?' she had asked the po-faced young doctor who had earlier lectured Frances.

'Ignore her,' Frances had said apologetically, seeing the look of confusion on the young woman's face. She took her sister by the arm and led her away. Once outside the hospital they both collapsed into fits of giggles.

They are driving in silence now. There is a weariness about all of them. Even Sinead is subdued.

Frances thinks of the car journeys they took together as small children, the three of them in the back seat, squabbling about whose leg brushed against whose, or whose turn it was to sit in the middle on the return journey. Their mother always kept the windows steadfastly closed as she chain-smoked the entire journey. 'But we'll catch our death!' she would argue when they requested some fresh air. Little Frances would lean her head back and stare up at the yellow nicotine patches on the car ceiling, feeling polluted by the smoke and longing for a bath. But it also worried her that death could be so casual. So easily caught.

...ed tiny Grim Reaper–shaped particles floating around ...here, just waiting for an open window to enter.

Sinead is sitting in the passenger seat, her head against the rest, her eyes closed. She looks drained of her usual exuberant colouring. She had been a terrible traveller as a child, her face always green-hued, forcing their mother to pull over regularly so she could vomit. She was certainly not built for New Zealand's kamikaze topography, with its winding hills and cliff-edged hairpin bends.

On one awful car journey, Frances can't remember the destination, Sinead, about six at the time, perhaps anticipating the nausea, had whined from the moment they sat in the car. She was never one to suffer in silence. Twenty minutes in and their mother could stand it no longer. She pulled the little Nissan abruptly into the hard shoulder, almost causing a pile-up behind her. She threw open her door so suddenly that a cyclist, swerving to avoid it, yelled angrily. Then she stormed around to the rear passenger door.

'Why do you always make things so difficult? Get out.'

Little Sinead refused to budge.

'I said, get out.' Her voice was menacingly low. Still Sinead refused to move, so her mother took her by the arm and yanked her out of the car. Frances and Conor sat as still as possible, staring straight ahead, too afraid to move and attract any wrath upon themselves. They watched, horrified, as their mother, her grip still tight on Sinead's arm, pulled their sister up the steep grass berm and pushed her down to sit. Then she came back to the car, got in, and drove away. Frances turned back to see Sinead sitting with her arms wrapped around her legs and her forehead resting on her knees. She stayed like that, not even bothering to look at the car as it sped off. Frances's heart swelled with concern for the little unmoving figure perched on the roadside. She wanted to speak up, tell her mother to go back, but the fear of the same thing happening to her made her keep her mouth shut. It was Conor who eventually spoke.

'I hope a car doesn't come and run her over.'

Frances's stomach flipped. She looked at Conor and wondered how he had dared to say it. But Conor had his chin up, and he met his mother's gaze with defiance in the rear-view mirror. Frances couldn't breathe with the tension. What was their mother going to do now? After what felt like a lifetime, it was their mother who averted her gaze first. Indicating, she pulled up once more on the side of the road. She turned around, her eyes wet, and gave her son a look that to Frances seemed almost fearful. But she did a U-turn and they headed back towards Sinead.

As they approached the spot where they'd left her, Frances could see a blue car had pulled up on the berm. A man was standing over their sister, who appeared not to have moved a muscle since they'd left. He was looking, bewildered, towards a wooded area beyond the roadside hedge, as though suspecting this little person to have come from there. Like some kind of ethereal forest nymph.

From their parking spot on the opposite side of the road, Frances anxiously watched the interaction between her mother and this concerned passer-by. She felt sure the authorities would be called and they would all be taken away after this display of parental negligence. However, much to her surprise, the conversation appeared amicable, both adults even laughing. The world of grown-ups was a mystery. Their mother led Sinead back to the car in a much gentler fashion than when she had removed her. She even gave the man a jaunty wave before driving away. The rest of the journey was spent in silence. And if Sinead felt sick again, she gave no outward display of it.

Now, Frances looks at Conor in the rear-view mirror. He looks so tired. She catches his eye and gives him what she hopes is a sympathetic smile.

'Sorry,' she says.

'For what?' He seems wary.

'Just, you know, what's going on in the media and stuff. But I think you will deal with it, get through it. You've always been brave.'

He looks a bit mystified but says, 'Thanks.'

—

Late that night Frances sits at the kitchen island, catching up on emails and admin for the PTA and the upcoming inter-school swimming competition, and scrolling through inane Swim Mom WhatsApp conversations to find any pertinent information. Sinead, exhausted, is fast asleep. Conor has retired to his bedroom, but Frances can hear him pacing and talking in urgent tones on his phone.

Harry had been sweet, waiting on Sinead, and made no mention of Frances's earlier outburst. But his concern was harder to bear than any grudge he may have held, and she was relieved when at last he left for Auckland ahead of a client meeting the next morning.

She has been cc'd into a tedious email argument between Lauren and another one of the Swim Moms, Donna, regarding the merits of a sports theme versus a carnival theme for the social being planned to raise funds to send the qualifying swimmers to Nationals. Lauren is leaning towards a carnival theme because they have a lot of the decorations already – courtesy of last year's circus theme – so could cut costs (and work for Lauren). Lauren writes her emails the same way she speaks. Bad grammar, shouty capital letters and exclamation marks galore. Donna prefers the sports theme because she is concerned that, as with the circus, the carnival theme would give the girls licence to turn up in all sorts of inappropriately sexy costumes. Sexy acrobats, sexy ringmasters, even sexy clowns, for goodness' sake. Donna is also worried about cultural appropriation. (*Are clowns a culture now?* Frances wonders.) Frances has been asked to make the final decision but finds she is quickly losing the will to live. For her own amusement she drafts a reply.

Hi Donna and Lauren,

Might I suggest an S & M theme? Harry and I have a whole collection of gear here: gimp masks, dildos, and whips etc. so we wouldn't have to buy much, which will work for everyone. Let's give the kids something to really get their teeth into,

Best, Frances

She logs in to her Instagram account. One of the Swim Moms has posted a graphic showing the results from the training session that Livvy missed earlier. *So many PBs today! Amazing! Go Tauranga!* It makes Frances feel panicked. She doesn't hit the Like button. That would be noted, no doubt. Scrolling through her newsfeed clogged with photos of overachieving children and macro-nutrient perfect dinners, she stops at a photo Andy has posted. A selfie of himself and his wife Cathy in a restaurant, smiling, cheek to cheek, with the hashtag *#datenight*. Cathy looks good, but has she had fillers? Her cheeks have that slight chipmunk-ish look to them. Maybe it's the light, but her hair is a bit brassy. *Dyed off her head*, she can hear Joy say. And Andy's smile is a little forced. She scrolls through his previous posts, looking for clues. Something that will tell her their relationship isn't as cosy as it appears. It's a futile exercise. Andy, like everyone, only posts the highlights.

'Stanning an ex, are you?' She has not heard Livvy come back from her night out at the cinema with friends. She shuts the page down quickly and reopens her emails.

'What does that mean?' Frances can't understand half of what Livvy says these days.

Livvy sighs impatiently. 'Stalking an ex. You know, like the song?'

'What song?'

'You know, Eminem? Never mind.'

Frances shakes her head, bewildered. 'Of course I'm not stalking anyone. I'm catching up on work.'

'Work?' Her tone is sarcastic. Frances still smarts from the time Livvy, aged five, had asked her, 'Mummy, why didn't you grow up to be anything?'

'Yes, Livvy, just because I don't get paid for it doesn't mean it isn't work.'

'Whatever. I'll be out of your way soon, just getting a snack.' She is still angry about earlier. Fridge and pantry doors are being opened and shut aggressively. 'There is literally never any nice food in this house. So dumb.'

Frances recognises that her daughter is communicating her hurt. She tries to soothe it. 'Look, Livvy, I'm so sorry for what I said at the hospital. I think it's a great idea reading to your gran like that. Even if she can't hear it, I'm sure it brings comfort on some level.'

'Whatever,' Livvy says again. Where is the little girl who allowed her mother to tenderly kiss her grazed knee then put on a plaster as she sat on the kitchen bench?

'So when you missed training again today, I rang Josh and he said he could do some extra work with you tomorrow morning after squad?'

'No, thanks. I'm all good.'

'But the comp is in a couple of weeks. Everyone's times are improving Livvy, you'll get left behind.'

Livvy shrugs and Frances can feel a pressure forming, like a pulse travelling from her chest to behind her eyes. It takes all her will not to scream at her daughter. Instead, she takes a breath. Counts to ten. 'I thought maybe we could talk about something that happened today with Sinead. She, well . . .'

'Chill, Mum. I got the memo. Dad rang me earlier and told me. So you can stop with the whole "Alcohol and drugs are dangerous" lecture.'

Frances finds herself annoyed at Harry yet again. Must he always be such a woke model of parenting virtue?

'Okay, it's just I know you get on well with her, and I didn't want you thinking it was, you know, cool to—'

'Jeez, Mum, literally no-one my age thinks drinking and taking drugs is *cool*. That's just your generation.'

Frances finds Livvy's new way of talking infuriating. She has developed a habit that involves her voice trailing off croakily at the end of her sentences. It's as though she's trying to communicate her complete disregard for the person she is talking to. As though even speaking to them is a massive effort. Vocal fry, Frances thinks it's called.

('I blame those fucking Kardashians,' Lauren says. Lauren likes to blame the Kardashians for everything.)

It is certainly frying Frances's brain. Do other mothers find their teenage daughters this annoying?

(Lauren would say yes. 'Girl, that's just God's way of making it easy to let them go!')

'Right.' She tries to lighten the tone. 'Well, you should count yourself lucky we didn't lumber you with siblings. Nothing but trouble your whole life, believe me!'

Livvy is on her way out the door. She stops and turns back when Frances says this. 'Lucky? Are you for real? I *hate* being an only child. It's like I've got to be perfect *all the time*. I feel like your little project. I just wish you had a job like other normal mums so I'm not your only focus. And of course you're involved in the PTA and swimming too, just so you can be controlling when I'm not at home. And you're not even focussed on me as I am, just a version of me you think I should be. I don't care about being perfect. I don't want to be at squad training every day. I don't care about making Nationals. I don't care if my backstroke is three-tenths of a second quicker than Scarlett's. Being an only child is just pressure, pressure, pressure like I'm going to explode. I feel like I can't even *die,* because I'm the only one!'

'What do you mean? Do you want to die?' It comes out as a shriek.

Livvy lets out a big sigh. 'See? You're just putting all *your* messed-up family shit on me again. Forget it, you're not even hearing me. I'm going to bed.'

'We can talk about this again later, Livvy, maybe—' But her daughter slams the door.

She looks at the collage of Livvy's baby photos, turned into magnets, displayed in a symmetrical design on the fridge. The memory of holding her newborn is strong, the physicality of it still palpable, and the thought she had when she cuddled her that first time. *I can make this right.*

She stands up and swipes angrily at the magnets, knocking them to the ground. 'Fuck you,' she says to the floor. To herself.

She sits again and reopens the draft email she composed to Lauren and Donna. She hovers the cursor over the delete button, then changes her mind and presses the send button aggressively. It feels so good to give in to this impulse. A minute later her phone pings with a message notification. It's from Lauren.

OMG FRANCES! HILARIOUS! S & M Theme!! Love it!! Mrs
Fucking Poker UP HER TIGHT ASS will DIE!! LOL

The adrenalin leaks away. Oh God, what has she done? She
groans and drops her forehead onto the cool marble benchtop.

CONOR

The next morning Conor sits on the large wraparound deck at the back of Frances's house drinking a cup of coffee. He closes his eyes for a moment, listens to the complicated trills and tics of some nearby tūī. The early sun feels pleasant on his face. The deck faces towards the glass-fenced swimming pool, glinting in the light, and the jasmine-covered pergola. Beyond the pool is a large expanse of summer-parched lawn, dotted with mature fruit trees, persimmon, fig, avocado. A couple of parakeets paint the kōwhai tree in the corner. Past the feijoa-hedged boundary of the lawn, the acre section backs on to bush. Two large prehistoric-looking gums tower over the other trees there, miniaturising them, even the gnarled pōhutukawa, which now retains only a few of its crimson flowers. He thinks of the tiny, treeless back gardens separated by low wire fences in their newly built estate in Navan that meant you could see into several other houses all at once. The light-eyed jackdaws and yellow-beaked starlings that congregated on the flat rooves of the garages. The concrete pavers under rows of clotheslines heavy with terry nappies and school uniforms and greying underwear. Women in pink polyester dressing gowns with cigarettes in their hands throwing plastic bags into the steel bins that stood outside the doors. He wonders how he and Frances got here. A place with covered verandas and backyard pools and long, dry summers and exotic birds and abundant trees of fruit that he'd never heard of before he moved here. It seems so unlikely. He sometimes has the feeling he has borrowed someone else's life. He wonders if Frances feels the same.

He spent last evening canvassing the board ahead of the extraordinary meeting that Trevor has called, and now has six of the eleven board members on his side. Enough to mean Trevor will lose the vote to remove him as CEO. But still, he feels strangely flat.

The original online piece has been picked up by several news outlets. Angie has been fielding a lot of requests for comment and interviews. She and Raewyn have reassured him that he just needs to tough it out for a few days before the media become bored and move on to their next scandal. Raewyn had bemoaned the fact that the story was published during silly season, parliament's traditional summer break. 'Thankfully the politicians are back this week to take some of the heat off. Shouldn't take too long for one of them to fuck up.'

Still no word from Lara. He told a much-recovered Sinead at breakfast all about his romantic woes. She reassured him, suggesting that Lara might just be lying low to avoid any attention on herself. She was sure she would be in contact later when all the fuss died down.

'Don't you think, Franny?' Sinead had asked her sister, who was loading the dishwasher as they spoke.

Frances had straightened up and glanced at Livvy, who was packing her lunch into her schoolbag. 'It doesn't matter what I think; you'll read whatever suits your own narrative into other people's actions.'

Sinead gave Conor a wide-eyed *Uh-oh, something's up with her* look and got back to eating her toast.

'Sounds like you've been ghosted, Uncle Conor,' Livvy announced before heading out the door to catch her bus.

'What does that mean?' Conor asked.

Sinead just shrugged her shoulders.

Frances said, 'Don't ask me. I've no idea what goes on in that girl's head anymore.'

The memories of the little house in Ireland make Conor think he should go and see his mother. He has nothing to do now anyway but wait. His fate is in someone else's hands. A disconcerting feeling.

In the car he backs carefully out of the long driveway, and just as he reaches the road a couple of young boys on bicycles whizz past, oblivious to the reversing vehicle.

'Are you tired of living?' he yells out the window at them.

He is surprised that these words have come out of his mouth. It is something his father used to yell at errant pedestrians or cyclists. That was before the accident, of course. Saying it after would have been unthinkable.

One of the boys turns back and gives him the finger and they carry on their way, laughing hysterically. He stays there at the end of Frances's driveway looking at the pair. He envies their energy, the joy in their physicality, but most of all the fact that they have no idea they will ever feel any different. He thinks of a line he's always loved from a Bob Seger song about wishing he didn't know now what he didn't know then. He remembers riding with his friend Philip around the streets of their housing estate in Ireland. Both of them on their Raleigh Choppers, doing skids on the dusty gravel that would skin the knees off you if you mistimed it. Or using the dirt mounds – from the new houses that seemed to be constantly in mid-construction – for their Evel Knievel stunts, until one of the builders would yell at them, 'Have yous no homes to go to?'

When he arrives at the hospital Bridget is in the room manipulating his mother's arms and legs in a series of stretches. She talks matter-of-factly through the manoeuvres. 'I'm just going to roll you this way, Mrs Tobin,' or, 'I need to bend your leg that way, Mrs Tobin.'

Conor looks at his mother's face when she is rolled on her side, one of her eyes popping eerily half-open, revealing a yellow-tinged sclera, her mouth lolling open in the manner of a halfwit, a glob of drool collecting in the corner.

How she'd hate this, he thinks. His mother who hated unnecessary touching. If you tried to give her a hug her body would go rigid, her hands dropping to her side. You could feel the relief as you pulled away, which you always did. Unfulfilled.

'Do you feel like helping, Conor?' Bridget says.

Conor does not. But he stands up and waits awkwardly for instruction.

'If you roll her over onto her side and just hold her up like that for a few minutes. It'll relieve some of the pressure on her spine.'

Conor has braced himself to push over a dead weight, but instead is surprised by how light she feels. Insubstantial, almost. When she is on her side the back of her hospital gown gapes open. He catches a glimpse of what looks like a diaper and quickly averts his eyes. He hasn't given much thought to the logistics of waste management but is now acutely aware of the catheter bag hanging from the side of the bed, perilously close to his leg.

Her back, like his, is deeply freckled, especially around her shoulders. Kisses from God, she used to call them. He remembers her once trying to console teenaged Frances about this when she was comparing herself unflatteringly to one of her olive-skinned friends. But then she lost her patience with the self-pity, her milk of kindness being finite, and said, 'Pull yourself together, Frances, at least you're not fat.' Sinead, who was present at the time, visibly winced and left the room.

That was their mother, giving with one hand and taking with the other.

He feels a creeping disgust now, touching her like this. He hates himself for it and he hopes Bridget cannot sense it.

'Can I . . . I mean, should I let her down now?'

Bridget nods and he releases her gently onto her back. Involuntarily he wipes his hands on his t-shirt. 'Sweaty,' he says when he realises Bridget has seen him.

'Well, I'll leave you two alone then. By the way, another bunch of beautiful flowers arrived for your mum this morning.' Bridget points to a display on the bedside locker.

Conor wonders if there is any gesture more redundant than sending flowers to a coma patient. It ranks up there with posting a message to someone on their social media page after they've died. *Hey bro, will miss you so much, have a great time in Heaven!* But he feigns interest for Bridget's sake and picks up the envelope placed in front of the vase. He opens it and reads the message.

Wishing you well, so that maybe you can learn to forgive yourself, as I have, B

An ambiguous, almost anonymous message to a nearly dead woman. Ridiculous.

He goes to put the card back in the envelope when Bridget says, 'Perhaps that's worth reading aloud to her.' Then she leaves the room.

He feels foolish, but Bridget intimidates him. He sits down beside the bed and opens the card again, reading the words slowly and loudly.

B. Billy? Surely not. How would that useless bastard even know? Billy Tobin, that paragon of fatherhood, who went as usual to work at the ACC Bank on Market Square one Friday morning a few weeks after the accident and never came home. Joy didn't seem to know, much less care, where he was. 'Hell, hopefully,' she said when Conor asked. He stopped asking pretty quickly. They all did. He allows himself to imagine that his father has been following his career from afar. Rejoicing in his son's successes and growing fame. Devouring any online information he can, learning of his abandoned wife's situation through the latest stories. For a moment he hopes his father doesn't believe the libellous recent reports. Hopes he is not ashamed of his son.

Then he tells himself to grow up. His father cares nothing for him. He left. His mother chose leaving, too. And it looks as though Lara has done the same. He considers ripping the card into pieces. Instead he walks to the vase, plucks the head off a white chrysanthemum, and crushes it. The petals fall to the floor, and he kicks them as he strides out the door.

SINEAD

She opens her laptop. She has been avoiding this for days. But Maggie has begun to leave giddy voice messages, and writing might be easier than ringing her. She clicks on the icon and sees new mail from Maggie. She stares at the subject line, New Novel, for a few moments, sighs, then opens it.

Darling Sinead,

Oh my love! I think we are onto something here. I passed the chapters you sent round the team. They're all in agreement. We all adore it! The terse atmosphere in the farmhouse, the visceral tension, so much left unsaid and yet still so evocative. And the characters, so beautifully realised; they hop off the page. We can't wait to know how it ends. Have you done more? Can you send it on? What about a brief synopsis? Do you know where you're going with it? So many questions!

Gina, who handles the film and television rights here, is
champing at the bit. She's imagining a *Brooklyn*-esque type
adaptation. I can totally see it too! I mean, there are no
guarantees of course, but I think it lends itself perfectly to a film.

Do you think June is doable for a first draft? Then we are
looking at a release date of next summer. Perfect timing! No
pressure, of course. I understand it's a horrible time for you,
darling, but honestly, I'm so excited by this. I always believed
in you. You're so talented, Sinead. There's no way there wasn't
another brilliant book in there somewhere.

Maggie x

She reads it through three times. Becomes intoxicated by
Maggie's effusive praise. Imagines another glowing review in
The Irish Times, a humble yet insightful acceptance speech for
a literary prize where she acknowledges the talent of the other
nominees, a glittering night at a television awards ceremony . . .

Then she remembers how she felt when she got that first
call from the agent who agreed to represent her and later the
news that several publishers were interested. When she experienced such elation, but also an overwhelming sense of imposter
syndrome, as though at any moment people would realise she
had no talent whatsoever.

And this time, if she carries on leaning on the little grey
book, she really *will* be a fraud. She sobers up quickly. Feels sick
with herself. She will write to Maggie later and let her know it's
another dead end.

She needs to get out of her head for a while so she borrows Frances's car and drives to a yoga studio on Eighteenth Avenue, directly opposite the hospital. She unrolls her mat near the back of the class next to a woman who gives her a friendly smile. She sits cross-legged waiting for the class to begin, regretting the teeny cycling shorts she has taken from her sister's neatly folded pile of gym attire. The fronts of her thighs are on show, exposing a crisscross pattern of silvery pink scars running down almost to her knees. She tries to pull Frances's singlet down to cover them, but it remains stubbornly fitted and short. Damn her sister and her toned, Lycra-worthy body.

So, she stares at the scars and imagines herself like a ringed tree trunk, each line representing not a year of growth but an episode of belittlement, a stunting. Here was the time she found out that Justin White had asked her out only as the consequence of losing a bet. Here was the time she snuck down to the kitchen at three in the morning and ate a whole box of Christmas chocolates. She was never the type to stick her fingers down her throat and flush her shame down the toilet like some other girls in school. No, she preferred to keep the food in her stomach and have her shame seep out her skin.

Although it has been years since she's done it, she longs now for the release that trickles out with the blood.

She is distracted by the woman next to her, who has turned her head towards her. Instinctively she places her hands over her thighs. She does not want to make small talk with a stranger. She shuts her eyes and considers some chanting to discourage any communication.

'Sinead Tobin, is that you?'

Sinead's heart sinks. She sighs and turns towards her accuser, but doesn't recognise the woman, who is now smiling in a maniacal way.

'It's me, Jessica Stevens – well, Thornbury now! From high school! Look at you! You're so skinny! It took me a while to place you. Oh, we must do coffee when the class is over. Dying to catch up.' She says this as though reconnecting with Sinead has been forefront in her mind for the last twenty-odd years.

The class is now ruined for Sinead. She distorts every pose to avoid catching a glimpse of Jessica, who somehow manages to achieve the most complex of positions with her head turned towards her in an encouraging grin. Sinead imagines her regaling her old posse with the miracle of seeing that fatso Sinead Tobin being able to balance in crow pose with ease.

After class Jessica suggests a café next to the studio, and they sit at one of those pretentious, low-couched tables Sinead despises, which give away the café's early aughts inception. There is no way to drink your latte without spillage as you hoist yourself forward and back to place and retrieve the impractical wide shallow bowl these places insist on using. Also, they are so close to each other their legs are almost touching, the artfully saggy and shabby-chic couch rolling them together each time Sinead tries to edge a little further away.

'So . . . spill the goss, Sinead. What's been happening?' Jessica says, as though she wants an update on her weekend rather than the last two decades.

'Well . . . I'm just here from Dublin for a few weeks. My mother, um, well . . .'

Jessica touches her knee sympathetically. It takes a huge effort not to recoil. 'I heard, you poor darling. Saw all the news articles. How devastating.'

Sinead waves her hand dismissively. She has no desire to get into it with Jessica. Feels nauseous at the thought. 'Oh well, shit happens.'

Jessica gives her a quizzical look, then emits a hesitant chuckle, as though she is sharing in a naughty joke. 'You were always so . . .' – she searches for a word – '. . . irreverent! What fun we used to have!'

Sinead wonders if perhaps she is confusing her with someone else. Jessica leans forward to get her coffee cup and as she does pushes her hair back from her forehead in a gesture Sinead remembers. Jessica's hair was always a wonder to Sinead. Thick and straight and shiny, it always fell just so. Rich girl hair, it looked as though it would emerge sleek and unscathed from a tropical cyclone.

Sinead touches her own shorn fuzz with a hint of regret. It had felt liberating when she'd taken the razor to it. ('You've done a Britney!' Franny had commented.) The first evening, when the effects of the little yellow pill she'd taken were new and intense, it gave her a kind of cooling release, similar to the first nick of the blade on the compliant flesh of her thigh. She wonders if Jessica is thankful for her hair or just takes it for granted. People like her take a lot for granted.

'Shit, do you remember the time we mooned those people from the bus on our way back from Auckland for that choir festival? It was the funniest thing ever. Far out! To be young again, eh, Sinead?' Jessica is properly laughing now, her eyes wet with nostalgic mirth.

Sinead feels her face redden. For the first time in high school, she'd been enjoying the company of her peers. Singing was something at which she excelled. She even had a solo part in a couple of the songs. Some of the other less assured singers followed her lead, and their music teacher Mrs Clarkin often called on her to show the others if there was a difficult piece of phrasing. They had won first place in the competition and everyone was in a good mood. Mrs Clarkin had even taken a detour so they could pick up milkshakes from the McDonald's drive-through, still a novelty to a bunch of Tauranga schoolgirls in 1992.

So, when Kim McMurtry suggested mooning the middle-aged couple in the car that was driving alongside them in the outside lane, Sinead, high on a newfound sense of pride and camaraderie, didn't hesitate. She pressed her bare arse against the glass with gusto and even gave an extravagant wiggle for good measure.

At the next set of traffic lights the bus paused for an unusually long time, then pulled up unexpectedly into the hard shoulder. There appeared to be a bit of a commotion at the front but the girls, still giggly and full of adrenalin from their prank, didn't take much notice. It wasn't until Mrs Clarkin, now drained of her earlier good humour, strode angrily down the aisle towards them that they began to feel concern.

'Girls, I am completely mortified!' Mrs Clarkin yelled. 'I am particularly disgusted and surprised by you, Sinead Tobin! You have brought the school into disrepute with your appalling behaviour! Exposing yourself in this manner! Just wait until the principal hears about it!'

Just as it was dawning on Sinead that Mrs Clarkin couldn't possibly have known which of them had been involved and that the couple in the car must have given an unflattering description of a fat perpetrator, it must have similarly dawned on the rest of the girls. There were a few stifled giggles, then Jessica piped up, 'But Miss, how do you know it was Sinead?'

The rear of the bus erupted. Mrs Clarkin, realising her faux pas, shook her head at Jessica and turned to walk back up the aisle. Sinead laughed along for a while. She even made a joke along the lines of using her arse instead of her face for a mugshot.

But when she got home that night she went straight into the bathroom. She took one of Conor's razor blades and sliced into the fleshy underside of her upper arm. As the blood seeped, she stared at her reflection in the mirror on the front of the small medicine cabinet above the sink, its white paint flaky and discoloured, and said aloud, 'Fat Bitch, Fat Bitch' over and over, like a mantra, until she almost felt hypnotised. And a little deader.

Jessica is wiping a tear from her eye. 'Gosh, the fun we had,' she says again. Then, sotto voce, 'How is that gorgeous brother of yours? We were all in love with him in high school, you know. And he seems to have got even better looking. I must admit to being a bit stalkerish, following his every move on social media. What's it like having such a famous brother?'

'It's exactly the same as having any other sort of brother. They can still be a total dick sometimes.'

Jessica leans in, eager for the inside scoop. 'You mean taking advantage of the intern and all that? I have to say he never struck me as the type.'

'No, I just meant in general.'

'Oh Sinead, you're such a crack-up. I love that you haven't changed a bit!'

This is even more tedious than Sinead imagined. Going to the hospital and sitting beside her comatose mother's bedside is looking increasingly attractive.

'I'm so sorry, Jessica, but I've got to leave, see my mum.'

'Of course. But look, here's my number, please call me. I'd love us to get together again. We've barely scratched the surface.' She puts a card into Sinead's hands and clasps her own around them. 'I've really enjoyed seeing you.' She says this so sincerely Sinead almost believes her.

The studio is a short drive from the hospital. There is no-one at the reception desk so she goes straight into her mother's room and is confronted by a shock of an empty bed, which makes her heart palpitate wildly. The bedside table is clear, the bed crisply remade, ready for the next occupant.

The practicality of it, the lack of sentimentality, moves her, and she unsteadily plonks herself down on the chair. Her hands are shaking as she takes out her phone to ring Frances, who answers impatiently. Sinead, in a quivering voice, describes the empty-bedded scene. It's the third time in the space of a few weeks that she has believed her mother deceased, and it's not getting easier.

'Shit, shit, shit. Sorry, I forgot to tell you; Conor rang to say he somehow expedited the move to the Mercy Private. He's paranoid about the press sniffing around. And the flowers spooked him.'

'The flowers? What do you mean? Anyway, the point is why nobody thought to relay this news to me? I'm always the last to know everything,' she says sulkily. She's always felt on the outer, as though things are being withheld from her. Or worse, that she is not deemed important enough to bother telling.

Frances says, 'It was just a mistake. I'm so busy at the moment. All this swimming comp stuff is starting to pile up. Anyway, can you please go over there? I can't get in today and I think it'll look bad if none of the family show up on the day she's transferred.'

'Oh sure, I've nothing better to do than drive around various medical establishments searching for a comatose old lady.'

'Well, you kind of don't, let's be honest.'

'Go fuck yourself, Frances! Meeting the girls from the PTA for a coffee does not constitute a busy day, you know.'

On the way over to Mercy she wonders if Frances is having some kind of breakdown. She seems so off the ball. She finds herself kind of missing Frances's micromanaging and constant organising of everyone else's life. It's throwing her off-centre a little.

The Mercy reception reminds her more of a spa waiting room than a hospital, with its oversized plants, watercoolers stocked with real glasses and tasteful hanging art. The lighting over-head is soft and flattering, the aircon perfectly controlled, the beige carpet plush and noiseless. She feels compelled to whisper when she approaches the elegant woman behind the desk. She thinks of the public hospital with its smell and noise and stuffy overheated air and harassed-looking staff, but she thinks she would prefer to die there amidst all the chaos. Dying *here* would feel like failure. It must be costing Conor a fortune.

She is escorted to her mother's room by a pleasant young man, job title unknown. She half expects him to offer to carry her bag. There is a doctor in the room. She introduces herself as Dr Sharma. She explains that Joy has handled the move well and is stable. 'All vital signs are good,' she says.

'Her brain hasn't magically healed itself though, I suppose.'

Dr Sharma gives a rueful smile. 'No, but we will continue to run tests to check for brain activity.'

'But there is no chance of her recovering, is there?' Sinead pushes. 'I mean, my brother refuses to accept it, but don't you think he should?'

If Dr Sharma believes Conor is wasting his money, she is not about to say so. 'All I can say is she is a very tenacious lady. Perhaps she has some unfinished business in this life.'

Sinead is surprised at this strangely alternative view from a medical doctor. The doctors at the public hospital were far more forthright in their prognosis. Perhaps some misplaced optimism is included in the package here.

After Dr Sharma has gone Sinead studies her mother for a while. It's true she is not looking as horrific as she did. Her colour is better, and the swelling has subsided a bit. But maybe this is just because Sinead is used to her appearance now, or maybe the

THE LAST DAYS OF JOY

lighting is more flattering here. Either way, it is less traumatic to look at her, and Sinead sits up beside her on the bed.

Her phone rings. It's Frances.

'How are the new digs?'

'Pretty swanky. To the point where I'm beginning to question Conor's protestations of innocence about the charity's funds.'

'Don't even joke about that, Sinead. Anyway, I forgot to tell you earlier, and as I don't want to be accused of leaving you out of stuff again, I'm just letting you know the police got back to me on how Mum got hold of the gun. You'll love this.'

'Let me guess, she made a pact with the devil? No, she'd already done that. Eh . . . granted sexual favours to an arms dealer?'

'Shut up and listen. She got it by mail order! She invented a firearms licence number and even created a fictitious police officer who confirmed all the details. Get this, Officer Marion Morrison, QIDWJH357.'

'Marion Morrison? Wait, wasn't that John Wayne's real name? Jesus!'

'I know, and apparently the licence name and number and the police ID were so authentic that they got by the store's checks.'

'The wily old fox. She was determined. It's almost admirable.'

After she hangs up, she takes her mother's hand in hers. 'Who are you *really,* Mum?' she asks. There is something in her back pocket digging into her bottom. She pulls it out. It's Jessica's card. *Jessica Thornbury, Life Coach.* Sinead snorts derisively.

She thinks again of Jessica's cruelty on the bus. Being the literal butt of the joke. And the million other cruelties she endured in school. She thinks of Maggie's email and the compliments. Remembers those few months ten years ago after her book was published once her sense of being an imposter had abated and she felt almost worthy of what was happening. The champagne launch, the book signings, the panel discussions, the radio interviews. The book festival in Clare where she headlined and where she went to the old pub on the last night and was surrounded by people who admired her, asked her opinion. Asked her about process and inspiration. About influences and style. Asked *her* for advice. And how she stood there, in the middle of them, these writers and publishers and readers, lovers of books all of them, and felt such a sense of belonging. These were her people. And the drink flowed and she stayed there till three in the morning sitting beside the session players and singing traditional songs, and the euphoria of it. She thinks of the photoshoot she did in St Stephen's Green for a women's magazine feature about young Irish female talent. She was so thrilled with the result when she saw it. She looked hot. And thin. But then one day something changed. The invitations stopped arriving. Reviewers no longer referenced her book. They moved on. They discussed other books. When she googled herself, the first thing she saw was a one-star Amazon review. *Might have given it another star if I'd have been able to finish it!* Her agent was always on another call when she rang. The thumbnail of her book that Maggie used to display under her email signature was replaced by another one. Someone else was asked to headline the book festival. A new list of young hot talent was drawn up. And all

Sinead was left with was a hangover, a squandered advance and a strangling clause in a contract.

She takes out her phone. Opens her email and composes a new message.

Hi Maggie,

Thanks for those kind words about the new manuscript. I'll have some more over to you in a few days,

Sinead x

JOY

Parthenogenesis. I roll the word luxuriantly around my mouth. Virgin creation. A reproductive strategy that involves development of a gamete without fertilisation. Sometimes considered to be an asexual form of reproduction.

I learnt this from the Encyclopaedia Britannica. Daddy and I used to pore over those weighty volumes together, delighting each other with newfound knowledge. I remember reading about this phenomenon being observed in captive Komodo dragons, and I feel my heart sing. Ahh yes, that's it. Holding this baby now, so pure, it feels like he has come solely from my bloodline – a wondrous genetic anomaly, with no relation to Billy or the grotesque act I feel obligated to perform. I can hear Mother, crude with gin, 'For Heaven's sake, Joy, it's not that hard to be married, just feed him and fuck him!'

And I feel myself powerful, just like the giant lizards. And a fierce protectiveness envelops the two of us and I imagine myself hissing away anyone who dares to come between us. Looking in my baby's eyes now, studying his features, I see nothing but me and Daddy. Daddy's eyes that were sometimes grey, sometimes blue, reflecting the light, just like his beloved Lough Conn where he spent happy childhood days fishing for trout. And when Billy wonders what we should call him, I say Conor. And Billy shrugs and says, 'What's wrong with Sean or Patrick anyways?' But he doesn't care, not really, and so Conor it is.

And Daddy is here now, calling to me, standing in the mist atop Nephin Mountain that rises above Lough Conn like a spectre in the morning fog. And he reaches out his hand, but I can't quite grasp it.

Because there are more babies now, two girls, one solemn, one a whirligig. And they need me. And I try, I do, but still most nights I lie in bed, regretting, vowing to be better in the morning.

But it's hard to reach through the pain to them. And the bloodlines that run through us aren't pure, they're contaminated. And the Komodo dragon is not a powerful protector but a poisonous predator, with a toxic tongue. Despised and alone.

I'm being taken somewhere else now. When I look around, I see I'm sitting at the back of a church. I have a curly-haired little girl on my knee. She turns to me and smiles a deeply dimpled lopsided smile. She wants to play peek-a-boo, but I tell her no, this is not the time to do that. The church is large and draughty, but all the dark wood and stained glass make it feel claustrophobic. And the hush of the place is unnatural and suffocating. There is a scarf covering my head and pulled tight under my chin. It exerts a heavy pressure. I feel out of place, like I shouldn't be here, but also that I'm integral to what's happening. Billy warns me to get out of here – 'I wash my hands of you, Joy' – as though I'm a disease. The pain in this place is palpable, all these people with so much grief.

And there is a procession coming down the aisle. They are carrying a coffin, so small it makes your heart ache, and as they pass I keep my head bowed, buried in the curls of this cherub on my knee. It's a mistake to be here. Worse to have brought the child.

She senses me. Because mothers always do. And she halts dead in her tracks and turns towards me. And I know her, I know those green eyes, I've seen them before. They are drowning in sorrow, and I understand it has something to do with me. I'm the reason her little boy is in a box and not in her arms. And I want her to come over so badly. I want her to hurt me. I want her to scream in my face and stick a knife in my stomach or fire a gun in my temple. But she simply turns away, dignified, and keeps on walking out the door.

Following her heart, which is now outside of her body and being carried away in the tiny coffin.

Billy is so angry when he finds out I went to the funeral. 'You stupid woman, adding insult to injury. Were you looking for forgiveness?' But the truth is I don't think I was seeking absolution. I was seeking annihilation. I fantasise that the funeral procession becomes an angry mob who rip me limb from limb. Or they throw me in the ground, coffin-less, and each take a turn to throw a shovelful of dirt onto my face. Until I suffocate.

Eventually I'm able to get close to Daddy. 'Who are you?' he asks, confused. 'I'm your Pride and Joy, of course!' But the words won't come out properly because I know they're not true anymore.

FRANCES

Frances stands naked in front of the full-length mirror in her bedroom. She remembers her thirteen-year-old self doing the same, desperately hoping her breasts would enlarge overnight before their school beach trip the following day. Not so large and pendulous that they would draw attention and ridicule the way her friend Leigh's did. But at least big enough not to draw ridicule for being non-existent.

Looking at her less than perky appendages – lemons in a sock, Lauren calls them – she would give anything to have those pert buds again. She once sounded out Harry on the topic of breast augmentation.

'I don't care if they're a bit saggy, they're attached to you and that's all that counts,' he'd said.

It was a lovely sentiment, but standing here now it doesn't help very much. She suspects Andy might be more critical. If you are going to have a lustful affair with someone, their body takes on extra significance. *He* is not invested in her ability to make a great curry or keep the toilets spotless.

And what about her dark pubic hair? Do young women even have hair anymore? Isn't there a whole generation of men who believe women remain bald their entire lives? And what about the rest of it? Isn't vaginal rejuvenation a thing now? Swim Mom Donna admitted, after several wines, to having a labiaplasty.

'No more lettuce outside the bun!' she said.

At the time Frances thought her ridiculous, trying to conform to some porn-approved version of womanhood. And Lauren was openly scathing. 'Jesus, Donna, is it not enough that your asshole is so tight?' That caused much tension within the group for a long time, especially when Lauren referred to Donna as Design-a-Vagina on one misdirected WhatsApp message. But now she is unsure. Would Andy feel let down by a less-than-tight cavity? Her saggy tits and saggy fanny?

What about contraception? When she turned forty, Harry finally gave up on the dream of having more children and had a vasectomy. She didn't even ask him to do it. He was concerned at the amount of time she'd been on the pill and thought it only fair that he shoulder the responsibility. The procedure was easy; in fact, Harry even enjoyed it. At the plush clinic – that performed the vasectomies only on a Friday, to make it easier for the clients – he was given a Valium washed down with expensive whiskey beforehand, was able to request his favourite music during, and was then *ordered* to recuperate afterwards by lying on the couch for the weekend watching the cricket. She was secretly seething with the unfairness of it. Imagine if getting an abortion was as easy. If men got pregnant, it would be. ('Listen,' Lauren said to her once, 'if men got pregnant we'd be able to get an abortion at a drive-through. Side of fries with that, darl?')

She can't imagine Andy getting a vasectomy. There is a vanity there that will prevent him from making himself feel anything less than virile. She could see him struggling to read the menu when they had met in the café, but he pretended not to, and certainly didn't take out reading glasses, as she had done.

Anyway, she remembers reading something about how few eggs a woman has left by the time she is forty-three. Basically, she and Andy could shag nonstop for the next year and she'd still only have a 2 per cent chance of getting pregnant. Isn't this supposed to feel liberating? After all, she spent most of her life trying to avoid getting pregnant.

Instead, it feels depressing. She looks at her lower abdomen in the mirror and imagines her ovaries hanging there like two shrivelled balloons deflating in the corner after a party. Livvy, on the other hand, will have about half a million eggs. What a cruel joke the universe plays. Giving you a beautiful, fecund, teenage daughter just as you hurtle towards menopause and procreational obscurity.

Once dressed, she rummages around in her jewellery box for some earrings. An oval pendant catches her eye. She recognises it immediately as the only piece of jewellery her mother ever wore. They must have given it to Harry at the hospital, and he put it in here.

It has a dark smudge on the front, and when she wipes it she is alarmed to see it leave a deep red stain on the tissue.

An unbidden image comes to her of her mother with a gaping wound in her skull. She sees the pendant has a hinge, is in fact a locket, and she is surprised. She opens it and at first thinks the black and white photo is of Conor. On closer inspection, she sees that although the likeness is uncanny, it isn't Conor. The chin is weaker and there is a solitary dimple on one cheek. She recognises the face as that of her grandfather. She knows her mother had a great fondness for him and that he died young. Some kind of accident, she thinks. Joy was always a bit vague, and they grew up never questioning too much. In their house, ignorance was often bliss. Spontaneously, she fastens the locket around her neck. It looks good with her new maxi dress and knee-high brown suede boots; a different vibe to her regular suburban mother uniform of designer activewear. She takes a patterned silk scarf from her drawer and ties it around her hair to complete the boho look.

She has arranged to meet Andy at his hotel on the downtown waterfront. Getting out of her car, she puts on a pair of oversized sunglasses and walks quickly through the lobby, head down. In the lift, she looks at herself in the mirrored wall. The dim light means she can only see a vague outline, so she takes off the glasses and is immediately confronted by a stranger. The red lipstick and over-powdered face make her appear clownish. She has a sense that she looks like a lame joke, a garish punchline.

Andy opens the door wearing a thick white robe with the hotel logo embroidered in navy on it. It gapes open to his narrow waist so she can see his smooth chest. She thinks of Harry and his tufts of unruly hair and the comfort she used to get playing with it as she lay nestled into his armpit.

She steps in and says, 'I can't do this, Andy.'

He nods, his face arranged sincerely. 'Hey, it's okay to be nervous, you know.'

'No, Andy. It's not nerves. I've just come to my senses. There's too much at stake. And this is not me. I don't do things like this.'

She thinks she sees a look of impatience or exasperation fleetingly cloud Andy's face, but it's gone before she can pin it down. He places his hand around her wrist and pulls her towards him.

'I understand how you're feeling, Frances, I do. Don't you think I haven't felt conflicted too? But shit, Frances, I want you so much. I can't stop thinking about you. Ever since I saw your profile again on Facebook. And then after meeting you last week in the café. It's driving me crazy. Every time I shut my eyes I can see you. I think of that look you used to get on your face when we had sex. Remember how I used to call it your fuck face? Like most of the time you were so self-conscious, but then you would just let go. Totally give in to it. It was such a turn-on. The thing is, you're so sexy, Frances, but you've no idea that you are. We were so good together once. The sex was mind-blowing. Don't you remember? I do. I remember all the time.'

She closes her eyes, thinks of herself and Andy in the dunes behind the surf club, thinks of herself under a table in front of him at a party. 'Yes, I remember.'

He takes her hand then and places it on the outside of his robe, and she can feel how hard he is. It's intoxicating to be so wanted again. And she feels a sense of power then, too. She opens her eyes so they are looking at each other. He rests one hand on her hip bone and slips the other under her bra and over her breast, and she feels a deep pleasant ache tugging between her legs. And it's like a drug. She could be twenty again, with luminous skin and eyes, a face not pummelled by years of broken sleep and worry, a virgin body unscathed by a caesarean scar or stretch marks or three years of breastfeeding, capable of blowing someone's mind. And they are kissing now, not the dry, almost chaste kissing of marriage, but deep and wet and probing. And it feels different, yet familiar somehow. She pulls his robe open as he unbuttons her dress and takes off her underwear and they press against each other with such urgency that it's like they could consume each other. And then he leads her to the end of the bed and pushes her down gently. And he peels off her boots slowly and with care. And it is so removed from the way sex happens with Harry, the *we're already in bed naked Saturday night* routine of it, that she feels almost like an actress in a film. As though she is being watched and she is acting for the camera. Performing her life. He kneels over her then and she raises her hips for him.

And then he is inside her and they are moving together and she moans and turns her head to the side and catches a glimpse of their entwined bodies in the full-length mirror on the opposite wall and the image is so bizarre, confronting, that she experiences an odd sense of dislocation. As though she is not really here anymore. Not performing for the camera but observing instead. Frances turns her head further and she sees her new dress, her disguise, thrown across the back of the armchair. And she moans again, but it is forced and she realises Andy has not made a sound. She turns her head back to look at him but sees his eyes are averted too. All she can think about now are the differences from Harry and she wonders if Andy is comparing her to his wife. Because suddenly it doesn't feel familiar at all. It feels strange and new. He is lighter, less substantial than Harry, and she feels she might float away. His skin remains cool and dry. And the bizarre silence. As though aware of himself at all times. Is he even breathing? Was he always like this? Has she just forgotten? Or has Harry been subsumed into her mind and body and memory?

He holds his breath for several seconds before he ejaculates noiselessly and tidily into the condom he rolled on. She thinks of Harry, vocal and breathy and eager, who falls away, sweaty and laughing and spent.

As Andy naps beside her, the endorphins having subsided, it occurs to her that what she wanted to return to was simply herself. Not Andy. And she feels a kind of resentment because she understands she has swapped one sense of obligation for another. She feels manipulated.

She hasn't thought much about the way they broke up all those years ago, but she recalls now Andy's behaviour towards the end. She fooled herself into a kind of smugness that she was the one to finish things because of the way he treated her. But thinking about it now, she wonders if he treated her that way to leave her no choice. He was contemptuous, putting her down in front of their gang while flirting with the girlfriends.

Not contacting her for days on end then accusing her of suffocating him when she demanded an explanation.

She gets up, her thighs dry, no clammy wetness like after Harry, and goes into the bathroom. The lights around the mirror are unforgiving. Her lipstick is smeared around her mouth, she looks paler than normal, the hollows under her eyes exaggerated. No rosy afterglow here. Why do hotel bathrooms make you look so bad? To induce guilt?

Andy calls from the bedroom. 'Frances Tobin, get your sexy ass back in here now!'

It bothers her that he has used her maiden name. It doesn't make her feel as though she is still young. Instead it feels proprietary. Like one-upmanship on Harry. 'It's McEvitt actually, Frances McEvitt,' she shouts back.

Silence from the bedroom. She puts on a bathrobe, embarrassed now by her nakedness, goes back in. He is sitting up, his arms wrapped around his knees, and looks sulky. There is a trace of her red lipstick across his cheek and it makes her feel nauseous.

'I'm perfectly *aware* of your married name, I was just having a bit of fun. You should try it sometime.' He says it in a pointed way.

He appears to her a man-child. Petulant. Mean.

'I should go.'

'Fine.'

She takes her dress from the chair, shakes it out. Thinks how different the mood is compared to when it was thrown there only an hour ago. She wonders how it's possible to feel so empty yet full of self-loathing.

He doesn't speak while she dresses and gets ready to leave. She has a sense that she could easily rectify the situation if she went to him and made herself agreeable. Coloured herself within the lines again, just the way he likes her. But she discovers she has no desire to do so, and walks out the door without looking back. In the lobby she has a sense of being untethered. She heads out to her car. She turns the radio up full volume, hoping to drown out the intrusive thoughts, flashes of Andy's naked body, Harry's open, trusting face. Livvy. There is a rising sense of panic now, her heart is palpitating wildly. She starts the car, not knowing where she should be headed or where she belongs. She drives in semi-awareness until ending up, surprised, at her mother's house.

She stares at the house for some time. It conjures up such intense emotion within her, so at odds with the humble weatherboard and flaking white joinery. She gets out of the car and fumbles with the stiff, rusting bolt on the gate. She feels keenly all those times coming home from school when her stomach did somersaults walking up the narrow path to the door, unsure of what lay behind. There were signs of course, clues. But sometimes she would be taken by surprise.

She can't bring herself to walk round to the back door. She thinks of the little note her mother taped there for her. So brief, it had angered her. Five short sentences. So inadequate for what she was about to do. She enters through the rarely used front door. In the hallway, the smell is familiar, a musty odour – despite Frances's rigorous cleaning every Saturday – that lies somewhere between soured milk and damp laundry. But there is another smell now too, that wafts on top of the staleness, and

Frances recognises it as bleach. Harry had come here and purged the kitchen of any of the detritus from Joy's misadventure. The police had told her about specialist trauma cleaning companies that could do it, but Frances felt too ashamed to have anyone else bear witness. Harry reassured her that it wasn't too bad.

'She had the foresight to put a sheet down on the floor,' he said.

Even so, there must have been blood spatters. She thinks of Harry scrubbing away at a stain on the wall. She feels a bubbling anxiety in her stomach, and as though her heart is pulsing now behind her eyes. She hits the side of her head to get rid of the image.

She walks into the small sitting room. In later years her mother barely used this room, but for Frances it is full of the ghosts of their childhood. The curved mahogany carriage clock still ticks away on the mantelpiece just as it did when they were young. She can see the three of them, sitting on the old red couch, watching Saturday-morning TV in their pyjamas with bowls of cornflakes balancing on their laps, or in Sinead's case often tipped on the floor so Frances would have to clean it up.

She walks down the hallway towards the bedrooms, stepping over the creaky spot just before her mother's door. Joy's bedroom is neater than she has ever seen it. Housework was never her forte, but the bed is made, sheet tucked in tightly, a pair of slippers placed with precision by the polyester valance. The top of the chest of drawers, normally cluttered with hairbrushes, redundant keys, glasses cases and hats for various purposes, is now bare and polished.

She goes then and opens the freestanding wardrobe in the corner and is surprised to see a solitary dress hanging in there. It's wrapped in plastic as though just back from the drycleaner. It is Joy's favourite, a blue silk that she bought for Sue's daughter's wedding at least ten years ago. She told Frances that many people had complimented it that day and she stuck with it ever since. It makes Frances sad to think of her mother, so unsure of herself. Of her own taste, her choices.

The military neatness of the room, the solitary shroud, the deliberateness of the whole scene strikes her, and she feels weak and sits down on the bed. She imagines Joy, choosing her burial outfit and cleaning her room to stand up to strangers' scrutiny.

She goes now to the little room she shared with Sinead. She looks at the narrow twin beds separated by a slim locker. She thinks of the teenager she was, idealistic despite everything. Dreaming of a life under her own control and of her own making, not subject to the moods or appetites of others. So many nights she was furious with Sinead because she kept the bedside lamp on late, reading. Despite Frances's complaints Sinead would never capitulate, so Frances eventually learnt to fall asleep with the room bathed in a yellow glow. Even now she prefers to sleep with the door to the ensuite in her bedroom open and the light on. Some nights she woke to find Sinead had stopped reading and was weeping softly under her duvet. Or other times she would wake to see the covers thrown back and Sinead gone. She knew she must be in the bathroom because she could hear the noise of the ancient cistern, and sometime later Sinead would sneak back in and carefully replace the pair of dressmaker's scissors she kept in the drawer of the locker. Frances knew what Sinead had been doing to herself, saw the evidence on her legs, but never confronted her about it. That was the way in their house. Keep your head low, say nothing.

She looks out the bedroom window and sees that Sue is in her garden next door deadheading her rose bushes. She steps back to avoid being seen. She thinks of everything Sue must know about them and feels the old anxiety she used to feel as a child. Other people were shame. Worse now, somehow, with all the judgement and knowing that comes with being an adult. She remembers Sue finding Joy wailing in the garden one night and helping Conor put her to bed. The way she looked around their untidy kitchen on her way out the back door, dirty dishes piled high in the sink, and Frances, eight years old, had walked over and started washing them up herself.

She closes the door to the bedroom and steels herself before entering the kitchen, but it gives no hint of the trauma. There is, however, a half-drunk bottle of vodka perched on the sideboard. She's surprised that Harry did not stow it away when he came to purge the place. She is enraged with him suddenly. And with Sue and her perfect rosebushes and pitying looks. And Andy with his sterile charm and petulance. But mostly her mother. She picks up the bottle, carries it over to the sink. She closes her eyes and sees herself there, eight years old with uneven pigtails and a dirty stack of dishes. She sees Sinead, baby-faced and dimpled, her outstretched arms ever hopeful but even then used to rebuttal. And she sees Conor, lanky and slight, just the beginnings of some fluff on his upper lip but already the weight of adulthood on his shoulders.

And she raises the bottle above her head and screams. 'It wouldn't have been that hard, Mum. Was it really that fucking hard?'

She brings the bottle down heavily on the edge of the sink and as the first shards of glass splinter into her palms her eyes fly open in shock, and she watches in wonder as a line of blood flows towards the plughole.

CONOR

That same day, Conor is sitting opposite Trevor in a private conference room in the Sebel waterfront hotel. Trevor asked to see him before the board meeting. His left hand is big enough to encircle the oversized coffee mug comfortably, while his right makes a karate-chopping motion in time to his words on the edge of the large leather and oak desk.

Conor thinks each hand looks big enough to carry a rugby ball the length of a pitch with ease. Or slip around the neck of a large adult. He examines his own slim hands. Hairless and smooth, with tapered fingers and oval nails; he has always felt self conscious about them. Piano-playing hands, his mother used to say. Though she'd never done anything about getting him lessons. He feels angry about that suddenly.

Trevor is saying something about the charity's brand being tainted. Conor tunes out, imagines himself in a parallel universe playing free jazz piano, a Kiwi Chick Corea, in an edgy underground club in New York. The chords untethered, transcendent.

His life a bit the same. Not sitting here listening to Trevor's discordant bullshit. He tunes in again.

'So, Conor, as you can see, there is no option for you but to resign. Just go nice and quietly, lay low for a while, take a few weeks in a vegan yoga retreat in Bali finding yourself or whatever and in a couple of months no-one will remember any of this. I've no doubt a pretty fella like yourself will pick up another cushy position with ease. It's all about optics these days.' Trevor leans back in his chair with a self-satisfied smirk.

Conor feels a rage pulse through his non-piano-playing hands. He imagines smashing his water glass on Trevor's oversized head, the blood running down his doughy face, like a fat malevolent Jesus, reddening his eyes and pooling on his ridiculous moustache.

Trevor, with his crown of glass, crying like a baby, begging him for mercy.

'As I've already explained, I've done nothing wrong. Maybe we could have been a bit more circumspect in our spending, but I wanted to promote a healthy culture within the organisation. Hire the best people and reward them appropriately. As they say, if you pay peanuts—'

Trevor sits forward again and interrupts. 'You think the PC police give a flying fuck about your promotion of a healthy culture? Your average donor these days thinks we should be running a charity with zero overheads. They think that every cent of their donation should be going to the recipients. As though we can operate on fresh fucking air. Then they see the hospitality and travel expenses and imagine we spend our time gorging on caviar and champagne and wanking off to the Hilton's pay-per-view porn. You're not just accountable to the board these days, Conor. The whole fucking world has a keyboard and an opinion. Just waiting to be outraged by something. Anyway, the money isn't the main problem. You couldn't keep your dick in your fancy Armani trousers and now those feminazis literally have a major bone to pick. Once those bitches have you in their sights you're toast. The only way to placate them now will be to appoint a fucking woman. Jesus wept.'

Conor knows Trevor has a wife, Greta, a small, quiet woman, but he wonders if he has children. He sincerely hopes not.

'How many times do I have to explain? Lara quit her position before our relationship started. She'll vouch for me.'

Trevor gives a sneery laugh. 'Lara? Jesus, Conor, you genuinely don't know?'

'Know what?' He has a sick feeling in his guts. Trevor looks delighted with himself. As though he is about to play a royal flush.

'Who do you reckon gave everything to the press in the first place? Christ, Conor, if you're going to fuck the hired help, make sure she's not a journalism student passing on juicy intel to her mentor, who happens to be an editor for *Stuff*.'

'Don't be ridiculous, Trevor.'

But even as he says the words it is like a whole collection of hitherto unconnected neurons start to fire in his brain, communicating signals along new pathways, all leading to one irrefutable conclusion. He thinks he might vomit.

Trevor says nothing. Just relishes the dawning of the Judas betrayal on Conor's face. He takes a letter from his briefcase and unfolds it on the desk in front of Conor.

'This is a resignation letter I had drawn up for you earlier. Sign your name on the bottom and we can all get on with the rest of our lives.'

Robotically, Conor takes the letter. The words on the page swim before his eyes but he knows it will contain the usual meaningless stock phrases. He refuses to look up and see the triumph on Trevor's face. He grips the pen that has materialised in his hand somehow and makes a shaky scrawl above his name.

'You've done the right thing, Conor.' Trevor's tone is softer now, conciliatory. 'I'll go give this to the board. You go spend some time with your mother. Get some perspective on things.'

Getting lectured on perspective by a man with the self-awareness of an amoeba should be galling, but all Conor's rage has gone.

He stays seated after Trevor has left the room. For the first time he feels directionless. Deplete of all purpose. If he stayed in this room for the rest of his life it would make no difference to anyone or anything. He will not manage to make the world a better place. The board will meet. A new, more palatable chief executive will be appointed. TheOneForAll will go on and people will forget its founder. His mother will die sooner or later, regardless of his intervention. Sinead will go back to Ireland. Frances will become consumed once more by her own life. Lara will make beautiful babies with someone her own age and he will simply be a footnote in her brilliant career. He imagines her giving an interview after winning the Pulitzer, humblebragging about Machiavellian methods, all in the name of truth and justice.

He thinks of the last time he saw her, everything now tainted with a different perspective. The concern for his mother, the offers of help with the charity's admin, the abruptly ended phone calls. The questions about his father.

His hands and feet feel numb, and he realises he has been hyperventilating. He tries to slow down his breathing, imagines it being controlled by the hospital ventilator.

Did his mother feel like this before she put a gun to her head? If so, he gets it now. It's not a tangible emotion; it's simply an emptiness, a lack. A black hole. And it's something you'd try to fill with drugs or alcohol if you were so inclined. And then at least you'd make sense of the yearning. You'd have a name for it. It would be an addiction you could be pitied or treated for. But then one day the drugs or the alcohol, or the food or the sex, wouldn't fill it anymore. Wouldn't even touch the sides of it. And what do you do then?

He leaves the room and goes to his car. His head is pounding and he leans over to open the glove box to retrieve a packet of paracetamol. Something falls out onto the floor as he does so. It's a reusable coffee cup of Lara's. He thinks of her sitting in the passenger seat, sipping her dairy alternative flat white. How her presence gave him a warm glow while he was driving. He turns the cup over in his hand. *Saving the planet one latte at a time* is written under the trademarked name. Lara, with her idealism, doing her best to save the planet but happy to destroy his life. He wonders if twenty-four paracetamol would be enough to kill you. Knowing his luck, he'd end up alive but in need of a liver transplant.

He doesn't start the car. He doesn't know where he'd go. Instead, he tries Lara's phone and is surprised when she answers. Her voice is hesitant.

'Conor?'

'How could you, Lara?'

There is a pause. Then, 'Look, it wasn't personal. I—'

He explodes. 'Not personal? What the fuck? You ingratiate yourself into my bed, my life, then you destroy me? And you say it's not personal?'

'I did like you, Conor. And that took me by surprise. I never intended us to become lovers. It just happened. And I never planned to leak information about the charity either. I just, well, saw what was happening and thought it should be exposed. There were some seriously suspect things going on, as far as I could see. And then I guess I was able to compartmentalise. I mean—'

He interrupts. 'How the fuck can you compartmentalise stuff like that? That's not normal, Lara. It's sociopathic.'

Lara's tone changes from placatory to angry now.

'You're having a go at *me* for compartmentalising? You're such a hypocrite, Conor. You preach charity like you're fucking Gandhi and yet you're really a complete narcissist who just wants to be in the limelight, like some kind of fucking rockstar. You don't give a shit about anyone's wellbeing. You want people to adore you. But just because someone hits the Like button doesn't mean a damn thing. Jesus, and I'm supposed to be the one from the superficial generation? You're trying to make up for whatever you feel you didn't get as a kid, Conor, it's so transparent.

And even your poor brain-dead mother now has to suffer the indignity of being kept alive for your own screwed-up agenda.'

He is so shocked by her outburst he doesn't know what to say. And hovering there is a horrible feeling of the truth of her words. So he says, 'At least I would never play games with someone's emotions and use them so cruelly.'

She laughs. 'Get over yourself, Conor. I was a pretty accessory to you, a prop on your social media feed. We were both playing a game, using the other. We were just using a different currency, that's all. Goodbye, Conor.' She hangs up.

'Bitch,' he says to the beeps.

Before Lara picked up the phone, Conor had to admit he still had a glimmer of hope that they could fix this. That maybe she was unaware of the damage she had done, that she had been manipulated by someone else into doing it. She's so young, after all. They would move on from this, resume their relationship, which, thus tested, would be even stronger. But now she feels like a complete stranger to him. Hard and remorseless.

He gets out of the car. The hotel carpark overlooks the harbour and he walks along the wharf, past the fish and chip shop, busy with lunchtime trade, to the children's playground on the waterfront. He sits down on an empty bench, one of seven in a semicircle formation, opposite a mother and her toddler son. The woman is young, mid-twenties or so, tall, attractive.

He observes them from behind his sunglasses, though they're too absorbed in each other to notice. They're playing a game whereby the little boy drops his hat on the ground and his mother picks it up, saying in a sing-song voice, 'Whoopsie, Luke's dropped his cap again!' They must do it thirty times while he watches, transfixed. Neither of them tires of the game. They just delight in the other's reaction, the little boy clapping and giggling excitedly and his mother revelling in his joy. Conor thinks he has never seen such pure love in his life. *You've hit the jackpot with this one, little Luke, mate. You'll never be loved by anyone like this again.*

His attention must have wandered because now the bench opposite is empty. He has not noticed Luke and his mother leaving. Panicked, he looks around to see if they are still in the playground. He spots them walking away towards the railway track that separates the waterfront from the strip of downtown bars and cafés. Luke moves slowly, holding on to his mother's hand, with the gait of a child learning to find its balance. She allows him to dictate the pace, but as they approach the crossing she swoops him into her arms and checks several times in both directions before purposefully walking to the other side.

Conor watches after them until they meld with the other pedestrians and he can no longer distinguish them. He feels their absence keenly now. He imagines them returning to their house, which is neat and small but plenty big enough for just the two of them. It's all they need. Luke will be put down for his nap in a room decorated in muted tones of white and beige. He'll drift off to sleep feeling safe and wake up with nothing but the expectation of more love from his perfect mother.

There is a freight train in the distance. It is moving very slowly towards the port, laden with at least thirty carriages of logs. Conor knows if he moves quickly enough he can get across the tracks before it comes and slows him down. And then he can find Luke and his mother once more on the other side.

SINEAD

Frances and Sinead are sitting at their mother's kitchen table. Sinead is doing her best to close the nasty gash on her sister's hand with some steri-strips retrieved from the lunch box-slash-first aid kit that has lived under the sink since time immemorial.

'What's the date on these things, anyway? Best before 1997! Jesus, do old people ever throw anything out? I think you might need to get stitches, Franny,' Sinead says, throwing the useless packet across the table.

'No, no, it'll be fine,' Frances says. She swipes Sinead's hand away and presses on the wound with her own good one. 'I'll just go to the pharmacy and get a few things to sort it.'

'Always the martyr!' Sinead teases. 'Just like a proper Irish Mammy.'

She means only to lighten the mood. Frances had rung her sounding odd, talking about a bottle and asking if she'd come over, and something in her sister's tone concerned her so she came straightaway, not knowing what to expect. It felt unusual to be needed by Frances like that. Sinead walked through the back door to find her sister standing over the sink, holding her bloodied right hand under a running tap, a glazed look in her eyes as she followed the stream of red down the plughole. For a moment, she thought Frances had slit her wrists. This house has seen its fair share of self-mutilation. 'I dropped the bottle,' Frances said. Almost in a trance.

But now Sinead's gentle teasing has the opposite effect on her sister.

'Martyr? Me? That's rich coming from you!'

'Hey, I'm only kidding around, Franny,' Sinead says, laughing. 'And what the hell do you mean by that anyway?'

'Oh, you know. Your poor struggling writer routine, feeling sorry for yourself all the time. The unbearable weight of the follow-up novel. I mean, how hard can it be? It's not like the first one required much inventiveness.'

She's pinched a raw nerve. 'Actually, the second novel is coming along very nicely, thank you very much. I've been in touch with my publisher and we're looking at a launch date of next summer. And I can't believe you're accusing *me* of feeling sorry for myself. The woman who lives in a mansion with a gorgeous man who adores her and a clever, funny, talented daughter, and who still manages to walk around with a face like a slapped arse. I mean, you should take a look at yourself, Franny. You've got everything and yet you're so dissatisfied with it all. It's all so comfortable for you. Your life is so sheltered.'

Frances opens her mouth as if to say something then seems to change her mind. She stands up, takes her bag from the back of the chair and goes towards the back door.

Sinead feels bad. 'Come on, Franny, don't get your knickers in a twist. I shouldn't have said that. You know me, speak first, think later. I love you really, sis.'

'I'm not *getting my knickers in a twist*. I'm just going to sort my hand out. And by the way, you talk about sheltered? You've no idea, Sinead. No idea at all. We've sheltered you your whole life.' And with this cryptic statement she leaves, closing the back door a little harder than necessary.

With Frances gone, Sinead cleans up the broken glass and wipes the blood off the sink. The smell of vodka is strong even after she's spritzed the area with a sickly floral antibacterial spray. The lingering whiff of alcohol barely disguised under a subterfuge of personal hygiene or cleaning products is one she knows well. A contaminated sort of clean.

It evokes the jumbled smell of the hospital, too. Disinfectant. Homogenous distant food being cooked. Vomit.

Desperate to distract herself, Sinead opens the high cupboard above the fridge that Joy always used as a drinks cabinet. It's empty. She checks the various hiding places around the house where she always managed to score a reward as a teenager. Whether her mother was hiding them from her children or herself was never clear. But the cistern of the toilet, underneath the base of the ancient lawn mower and the electrical fuse box in the garage are all empty. Likewise the bathroom cabinet.

She is interested to see there is an almost-full bottle of sleeping pills there, though. Why didn't her mother use these instead of blasting her skull open with a handgun?

As a last resort she lifts the edge of the pink polyester quilt and checks the dusty underside of her mother's bed. There is no bottle but there is a small hard-shell suitcase that Sinead has never seen before. It's old – the kind of carry-on case you'd see in the hands of people alighting from trains in wartime movies – and somewhat battered. The exterior pattern is a mustard and black tweed, with black leather trim and two sturdy brass locks. Sinead thinks it is quite beautiful.

She pulls it out and runs her fingers over the textured exterior. Unlike the space under the bed, it is dust-free, as though it has been regularly handled. She hesitates for a moment, then presses on the locks and lifts the lid.

It contains a collection of papers, photos and handwritten letters. The flotsam and jetsam of a life. Sinead thinks she cannot look through it at this moment without something to fortify her, and is about to close it again when a blue envelope addressed in her mother's elegant cursive – as unique as her fingerprints – beckons her.

The name and address strike her as subconsciously familiar though she can't quite place either. *Mrs Belinda Smith, 9 Rathdown Heights, Navan, Co. Meath.* The stamp is a New Zealand one and it is postmarked. The date is smudged but she can make out the year, 1983. She turns it over and written on the back is her mother's name and address. Underneath, in capital red letters, are the words RETURN TO SENDER.

It is unsealed, a shred of Sellotape attached to one side, as though it has been opened and resealed previously. She goes to pull out the contents and suddenly the carpet is littered in flakes of paper. Her mother's words lie fragmented and incomprehensible around her. She catches glimpses of a narrative: *broken, son, undo, forgive*. Whoever tore it apart did a thorough job. The anger is palpable.

Sorry now that she found it, she stuffs the shards back into the envelope, closes the case and shoves it with some force into its shady resting spot.

That box under the bed will bring her no peace. She is sure of that much. And neither will this haunted house with its spectres of unhappiness everywhere.

She has a pressing need to see Conor. To be the baby again, maybe. She calls his mobile and is surprised by a woman's voice.

'Hello?' Whoever she is, her voice is shaky.

'I'm looking for Conor?'

'Conor.' It is said almost as a clarification.

'Yes, Conor. The person whose phone I'm ringing. Is he there?'

'Are you his wife?'

'No, his sister. Look, could you just put him on, please? Tell him it's Sinead.' She is impatient. Imagines Conor getting the nearest bystander to answer his phone while he tends to other more important tasks.

'Sinead. Are you here in Tauranga?'

Sinead's impatience turns to concern now. Something about this stranger's tone. 'Yes, why?'

'Sinead, do you think you can come here? I think your brother might need you.'

JOY

There is a searing pain in my head, so strong it turns into a
piercing shriek. Like the wail of a banshee. And I know death
is in this room with me. I am thirty-one years old and I am
sitting by Mother's bed. Daddy's sister, Mary, is trying to thread
rosary beads through her stiff fingers, and I swear Mother, even
in death, is making it more difficult for her. She'd be horrified at
this Catholic defilement. The clock on her bedside table has been
stopped. The mirror on her dressing table is covered by a white
blanket and even though it's a cold February night the window
is wide open. To stop her soul getting trapped, Mary says.

Daddy's sisters wouldn't want her hanging around any longer
than necessary.

I think how much Mother would hate all these superstitious
customs. Gypsy nonsense, she'd say. Wrap me in a simple shroud
and throw me on the pyre and be done. None of your ridicu-
lous idolatry.

But she'll be buried beside Daddy in the papist graveyard for a restless eternity instead. It irked her that I was educated by the nuns. This will infuriate her even more. Stomach cancer. I imagine all that bitterness forming bilious growths on her insides. Her face is different to how it was in life, though. Softer, less lined. As though death came as a relief.

There is a man at the funeral I haven't seen before, a barman from Mr Reilly's pub, which Mother has run since Mr Reilly died. He is handsome and dark, recently come from New Zealand, he says, to play rugby. It is a place I know little about, but the name inspires hope and fresh starts. He is soft-spoken but eloquent, and as we drink whiskey together at the wake he tells me stories of his home. Of the god of the forest prising apart the earth and the sky to form the world; of eyes being hurled to the heavens to form the stars; of mountains battling against each other for love; of star-crossed lovers; of whales and canoes and lakes and the fecund Pacific Ocean.

There is a deep connectivity in these legends that is tantalising to me, when I feel so adrift. I listen, rapt, finding the way he rolls the Māori names and words around his tongue exotic and sensual. I can feel a pagan fire lit within me when he speaks of his ancestor gods and their adventures.

There is a tuft of black just visible above his shirt and I have to stop myself from reaching out to touch it. I imagine the line of hair snaking down his abdomen to his groin. I wish everyone would leave this room because I know I could be with this gentle person. Without shame.

In the cold grey of the morning he leaves me alone again in this bed. Anchored down with the weight of myself, the holy water turning to poison in my head. I plan my escape from here. I will use my inheritance to start again in New Zealand. It feels like a small victory over both Mother and Mr Reilly. I dream that I am like the very first woman in the Māori creation myth, being rebirthed from the rock and dense clay of a new promised land, my bones fashioned from trees, my blood from molten lava and my breath from the misty air. My flesh bears children who are proud and strong.

And I try to move but I am paralysed, and I try to call out but my mouth won't open, and Mother is sitting beside the bed now, our roles reversed, like in that game she played with me once, Vice Versa. She is laughing. Rigor mortis, she says, now let's see how you like it. And she lights a cigarette and blows the smoke in my face.

I should have known. Of course I'm no great Māori forbearer. I'm simply a fallen child of Eve, with her sin and my shame destined to be carried on in the souls of our children.

FRANCES

When Frances arrives home that evening after being at her mother's house, she is surprised to see Harry's car in the driveway.

'I thought you weren't back till tomorrow,' she says, walking into the kitchen to find him standing at the stove, beer in one hand, wooden spoon in the other. The place smells like beef casserole, his signature dish.

'Great to see you too, darling,' he says, but he is smiling, and he puts down his implements and embraces her. He holds her at arm's length then. 'Nice dress, by the way.'

'Sorry, yes, of course it's great that you're here, I just wasn't expecting to see you, that's all.' She extricates herself from his arms and starts busying herself with stacking the dishwasher with the myriad of bowls, chopping boards and cutlery littered on the bench. Harry's cooking always involves more work for her rather than less.

'There was just a social evening planned for tonight with some of our clients. I excused myself on the basis that I have a very beautiful wife at home in need of some TLC. Now taste this and tell me it's not the best beef bourguignon you've ever tried.'

He holds the spoon up to her mouth, but she pushes it away. A few drops of thick red sauce fall on the floor.

'I know what your beef stew tastes like, Harry.' She bends down and wipes the spilled sauce with a cloth.

'Bourguignon,' he corrects.

'Throwing a splash of red wine into your stew doesn't make it into a classic French dish, you know.' She knows she is being hateful but she can't seem to stop herself.

He looks hurt, turns back to the stove and starts stirring.

'I'll set the table,' she says, trying to make amends.

'Sure, thanks.'

They finish the meal preparations in silence.

As he dishes up, Harry asks, 'Will Sinead be joining us tonight?'

'No, she texted to say she and Conor are going to spend the night at Mum's.'

'Oh, strange.'

Frances shrugs. 'That's my sister for you.'

Harry calls Livvy from her room to come and eat.

'So, how was your day, Livvy?' It is the same question she has asked her daughter at the start of dinner since she started school as a five-year-old.

'Fine.'

'And how are you feeling about the comp?'

'I think you know how I feel. I just wish you'd stop banging on about it.'

'What's the issue?' Harry asks Frances.

It is his asking that is infuriating. As though everything is her responsibility. Like those men who talk about babysitting their own children.

'Well, she's missed a lot of training and the big qualifying comp is the week after next. And she doesn't seem to care.'

'Not to worry,' says Harry. 'There'll be other competitions. How's Joy?'

The way he is so dismissive, she has to force her voice to sound steady. 'No change. It just feels like we're in a holding pattern. I mean, it could stay this way for months.'

Livvy says, 'How inconvenient for you.'

'That's out of order, Livvy,' Harry says.

'Sorry, Dad.'

Frances can feel tears start to well. She presses her hand to her eyes so no-one can see.

'What happened?' Livvy asks, nodding in the direction of her mother's bandaged hands.

Frances has rehearsed her answer. 'Oh, this. I was at Mum's house airing the place out and I was putting a bottle in the recycling bin when some broken glass that was already in there caught my hand. It's just a little cut.'

'You managed to cut both hands doing that?' Harry asks.

'I know! It was so silly. Whatever way I put my hands into the bin . . .' She tries awkwardly to mimic a hand movement.

'So, you didn't do it at the Sebel hotel then?' Livvy asks.

Frances almost drops her fork. Harry looks at her quizzically.

'How did you know I was at the Sebel?' *Breathe, Frances.* Her heart is pounding wildly. Her brain thrashes around trying to think of something plausible.

'That dumb app you made me download on my phone when I started high school. You know, the one that lets you stalk my every move, like the helicopter parent you are? Well, it works both ways. I can see where you are too. Haven't you ever noticed that little arrow in the corner of your screen?'

Come to think of it, she has noticed it, but thought it was something to do with Google Maps.

'Right. Well . . . I was just there meeting a friend for a coffee.'

'That's a funny place to meet for a coffee,' Harry says.

Her mind is spinning. She wonders if she should say it was Andy. Where's the harm in a coffee? Then she starts to worry that Livvy can pinpoint her exact location within the hotel, see that she was in a bedroom. She can't think straight.

'Yes, well, it was an out-of-towner, Rachel, who I went to school with. She's here for work so that was the easiest. Gosh, the bedrooms are stunning! I went up there for a look around, ended up ordering room service champagne on her company expenses. Quite the degenerates, we are!' She is babbling.

'Rachel? I've never heard you mention her.' Harry is leaning back in his chair now, studying her, fiddling with his glass of red wine.

Frances can feel a creeping heat up her neck. 'For goodness' sake, Harry, I don't give you the third degree about your comings and goings during the day.'

Harry raises his eyebrows. Livvy pushes her plate away.

'Thanks for dinner, Dad.'

'You're welcome, sweetheart.'

Frances looks at the barely touched meal in front of her daughter.

'Is that all you're going to eat, Livvy?'

'I've decided to become a vegetarian,' Livvy says, carrying her plate to the sink.

'What? Why? But you love meat! And with all the training, you need it.'

'Maybe, but meat production is literally ruining the planet. We've been watching documentaries in school about it. We all need to eat less so there's less strain on the earth's resources. Also, it's cruel. Like, pig crates and battery hens. Disgusting.'

'Not necessarily. I always buy free-range. And why are we paying huge private-school fees for you to be shown crazy hippy documentaries? Those people don't take account of what athletes require. It's vital at your age and your level of competition that you get enough protein and iron. You'll become anaemic. I'm not letting you.'

'Mum, it's my decision. Stop trying to control me! And by the way it's David Attenborough, not crazy hippies.'

She leaves the kitchen. Frances is so tired of slammed doors.

'What do you think of that?' she asks Harry, annoyed that once again he has not stepped up.

He takes a deep breath. 'Actually, I think she's right, Franny. You've got to let go, start trusting her decisions. Treat her as an equal.'

'Treat her as an equal? It's not our job to be her friend. We're her parents, for God's sake. Something you seem to forget. And why aren't you saying anything to her about her training? The whole year we've been prepping for Nationals and now she'll blow it all at the last minute. You constantly make me look like the bad cop while you indulge her every whim.'

'That's unfair.'

'Unfair?' She hears her voice rising but it feels distinct from her, as though it is its own autonomous entity. 'I'll tell you what's *unfair*. Unfair is that I spent my whole childhood trying to keep everything together and now even with a family of my own it's the same old shit.'

Harry holds up his hands in a gesture of surrender. 'Franny, I understand that your childhood was no picnic. I even understand your need to impose order on everything. Christ, it's part of you and I love you for it. But I don't understand why I've become your punchbag. I'm the innocent party here.'

The lyrics of an old Billy Joel number float through her head and she imagines Harry sitting at a piano, crooning about being an innocent man. She has an inappropriate urge to laugh. She feels unhinged. Harry pours himself some more wine and it sets her anger off again.

'Haven't you had enough to drink? I'm sick of watching you and Sinead like a couple of old soaks every evening. Like alcohol hasn't done enough damage to this family.'

'Maybe I drink to take the chill off.' He raises his eyebrows at her. 'Anyway, you're the one with the alcohol problem, not me.' He takes a long, noisy, antagonising gulp.

'That's ridiculous. I never have more than a glass or two.'

'Exactly. You're terrified of alcohol. You've got to have your carefully measured pour every evening, otherwise it will control you. Actually, it already controls you. Your moderation of your alcohol intake requires a massive effort.'

'What utter pop psychology bullshit, Harry.'

But later that night, alone in one of the spare rooms, his words burrow away at her. Contaminating a part of her that has always felt virtuous. She has always felt herself to be the opposite of her mother. How dare he suggest they are the same. She is furious he has done this to her.

She enters their bedroom where he is sleeping and turns on the light.

'Wake up, Harry. We need to talk.'

CONOR

'There's no need to call an ambulance. I wasn't trying to kill myself. This is just a stupid misunderstanding.'

The young police officer frowns and Conor regrets using the word stupid.

'But, Sir, the train driver said you ran on to the tracks then appeared to stop and turn towards the train. She only managed to stop in time because of the very low speed she was travelling at.'

'I think maybe I just got a fright. It paralysed me. Like, you know, a deer in the headlights . . . or something.' He is aware of how unconvincing this sounds.

The police officer turns towards the train driver, who shrugs her shoulders. 'He did appear to be in a bit of a trance. I spoke to his sister just after I rang you. She's on her way.'

'Sir, I think I would be failing to do my job if I didn't have you properly assessed by a mental health professional. They can decide on your intent and let you go home if they deem fit. I'm not qualified.' He turns away and speaks into his radio.

Conor contemplates making a run for it but doesn't fancy his chances against this young man. Also, it would not be a good look. He imagines the headlines. Disgraced Charity Boss Chased by Cops through Downtown Tauranga.

A small crowd of parents and their children are openly staring from over the railings on the playground side of the tracks. A couple of them are taking photos. Conor gives a wave. 'Nothing to see here,' he shouts over.

—

A few hours later, after being assessed by a triage nurse, an emergency doctor and finally a psychiatrist, he is deemed not to be a threat to himself or anyone else and allowed home. He is grateful in the end that Sinead was with him as his advocate. Her banter and good humour with the various professionals lightened the mood. He thinks that if Frances had been there her default demeanour might have landed him in a transfer to the local secure mental health unit.

'So,' Sinead says as they pull out of the hospital carpark, 'do you want to tell me the real reason you stopped in the path of an oncoming train? I mean seriously bro, that poor train driver, you've totally ruined her week.'

Conor feels bad about that. 'I was just following a woman and her little boy I saw at the park. I'm not sure why.' He thinks about them again. Luke and his Thomas the Tank Engine cap, his mother's strong brown arms as she swooped him up.

Sinead looks at him, eyes wide. 'Jesus, Conor, now *that's* batshit crazy. Thank God you didn't tell that to the psychiatrist.

They'd have locked you up for sure. And I think I would have concurred. You were stalking someone?'

He feels exhausted now, all out of reasonable explanations and rebuttals. He fixes his eyes on the rear of the car in front. The back window is decorated with those stick family figures. A smiling nuclear family. Mum, Dad, two kids, dog. He doesn't see the point. Those and the Baby on Board signs. Even our cars are now signifiers of our happy domestic lives.

'No . . . I mean, I don't think so. It seemed to make sense at the time. And then when I was on the tracks, and I saw the train, that made sense too. I had this moment of hesitation, as though my self-preservation reflex had deserted me. You know when people talk about adrenalin coursing through their bodies, the flight or fight reaction? Well, I just felt the opposite. This overwhelming feeling, like everything was too much, too big. It made me so tired. And then all I wanted was to lie down right there and then, on the tracks. I can't explain it.'

He turns and looks at her and says again, 'I can't explain it, Sinead. What if I really meant to . . . ?'

He doesn't finish. He starts to cry. Sinead pulls up in the hard shoulder, rubs his back in silence as heaving sobs convulse his body. When he finally stops she says, 'Now, should I drive you back to the mental hospital?'

He laughs. He is grateful for her again.

But she doesn't make any attempt to drive on. She turns on the hazard lights and they stay in the hard shoulder. Conor begins to talk. He tells her about Trevor and the board meeting. And about Lara giving information to her editor mentor, and the online stories. Once he begins he can't stop. He tells her about the charity's money, the parties, the trips away. And before all that, the kernel of emptiness that's been seeding inside him for months, maybe years. And how the emptiness feels so vast lately that he's lost in it. He doesn't worry about how the words sound. He just needs to say them. He finds he is not angry anymore, or defensive. He doesn't try to spin anything, nor is he apologetic. He is simply telling a story. He doesn't feel any happier after he tells her but neither does he feel worse. There's just flatness. As though he is not talking about himself but reporting on a story for a news channel.

When he finishes, he leans his head back on the rest and closes his eyes. Sinead says nothing but he feels the engine start again and the car pull out. When they stop again, he opens his eyes and sees they are outside their childhood home. He has no feelings one way or another about that. It's just where they are.

Sinead walks round and opens the door for him. She takes his hand and leads him through the whiny gate, along the path that passes down the side of the house and through the back door. He hasn't been here since Joy's suicide attempt. He felt guilty when Harry said he was going to go and *sort the place out*, as he put it. Solid, unflappable Harry. He should have gone too but he was terrified. Now, though, as he is led through the kitchen, he feels no sense of trauma. It could be any neat but dated kitchen. Anywhere.

He allows Sinead to lead him into the bedroom she once shared with Frances. It doesn't occur to him to wonder why she brings him here and not to his old room. She sits him down on the bed and hands him a pill and a glass of water. He swallows dutifully. She pulls back the duvet and he kicks off his shoes and climbs in. He has to curl up in a foetal position in order to fit. She leans over and kisses the top of his head. And as he closes his eyes he hears her switch off the light, but instead of leaving the room she gets into the other bed. He wants to thank her, but he is too tired to speak. Their heads are so close, he is aware of her breathing, even and slow. Soon his breath synchronises with hers, and he is soothed into a dreamless sleep.

SINEAD

She waits till she is sure he is asleep to get up. The pill she has given him will mean he won't wake till morning. In her mother's room she opens the bedside drawer and takes a cigarette from the packet she guesses correctly is there. As she walks out past the bed, she sees the corner of the little black and yellow case poking out. She kicks it back in with her foot as she passes.

It is a humid, sleep-denying kind of night. She sits on the front doorstep and notes the many lights still on in the cul-de-sac. She imagines the occupants, tetchy and hot, wandering in pyjamas to down glasses of water or to soothe grizzly children back to sleep.

It's a few years since she last smoked. The first drag surprises her lungs with its sting and she coughs, but by the third or fourth they remember how it's done. She enjoys the head spin. Remembers those first illicit cigarettes as a twelve-year-old, hiding behind the tin shed in the backyard. Frances, sniffing the air like a bloodhound when Sinead came back in, wrinkling up her nose and eyeing her suspiciously. Joy must have known she smoked, surely noticed the unexplained depletion of her supply. But she never said anything. Sinead suspected she approved, if only as a (not very successful) weight-loss method for her rotund daughter.

She stubs the butt out, throws it on the lawn and thinks about going to get another one. A car drives past slowly, briefly pausing outside the house, before turning at the bulbous end of the road and driving back again. It pulls up on the opposite side of the street. Sinead, still seated and so hidden from view by the hedge, waits for someone to emerge. Several minutes pass and still no-one gets out. The interior light comes on and Sinead sees it's a man. His profile looks familiar, and she racks her brain trying to figure out where she knows him from.

He gets out of the car and starts to walk towards the gate. That's when it clicks. The hospital. The last time she saw him he was in the hospital.

'Can I help you?'

He visibly starts, casts his eyes around looking for the owner of the voice. She stands up so he can see her. She is nervous now and thinks maybe she should run back inside, lock the door and try to rouse Conor. Not that he'd be much use in his current state.

'I'm sorry, I didn't see you down there. I just saw the lights on and . . .' He trails off.

'What do you want?'

He holds up his hand. 'It's okay, Frances. I'm not going to hurt you. I'm glad you're here. I've been working up the courage to talk to you all for the past couple of weeks, ever since I heard about your mother. I'm Brendan. Smith. Declan's brother.' He says this with gravitas, almost like it's a confession.

Smith. She thinks of the envelope in the case under her mother's bed. She is certain she is on the cusp of something and does not want him to stop talking.

'Okay.' She senses she has nothing to fear, and moves towards him.

He waits for her to say more, perhaps taken aback at her muted reaction, then carries on.

'It's kind of insane that we all ended up here. I live nearby. In Hamilton.'

'That's nice.'

He looks at her strangely. 'Yeah. Right, well when I read about your mother's . . .'

He struggles for a word. Sinead helps him out. 'Incident?'

He looks grateful. 'Yes, incident. Well, I felt so bad for her. I needed to come and share something with you all. About that day. I've been carrying it around for such a long time. You see it wasn't her fault. I know she blames herself, but you see, I . . .'

He is unable to finish and, to her surprise, begins to cry. She pats his shoulder awkwardly. He takes a deep breath and composes himself.

'Sorry, it's difficult to talk about, even all these years later. I'm sure it's painful for you to think about, too.'

He looks at her kindly. He is so sincere, this man. There is something so attractively vulnerable and open about him. She should come clean.

'Look, Brendan. I've got to be honest, I've no idea what you're talking about.'

'But what do you mean? You were there, you saw what happened.'

'I'm not Frances, I'm Sinead.'

'The baby?' It seems a funny way to be described, aged forty. But she nods.

'But, even so, didn't they . . . do you not . . . ? Surely you know?'

'It appears not.' It feels too big, suddenly. She's not sure anymore if she wants to hear what he has to say.

'Shit. Look, I should go. I'm sorry. I thought . . . I'm sorry.' He doesn't finish and is so distraught Sinead feels genuine sympathy for him.

'No, wait, please, tell me.'

He shakes his head. 'It's not my place. Please just ask your family. Again, I'm sorry.'

He makes to leave, then turns back again and says, 'Please take this. Maybe you could ask Conor to ring me? We used to be friends. When we were kids.' He hands her a business card then almost runs back to his car. For a moment she thinks about following him but feels weak. She sits down again on the door-step, wrapping her arms around her thighs, head down between them, looking at the ground. Her classic carsick pose.

There are ants scurrying around her feet. Ants always make her feel as though she should be doing something. She sits up.

She goes back inside, gets the pack of cigarettes from her mother's bedside locker before checking in on Conor. He is lying prone on his back, his long legs hanging over the side, and is so still that she leans over him, suddenly fearful, to make sure he is still breathing. She goes into the kitchen and tunes her mother's ancient radio into an all-night station. One with the kind of easy-listening tunes that appeal to middle-aged insomniacs.

She lights up one cigarette after another and inhales each drag so deep it seems to reach the pit of her stomach. She smokes so much her chest begins to burn. But she carries on anyway. The pain feels good.

She takes out her phone and checks her emails. A new one from Maggie. She opens it with a sense of dread.

Darling!

So, exciting news! Given the progress with the second book we've decided to bring out Motherload on eBook. It would be July/August timeframe. I think what with the new novel round the corner it's perfect timing. And then we could include the first chapter of the new book at the end? Would you be ok with us sending it for proofs? Although it's damn near perfect as it is. We can really ramp up the anticipation. It's all coming together beautifully! Are we still looking good for June for a first draft?

Another from the publicist, Tara, telling her she's heard about the new novel and suggesting she write a feature essay or two now to generate renewed interest. Get her voice out there again.

I'm thinking prolonged writer's block as the subject. People love that confessional sort of thing. Other people's failures are always so reassuring. Then you mention the new book and the inspiration for that. (Could we somehow tie in your mother?

The shock jolting you into creativity? Just a suggestion?) The
papers will be all over it! I'll line up a couple of interviews.

A shot of euphoria courses through her. Her breathing
quickens, becomes shallow. She knows exactly the essay she
would write. She loves when this happens. When she can see
clearly how to tease out an idea. When she can see the opening
line. The progression of the narrative. Then how to tie all the
strands together and deliver a devastating final sentence. The
satisfaction she gets from its conclusion. Impulsively, with the
adrenalin still running through her, she fires off two emails in
quick succession, one to Maggie and the other to Tara.

Wonderful . . . Of course . . . June, no problem . . . Brilliant . . .
Great idea . . . Can't wait . . . Have it with you in a few weeks . . .

She is doing this. She is really doing this. The adrenalin leaks
away and her breathing becomes normal again. The rush has left
her now with a pulsing head, like a hangover. She closes her eyes,
and she must have drifted off because now Conor is standing in
the kitchen doorway, looking groggy, and there is a cool grey
light coming through the window above the sink. She sits up.
Her back feels stiff and her lungs heavy. Her cheek and hand are
wet with drool, and she wipes them with the sleeve of her dress.

'How did you sleep?' she asks him.

He furrows his brow. 'It was weird, I feel like I've been
unconscious rather than asleep. I wonder if this is how Mum
will feel if she wakes up.'

'She's not going to wake up, Conor.'

'I know.'

Sinead is surprised but does not say anything.

He walks over to the sink and takes down a glass from the cabinet beside it. 'Bloody terrible metallic taste in my mouth.'

'Yeah, that'll be the sleeping pill. Haven't you taken one before?'

'No. I've never needed one.'

'That's a gift.' She remembers Conor as a child was always loath to even take an aspirin. As though admitting pain or illness was weakness. She thinks admitting to being depressed must seem the ultimate failure to him.

She takes a deep breath. 'Does the name Brendan Smith mean anything to you?'

He is facing away from her, filling the glass from the tap. Now he puts it down on the counter without taking a drink and turns around to look at her.

'Why are you asking?' There is an edge to his voice.

'He was here, last night. And I recognised him as the guy I saw in Mum's room that time. He thought I was Frances at first, and started talking about some incident involving Mum? He was saying something about feeling guilty. How it wasn't really her fault? When he realised I didn't know what he was talking about he got all upset. Said I should talk to my family when I asked him what was going on. Then he left.'

Conor looks confused. 'Brendan Smith? What the hell? What is he doing here?' His expression changes, as though he has worked something out. 'Oh Jesus, that's who it was. I thought he was a journalist or something. Shit, shit, shit.'

'Okay, I'm surmising from your reaction that this is not a happy story.'

He sits down at the table facing her, takes a deep inhalation, then exhales slowly.

'Correct. Are you sure you're ready to hear it, Sinead?'

JOY

I feel proud of myself after hanging the new stripy hammock between the two magnolia trees in our back garden. It's far from a hammock you were raised, Joy! I can hear my mother's voice in my head, but I tune it out and rock gently with my eyes closed and feel the warm New Zealand sun on my face. Her voice is there again. Wear a hat, Joy, you know how much you freckle. It's so crass! Well, I don't care, Mother, today I don't care. I can hear children's voices floating from nearby. They are happy, sing-song voices. The irresistible timbre of a girl's giggle, the still unbroken sweet teasing of a young boy. I think of my long-ago friend Deirdre and our games together. How we collected petals and wild blackberries to make undrinkable juice concoctions when the sun shone. Or made mud pies when it rained. And the memory is bittersweet because I can't quite connect with the child I once was, who was content in such innocent pursuits.

A high-pitched whine irritates my left ear and I swat blindly at the lurking mosquito. The damn things never leave me alone, my Celtic skin overreacting to every bite, swelling and itching with the poison. Just thinking about it makes me want to scratch. I can feel welts rising on my shoulders, heels and buttocks, but I'm so sleepy my brain can't summon my hands to reach them. I try to turn over to relieve the pressure, but the hammock is too narrow. And I feel trapped now, and the gently swaying bed feels more like a straitjacket. I try to call out, but the children's voices have faded away and I'm alone save for the relentless shrill echo in my ear.

I wish the children would come back and play their games. I wonder what games the little green-eyed boy used to play. Declan. The name comes to me. Did he like to ride his bike downhill, his legs free of the pedals, the momentum lifting his dark hair off his forehead and accentuating the cow's lick there? Or did he prefer to line up toy soldiers in a row or throw a ball against a wall, over and over? Or did he lie on his bed reading, dreaming about adventures in places beyond the confines of his little world? Did he daydream about being a pilot, or a zookeeper, or a professional football player?

All those big dreams in tatters on the tarmac, strewn beside the spilled contents of a schoolbag; a half-eaten jam sandwich and an apple core.

Where have the children gone? I miss them suddenly. I'd do anything for a pair of chubby arms around me and damp, sweet breath on my neck. It wouldn't feel like a burden now. This time I'd cherish it. I see the face of another bereft mother above me, with eyes green and soft, just like him. She is crying and the tears fall onto my temples, the salt stinging my irritated skin, and run down into my hair. I want to brush them away, but my arms refuse and anyway I deserve the discomfort. Without saying a word, her grief shows me all I have squandered.

I mouth the word sorry over and over, but she doesn't understand and eventually her face fades away and I'm alone again, the only sound the rhythmic creaking and clicking of the hammock as it strains under my weight. The noise becomes so loud I fear I haven't secured it properly and it will break at any moment. And Mother's voice again. Stupid Joy can't even get the simple things right. Inept, just like your father!

Oh Daddy, did you mean it? Or was it just a mistake? Did you lie down, weary, just meaning for some respite? Did you not hear it? Were her hateful words ringing in your ears, so you weren't aware of the danger? You wouldn't have left me on purpose, would you?

There was always an unreachable part of you, though. As generous as you were with your affection, you held something back. I felt it. Felt it when we'd take walks together in the summertime, down by the Dodder. Those long summer-evening walks when it never really got dark; the day just petered out into a soft twilight. And Mother always refused to come, claiming she hated the little midges that were everywhere that time of year. And though you always asked her, I knew you were glad too that she wasn't there.

How I loved those walks, hanging on to every word you said. Look at how green everything is, you'd say, have I ever told you how photosynthesis works? You had, many times, but I'd just shake my head and let you tell me again, just for the pleasure of hearing you explain it to me. Revelling in having you all to myself. But sometimes with no warning you'd go silent, my questions ignored or unheard. I knew then to stop talking and wait for you to come back to me again.

And there were the days when you'd come home from work and go straight to your bedroom, refusing even to eat dinner. But you'd come out eventually, tousling my hair as I sat eating my porridge in the morning, telling me to eat up so my brain had enough energy for school.

After you died, I felt your presence for such a long time. In my darkest moments I used to feel you, like sunlight giving me strength. I imagined it as though the chemical reactions that were formed when we interacted had remained, even after your physical presence was gone. It's a terrible thing, but now I can't for the life of me remember what your voice sounded like. And when I try to picture your face, it's a vague outline. It floats tantalisingly in front of me, like a barely remembered dream in the morning, but I can't put your features into a coherent whole.

And I'm not sure why that matters so much, except maybe I'm afraid that you weren't real. That if I can't remember your face and voice properly, then maybe I'm misremembering the love too.

And that maybe there wasn't a reason in the world to stop you from lying down on those tracks.

FRANCES

'Is this a joke, Josh?'

Frances hopes that she has misheard Livvy's swim coach.

'Sorry, Frances, but no, she's definitely drunk. A couple of the mums are looking after her. I think you should get in here asap.' He says 'asap' as one word. Aysap.

She drives in a panic to the aquatic centre, forgets to give way at a roundabout, narrowly misses a collision and gets a blast from a horn and angry hand gestures from the other driver. Josh is behind the desk at the reception area when she arrives. One of the Swim Mums, Meg, is leaning on the desk talking to him. They finish their conversation abruptly when they see Frances.

'Hi, Frances,' Meg says. 'You've managed to miss all the drama.' As though Frances has planned it that way.

Frances's mouth forms a tight line. Everything feels pulled and constricted inside her now.

Josh walks around to her.

'Frances, thank you for getting here so quickly.' He is only twenty-two, and his manner now, all formal and supercilious, makes her feel uncomfortable.

'Of course. To be honest, I'm in shock. I can't quite believe it.'

'I know. It's not something I ever expected from Olivia either.'

Olivia?

'What happened?'

'Well, according to the other kids, she had a bottle of vodka in her swim bag, was offering it around before training when they were in the changing rooms. They all declined but stupidly didn't think to tell any of us. I didn't notice anything until she was walking along the side of the pool and lost her balance. She was lucky she didn't smash her head open or fall in and drown.'

'Jesus, fuck.' When she sees Josh's eyebrows rise, she says, 'Sorry.'

'It's okay. But yes, exactly.'

Frances reminds herself to breathe. 'How is she?'

'She's vomited heaps. I don't think there's anything left. It's probably safe to drive her home now.'

'I'm so sorry about this, Josh.'

'Yes, indeed.' *Indeed?* She wants to retract the apology. 'The whole training session's been a write-off. I had to send the other kids home. There'll have to be an investigation too. Health and Safety and all that. She's put herself and everyone else in danger. So close to the big comp, it's a massive disruption.'

Josh has always been a pushover. A lamb to the slaughter in the midst of all the Alpha mums. But Frances senses a different energy from him now. Superior. Righteous. He is short with a square head and an overly developed upper torso; he's always reminded her of a Lego figure. As he talks to her his stance is wide and his hands remain on his hips, as though he's trying to take up as much space as possible.

She has never so desperately wanted Harry by her side. Harry, relaxed and jovial, able to handle any situation. Except for last night, when she'd seen a side of him that shook her. He'd sat up in the bed when she turned on the light. Rubbed his eyes in confusion, looking like a sleepy little boy. And then tried to make sense of what she was saying. 'Am I dreaming?' he asked when she told him about Andy. And then she realised what she had done. Realised as the words were coming out of her mouth, the utter stupidity of it all, the thought of Andy making her feel physically ill. She tried to stop talking, but it was like she was outside herself again, moving inexorably to a point of no return, looking on with a sense of disgust yet unable to stop. She'd fucked up so badly. No, fucked up implied some sort of accidental misdemeanour. Looking at Harry's shocked face, she realised she'd deliberately sabotaged them. Maybe she'd always meant to do this. Maybe she'd always known he was too good for her. And now, was her daughter the collateral damage?

'Where is she?'

'I'll bring you through.'

Josh turns and she follows him past reception into the windowless back office. The smell assaults her as soon as he opens the door. The sterile chlorine is no match for the contaminated stench of puke. Will this odour follow her forever? Livvy is sitting on a chair behind the desk, a small metal bin beside her, her head resting on her hands. Donna is on a chair beside her. Lauren is sitting on the desk, flicking through a magazine, her legs swinging. She gives Frances a sympathetic grimace. As soon as Donna sees Frances she starts to rub Livvy's back, her eyes locked on Frances. Frances recognises she is gloating. She hasn't seen her since the bondage email. She feels a violent urge to slap Donna's hand away from her daughter.

'Hi, Frances. Don't worry, we've had everything under control here,' says Donna.

Livvy raises her head from her hands. Her usually bright face is lopsided, gormless. Frances thinks of Joy. The way her face would lose its shape after a few drinks. Collapse in on itself.

'Hi, Mum. Sorry, Mum.'

'Let's get you home.' Frances walks around the desk to her daughter. As she does, Donna puts her hand under Livvy's arm and starts to pull her up.

'It's okay, Donna, I've got this,' Frances snaps.

Donna raises her hands. 'Only trying to help.'

Livvy stands unsteadily. Frances takes her hand and leads her towards the door.

'So can we do anything for you, Frances? Is everything all right at home? Livvy was saying something about Harry being away?'

Frances can feel Livvy's hand tense up in hers. She is terrified at what she may have overheard last night. Was there shouting? She can't remember. She remembers the 'Why?' from Harry, though. Over and over. 'But why?'

'All good, he just has a business trip.' That's what she'd told Livvy. He's actually gone to stay with his brother in Wellington.

'Oh, sure,' says Donna, in a tone of pure passive aggression. 'In that case, before you guys leave should we discuss what's going to happen with the competition? Just to clarify the situation? I mean, obviously after this Livvy is out, so we'll have to discuss tactics and relay positions. And then there's the question of who will chaperone them down to Dunedin for Nationals seeing as you're out, Frances, and—'

As Donna speaks, Frances feels the intense pressure behind her eyes again. She becomes aware of Livvy's hand dropping from hers. She looks at her daughter, whose head is down, eyes on the floor. Frances turns to Donna and interrupts, 'Not now, Donna, please. Just not now.'

Then she opens the door, noting Lauren's delighted face as she does. Lauren makes an *I'll call you* gesture with her hand.

Josh follows them out. 'Maybe you could all come back in, Frances? Sometime in the a.m.? Talk about the repercussions of this?'

Repercussions? Frances ignores him and walks through the automatic doors.

She drives Livvy home in silence, stealing glances at her along the way. Her profile, the straight nose, the high curve of her cheek, the distinctive cut of her jawline, is all Harry. Perhaps he, with his happy, uncomplicated bloodline, was their only chance for redemption. And now she's blown it.

As he was packing a bag this morning she had gone on the defensive, trying to justify Andy, make out that it was just one mistake. One little mistake in twenty years of doing the right thing. He'd turned to her and said, 'It wasn't just one mistake. Cheating is a series of decisions. And I always knew you weren't perfect, Frances, that's never what I wanted anyway. But up till now I always believed in your fundamental integrity.'

And then he was gone, pulling his black wheelie bag behind him.

Now, halfway home, Livvy starts to roll down the window.

'Livvy? Livvy? Are you going to be sick again? Jesus, give me some warning! What have you done to yourself?'

'Do you think I want to feel like this, Mum?' she slurs.

Frances pulls in quickly to the hard shoulder of the dual carriageway. Livvy opens the door, leans out and starts to retch.

She looks at her daughter's convulsing back. How did they get here? She thinks back to when Livvy was a newborn and Frances was immobilised by exhaustion. *It gets easier*, everyone said to her. Except Joy. She never was one for platitudes. She remembers the first time Joy held her granddaughter. Livvy was almost hysterical from overtiredness and Frances was only too happy to hand over her screaming child. She was surprised by the look of fierce love on Joy's face.

'There, there, precious girl. I'll make it better,' Joy said over and over to her granddaughter. Frances wonders now if there was a deeper meaning behind those words. Certainly, she can empathise with the regrets of motherhood. The feeling that she could have done it better given a second chance.

'No-one is ever the mother they think they'll be, Frances,' Joy had slurred once, a rare moment of drunken insight.

And no-one gets the mother they think they deserve, Frances had thought.

In the driveway she cuts the engine, but neither of them make any effort to get out of the car.

'Well, aren't you going to yell at me?' Livvy says. She speaks slowly, over-enunciating the words.

'I thought I'd wait until you woke up with a raging hangover tomorrow before I did that.'

Livvy giggles. 'You're legit funny, Mummy. I love you. I'm sorry.'

'I know. Me too. Now let's get you into bed.'

Sinead is back, sitting at the kitchen island banging away at her laptop when they enter. She looks on wide-eyed while Frances bundles her dishevelled daughter to her bedroom. Frances hears the fridge door being opened as she walks down the hall, and knows that Sinead will have a bottle of wine and two glasses waiting when she gets back.

Livvy passes out almost immediately. Frances sits on her bed for a while, making sure she stays lying on her side. She remembers Conor doing this for their mother. She'd walked into Joy's bedroom one night and found him sitting there, keeping guard. She'd asked him what he was doing, and he said he was just making sure she didn't choke on her own vomit. The idea of it has terrified her ever since. Conor couldn't have been more than eleven or twelve at the time.

Sitting beside her daughter, fragments of Harry's accusations from last night come back to her. How he'd felt sexually rejected by her for a long time. How it was as if she'd had no need for him in that way since Livvy was born. That her daughter's embraces seemed to be enough for her; they fulfilled any physical needs she had. So how devastating it was for him to know she sexually desired another man.

And then, as though something had just occurred to him.

'Oh, Jesus. Last week, when you came home from the hospital that day, you know, the day you stopped on the way for a swim at the beach. And you came in and for the first time in years you initiated sex with me. And you were almost insatiable. I thought maybe it was some kind of reaction to your mother. Like, you know, you were trying to feel more alive in the face of death or something. But I didn't care because it felt so good to be wanted by you again. But that wasn't it, was it? You were thinking of him, weren't you? You were fucking him in your head.'

'No . . . no!' she'd shouted. 'No, that's not it.' But he'd looked at her with such knowing disgust, it felt pointless.

Thinking about it, maybe she is only capable of a finite amount of love and affection. Isn't the perceived wisdom that women are capable of an endless amount of love? That's why they can have twenty children and love them all equally. Harry's mother Patsy – Saint Patsy as Sinead refers to her – always says, 'The more you have, the more you love.' Well, maybe she, Frances, is different – defective, even. Harry should be thankful they only had the one. Livvy has used up the quota and now there is no more to go around for rejected husbands or alcoholic mothers. Maybe that is just as well, because she has lost both anyway.

Livvy's breathing becomes deep and even. Frances wedges a pillow behind her neck. When she walks back into the kitchen,

Sinead pushes a glass towards her and says, 'Wow, I thought *I* was having a rough day. You look like you could do with this.'

Frances does not argue that it is too early or that drinking alcohol is hardly the most appropriate response to an errant, intoxicated child. She takes the glass from her sister and inhales the straw-coloured liquid.

She puts the empty glass down. Sinead refills it wordlessly.

'I slept with Andy Wright. I told Harry; he's gone. Which might explain why Livvy took a bottle of vodka to swim practice and got shit-faced.'

Sinead's face looks almost comedic in confusion.

'Andy Wright? That vain, jumped-up little prick? Why? He was such a cock. He flirted with everyone. Even me. Always had something to prove. How could you do that to Harry?'

Frances bristles. 'Andy's okay, and anyway, it's not like Harry's perfect.'

'Maybe not, but he's perfect for you. But please, go ahead and tell me the whole story so I can chastise and judge you harshly.'

Frances smiles grimly. And as she tells her sister, as she hears the story told out loud, her words come back to her like a delayed echo on a faulty phone line. The words form a story, not of an unappreciated wife rekindling a romance with an attentive lover, but of a deluded, middle-aged fool, throwing away a life of integrity, if not exactly wild excitement. A small life maybe, but one full of tenderness. Of meaning. All in the pursuit of an insincere player who had broken her heart once before. Because though she'd fooled herself into thinking it had been her, he had done the heart-breaking.

When she finishes, she says, 'I'm a total dick, aren't I?'

'Yes,' says Sinead, but it is not unkind. 'It seems it's been a revelatory day for all of us.'

'How do you mean?'

'Conor told me about Declan Smith.'

The name is like a kick in the guts. Frances feels as though she is too winded to speak.

'I can't understand why you kept it from me, Franny.'

Frances thinks of Joy standing in the carpark, bewildered. *It was the baby, the baby was crying.* 'It wasn't something we decided on. We were so little when it happened and even though we knew it was bad, we didn't understand all that much. I think we understood though not to mention it in front of Mum, for fear it would send her off the rails. I mean, I don't know if you remember that time Mum kicked you out of the car?'

'Yeah, of course.'

'Well, when we drove away, Conor said something along the lines of "I hope she doesn't get run over." You should have seen the look on Mum's face. I think it was the only time it was referred to. Even indirectly.'

Sinead puts her head in her hands. 'Jesus.'

'Leaving Ireland was a way of leaving it behind, I guess. Starting over. Conor and I never discussed it. We never decided not to tell you. But I suppose we just thought there was no point in you knowing. I mean, why should you have to carry that around too? And then it sort of faded from my consciousness. And I never heard Mum refer to it, not once, in all these years, so I wonder if it was the same for her. Sometimes I wonder if it even happened at all. If it was just some kind of bad dream.'

'Well, seeing Brendan Smith last night was certainly no dream.' Sinead tells her the story of Conor and the train and of Brendan turning up on their mother's doorstep. And how it felt as though he wanted to confess something to Joy, as though he'd been carrying round a great weight.

When she's finished, Frances thinks of how bitter she's been because she's felt her life to be so small and conscribed. Prosaic, as her mother would say. But Frances must have built it that way on purpose, because now she's floundering about, the boundaries all moved, and it scares her. And now it's also beyond her control as to whether Harry will come back or not.

Frances picks up the bottle of wine, is surprised to find it's empty. 'I'll open another,' she says, oblivion less frightening than the abyss she's facing.

'Actually. I'm going to get back to my novel. All these revelations must surely translate into some dramatic tension.'

For her part, Frances channels all the drama into violent scrubbing of her already pristine pantry.

CONOR

Conor has nearly finished his coffee by the time Angie arrives. He woke at 4.00 a.m., and lying there in his sister's spare room, a whole day of nothing stretching in front of him, he had felt a wave of panic. As though without a purpose he might end up lying down again on some train tracks or harassing some young mother in a playground. So he caught the 6.10 a.m. flight from Tauranga to Auckland on a whim.

It had felt strange to be sitting amongst all the besuited businesspeople on the plane – banging away on laptops or reading plastic-covered reports – and feeling removed from their industriousness. He had tried to make conversation with the man sitting next to him, who gave him a polite closed-mouth smile then went straight back to his open document.

Conor rises to greet Angie with a kiss, but she pulls back so he ends up giving her an awkward shoulder pat instead. She appears flustered. It had taken five attempts before she'd eventually answered her phone. She'd sounded wary, agreeing only to meet him when he insisted it was purely social. 'We're friends, aren't we?' he'd asked. He always imagined they were, anyway. That the relationship ran deeper than a simple boss and PA transaction.

'I can't stay long,' she says when he asks if she'd like something to eat. Before she arrived he took the liberty of ordering a latte, her usual choice, and she appears annoyed when the waiter brings it over.

'Of course. So, how are you? How's Troy?'

She softens at her son's name. 'He's good. Still mad for that bike you got him for his birthday.'

'Good boy, I remember being the same as a kid. And you're coping without me in work?'

He meant it light-heartedly, but Angie frowns. 'Look, Conor, this is all a bit awkward. Once you handed in your resignation, Trevor told us we needed to distance ourselves from you. We were told not to answer your calls or give you any information on what was happening within the organisation. I feel very compromised just by being here. I want to stay working there, and if anyone were to see us . . .'

He is surprised at how quickly her loyalties have switched. He was only forced to resign a couple of days ago. 'No, Angie, I'm not here to get info from you. Honestly, I don't care anymore about all that. Well, maybe *don't care* is the wrong way to put it, but I'm done with it. I've no interest in fighting Trevor. I asked to meet you because I wanted to see you, that's all.'

She looks unconvinced. 'I hope you didn't fly here especially. As I said, I only have a few minutes.'

'No, no, I've got a few loose ends to tie up while I'm here.' The only thing he can think of is maybe checking on his apartment. But he does not want to go there. It reminds him too much of Lara.

They lapse into silence. He thinks of how easy it used to be between them. She is fiddling now with a packet of brown sugar. He notices she has not touched her coffee. 'Do you mind if I ask, Angie? Was I a good guy to work with?'

She places the sugar back in the bowl, keeps her eyes down. 'I'll always be grateful to you, Conor. For giving me a chance.'

'That's not what I asked.'

'As my boss, yes, you were a good guy to work with.'

'What aren't you saying?'

She takes a breath, looks up. 'There were things . . .' Her voice trails off, perhaps discomfited by the puzzlement in his expression.

'What do you mean "things"?'

'Sometimes it seemed to me that you cared more for your own image than the people we were supposed to be helping.'

'What are you talking about? That's all I cared about, helping people.'

'Do you remember that little girl, Katie? She had leukaemia. You posted a photo of her with her Beads of Courage when TheOneForAll donated money to the children's hospital.'

'Of course. Cute little thing.'

'She died, Conor. She *died*. Before you posted the photo. And for whatever reason, you didn't check with her family or anyone before using it. I never said anything to you because that's around the time your mother was hospitalised. But I couldn't stop thinking about her family. About how her mother felt seeing a photo of her dead daughter being used like that, to promote the charity. Every Like it received must have been a kick in the guts for them. It made me feel sick.'

Conor groans and puts his face in his hands. 'Oh no.'

He looks up. Angie has tears in her eyes. She carries on. 'And there were other things.'

'Like?'

'You put us all in a terrible position with Lara.'

'What do you mean? Everything was above board! She finished volunteering there as soon as our relationship started.'

'You're twice her age, Conor. It was totally inappropriate. You shouldn't have gone there. You were taking advantage. It was your Bill Clinton moment.'

'Bill Clinton? You can't compare . . . Taking advantage? She initiated everything, for Christ's sake! My God, as we all know now, she was scheming and manipulating the whole time. Feeding information to her journalist mate. How can you possibly accuse *me* of taking advantage?'

'She's so young, Conor, trying to impress her mentor or whatever. Yeah, she was stupid to have done that, but *you* should have known better.'

He feels too tired to argue anymore. Angie starts to organise herself to go, pulls on her jacket, places her handbag over her shoulder.

He wonders if this will be the last time he sees her. How easily people leave your life. Fathers, mothers, friends, girlfriends, colleagues. You assume they'll always be there. Years spent with them, intimate moments shared, and then all of a sudden they've gone. And most of the time you never even realise when it's happening. It's so hard to see the end of things. How can you know that this cup of coffee, or that phone call, or that drink after work, or that hug, will be the last? You only realise after the fact. A sad footnote to the story of the relationship.

'Take care of yourself, Angie. I'm sorry I let you down.'

She says in a kinder voice, 'I'm sorry too, Conor. I didn't come here to lecture you. Deep down you're a good person, I know. I think you're just a bit blinkered, that's all. You've made some bad choices. At the end of the day we're all just making choices. Some good, some bad.'

When she's gone he sits for a while, unsure of what to do, where to go. A young couple in their twenties, at a table in the opposite corner, are staring in his direction. The man is wearing a *Ghostbusters* sweatshirt. Conor is not sure if it's meant to be ironic. Isn't that the way of things now? Making self-aware fun of yourself just to show how enlightened you are? Or was it always that way? He can't remember. He feels tired now of the disingenuousness of it all. The young man's phone is pointed in Conor's direction, and he puts it down quickly when he sees him looking. He says something to his girlfriend and they both laugh.

Feeling self-conscious, he takes out his own phone. There is a text from Sinead.

U ok? Where r u? Thought you might find some use for this

There is an attachment, an electronic business card. He opens it and finds a number for Brendan Smith. There is also a GIF attached depicting Barack Obama at his Oval Office desk, looking his most presidential and making an obviously important diplomatic phone call. The GIF makes him smile.

As he leaves the café he stops at the table of the young couple, and gesturing at the man's phone says, 'May I?'

The man looks at his girlfriend, confused, then shrugs and hands the phone over. Conor holds it up, switches the camera to selfie mode, and pouts extravagantly into the lens. He hands it back to the man and says, 'There you go, mate. See how many Likes that gets you.'

SINEAD

Sinead has come to visit Joy to escape the atmosphere in her sister's house for a few hours. She sits at her mother's bedside, takes her hand. Thinks of the horror of the accident. Of poor little Declan Smith. She should say something to her mother about it. Let her know she knows. But what is there to say? She thinks of what Conor told her about Joy crying, 'It was the baby, I just got distracted by the baby.' And she feels angry then. Lets go of her hand.

She has brought her laptop. There is a mahogany and leather desk in her mother's room, which amuses her. As though sickness and death are not enough to stop the busy lives of private patients. She sits at the desk. The little grey book is peeping out of her bag. Funny, she doesn't remember putting it in there. It doesn't matter; she doesn't think she needs it today. The story Conor told her about the accident will surely inspire her. All that pain. The tortured artist. It's not just a trope. And she has finished her piece on writer's block and it's good. Her editor friend at

The Irish Times was keen when she approached her with the idea. She opens the manuscript, stares at the last paragraph. It is so raw. Connie reflecting painfully on her infertility, the inadequacy of her own body, in the midst of all the fecundity of the farm. What good is her body if it can't procreate? Is she even a woman? But she can match it with her own words. No need to revert to the book. She types a sentence, deletes it. Types another, deletes that. Brilliant ideas – she's sure they are – float, half-formed, before her, but she can't quite grasp them.

Her mother makes a sound somewhere between a gurgle and a moan. It startles her and she turns around, knowing she shouldn't read anything into it. The doctors have always dismissed these noises as involuntary. 'Mere functions of the intact baser parts of her brain.'

She turns back, closes her eyes, tries a different line. It doesn't work. Nothing works. She tries to imagine how it would feel to want a baby so badly but not be able to conceive. But it is so far removed from how she feels that she can't find the empathy to write it authentically. Clichéd phrases of longing and barrenness fill her head.

She looks at her bag. The little grey book calls to her. She can be strong and resist. But it is so insistent. It boasts of its own simple elegance. No-one will ever know. How many times has she googled it now and still nothing? She can't even find anything on the now defunct New Zealand press that published it. She takes the book out of her bag. As she does, a little card falls out. It's the one Brendan Smith gave her. Under his name is written *Gardener/Landscaper*. She likes that.

She opens the book. Maybe she's actually doing it a favour. Maybe she's helping the world rediscover a work of art. Artists do that all the time. The Dadaists had their literary cut-up technique. Didn't William S. Burroughs do that too? Take text and rearrange it? And she is setting the book in Ireland. Changing crucial details. Giving it a whole new landscape. She will have to do a lot of her own research in order to make it authentic. So, it's hardly plagiarism. And musicians sample other people's music all the time. It's practically expected. There are only a certain number of ways you can arrange the same notes. Likewise words and stories. And she'll just use a line or two. Just a little bit to get her started. Get her confidence up. She can stop using it anytime.

She thinks of Brendan Smith. She imagines him planning, pruning, planting, cutting. And she is doing the same. She is transplanting the little grey book. Grafting it to something else. Cultivating a hybrid. Nurturing it. Helping it flourish.

She starts to type. The rhythmic tapping of the keys and the comforting appearance of text on the screen fill her with renewed purpose. She is a writer. Yes.

JOY

She takes me by the hand, this curly-haired cherub, and leads me to the car. I don't want to go. They'll be fine to walk home, sure a drop of rain never killed anyone, as Daddy used to say. And I've been here before, I know what happens. But I think of little Franny, holding on proud as punch to her big brother's hand, her skinny wee legs glistening with rain, doggedly trudging home, her determined mouth set, and a rush of love fills my heart.

This morning has been bad. I've had images in my head that only a nip of gin could shake off. I took the bottle down from the press and set it on the table in front of me. Flashes of red flesh and dark springy hair coming towards my face, and that smell. Like sour milk.

She grizzles a little as I place her carefully in the back seat, a blanket tucked around her body. Another morning she has resisted her nap, the scallywag, so she's tired. To be honest, I don't mind all that much. I hate when it's too quiet in the house and I'm alone with my thoughts.

We are turning out of the estate and onto the straight stretch of road that leads to the school. It's a suburban road like any other. I've driven or walked it so many times that I take no notice of anything. I take no notice of the pebbledash and brick semi-detached houses on my right that form the front row of our housing estate, facing the main road. Or the petrol station beside them where I sometimes send Conor to buy me cigarettes and a ten-penny bag for himself. Or the road to my left that leads to the shopping mall; an eclectic collection of post office, newsagent's, shoe repair place and chemist we refer to simply as The Shops. Or the newly built red-brick Catholic church beside it to cater for all the believers – or those who still pretend to – in the housing estates now being thrown up, where once there was nothing but rich Meath pastureland. I fail to take any real notice of the cul-de-sac just before the school that leads to eight established detached houses, shrouded behind walls and mature hedges, as though trying to retreat from the onslaught of homogenous semi-d's that have had the audacity to spring up all around them.

And though I've been on this road countless times before and will travel it again after, this time feels like the first and the last. And while I take no real notice of any of the surroundings, they are imprinted on my brain now in agonising clarity.

Still, it rains. Not the drenching, thunderous downpours that sweep in and out quickly from the Pacific, but that insipid Irish drizzle that settles in for days. Content to linger and dampen. They would have been fine to walk the short distance home, their yellow raincoats protection enough, and a fire and a bowl of oxtail soup when they got in to warm them. But Frances is so wee, and hates being wet, and Conor has probably forgotten to put his coat on. And my heart is full when I think of them both.

The rubber on one of my Hillman Hunter's wiper blades has become dislodged, and the regular drag and squeak of them irritates me. I turn them off. The rain is light enough to only need them intermittently. Perhaps the rhythmic sound was hypnotising Sinead though, because now they're off she starts to cry harder. I sing to distract her. Dance for your daddy my little lassie! She delights in my singing; God knows why. Not a note in your head! Mother used to say. She claps her hands, and when I get to the line You shall have a Fishy on a little Dishy, I sing in an exaggerated Welsh accent, which makes her giggle with excitement. I've never heard a sound as sweet.

I need to concentrate. The bell has rung and there are children making their way out of the school gates. I don't want to miss my two, so I scan the faces to see if I can spot them. The lollipop lady walks into the centre of the road, and we stop as she waves some children across. Sinead starts to whimper again, then it turns into a wail. I know by the sound that she may have passed the point of being pacified. Shush my love, shush. This makes her wail louder. That child has some pair of lungs on her, a neighbour of ours once said in a barbed kind of way. I'm secretly proud of that. She laughs and cries with equal gusto, this child of mine. I think she'll be a force to be reckoned with.

But she is distracting me now as I pull into the carpark, still scanning the faces spilling out of the school doors. Happy faces, *innocent faces, that will soon turn to shock, tainted by an image that will stay with them into adulthood.*

Sinead, please stop, I can't think with all that noise. Shush now, shush. I hand her back a banana. She loves her food and it's usually enough to placate her. Not this time. She hits it out of my hand and her wailing turns into a screech.

The car is too small for the two of us right now. I feel my temper rising. Naughty girl! And I hate my voice like this because it sounds like my own mother's, with its constant undertone of criticism and disappointment. I pull into a space and jerk on the handbrake with some violence. I spot two yellow-raincoated figures of similar size to Conor and Franny approaching, but no, it's not them. It's the Smith brothers, nice gentle little boys, who live around the corner from us. The smaller one gives me a wave, but I don't acknowledge it as Sinead's screeching is monopolising my head, leaving little space for social niceties. I think about this a lot. After.

Still no sign of the two of them. The avalanche of children coming out the doors has dwindled to a few sporadic dawdlers. It wouldn't be like Frances to be one of the last; despite being the younger one, she'd make sure Conor didn't tarry. I think with all of Sinead's noise I must have missed them. The rain is getting heavier, so I turn on the faulty wipers. I can feel the drag of them in my nerves. Whoosh-click, Whoosh-click. I look over to the crossing and think I can see two familiar figures. Now see, Sinead! You've made me miss them! I'm shouting now and Sinead looks a little taken aback by my voice. There is a brief pause before she starts to cry again; not the frustrated wails of before, but a despairing, heaving sob.

I let off the handbrake and put the car into reverse. If I go quick enough, I'll catch them before they take the path at the top of our estate that leads through the playing field and serves as a shortcut home. The echoes of my mother's shrill voice, and the grotesque images that have replayed in my head all morning, have made it vitally important that they know I've come to pick them up. I glance quickly in the direction of the doors one last time and put my foot on the accelerator.

There is a sickening bump. It's enough to stop Sinead's cater-wauling. Not comprehending, I turn around and look out the rear window where I see the older Smith boy, a few feet back, his hand over his mouth, eyes wide in horror. For a moment I think I've backed into another car, dislodged the bumper. But maybe I knew all along because I stay rooted to the seat, unable to get out and investigate. A loud wail goes up but it's not Sinead this time, she's mute, and I realise it is coming from outside. Suddenly there is commotion everywhere that I register only as blurry movements. A face appears at my side window, it's Conor, and he's crying, and I roll down the window and look at him. His eyes say Mammy, Mammy, what have you done?

I get out and walk around to the back of the car. I spot the schoolbag first. It's a green and brown satchel, the ties open, the contents spilled out on the wet tarmac. And then I see an arm. It's sticking out at an odd angle from behind the wheel. And the older Smith boy is crouching down now and he's saying It's okay, Declan, it's okay, as he puts his own raincoat under his brother's head. But I know by the odd angle of the yellow arm that it's not okay. That it will never be okay again.

There are lots of people now, crouching around the car. I stand back, paralysed. There is a low moaning coming from somewhere and at first, with horror, I think it's little Declan, but then I realise it's coming from me. I didn't see him, I didn't see him, I was seeing to the baby. But no-one is listening to me. I look round to find someone to explain it to but the only people paying any attention to me are Conor and Frances. They are standing side by side, holding hands and looking at me in a way I can't even interpret. Pity? Horror? Shame? It was Sinead, she was crying, I try to explain, but Conor turns away from me, puts his arm around Frances's shoulders and leads her over to the grass verge beside the gates. They sit down, Conor's arm still around his sister, and stay huddled together, eyes fixed on the ground. A solemn tableau amidst the drama in the carpark.

And soon there is an ambulance that arrives in a hurry with flashing sirens but has no need to leave in a hurry. Someone has run to the church and got the priest, who is kneeling by the wheel, bent forward and whispering into the unhearing ears of little Declan. There is a garda talking to me. He is asking me questions and writing things in his notebook but all I can say is I didn't see him over and over so eventually he sighs, puts his notebook away and offers to bring me home.

I sit into the back of his car, and Conor and Frances reluctantly join me. I become aware of the group of teachers and parents looking in my direction. One of the teachers, Mrs Connell, walks over to the driver window and knocks on the glass. She forgot the child in the back of her car, she says to the garda, avoiding any eye contact with me, and that's when I look over and see Sinead, her face pressed in despair against the fogged-up window of my Hillman. Ignored.

We make the short journey home in silence. Nearing the corner before our cul-de-sac I see another garda car on the street and realise it's parked outside the Smith house. As we drive past the door opens and I see her. Her feet are clad in purple fluffy slippers and she is wearing an apron. I wonder if she has been baking, an apple pie or a Victoria sponge, some kind of treat for after school. She is yelling and trying to get to the green Volkswagen Beetle parked in the driveway but there is a ban garda there holding her back. I turn away and squeeze my eyes shut but Conor sits up, and keeps his head turned in their direction until we round the bend to our own house.

Of all the days, Billy is home early from the bank. The garda delivers me to him like I'm an errant child and Billy sends the children upstairs to their bedrooms and tells me to go wait in the kitchen. I hear them talking in low voices on the doorstep. Billy is saying Sorry, garda. I'd say he is most sorry for ever having met me. When the garda leaves he comes in, goes to the cupboard, and pulls out the bottle of gin. That was on the table when I got home, he says and slams it down in front of me. You stupid woman, what have you done to us all? He stares at me, but I say nothing.

I don't tell him that I was tempted to, but that I didn't drink any of it. Not today. I don't tell him that I only do it anyway to keep the awful pictures in my head at bay. I don't say a word. So he walks out, and I hear the front door slam behind him.

And what's to do then but pour myself a glass?

FRANCES

It's true what she said to Sinead about the accident. They did, in a way, leave it behind in Ireland. In truth, she can't remember much of it anyway. It's as though events have been filtered down to a few concentrated flashbulb memories of that day and the time that followed. And sometimes she wonders if the memories are even of that day. Or if she's lumped all her memories of their life in Ireland together in her mind, to create a compact and ordered narrative. She feels, in a way, like it was a parallel life lived. That it didn't happen years ago, or even in the past, but rather in another dimension. When she thinks of their life in Ireland it doesn't seem as though she is reaching back in time, but to another place within herself.

But she does remember with clarity how Declan Smith, who was in her class, had the same yellow raincoat as her and how that was mortifying because Alan Kane – also in her class and whom Frances loathed – said that meant they were going to get married. She remembers seeing a mangled raincoat on the wet tarmac and – she recalls with shame – feeling happy because she was sure it looked too wrecked to be worn again. That surely was *that* day.

She also remembers kneeling on her bed under the window, in the poky box room that faced the street, and watching her father storm out and into his brown Escort. She stayed there till it got dark. She was hungry, but too scared to go downstairs. And when she finally did she found her mother passed out on the kitchen table. Of course, that could have been any number of occasions.

That is the last memory she has of her father. Even though she knows he didn't leave that day, that he actually left weeks later, that moment has come to represent his abandonment. *There, I'm done with her, you're on your own now, kiddos.* She wonders about what Livvy has witnessed. Did she see Harry leaving the house, yanking his trolley bag behind him? Did she see him put his head down on the steering wheel momentarily before steeling himself and driving away? Was she unsurprised? Did she simply think, *Ahh yes, so here it is, the day my father has had enough*? Will that be another scene, perhaps deemed inconsequential now, that later proves to be a defining moment of her life? The Day My Father Left.

Her phone pings. *Please let it be Harry.* She feels a kind of disappointment, bordering on disgust, when she sees it is from Andy. Suddenly all the attributes she once thought of as sexy and charming make her feel uneasy. Soiled. His smile too white, too orthodontically perfect, like a leering Cheshire Cat. His clean-shaven face, barely a hair follicle in sight, moisturised and almost poreless. His loafer-clad feet that despite being sockless never smelled. How is that even possible? His overly lean, marathon-running, carbohydrate-denying, teetotaller and vegan physique. Incongruous with the bloated, environmentally hazardous Range Rover he drives. The exaggerated way he'd lean forward, chin on hand, to listen when she talked, as though he was so involved. The way he is so aware of himself at all times.

She opens the message reluctantly, her heart racing.

You forgot your necklace 🖊

His stupid emojis. Lauren is right. Deeply unsexy.

Damn. Her mother's locket. She doesn't know how to respond to this. Is he wanting to meet up to give it back? Is it a threat? A ransom? She realises that is exactly what he wants. To make her doubt herself. This is always what he wanted. She replies,

Can you post it to me, please?

Nothing. She can almost feel his petulance through the phone. What should she do now? Will he post it or not? Does she need to text him again? If it was any other necklace . . . She gives it some time, then texts.

Andy??

Maybe the double question mark was too much; a bit desperate. This time he gets back immediately.

Sorry, forgot to reply! I left it at hotel reception. Cheers, A

Cheers? The breezy tone is contrived, but that will do. She considers texting back and saying thanks, then thinks *No, fuck him.* Instead, she deletes his contact details from her phone.

With that taken care of, her mind turns to the insurmountable problem of her marriage. She has respected Harry's request for space, and not tried to contact him. However, he needs to know about Livvy.

He answers his phone straight away. 'Frances.'

She launches in, nervous and stumbling. 'Sorry, I know we agreed you'd contact me when you're ready, but it's Livvy. Something happened yesterday.'

'What?' He sounds terrified.

'She got drunk at swim practice.'

'What?'

'I know, it's insane. But look, I was wondering . . . if it's okay, if you'd come home. Just for a while. Josh wants to discuss what happens now going forward. And I don't think I can do it on my own. Do you think that's possible?'

'Yes. I'll fly back first thing.'

'Thank you so much, Harry. I appreciate it. And I—'

He cuts her off. 'No need to thank me. Of course I'll come back. For Livvy.'

'Of course. For Livvy. Obviously.'

Twenty years of knowing Harry, and she's never heard that dead tone in his voice. She's watched friends go through divorces and marvelled at the speed with which love could turn to animosity. Secretly, she had thought those friends were lacking in character to allow matters to deteriorate so badly, unable even to keep things civil for the sake of the children.

Now, as she sits in the fading light of the kitchen, she thinks how precarious it all is; we all teeter on the edge of one bad decision, one temptation, one momentary lapse in concentration. It's like living your life with a cocked gun in your hand.

CONOR

He is just about to hang up when a tentative voice says, 'Hello?'

'Is this Brendan?'

'Yes?'

Conor takes a deep breath. 'This is Conor. Conor Tobin.'

Then, 'Wow. Conor. Thank you for calling me.'

'God, don't thank me. I've been so angry, imagining you were a journalist out to ruin me. And, I mean, everything that happened. At the school . . . I'm so—'

'No, please,' Brendan interrupts. 'Look. I'm happy you rang. There's a lot to say. I'd love to meet up with you, Conor. Talk about stuff. Maybe, with your permission, spend time with your mother? Explain things.'

Conor can't understand why Brendan would have any interest in spending time with the comatose woman who was responsible for killing his sibling. But he is tired and past caring. Let someone else figure that mystery out.

'Look Brendan, to be honest, I'm of no use to you just now. I'm at my apartment in Auckland, packing. I've got to go away for a while. Business trip, you know? I'll give you Sinead's details. She'll help you out, I'm sure.'

'Okay.' He sounds disappointed. 'Maybe we could get together when you get back? It would be good to, you know, talk, after all this time.'

He manages to say in an upbeat way, 'Sounds great, Brendan. Looking forward to it. Sorry to cut it short but I've got to run. Plane to catch and all that. I'm forwarding that number to you now, though.'

Once he's sent the message he puts the phone down on the couch beside him and picks up the remote. He flicks through the channels and stops on a game of cricket. Some domestic game being played in brilliant sunshine. The players are dressed in garish colours, pink and yellow, which surprises him. He thought they always wore white. Cricket is not a game that has ever really interested him. Maybe it's because he came to it late, spending his formative years in a country that never took to it. Too English, too stiff upper lip. He prefers football, which seems far more egalitarian. However, the cricket suits his mood now; there is something pleasingly hypnotic about it.

All the blinds are closed in his apartment. He didn't bother to open them when he came in. It gives the place that unnatural gloom that comes from blocking out the sun on a hot day. He looks around and wonders why he paid a lot of money for an interior designer to style this place in such a sleek way. Fulfilling a design aesthetic that he cared nothing for. Minimalist meets

Industrial Chic, she'd called it. The lack of possessions on show supposed to reflect an absence of consumerist desire. This, he discovered, was ludicrously expensive to achieve. He could be anywhere, in any apartment, in any city, in any season. In any life. He remembers details of their old house in Ireland. No minimalism there. Houses back then were places where the messy act of living took place. The mismatched brown and yellow dinner plates – delph, Joy called it. The doily tablecloth and net curtains. The mid-century mahogany and mustard polyester dining chairs, the sofa (settee, their father called it, which drove Joy mad) covered in a brown velour pattern. She'd never been hugely houseproud; wasn't one to get upset by errant toast crumbs or an abandoned tea mug, but she'd lost all semblance of interest in home décor by the time they moved to New Zealand. He always felt slightly embarrassed by the shambolic interior when friends came over. Although he learnt to keep *that* to a minimum. They all did.

He washes down another pill – Was it his second? Third? – with a swig of the eye-wateringly expensive whiskey he received from some client or other several years ago. *Uisce beatha*. He remembers the Irish for it. Water of life. He usually steers clear of the stuff, finding it too strong, but this is surprisingly mellow on his palate. *Should have opened it sooner*, he thinks ruefully.

The television camera scans the crowd at the cricket, pausing at a group of sunburned men who, judging by their French maid outfits, appear to be on a stag do. One of them looks straight into the camera, raises his can of beer and winks. 'Cheers!' Conor says aloud, raising his own glass towards the television.

Should have got married, he thinks. Settled down with one of those perfectly nice girlfriends. God knows there were a few who were willing. *Should have stayed at the law firm.* Spent weekends at cricket matches, evenings quaffing single malts after the kids had gone to bed.

He is bone-meltingly drowsy. Like his entire body is inconsequential. Air. He takes a look at the bottle of pills he has swiped from his mother's house. It had been a spontaneous action. At the time he was only half-aware of stuffing it into his jeans pocket, but he was cognisant enough to not let Sinead see. He struggles to understand the violence of his mother's choice of exit from the world. Cricket, a single malt, and some pills. Far gentler.

The action on the pitch is getting blurry. His eyelids start to droop, but then the reverie is broken by the players in pink screeching loudly and jumping in the air, fists pumping. 'That's just not cricket,' he says aloud, then starts to laugh. The player at the crease takes off his helmet and walks off the pitch. Before he disappears into the tunnel he raises his bat in salute at an appreciative crowd. 'Good on ya, mate,' one of the commentators says, as though addressing the exiting player. 'You can leave now with your head held high.'

If only I could say the same, Conor thinks. Then he lays his head down on the smooth leather of his beige Italian sofa.

SINEAD

Sinead studies Brendan's profile from the passenger seat of his work ute. He is concentrating on negotiating some gnarly bends over the Kaimai Ranges on the route from Tauranga to Auckland, so is unaware, or at least pretending to be, of her attentions. She finds she could look at him for a long time. The large eyes framed by long, dark lashes. The straight nose. The full mouth. His hand rests on the gear stick and she notes the dirt under his fingernails. She likes this, the earthiness of it. The usefulness of what he does. He is not her usual type – if indeed one could say, musing on the eclectic collection of men (and the occasional woman) she has been with, that she has a type – but there is something unique about him, for sure. An openness, a vulnerability. But not the tiresome fragility displayed by many of the men in the circles she moves in. The creative types with their easily bruised egos, who swing between elation and despair. His vulnerability is more solid than that, one rooted in real pain.

He had rung her less than two hours ago, explaining that although he didn't have much prior experience to go on, he thought that Conor had sounded a bit strange on the phone; distracted, even.

'Like he had other things on his mind?' she'd said.

'Yes.'

'Don't worry, he always sounds like that.'

'I guess he did mention something about catching a plane for some business trip.'

'Oh, fuck. Well, unless he's managed since yesterday to secure a high-flying job that necessitates an immediate trip, that sounds like a crock of shit.' She thought it best not to mention that he had form in this regard. She did not want to freak Brendan out with talk of close calls with a train.

When she had said she was going to drive up to his apartment to check if he was okay, Brendan had offered to come. At first she declined politely; no need to involve anyone else in this family's dysfunction. Although, in a way, he was already involved. And he seemed so eager, and she thought, why not?

'I can drive, if you like? I'm just in Cambridge working today. Could swing by in an hour or so and pick you up?' he said.

Now she asks, 'So, tell me, how did you end up in New Zealand? It seems so weird that you did too.'

'I know. Of all the places, etc. But if you're going to run somewhere may as well make it epic. My dad moved to Australia after my parents separated. I joined him there as soon as I left school. He had set up a landscaping business and I went to work for him. Then I came here to New Zealand a few years ago, decided I needed a change of scene. Relationship break-up, yada yada. I love it now.'

'Did your parents separate because of what happened?'

'Probably. They tried but I think they dealt with it so differently that it drove them apart. Mam couldn't understand Dad's way of handling things. She just wanted to talk about Declan all the time. She ended up getting together with a former priest, of all things. I think she enjoyed the confessional aspect of their relationship. She died young, in her fifties. Her heart just stopped. Sometimes I think she was waiting to go, to see her baby again. And poor Dad went all stoic and retreated into himself. I wonder if landscaping was the best thing for him to do. Too much time alone and all that. He died young too. Brain aneurism. I reckon it was all those feelings that he suppressed that finally made his brain explode.'

More casualties. 'I'm so sorry. And you? Is it the best thing for you to do?'

'Probably not.' He glances over and laughs. 'So what about you, what do you do? Apart from driving round the country to check on your siblings.'

'I ran the other way. Went back to Ireland. I wanted to be a writer and it seemed more conducive to that lifestyle. I think people in Dublin are more accepting of the struggling artist persona I try to project. New Zealanders would be deeply suspicious of someone who doesn't appear to do anything.' She grins. 'Writing is another terrible occupation if you shouldn't be alone with your thoughts.'

'Quite the pair then, aren't we?' he says, looking at her. It gives her a warm feeling.

'Indeed.' She smiles at him.

'And you love being back in Ireland?'

'It's more like I belong there,' Sinead says. It's true. Ireland is in her DNA. Sometimes as a teenager, reading about Irish history, she mused if even her fraught relationship with food was some kind of famine-related inheritance. Maybe her genetic memory caused her to overeat. She said as much one time to Frances, who was disdainful of the portion of the takeaway she was serving herself. Frances rolled her eyes and said, 'Gimme a break. Doubt our ancestors back in Ireland gorged themselves on chicken tikka masala once the famine was over.' And when, aged twenty-five, she first landed in Dublin – no, even before the plane landed, on approach to the airport – she looked out the window, saw the grey-green water and jutting coast, the striped Poolbeg chimneys and Bailey Lighthouse, the patchwork of small irregular fields enclosed by hedges, the white houses dotted sporadically, every cell in her body seemed to relax, and to say, *You're home now.* She'd walked almost fearfully up to passport control, half-afraid they'd turn her away. Expose her as a fraud. Immigration officers and police always terrified her. But she showed her new Irish passport and the man behind the screen smiled at her and said, 'Welcome home,' and she said, 'Thanks a million!' like she'd heard her mother say, and walked away grinning.

'Funny,' says Brendan. 'I feel the same way about here.'

'Your spiritual home, maybe.' And that's how Ireland felt for her. She drank in the scenery on that first trip into the city centre.

Kiwis who'd never been always said they'd heard that the two countries were similarly hued. But it wasn't true. The audacious green of the Irish countryside was a revelation. She knew that was the result of almost daily rain, but even the weather suited her and every centimetre of her freckled, melanin-poor skin. In the few times she came back to New Zealand in the following years, she never got the same feeling of home when she landed in Auckland. She loved the Māori carved gateway, or *tomokanga,* when she landed at the airport and walked through to arrivals. But it was more like an anthropological appreciation rather than the comfort of home; she felt *that* looking at photographic portraits of Irish faces that lined the walkway of the shiny new terminal in Dublin airport. And when leaving Auckland airport, the Phoenix palms and the timber houses, each one different to its neighbour, felt jarring. Though she'd spent most of her life in the country, it always felt foreign to her, as though she was arriving on holiday for the first time.

'I suppose they're similar countries in a way, though. Both on the edge. A little apart.'

She nods. 'I guess. And it can be good to be on the outside a little.'

'That's probably what makes you a great writer. Being an outsider.' He smiles at her. She doesn't feel worthy of it. 'What are you writing at the moment, by the way?'

'My second novel, actually. I had terrible writer's block for years but it seems to be practically writing itself at the moment.'

He looks delighted. 'That's so brilliant, Sinead. You must be thrilled.'

He is so genuine, his face lit up like a little boy's. She feels sick now. 'Mmm,' is all she can manage. Why did she justify the plagiarism to herself by comparing it to Brendan's gardening? She can't imagine him ever being deceitful like that.

They drive in silence for a while. Sinead tries Conor's phone but again it goes straight to voicemail.

'Kia ora, douchebag. I'm coming up to see you because you won't answer your phone. I'm going to be pissed off if I find out you're snorting cocaine with some hot young model, or whatever you high-flyers do when you're on gardening leave. Oh, and Brendan Smith is coming too. Ciao.' After she hangs up she says, 'Dunno why I bother, he won't listen to it.'

Brendan laughs. 'You're lucky to have siblings.'

'Look, Brendan, I don't mean to sound insensitive, but I think, as you may be beginning to see, they are right pains in the hole sometimes.'

'Yeah, but no-one will ever get you the way they do.' There is no self-pity in his voice. He says it matter-of-factly.

'Speaking of siblings, tell me, what was Declan like?' She instinctively feels comfortable to ask him this.

'Well, like all younger siblings he could be a pain in the ass,' he grins at her, 'but he was a cool little guy. Really bright. Liked to collect things. I always thought he might have made a good scientist if . . .' His voice trails off. 'My mother built a sort of shrine to him in the house. She covered a whole wall in photos and drawings or bits of writing he'd done. It used to freak visitors out. I think it's one of the reasons I left as soon as I could. I felt like *her* life stopped that day too. She could never move on.'

Sinead thinks of Joy, her life stalling on that day too. 'This is super nice of you, Brendan, and thanks for doing it, for coming with me. But I'm dying to know why you would want to spend time with the family responsible for your brother's death. The other night, at my mother's place, you mentioned something about needing to share something?'

He looks so troubled suddenly. He takes a deep breath in, then exhales heavily. As she looks at him it's like a shadow crosses his face, which was, a moment ago, as open and easy to read as the sky. He says, 'That's the thing. It wasn't your mother's fault. Can I tell you a story?'

—

Conor's apartment is down a side street in Ponsonby. It's a small, exclusive development over four storeys and containing only eight dwellings. Conor's is the penthouse, tinted windows facing the street. The blinds are drawn. No sign of life.

Sinead holds the buzzer down. No answer. A woman, maybe in her sixties, well-dressed, impeccably made-up, exits the front door.

'Excuse me,' Sinead says. 'My brother Conor lives in number eight. He's not answering the doorbell and I'm worried about him. Do you think you could let us up?'

The woman looks them over. Sinead realises they are probably not creating a good impression: Brendan in his gardening clothes, she with patchy regrowth on her head and an ill-fitting tracksuit scrounged from Franny.

She says, 'Okay, I'll bring you up. The lady who cleans the apartments, Sharon, is around today. Perhaps we can ask her to let you in.'

Several bangs on the door go unanswered, even though they can hear noise from the television. Sharon is found, and after some minutes of persuasion relents and unlocks the door.

When they enter, the darkness is a shock. Sinead's eyes struggle to adjust but then she sees him, lying on the sofa and bathed in the blue glow of the television. *Cricket, that's odd*, she thinks, then sees his right arm is flung strangely over his head, as though attempting some sort of salute.

JOY

It's Conor's tenth birthday today and he's all out of sorts. Last night was Hallowe'en, normally his favourite night of the year. There's always been something a bit other-worldly about him. But it was a let-down. It's a holiday viewed with suspicion here. Too mystical, too Catholic, maybe. (Mother would approve of its low status though. You Fenians and your hocus-pocus, Virgin-venerating voodoo! she'd sneer at my father.) And the season all wrong here for it too. Spring is a season for birth and new life. Not honouring the dead.

I wouldn't let Conor go trick-or-treating, afraid of the reception he might get. We were ready here with a bowl of sweets, just in case. But there wasn't a single knock on the door.

So the four of us sat and ate all the sweets and I wondered if I'd made a big mistake, transplanting these little lost souls to this upside-down, back-to-front place that could not be farther away from home. (And that's precisely the point, I told my aunt, when she exclaimed with horror at New Zealand's distance from Ireland. I was showing her its position on the old globe that once belonged to Daddy. Are they even civilised there? Are they like us? she asked. God, I hope not, I thought.)

Had I been naïve, though? Listening to those beautiful Māori myths that depicted such a deep connection to the earth, and feeling myself dislocated in Ireland? Imagining I could somehow start over here? That my children could start over here?

I worry for Conor. Worry for them all, but him especially. Despite the way he appears, so self-possessed, he's less resilient than his sisters. Wanting to salvage the day for him, I take them to the beach for the first time since arriving here. It's a late spring morning, and though the weather is sunny there's a blustery westerly coming in. The children build sandcastles and I marvel at the golden expanse of beach that stretches for miles and the swirls of pink and grey at the horizon. The light here is so different from home, so saturated.

I think of Daddy's beloved Mayo, the rugged Clew Bay at the foot of Croagh Patrick. I think of the wild Atlantic Ocean. Moody and turbulent. Where you'd look out and think of America. All a world away now, and I wonder if I'll ever see it again. I wonder if this place could ever inspire the same deep longing in these children once they're grown.

Despite the brightness of the day, a kind of melancholy grips me. I think of mists and glens, gentle rolling hills and yellow meadows, bluebell-carpeted woodlands, shady overgrown country roads and small fields surrounded by hedgerows, and I miss home.

We take a walk around the base of the dormant volcano, Mauao – Caught by the Dawn – that stands at the very tip of the peninsula. Then we climb partway up the hillside and stop and sit for a while, facing out to the vast ocean, murkier now that the sun is hiding behind a cloud. There are tufts of wild grass between stubby grey boulders and stunted, wind-bent trees and small pebbles of sheep shit. For the briefest of moments, we could be somewhere in Ireland. Then I look behind me, the illusion shattered by the steep rise of the volcano, lushly packed with pōhutukawa and silver fern and mānuka. Imagining the blown-open crater at its summit makes me think of the precariousness of the new land we've come to. The potential for violence. The earth gave a deep rolling shudder last night and we were all terrified, never having experienced an earthquake before.

I chose Tauranga because of its meaning. Safe Anchorage. But I'd never heard the name the first European settlers gave this land: The Shaky Isles.

We find a pebbly beach, sheltered from the surf by jagged charcoal rocks: perfect to explore. The waves are rough and getting stronger, riled up by the wind and hitting the rocks with some force. While I sit with the girls, fossicking for treasure in the gravelly sand, Conor climbs the tallest rock and stands, hands on hips, facing out to the ocean. As the surf froths on the peak next to his I start to worry and think I should call to him to get down, but Frances taps me on the shoulder to show me a shell she's found. I admire its unusual smoothness and colour and turn back again, intent on warning him. He is gone. A terrible fear grips me, and I stand up, sure a rogue wave has taken him. I run to the rock he was on and scramble up it. Conor, Conor, I scream, and all I can see in my head is the lifeless body of a little boy lying under the wheels of my car.

At the top now, I look down and there he is, bent over and peering into a rockpool, oblivious to my distress. Conor! And this time he looks up at me, his large eyes questioning. And I should hop down, wrap my arms around him and tell him that I am weak with relief, tell him how much I love him, tell him how special he is. But I say none of that. Instead I grab him by the arm and march him back to where his sisters are sitting. And he cries because I have frightened him, but instead of comforting him I angrily pack our belongings together and tell them the day is ruined and we are going home.

I storm back to the car, the children trotting behind me. And I won't look back at them. I don't want to see the confusion and disappointment on their faces. As we drive back home in silence I know it would just take a kind word, a simple gesture to fix it. But once again I am struck dumb and paralysed by my own sadness.

FRANCES

'So, Olivia, how are you feeling today?'

It's been two days since Livvy got drunk at practice. She, Frances and Harry are sitting in the claustrophobic back office of the aquatic centre with Josh. The shouts and screams of excited children playing in the pool seep through the walls and creep inside Frances's brain. She is finding Josh's condescending manner unbearable but she is hoping the swim competition can still be salvaged, so she tries to hide her irritation.

'Fine,' Livvy says, with a tilt of her chin that makes Frances nervous. She is sensing that Livvy may not be about to act as contritely as the current situation requires. Any remorse she expressed earlier has been replaced with a monosyllabic abrasiveness that Frances has been too scared to challenge. She is in no position to take the moral high ground. So they've skirted uneasily around each other, with Harry's arrival home providing a welcome relief.

'One of the many benefits of being young, eh, Josh? No two-day hangovers for you guys.'

Frances has to fight hard not to throw Harry a warning look. Again, no moral high ground allowed.

Josh gives a tight smile. 'I wouldn't know, to be honest. I don't drink myself.'

Inwardly, Frances rolls her eyes. But she says, 'Very wise, Josh, it's a terrible thing, alcohol. We should all steer clear.'

Livvy gives a derisive snort.

Josh says, 'So look, do you want to tell us, Olivia, why you did what you did?'

Harry interjects, 'Yes, Livvy. I mean, blue label vodka? I thought you had more class that that!'

This time Frances does shoot him a look, but he refuses to catch her eye.

'I don't know,' Livvy says, ignoring her father's mortifying dad jokes. 'I was angry, I suppose.'

'About what in particular?'

Please don't say it. Please don't say because my mother's been having it off with an ex-boyfriend.

'Just different stuff. It's hard to explain.'

'Please try.'

'Yes, darling, please. We just want to understand,' Harry says.

Livvy takes a deep breath. She looks down at the floor and starts to talk. 'Everything's been so weird. Since Gran tried to kill herself. Everyone's acting so self-absorbed and crazy. Mum's been dressing differently and wearing lots of makeup, sneaking around with her phone all the time.' Harry makes a weird exhaling sound, which stops Livvy for a second. She throws her father a look then carries on. 'And then I heard Dad yelling at Mum the other night. Dad *never* yells. And then he left at the crack of dawn, making up some business trip when I know he went to stay with his brother. And there's been all this stuff online about my uncle, who's apparently been defrauding his charity, and ended up in hospital after taking an overdose—'

'No!' Frances says, seeing the shock on Josh's face. She leans forward. 'He just took a couple of sleeping pills and was a little hard to wake, that's all, and he may have overspent a little, but he was just trying to promote a culture where everyone felt valued and—'

'Frances?' Harry interrupts her. 'Let Livvy finish.'

Frances sits back.

'And now my gran is lying in a coma in hospital, and no-one seems to care. And it's like they're all ashamed of the fact. Like, my mother still talks about *committing* suicide like it's a crime. Or they use dumb words like her 'incident'. I know she drank too much sometimes, and I know she wasn't the greatest parent, but I loved her. *Love* her. And I miss her. We'd eat dinner on our laps and watch old movies together and she didn't care if I spilled crumbs on the couch. Or was in danger of becoming anaemic because I hadn't eaten any red meat. Or spent too much time on my phone. I'd show her YouTube videos and stuff off the internet, and she'd actually pay attention. Not like just pretending, the way most adults do. And she didn't care if I went to bed late. Or if I'd done my homework or tidied my room or was class prefect. She didn't care about squad training or how fast my fifty-metre backstroke was. She'd ask about my swim comps but only so we could laugh together about all the pushy parents. The Swim Bots, she called them. She was really funny like that. I could just *be* with her without the need to be so perfect all the time. And the absolute worst thing is, she must have been in so much pain, and I didn't see it.'

Josh looks out of his depth. He looks to Frances, but she is struck dumb. By shock, but also a creeping shame.

Josh flounders. 'Well, I mean, I'm sure it's not really your fault—'

Livvy interrupts him. 'It is, though. You don't understand. She kept talking about when she'd be gone and how she thought it would be better for everyone. I thought it was just the way old people carry on sometimes. You know, being nearly dead anyway and all that. But now I realise she was trying to tell me. I think she was saying goodbye.'

She puts her head down again and starts to cry.

Harry moves to put his arm around Livvy and comfort her. Not for the first time, Frances feels envious of his ease with their daughter. His generosity with his affection. The thing that drew Frances to him in the first place, the simple straightforwardness of him, has now become a source of resentment. And she hates this mean-spiritedness within herself but can't shake it. When she reads a Hallmark-style inspirational quote that one of her friends posts online, she may inwardly roll her eyes, but she also feels a kind of sadness, as though she is the only one incapable of big-heartedness. In the wee small hours, reflecting on her day, she has lost count of the times she resolves to be a nicer person in the morning. But the same old bitterness resurfaces with the sun.

Josh says, 'Look, maybe Olivia doesn't need to be out of squad after all? I mean, listening to this, the stuff she's been going through, I could give her another chance. I might have to smooth things over with some of the other parents but I think everyone will understand. And she is our star performer.'

As Josh speaks, Frances looks at her daughter's distraught tear-streaked face. Remembers picking her up after a fall to comfort her. Remembers the sensation of her chubby little arms around her neck as she swooped her up, her hot sweet breath on her shoulder. Can feel it, almost. She sits forward.

'Actually Josh, I think Livvy needs a break. We're withdrawing from the competition.'

And Livvy looks at her and gives her a small, grateful smile that almost breaks Frances's heart.

—

At home, with Livvy gone to her room to listen to music, Frances and Harry sit out on the deck with cups of tea. Though she'd wanted one desperately, she didn't suggest wine.

'I'll stay for now,' Harry says. 'I don't think Livvy should be put through any more upset.'

'Thank you,' she says. 'I mean, I know you're not doing it for me, but thank you anyway.'

'So that'll make two of us in this gig out of a sense of obligation.'

'That's not true, Harry! That's not what this is for me!'

'It is. It's like much of what you do, Frances. It's done out of a need to be seen to be doing the right thing. A sense of duty that you resent deep down.'

He is right, but she also feels the unfairness of it. She does love them, her family, all of them, even her crazy mother, but isn't that just what family is? An obligation? Your duty? No matter how much you love them? What mother or wife or husband or father hasn't at some point longed for those carefree pre-family days? Who hasn't fantasised about sport-free Saturday-morning lie-ins? Or spontaneous not-too-tired-for-it sex? Or the wild abandon of nights out with friends that you know can be followed up by indulgent Sundays on the couch? Who hasn't felt, even fleetingly, the pang of resentment towards their family for that burden of love?

But she doesn't argue. She wonders, if she and Harry were to somehow salvage their marriage, if it would be this way forever. Him righteous, her debased. In a weird reversal of roles, where everything he did was beyond reproach. Maybe that's how some marriages worked. Maybe that's *why* they worked. Could she live like that? Could he?

Harry goes inside but she stays. Sits so long the male cicadas stop their racket. *Happy are cicadas' lives, for they have voiceless wives.* Just like future Harry, she thinks grimly. Sits so long the sunlight starts to diffuse into the low cloud on the horizon. The colours change from pink to yellow to orange. Although barely dusk, a solitary star is visible. Venus. She remembers sitting out here with Harry one night and he told her what it was. She thought he was mistaken. Astronomy and the solar system, anything celestial in fact, had always seemed unknowable and mysterious to her. Too big. The infinite nature of it too uncertain. The idea that you could just look up and see another planet was astounding. Harry wasn't condescending about it and didn't make fun of her – he'd never do that – but still she felt foolish for not knowing. Like she had failed to recognise the moon or the sun. Harry had an easy connection to the natural world that she envied. He had grown up in a family who'd rewarded his curiosity. She, on the other hand, had stopped asking questions. Or perhaps she never asked in the first place.

Prosaic, down-to-earth, practical. Uncurious. She hears her mother's descriptions of her personality traits. *Your father's child.* As though she couldn't bear to believe she'd played any part in the creation of such a pedantic little thing.

Venus has been joined by many stars now. Frances looks for the Southern Cross and smiles. It *is* more kite than cross. Shortly after they had moved to New Zealand, Joy erected a hammock between two magnolia trees in the garden. She had been proud of her handiwork and spent many hours that first summer gently rocking herself in it. Late one evening, Frances, unable to find her mother anywhere in the house, went outside to see if she was there. She saw the familiar sag in the hammock and approached cautiously, not wanting to wake her if she was asleep. But Joy's eyes were wide, staring up to the heavens.

'Mammy?' Frances asked. 'Are you coming inside?'

Joy turned her head and looked at her. 'I can't find it anywhere,' she said, and turned her gaze upwards again.

Frances tensed. She knew she had to ask, but there was always a chance she would irritate her mother with a question. And sometimes the answers were so perplexing anyway, she was left more confused. 'Can't find what, Mammy?'

Joy didn't look at her again but said, 'The Plough, of course. I can't find the fucking thing anywhere. All I can see is that damned kite!'

Frances sidled away, figuring her mother to be in one of her unreachable moods. Also, she had cursed, which could only mean one thing. When Conor asked what Joy was doing, Frances told him their mother was looking for something in the magnolia trees. Conor shrugged and took himself off to bed. But she stayed up, watching from the kitchen window as Joy's outline swayed in the hammock.

Frances didn't know what her mother was looking for. But she had a feeling that whatever it was, it could never be found.

CONOR

'You're not very good at this killing yourself malarkey, eh, bro? I mean, three sleeping pills? That might have worked if you were, say, a small rodent, but not a six-foot-two hunk like yourself. Not to mention choosing a freight train moving at approximately five miles per hour to lie in front of. What's next? Hanging yourself with sewing thread?'

He laughs. It feels good. It's been a hellish couple of days. Sinead has picked him up from the hospital and they are eating a takeout breakfast at his apartment. He has been discharged on the condition he remains in her care, with an immediate referral to a mental health worker. He doesn't know when or how she has turned from basket case to his dependable saviour, but he is grateful anyhow.

'Yeah. It's obviously a family failing,' he says.

'Come on, though. Joy's method displayed a greater degree of . . .' – she searches for a word – 'assiduousness.'

'You always had a way with words, sis. Have you ever thought of being a writer?'

'Ha ha. You're hilarious!' Her expression changes. 'But seriously. Did you mean it? Did you . . . *do you* . . . want to die?'

He thinks for a while. He has faced many questions from concerned health professionals over the last two days, but it's all such a blur he can't remember if he has answered honestly or just told them what he thought he should say.

'Thinking about it now, no. I definitely want to be alive. But then, it seemed sort of poetic. I know that sounds stupid. But it's like my thinking was all distorted. Like, you know the way when you're a bit drunk and you embark on some form of self-sabotage? Like texting an ex out of the blue? You sort of have a faint nagging feeling that you shouldn't be doing it, but that gets overridden by the euphoria in the moment. That possibly it's going to have a brilliant outcome. That she'll be delighted to hear from you. That you were meant to be together all along and this time it's going to be amazing. Well, it was like that, and the outcome, which was my death obviously, was somehow going to be noble and uplifting. That people would be . . . *grateful* to me, somehow. I mean, I imagined myself leaving this world to a barrage of cheering, like I was some kind of heroic sportsperson. I know that sounds deranged. But I wasn't scared. I was kind of happy in a weird way.'

Sinead nods. 'I get it. I mean, don't get me wrong, *no-one* would have been happy that you were gone. But I get that sense of relief you must have felt.' She pauses. Then, 'I worry about how Mum felt at the end. That she was in excruciating mental pain. Or was terrified. Or simply tired. But maybe, just maybe, there was a little peace there, too.'

Conor shrugs. 'Maybe.' He feels a compulsion to ask her then, 'And what about you? Have you ever felt like it? Dying, I mean?'

She exhales heavily, then looks up at the ceiling as she speaks, as though articulating what she is thinking requires divine assistance. 'No. Not dying as in ever wanting to end my life myself. But I have thought about death. The relief of it, sometimes. When everything gets too big. I've even sort of fantasised about it. About how it would happen. Like, I'm walking through, say, the Phoenix Park – the location is always quite specific – and I imagine a guy jumping out from behind the bushes and stabbing me. Or if I'm crossing the road, I imagine a big bin truck taking me out. It's weird, though. I mean, I don't want it to happen, but it's like a sick fantasy.'

'Wow. I can tell you something, little sis, my fantasies are *much* more fun than yours. Haven't you ever watched porn? Imagined some hunky plumber calling round to—'

'Ewww,' she interrupts him. 'I hope you weren't about to say something gross like *attend to my pipes*. Believe me, my sexual fantasies are far more imaginative than that. Anyway, at least I don't still possess white saviour complex even when face to face with my own mortality.'

He grins and gives her a gentle punch on the shoulder. 'I knew I shouldn't have told you the heroic sportsperson bit.' He leans back in his chair, hands behind his head. He feels lighter. 'We're some pair, eh?'

'That we are, bro. That we are.'

'So anyway, what's happening with the new book? You said something earlier about having made a good start on it?'

She looks pained. 'Jesus. Look. As we're in a sort of confessional mood. I've done something and I'm not sure how to get out of it.'

'Can I help? I mean, my close brushes with death have probably given me some profound insight and wisdom.'

She laughs. 'I doubt that.' Then she covers her face with her hands. She takes a breath, then speaks quickly, the words tumbling over each other. 'But okay, here goes . . . I . . . oh God . . . I was so desperate to get something to my publisher, to fulfil my contract, that I plagiarised a book I found on Frances's bookshelf. I've been sending in excerpts, passing it off as my own work. And now the publisher loves it. And there's this whole new buzz around this new book and I don't know what the fuck to do because I get so excited when I get these complimentary emails about how good it is and I think I can get away with it, and I've been plunged to the depths of self-loathing thinking I can't write anymore. And this seems like the way out even though I know it's wrong but I also don't want to go back to feeling like a failure either.'

She takes her hands away from her face. Exhales.

He nods slowly, thinks for a moment. 'Okay, well, okay, I see. I don't know if this helps at all, Sinead, but . . . I've been so unhappy, you know? And I thought other people admiring me or loving me could fix it. And them telling me I was great because of the philanthropy or liking one of my posts, whatever, well it made me feel good for a while. Like a tiny hit of a drug. But then the same old dislike of myself would resurface. I guess what I'm trying to say, and I know you know this anyway, is that you'll never feel good about that book. Even if you're never found out. Even if you win the Booker Prize for it.' He smiles then. '*Even* if Frances likes it.'

She smiles back at him.

He carries on. 'And I can help you, if you like. If you think you'd like to stop it all, come clean, but you're scared? Maybe I could talk to your publisher for you? I mean, I haven't been much of a big brother lately, so it might be time to step up.'

She reaches across and touches his arm. Her eyes are wet. 'Thank you. But no. It's time for me to put on my big-girl pants.' She leans back, wipes her eyes. 'Now, enough of my problems. I shouldn't be burdening you anymore. You might decide to go and put a water pistol to your temple.'

She barely lets him out of her sight for the rest of the day, but rather than making him feel claustrophobic, her presence comforts him. The apartment feels less sterile with her mooching about. And mooch she does. She boils the sleek black kettle constantly. She had to pull it out of the cupboard where it lived unused. Then she'd yelled at him from the kitchen, 'Where the hell is your toaster?'

'I don't have one.'

'What kind of a person doesn't own a toaster? You know it's like someone Marie Kondo'd the fuck out of your home.'

She can't sit still for long, turns the TV on and off in the quest to find something entertaining. He is amused to learn that she loves daytime quiz shows, shouts the answers at the screen. She likes to listen to the *Desert Island Discs* podcast. ('But only the people who are dead now; it makes my problems seem less awful somehow.') She opens and closes the fridge and cupboards a lot, like a teenager hoping that something new will have appeared since the last time she looked.

After one unsuccessful forage for food she said, 'You're like one of those guys on a true crime show. You know, when they finally get a warrant and search his apartment and they realise he's a total psychopath and must be the serial killer because all they can find is some caviar and a gimp mask.'

He finds it strange, but also nice, to be learning new things about this person he has known for forty years. He can't really remember her personality as a child. Baby Sinead appears in his memories as a shadow, an outline. An extra in the film of his life. A person who shared the misery of their upbringing but to whom he was never deeply connected when they were going through it. He sometimes feels as though he and his sisters had grown up completely separately, as individuals in the same house, but not a family. He finds it sad but maybe that's just how you survived. Self-reliance and self-preservation were key.

Her energy makes him wonder how she ever has the discipline to sit at a computer for hours or even teach a yoga class without getting distracted. But it's just what he needs. It makes him think of how it felt to have Lara around. And even though he doesn't feel angry now when he thinks about Lara, it occurs to him that he would rather have Sinead here. This surprises him. Maybe it's an age thing. He can't imagine telling Lara some of the things he has admitted to his sister.

That night as he gets ready to go to bed, she is sitting at his kitchen island typing rapidly on her laptop.

'So, what's that you're working on?'

'A short story. Brendan's inspired me.'

'Okay, just as long as it's not about me.'

'Christ, Conor Tobin, you think the world revolves around you! I blame Mommy Dearest.'

And he laughs, and once in bed surprises himself by slipping easily into a deep, and this time drug-free, sleep.

SINEAD

A week later Sinead pulls the old black and yellow case out from under the bed. God knows what she is doing back here in her mother's bedroom. She'd only come to check the place and clear the mail. But it's as though spending time with Brendan and listening to his story about his little brother, his confession about the day of the accident, admiring his desire to be truthful, has ignited a willingness in her to confront what she fears may be uncomfortable. She had asked him if together they could write a short story about what happened. Said it helped, committing things to paper, rather than having it all flailing around inside, messing with your head. You could make something worthwhile from the pain. At least that had been her experience with her first book. He told her he would like that. Very much.

She has never encountered anyone like Brendan before. There is a childlike quality to him that she finds compelling. As though he has somehow retained a little of his brother – the boy who was never allowed grow old – within him. He is thoughtful and serious, but not in a way that makes her feel bad about her own glibness. In fact, he seems to enjoy her lack of reverence.

Since Conor was released from hospital, she and Brendan have seen each other every day. At first she was wary of her attraction to him – the history between their families so entwined and painful that it seemed almost perverse to be having such feelings. But eventually she gave in to them, and when they had sex last night, it was the first time in years, maybe ever, that she'd done it sober. She wasn't sure if it was because of that, or because of Brendan, but it was also the first time that she'd felt present during it. Every other time she'd had sex with somebody it had been done out of a sense of obligation. *Well, we got high together so may as well finish the job.* Or something to do once the high was wearing off. Or a desire to be liked. Or to be considered nonchalant and edgy. Maybe just a way to not be alone. She had never felt pretty, but she knew how to act sexually forthright and open, which increased her attractiveness for a certain type of man.

But the act itself had always left her feeling diminished. A little degraded. Like the way she felt after she pierced her skin with a blade. Relief mixed with shame. If she was honest, she wanted one of those partners to fall a little in love with her. Maybe instead of telling her, over a post-coital cigarette, that *it* had been amazing, she would have liked, just once, for them to say that *she* was amazing. Or even just worthy.

Brendan didn't say anything like that. Didn't need to. During, he was an endearing mix of enthusiastic and shy. Afterwards, he buried his face in her neck and said, 'Can we please do this every single day for the rest of our lives?' And it didn't feel like a line, a throwaway remark from one jaded participant to another. A flippant reply sprang to her lips, but she held it back and said, 'I'd like that.' And she meant it.

Maggie rang while she was lying beside him. She has been avoiding her for days now. Interviews are being arranged. The most recent extract she sent admired. She picked up the phone, then, when she saw the name, dropped it quickly on the floor.

Brendan said, 'Wow, you *really* didn't want to speak to that person. Do you owe them money or something?'

'In a way.' She covered her face with a pillow.

'Shit, sorry, I was just kidding. I didn't mean to pry.'

She took the pillow off. 'It's okay. It's just I've done something stupid and I need to make it right.'

'Can I help?'

She studied his face. His expression was so direct, straightforward. Maybe it wasn't so complicated. 'I think you may already be helping.' And she kissed him.

Now, she hesitates. Closes her eyes and runs her fingers over the textured exterior of her mother's case. It feels like Braille. Is there a hidden message telling her to stop? But then she thinks of Brendan, how he overcame his fear to talk to them all, and presses down on the brass locks.

She sees the shredded letter lying on top. She imagines Mrs Smith going through her mail on an otherwise uneventful morning. How the handwritten letter postmarked New Zealand – even back then, when handwritten letters were not almost obsolete – would have stood out amongst the bills and circulars. How it would have been the first thing she had gone to open.

Curious, excited even. Racking her brain as to what it could be. Who did she know in New Zealand?

And then the shock when she turned the envelope over and saw the return name and address. How the grief and anger she might have tried to subdue, or at least learn to live with, would have come crashing back. How she would have gone ahead and opened it anyway despite her misgivings, read a few lines even, before the rage became too great and she ripped the thing in a hundred pieces. She might have sat down then with the intention of composing a letter of her own, an accusatory riposte, perhaps containing all the things that over the years she had imagined saying to Joy if she had ever had the opportunity. But then realising that she could never adequately put those feelings into words. They were too massive to live within the constraints of a sheet of Belvedere Bond. And so, she had simply stuffed them back into the envelope and written in a red hand that conveyed her response succinctly: Return to Sender.

And she imagines Joy, in the weeks after she has sent the letter, checking her mailbox each day, half hopeful, half fearful. Cursing the slow speed of the New Zealand and Irish postal services. Contemplating the unfathomable distance between the two countries; the planes, the ships and the trucks required. The last leg of each journey taken on foot or by bicycle. Waiting for a reply. Waiting for absolution. And then the disappointment, the shock, of seeing her own words sent back to her, the message unambiguous.

Had she written the letter in the hope that the answer would give her passage back to Ireland? And did the response mean she gave up all hope of ever returning? She had never gone back. Not even for a holiday. She'd never expressed a desire to or talked longingly of the old country like other exiles. It had been a total and violent separation.

Did she go then and open a bottle of vodka and drink herself into oblivion so she could no longer see those red letters and her own torn words? Telling her no, she was not forgiven; she would never be forgiven. Did they come home from school that day to find the curtains drawn, the milk still on the doorstep, the other mail strewn across the table untouched? A bottle half-drunk beside an overflowing ashtray. The sickly sour smell coming from her bedroom.

And she'd kept it. That bitter missive. Placed it amongst tender keepsakes and memories. Why? Self-flagellation? Maybe the same reason she herself used to take a pair of scissors to her thighs. Maybe the pain was a kind of release. Maybe when she couldn't understand the depths of her own sadness, the letter served as a tangible focus. A pain she could explore and feel wholly. A pain she could make sense of.

Sinead stands and takes the letter in to the kitchen, hesitating a moment before putting it into the bin. She goes back to the bedroom and looks through the other contents of the case. There is a small hardback copy of collected poetry. It looks well-used. The edges are frayed, the indented title on the cover smoothed with the years. The opposite of a human face.

There is an inscription on the inside cover. *To Joy, September 1964, Remember, when power corrupts, poetry cleanses. Miss Lally.* She inhales the scent of the pages deeply. It reminds her of one of her favourite places in Dublin, the Long Room in Trinity College, where she's always struck by the scent as she enters. Thinks how wonderful it would be if only she could bottle this smell. She flicks through the book and finds a small colour photo tucked into a page with the Yeats poem 'The Stolen Child'. The photo is of a group of children and is quite blurry, so it's not obvious at first why her mother would have kept it. A bookmark, perhaps?

She knows the poem vaguely. She has heard it put to music, but reading it now she finds the melancholy almost unbearable and has to stop reading when she reaches the line about the solemn-eyed boy. She looks at the photo again and sees it is a group of small boys playing football on a gravelly road. One of them is Conor; she would know his boisterous curls anywhere. He can't be more than seven, which means it must have been taken in Ireland. One of the other boys in the photo catches her eye. He is smaller, a bit apart from the others, not playing football, instead sitting on the kerb, dark head bent over as though studying an object on the road. There is something so innocent about his pose, so earnest. His spindly little legs cause a rush of yearning. She pockets the photo to show to Conor later.

There are several other photos in the case. Some of herself, Conor and Frances as young children. One makes her laugh out loud. Conor is sitting on his bike, an old red Raleigh Chopper. He is leaning back against the rear of the curved seat, legs planted firmly on the ground, arms folded. Frances is kneeling on all fours beside him, looking grumpy, a tiny Sinead on her back. *Horsies, Franny! Please play Horsies with me!* And Frances always obliged, though several moments in she would grow tired of it and try to dislodge her mount, who held on with a simian tenacity.

They were just a normal family sometimes, weren't they?

There are a few black and whites of her maternal grandfather. He looks kind. There is one that attracts her more than the others, and from its worn edges she thinks it must have been a favourite of Joy's, too. He is standing leaning one arm on a shovel and in the other hand is a pipe he is holding up to his mouth. He is wearing a white shirt and braces, his sleeves rolled up, and he's looking frankly into the camera. She imagines the warm smell of the earth and the tobacco and feels sad for never having known the comfort of a grandfather. A love she imagines as playful and wise.

There is another letter underneath the photos. It is addressed to her mother at their old address in Ireland and postmarked June 1981.

Joy,

Why? Why are you doing this to me? And why now? When you are a married woman with your own husband and children who surely should be your utmost priority. They will not thank you for doing this, Joy! I understand it has been a trying time for you after the death of that poor little boy, but do you really want to make yourself more of a pariah? Haven't you brought enough shame upon your family? And why are you making such disgusting allegations against a man who is no longer alive and able to defend himself? A man, let me remind you, from whom you will benefit most generously when I am dead and gone. Which, to be frank, I wish upon myself sooner rather than later given the grotesque accusations you have made.

I know how in thrall you were to your father, so I can only assume this is the reason behind your attempts to besmirch your poor stepfather, a man who was only ever generous and giving. But your father is long dead, Joy. He chose to leave me. He chose to leave you. That is the bare cold truth of it. Therefore, your loyalty towards him and continuing adoration of him is misplaced, to say the least.

I hope that the filthy letter you sent me is the only medium in which you have made your hideous and untrue charge. I have destroyed it and appeal to you to never ever make mention of this subject again. It will kill me, Joy, though I fear that would only act as an incentive to you. You have always treated me most coldly.

Yours faithfully,
Mother

Sinead reads it through several times. Each time, a chilling new realisation hits her. It is hard to know what aspect of the letter is the most distressing. *You never stood a chance, Mum.*

She picks up the poetry book and places it in her bag, and though she hardly knows why, she calls a taxi. When the operator asks where to, she is surprised to hear herself say Mercy Hospital.

Once there, sitting beside Joy, she is not sure what to do or say. Then she thinks again of Conor's revelations about Declan. She clears her throat.

'So, Mum, Conor told me about Declan Smith.' She allows a polite pause, as though her mother might respond.

'And I just wanted to say how sorry I am that you've been carrying that around for such a long time. I can't even imagine what that's been like for you. But, well, I also wanted to say that growing up, I always felt that you were angry with me about something. Long before my book came out. And I could never make sense of it. I figured it was because I was so different from Franny, who was always *good*, and let's face it, I was a bit useless and prone to getting into trouble. I often thought it was because I was fat. You were always so slim, Franny too, and I thought I disgusted you. I disgusted myself. But now, after talking to Conor, I think I know what the problem was. He said when you got out of the car, and saw what you'd done, you started wailing and said, "I just got distracted for a second, the baby was crying, I had to comfort the baby."'

Sinead feels her mother's hand twitch, and her heart misses a beat, but then she reminds herself that the doctors have always dismissed any movement as involuntary. She carries on.

'He wasn't saying it to upset me, he was simply retelling a traumatic experience as he recalls it. I mean, it seems ridiculous that anyone could think it was my fault. But you did, didn't you? Maybe not consciously, but buried somewhere, in that part of you that surfaced sometimes when you drank. I felt it, Mum, I really felt it.'

Sinead is crying now. Great wracking sobs that shake the sturdy bed and deposit fat tears on her mother's papery hand. They subside after a while and she says, 'I was just a baby, Mum. I needed you to love and protect me. I needed your face to light up, even just once, when I walked into a room. That's all.'

She feels lighter. She pats her mother's hand, places it down on the bed, looks closely at it. She imagines the hand young again, erased of its brown spots and gnarly raised veins. She imagines the courage it must have taken to pick up a pen in that hand and write that letter to her mother, hoping, at the very least, not for retribution but recognition. Something, if not maternal, then at least human.

She takes her mother's hand again and places it over the small poetry book she has put on the bed, then she leans forward, brings her mouth close to her ear and whispers, 'I believe you, Joy.'

And she feels her mother's courage inspire her now too. She takes out her phone, scrolls through her contacts. A groggy voice answers.

'Maggie, I'm sorry it's so late, but there's something I need to tell you.'

JOY

I'm back at school now. It feels good to be here, away from her. And him. She wants me to call him Father, but my lips refuse to form the word. So I don't call him anything. I don't call him anything when he asks me to pass the salt at the table. I don't call him anything when he gets me to help out behind the bar at the weekends. I don't call him anything except under my breath, you disgusting fucker, after he's left me shaking and sore in the grimy and dark storeroom out the back of the pub. It's here I've taken my first swigs of gin, topping the bottle up with water as I go.

My English teacher, Miss Lally, is reading a poem. It's Yeats's 'The Lake Isle of Innisfree'. Miss Lally loves Yeats. And she gets a faraway look in her eye when she talks about Keats or Wordsworth. She is a real Romantic. She says that in her opinion – Miss Lally isn't one of those adults who demands that they are right, another thing to love about her – the best poems are the ones that seem as though they were easy to write.

Deceptively simple, she says, but still, I prefer the Metaphysicals. I like how you have to think about what they say, rather than let it wash over you prettily. It's like a puzzle you have to piece together. I like how they can shock you with a conceit. I like their irony. I never spoke to Daddy about it, but I think he would have liked the scientific vocabulary they use. There is a lot of religion in their poetry but at least it is intelligent and philosophical, not the quasi-superstitious beliefs of most of the people in this place.

The bell goes and Miss Lally asks me to stay behind. Some of the other girls give each other a look. They think I'm odd. Even Deirdre, who used to be my best friend, steers clear of me now. She'd prefer to be with the other girls who talk incessantly about boys and dances and dresses. I find them all tedious, so I don't care if they exclude me. Prefer it, in fact. It's easier not to have friends, I've found. Other people make you feel bad about what you lack.

Miss Lally is asking me how I am, how things are at home. She has a way of looking at you, big brown eyes wide in empathy, that makes you want to spill your soul. She says she saw me last week behind the bar in Reilly's pub and did I like working there? And did Mr Reilly treat me well? She says I look unhappy, and she worries that I've stopped raising my hand to answer questions in class. And she knows I know the answers because I'm one of the best students she's ever had. This gives me such a warm feeling I want to throw my arms around her in grati-tude. But I say, It's fine, everything's fine, Miss, it's just been a bit hard with Daddy gone.

She nods, then opens a drawer and takes something out of her desk. It's a little grey tome, The Faber Book of Verse. *She takes a pen and writes something on the inside cover then puts the book in my hand. I read what she's written.* To Joy, Remember, when power corrupts, poetry cleanses. Miss Lally. *And she asks me if I know who said that and I guess Wordsworth and she throws back her head and laughs in such a pretty way and says no, it was John F. Kennedy! And we smile sadly at each other, because we all loved Jack. I remember how she cried in class last year when she talked about how he'd been shot. And how that set the whole class off and then Sister Josephine, obviously hearing something from out in the corridor – where I imagine she spent her days policing in the hope of coming across some errant behaviour from student or teacher – marched in and told us to immediately desist with our hysteria! As she turned on her heel, her broad black-clad back sailing towards the door, Miss Lally caught my eye and I swear she gave an almost imperceptible eye roll which was enough to stop me feeling sad about poor JFK for a moment.*

Miss Lally is telling me to come to her if I ever want to talk, and she looks at me with such kindness that I am half-tempted to tell her about the disgusting things Mr Reilly makes me do, but I feel so ashamed I can't bring myself to say anything. I couldn't bear for her to regard me in that way. The way he says I am. He tells me I ask for it. I don't think I do but there is something wrong with me. Something amiss. Mother sees it, he sees it. I don't want Miss Lally to see it too.

It's lunchtime and the other girls congregate in small groups around the school grounds, eating their corned beef sandwiches and apples. I find a spot near the chipped blue statue of the Virgin Mary that everyone is a little afraid of now since Jackie O'Neill said she saw blood coming from its eyes, and take out my book. I run my fingers over the raised gold title, then open it on the first page.

And I read it like that, every poem, one after the other, moving between Shakespeare and Donne, Milton and Hopkins, Keats and Yeats. And there's some I don't understand but there is much that I do. There is comfort here; in the oddness of Emily Dickinson, the only woman, with her funeral-in-her-brain strangeness that makes me feel not quite so alien; in the tortured, sometimes violent conceits of Donne; in Yeats's regret; in Shakespeare's longing. Solitariness in all of them, it seems to me.

And reading these words, I don't find myself so alone anymore.

FRANCES

Frances pulls into the carpark of the Sebel waterfront hotel. She takes a miniature vodka bottle from her bag, unscrews the top and knocks it back. She has told Harry that she is going to the supermarket. Not that he'd asked where she was going. There hasn't been much conversation in the past week since he returned. She puts on a baseball cap before getting out and heading into the lobby. A top-hatted doorman bows as she walks past. The young woman behind the desk is all sleek hair and sharp angles. She wears false eyelashes so long that Frances wonders how she manages to keep her eyes open. Her name tag says Rosie, which seems too jaunty for this contoured creature. Frances wonders if her parents were expecting a different sort of child. She feels suddenly frumpy. She has not even showered this morning.

'How can I help you, Ma'am?'

She hates the word, but it's the way she's addressed now. Sometimes she looks around to see who the addressor is speaking to. And her heart always wilts a little when she realises it is herself. *Just you wait,* she thinks, *just you wait, Rosie. One day soon, much sooner than you could ever think possible by the laws of physics, out of the blue a waiter will call you that when he comes to take your order and your heart will die a bit. And he won't flirt with you, but even if he does, you'll be suspicious.*

'Is there a package there for a Frances McEvitt?'

Rosie rummages around beneath the counter.

'No, I'm sorry, nothing here.'

'Oh, are you sure? It will be very small.'

Rosie sighs, looks impatient. She gives another half-hearted pilfer and says, 'No, nothing.'

Andy, you little shit. She stands there, unsure what to do.

Rosie, perhaps keen to get rid of this dishevelled-looking distraction, says, 'What is it exactly you were expecting?'

'Eh, just a locket I left behind last week.'

'Which room number were you staying in? I'll check with housekeeping.'

'I'm not sure of the number, it was on the second floor. Or maybe third. No, second, I think . . .'

Rosie gives her a withering look. Frances wonders how she ever got a job dealing with the public.

'What was your name again? I'll check our records.'

'It wasn't my room. It was my friend's. I just eh . . . visited him there.' She feels her face reddening.

Rosie looks up from her computer. Blinks her bovine lashes. Frances swears she sees a glimmer of a smirk on her face. 'And can you tell me your *friend's* name?'

'Andrew Wright.'

Rosie taps her computer. Her nails make a loud clicking sound. 'There is no record of a Mr Wright staying here in the last few weeks. Are you sure that was his name?'

Frances would like to punch Rosie in her pouty little mouth. 'Yes, of course I'm sure.'

At this point Rosie is joined at the desk by another equally sleek young woman. Her name tag says Madeline.

'Is everything all right here, Ma'am?' she says to Frances.

Rosie says, 'This lady left a necklace in a gentleman's room last week. But she can't remember the room number. Or the gentleman's name.'

'I *can* remember his name!' Frances feels her voice rising. 'I just told it to you, Andy Wright!'

Rosie looks at Madeline. 'There doesn't appear to be any record of a guest of that name.'

Madeline raises one perfectly micro-bladed eyebrow and taps away at the computer. 'Are you sure that was his real name?'

'Obviously, I'm sure! I've known him for more than twenty years!' Her face, neck and décolletage are scarlet now. Indignation and that damned Celtic curse, rosacea, conspiring against her. She wants to leave but she's not sure which would be more humiliating: staying here while they condescend to help her or turning her back in the certain knowledge that they will erupt once she's out the door.

She hears an impatient clearing of a throat behind her. She turns to see a man in a pinstripe business suit tapping his foot next to his black Samsonite suitcase. She scowls at him, then turns back again.

Madeline says, 'Perhaps you could just give him a call and find out what he's done with it.' Rosie nods her head in agreement.

Thank you, Madeline/Rosie, for that wonderfully insightful and creative solution to my problem. I'd never have thought of that all by myself. Hope you get a pay rise! But she does not say this. Instead, she says tightly, 'Great, thanks, I'll do that.'

They look at her expectantly. Frances wonders if they are waiting for her to leave or perhaps to make the phone call right now. She is so addled she stays standing at the desk, takes out her phone and starts to look through her contacts. It is only when she scrolls between *William Lily's Dad* and *Yvonne PTA* that she remembers she has deleted Andy's details.

'Oh, that's right, I don't have his number anymore.'

Cue another meaningful look between her tormentors.

'WhatsApp, Messenger, Snapchat?' Rosie suggests, perhaps reinvigorated to be helpful with the possibility of further humiliations to be laughed over in the staffroom later. Swanky hotels must be rich comedic fodder for young staff. All those ageing Gen Xers and Baby Boomers, their desires and appetites made pathetic by their decrepit bodies.

As she stands there, she hears the man behind her answering his phone. She catches snatches of his conversation.

'. . . be with you soon . . . trying to check out . . . woman in front . . . wittering on about something . . . petty . . . yeah, okay . . .'

It's the word petty that does it. Something snaps. She feels as though the flimsy scaffolding that has long been holding her up, the frayed threads that have been holding her together, holding her in, the fragile order that she has so long cultivated and imposed, is collapsing inside her, and a wild, unpredictable rage takes over. It occurs to her that she has been hungry for forty years. She has been on edge forever. And she can feel herself tip over. She can feel the adrenalin that has been produced through all the years of anxiety shoot frantically through her limbs. How dare they. How dare they assume that her life is petty, that her time is less important. How dare they assume that she is uninteresting and practical and uncurious and prosaic and dependable and pedantic.

'It is *not* a petty issue,' a woman yells. Frances is that woman. 'I am trying to retrieve the only piece of jewellery my fucking mother owned. And now she's lying comatose in a hospital bed with a giant fucking hole in her head and will die, so yes, I have come to get it back for her. Because that's what I do. That's what I always do. Find fucking everything. Wipe the kitchen bench down twenty fucking times a day. Sort every fucking little thing out.' She shuts her eyes and screams so loudly her lungs burn. 'AND I'M FUCKING SICK OF IT.'

She opens her eyes. Every head in the lobby is turned towards her. The businessman's mouth is agape. No-one speaks. It seems as though even the muzak that was being piped through the speakers has stopped. All she can hear is heavy ragged breathing. It is her own. Her chest hurts. Her head pounds. She feels dizzy and disoriented. Everything seems to be happening in slow motion. Madeline and Rosie are looking at each other, their eyes wide. She sees Madeline pick up the phone. She feels a firm pressure on her arm.

'Ma'am. I'm afraid I'm going to have to escort you off the premises.'

A man in a top hat and tails leads her to the door. His hand is gripping her arm. He is wearing white gloves. He is the ringmaster leading her away after her circus performance. The polished concrete floor is waving. She wishes she could drown in it. The automatic door is opening. She wishes to be swallowed by it.

Someone taps her shoulder gently. She turns to see Rosie looking at her, her face softer now, her eyes concerned.

'Is this what you were looking for?' And she hands her an envelope. Frances looks at it. The words undulate at first but gradually come into focus. **F. TOBIN** is written on the front. She almost laughs at the pointedness of her capitalised maiden name.

Fucking Andy. He had to get the last word in.

'Thank you, Rosie,' she says, quietly. And she races to the safety of her car.

CONOR

Conor is just about to go through the doors of Mercy when he feels his phone vibrate. It's a message from Raewyn, the lawyer for TheOneForAll.

Good News! Initial review through from Charity Regulator. No evidence of any financial mismanagement. Not proceeding with full investigation. Have sent email with all the deets.

He doesn't know how to feel about this. 'Okay,' he says aloud. He puts his phone away.

Dr Sharma is at the reception desk when he enters.

'Conor, thank you for coming in. Let's go into my office.'

The walls of the office are covered in various framed qualifications. Undergraduate, postgraduate, diplomas. Once they are seated, he gestures towards them. 'That's an awful lot of studying.'

'Too much, perhaps. I fear I may be a little addicted.'

'There are worse addictions.'

'Try telling that to my husband.' She points towards a large framed photo of a man on her desk. 'He put this here himself so I wouldn't forget what he looks like.'

Conor smiles. Then, 'So I've a feeling this isn't good news.'

Dr Sharma leans forward. 'We've run more tests. It's my opinion, and that of my colleagues, that there is no hope of recovery. I think that you and your family should talk about withdrawing her ANH.'

'Her what?'

Dr Sharma shakes her head as though irritated with herself. 'I'm sorry. ANH stands for artificial nutrition and hydration. Her feeding tubes. Nutrition at this point is, I believe, medically futile, perhaps even uncomfortable for her. She's had a chronic infection at the point of entry for the tube. I believe letting her go would be the greatest kindness.'

'But it seems wrong, like we would be starving her to death.'

'Conor, it's important to remember that your mother, in her state, does not feel things the way we do. Pain, hunger, thirst . . . these are all constructs that we as conscious individuals impose on those in a coma. She simply doesn't feel any of these things anymore. She has no awareness of anything. Not even of herself. I understand how inhumane it might appear, because we view food and water as such a fundamental right. A basic care. But you need to understand that her feeding tube is as much an artificial and technological intervention as the ventilator was. Your mother *will* die when we remove the tube, but not from hunger or dehydration. She will die from the massive brain injury she received.'

'Will she suffer?'

'You know, we find that many conscious patients at the end of life often refuse food and drink anyway. We think this might even bring analgesic benefits to them. I think we would be freeing her from suffering.'

Conor nods. It's almost a reflexive action. 'Yes, you're right. I think she's probably ready to go.' He doesn't know exactly where those words have come from. The idea that they should let her die has never occurred to him until this moment. But he feels at peace with the words. And the sentiment.

Dr Sharma covers his hand with her own. 'And I think that maybe *you're* ready now to let her go.'

When he leaves her office he goes to his mother's bedside. He takes her hand and imagines his own body in her place, features slack yet limbs rigid. He thinks about the near miss with the train and the pills, and shudders. He says aloud to her, to himself too, 'I didn't mean it. I didn't want to die.' He exhales deeply, because he feels an enormous weight lift from him. And maybe it's just his own tension releasing, but he feels a softening in his mother's hand too.

He puts his head down on the bed. He'd slept beside her for a few nights once. After Declan. After their father had gone. Unable to sleep, disturbing images appearing behind his eyes, he crept in after Joy had gone to bed and lay down on what used to be his father's side. He remembers wondering why she still stuck rigidly to her own side. Why didn't she spread out like a starfish? That's what he would have done if he'd had that double bed all to himself.

She'd never acknowledged his presence those nights. But after he'd been lying there for a while, he noticed her breathing slow down and deepen until it synchronised with his own. Then he could leave and go back to his bed and find it easier to drop off himself. Looking back, he wondered if he went in there to look over her. Keep watch. Make sure she didn't leave like their father had, not yet knowing that her leaving would take a different form altogether.

Now, he starts to fall into a dream. One of those semi-lucid ones that come with daytime naps. He is standing on train tracks in the middle of the countryside. In the distance he can see a plume of smoke. At first he thinks it's from a bonfire but then he realises it's getting closer and belongs to a moving train. He goes to move off the tracks but his legs feel leaden, and try as he might he can't move them. He starts to panic, but then hears a voice beside him. He turns to see his mother, young again, and she holds out her hand. He takes it and allows himself to be pulled to safety. She holds him close, waiting for his shallow breathing to deepen in time with hers, and says, 'I knew it. I always knew it.'

SINEAD

When she arrives at Mercy her brother and sister are already there waiting for her in their mother's room. They look up when she walks in.

'Here we go again,' she says. 'Third time lucky!'

It is deliberately provocative. She looks at Frances, expecting a telling off, wanting one, but her sister gives a rueful half-smile. She looks undone. It frightens Sinead.

Conor gets up and hugs her. 'Thank you,' he says.

At first she thinks he means about coming to the hospital, and she is confused. He sees her confusion and says, 'For the photo.'

She had given the photo she found in her mother's poetry book to him yesterday. He'd studied it for a long time and said, tears in his eyes, 'I remember.' And then he'd told her a story. They'd been kicking the ball around casually on the street, him and Brendan Smith, a few of the other lads from their estate. Little boys with nothing heavier on their minds than dreams of being Pelé. He hadn't remembered Declan, sitting on the kerb, but that wasn't unusual. He was often on the periphery, Brendan's little shadow, watchful and thoughtful.

They had decided to start a proper game. As usual there was an argument over who would be in goals. No-one wanted to do it. Usually they managed to cajole Barry Martin on account of him being a bit chubbier and slower than the rest of them. But Barry was steadfastly refusing that day. Said he was sick of always being the goalie and anyway his mother had warned him about getting dirt on his new shirt. *But she'll kill me*, he said over and over to the other boys' accusations of being a wimp. They stood around arguing the point, some of the boys sulkily threatening to go home, so it looked like the game would be called off.

And that's when it happened. (When Conor recounted the tale to Sinead, he became almost rapt at this point, as though he had been a witness to a miracle. Jesus walking on water, or some such.) Joy emerged from the driveway and offered to be goalie. At first Conor thought it was a joke and dismissed her with an embarrassed wave, but Barry, seeing a way of escaping either being branded a spoilsport by his friends or getting an earful from his mother, embraced the offer with enthusiasm, until one by one they all came around to it and soon Joy was *in situ* between two rolled-up jumpers on the ground. And she acquitted herself well, Conor remembered, hurling herself fear-lessly at each on-target shot. He was proud. When the game was over she walked away to shouts of *Thank you, Mrs T! Same time tomorrow, Mrs T!* And she raised her arm in acknowledgement, like a professional leaving the field.

Sinead sits on the edge of the bed. 'I didn't sleep a wink last night thinking about today. I had this weird sensation of simultaneously having complete conviction in what we're doing and also complete revulsion. It was a new feeling. Not the revulsion. It's just normally I lack any sort of conviction in anything.'

'I keep trying to reason with myself that it's like euthanising a sick animal or something. I mean, you'd never hesitate to do that,' Conor says.

'Yes, but it's different with a human being. It's like we've deemed ourselves to be so much more important than animals, of such a higher state of mind, so *evolved*, that it's unconscionable not to do everything possible to keep someone alive.'

'Maybe this is how soldiers feel going into battle. Or surgeons about to perform amputations. It's the right thing to do, but it doesn't make it any easier.'

Frances rolls her eyes. 'Get a grip, you two. We're hardly being heroic here.'

That's more like it, Franny. 'Where are Harry and Liv?'

'We decided there wasn't much point in them coming today. According to Dr Sharma it could take a couple of weeks for her to pass away anyway.'

'I think it might be even longer. She never cared that much about food. I don't think she ate when she was on one of her benders. And anyway, she'd be used to being chronically dehydrated.'

Conor groans and puts his head in his hands. 'Don't. It makes me feel like we're being cruel. I wish the doctor could just administer some kind of lethal injection or something.'

Sinead rubs his arm. 'Sorry, I'm being facetious. We've got to remember what Dr Sharma said. She doesn't feel any thirst or hunger. She'll die from her brain injury, not starvation.'

As if on cue, Dr Sharma and two other doctors enter. 'So, are you all ready? Any more questions?'

'I think we're good,' Sinead says, looking at her siblings. They both nod. She thinks back four weeks to when her mother was taken off the ventilator. (*My God, was it only four weeks ago?*) She felt so removed from what was happening then. Maybe that was just shock, or jet lag, or her little yellow pills, or a combination of all three. But she feels grateful now for the last few weeks. In a funny way she feels grateful for last night's insomnia, even for the anxiety clawing at her guts right now. They are sensations that make sense to her.

The doctors are gentle yet efficient and the procedure to remove the gastric tube only takes a few minutes. After Sinead's restless night, peppered with vivid semi-conscious dreams, it feels anticlimactic. The doctors leave and they are alone again with – it strikes Sinead fully – their dying mother.

They sit in silence for a while. Sinead studies her brother and sister; Frances with her arms wrapped around herself, so skinny they could almost meet at the back; Conor, his elbows on his knees, chin resting in his hands, greyer at the temples than she's ever noticed. She feels a great and protective love for them. They appear to her, despite their middle-age, like children, made vulnerable by the ebbing away of the life of their mother in the bed beside them. Motherless children. The term fatherless children doesn't contain the same poignancy. Mothers are so integral to everything, happiness or unhappiness. They are to adore. Or to blame. No middle ground.

Sinead thinks about their father. She wonders if he is still alive. She wonders why they all carry more anger towards a woman who at least stayed – imperfectly, it's true – than towards a man who left. She wonders whether the death of their mother would leave them orphaned. Silly way to put it, really. Surely only young children can be orphans. But it seems appropriate in a way, looking at her siblings now.

Sinead's holdall is on her lap, and she puts her hand in and fingers the edge of the cardboard folder contained within. She clears her throat. She feels nervous suddenly.

'Do you have time to listen to something I wrote? Just a short story? I thought now might be a good time. It's for Mum, but I think you guys might appreciate it too.'

They both look surprised. Frances says, 'Okay,' though she sounds wary.

Conor says, 'I'd love to hear it.'

'Well, when I say I wrote it, I mean I wrote it with Brendan. It's his story. He wanted Mum and you to hear it. I've just transcribed for him. Put his words on paper.'

'Oh, is this the reason you've been spending so much time with him lately? You've been *transcribing*?' Conor gives her a wink. Sinead pulls a face at him.

'Right. It's called . . . well it doesn't have a name yet, actually. Let's call it "Declan".'

She sees them both react to the name. A subtle flash in the eye, a rearrangement in their seats, an audible exhalation from Frances, Conor's palms rubbed along his shorts. She moves her chair closer to their mother's bed, turns her face in her direction.

DECLAN

The thing about Declan was that he had an unusual amount of stillness for a young boy. There was a wisdom about him, a serenity. Mammy used to say, *He's an old soul that one, he's been here before*. She claimed that he came into the world without a peep, just looked around at the nurses and doctor, taking in his new surroundings noiselessly. (I, on the other hand, she told me, screamed blue murder, annoyed at having been evicted from my cosy dwelling.) At first, she feared there was something wrong with him. She said she asked the nurse to hold him upside-down and slap him, like they do in films, to get some kind of reaction from him. She said that the old nurse just laughed at her, wrapped him up, handed him to her and said, 'He's your solemn little angel, your *chuisle*.'

And Mammy said it was the first and last time she ever contemplated slapping wee Declan. She'd say this giving me a rueful look, as though she had contemplated slapping *me* hundreds of times.

His temperament was such that, even when he was a wee mite, she would get him to cream the eggs and the sugar together when she made a sponge cake. He never cared how long it took for those two ingredients to eventually bond together to form the stiff peaks she was after. He seemed to enjoy the process and delight in the resulting alchemy. *No need to buy one of them fancy mixers with this lad in the house!* she'd say, so full of pride and love in him. She never asked me to help her, knowing I'd be too fidgety, longing to get back outside to kick my ball, interested only in the reward of getting to lick the bowl when all the boring stuff had been done.

But I could never be resentful towards Declan. No-one could. He wasn't that sort of a lad. He was too sweet to invite any sort of ill feeling. He had dark hair and black eyebrows that grew in two straight lines across his forehead. And his eyes were the colour of moss after a heavy drenching, kind of green and kind of brown. He was small for his age, a bit skinny. I don't think he cared much for food. He ate slowly and care-fully, whereas I always wolfed my food down, and sometimes it irked me that I had to wait an age for him to finish just so that I could get my ice cream. But like I said, you could never really get mad at Declan.

And he looked up to me. I could never understand why; he was so much better than me in every way. Except for sport maybe. He would sit and watch me and the neighbourhood boys play football for hours. Sometimes we might be short a player or two and one of the boys would ask him to join. He'd shake his head shyly and look down at the ground. The boys didn't mind his reluctance though, knew how he was, and they never pushed it with him.

Declan liked to collect things. Keyrings, coins, cereal-box cards. But his rock collection was his greatest treasure. He sorted it into different categories, which he then labelled and documented in a large copybook. Mammy got him a large, serious-looking geology book that he used for research if he ever came across a new type of rock. He kept the collection in three cardboard boxes that had originally housed Christmas baubles. He would take those boxes down from the shelf in his wardrobe at least once a day and lay them all out in various formations on the floor. Categories that no doubt made geological sense to him, but to my ignorant eye looked random.

I didn't have much interest in collecting anything, but I did pay attention for a brief time to his rock collection, after the Pet Rock fad swept through America and belatedly made its way to Ireland. Pet Rocks were basically smooth stones sold in their own little cardboard carry boxes with holes. It was as stupid as it sounds. Of course, like most imports from that country, we adopted it in a peculiarly makeshift way. There was no way any cash-strapped Irish parents were going to fork out a few pounds to buy what was basically a stone. You'd be laughed out of the house for even asking. *Buy a stone? Have you lost the run of yourself altogether?* So, we just collected them ourselves from gardens and roads, put them in an empty cereal or tea bag carton, and gave them lifelike monikers such as Sean or Fiona. The flat ocean-worn rocks that American kids bought were surprisingly difficult to come by in our part of the country, being inland, so for a few brief months in 1980, finding a suitably smoothed and shaped stone was a popular pastime.

One day Mam asked me to go with Declan as he wanted to hunt for a new rock. There was a barley field at the top of the estate that adjoined a quarry, and although we were strictly forbidden to go anywhere near the quarry, we figured that there may have been an interesting specimen or two that had made its way into the periphery of the field. As we walked up towards the field we passed the Tobins' house, where one of my footballing buddies Conor lived.

It was a warm day, late August, just before the dreaded start of the school year. Mrs Tobin was sunning herself on a deckchair in the front garden. She was wearing white shorts and a red strapless top. She had a pair of oversized sunglasses that made her look glamorous. Sunglasses would have been considered a bit showy for Navan in 1980.

I knew Mrs Tobin wasn't popular with some of the other mothers in the neighbourhood. She was never invited to the Tupperware parties or asked to play bridge in the evening. Mam used to say she was standoffish. I once heard Mam and her friends laughing about her when they were drinking tea and gossiping in our kitchen. *All fur coat and no knickers that one!* I didn't know what they meant but I always thought she was nice. Different to the other mothers, but nice all the same. She played football with us one time, went into goals. Was good too. I couldn't in a million years imagine Mam doing that.

Anyway, this day, she waved as we passed and called out to us, 'Where are you two intrepid explorers off to?'

We stopped outside the fence, and I said, 'We're going up to the barley field to see if we can find a rock.'

'Is that so?' she said. 'And do you think you will require some sustenance to assist you on your journey? I have a nice cold beverage in the fridge!'

She always talked like that, used long words even when she spoke to us kids. I think that was one of the reasons why my mother disliked her. *Thinks she's better than the rest of us! Well, I heard her mother was a stuck-up Proddy, that'll be why.* Protestants, even half-ones, were glamorous but damned. Definitely other. Having a *Proddy* in your neighbourhood was about as diverse as Ireland got back then.

Declan looked at me for guidance. 'Do you think it would be okay?' he asked. I think we both knew Mam wouldn't be delighted about us taking a drink from Joy Tobin.

But I shouted back, cocky as anything, 'That would be grand, Mrs T!'

'Rightio, come in and I'll get it for you.'

She got off the deckchair and walked through the front door, down the narrow hall and into the kitchen. We followed, me in front, Declan rather sheepishly behind. I could see through the window out to the back garden where Conor was lying on his back, hands behind his head, just staring up at the sky. His little sisters were stark naked and splashing in a paddling pool. I was mortified at this and turned my back to the window. I was surprised at how messy their kitchen was. Cornflakes and Rice Krispies boxes still on the table from breakfast even though it was past lunchtime. Dishes in the sink, countertops littered with cups and utensils. Mam always kept our house spotless. But some of the glasses on Mrs Tobin's counter looked like they could have been sitting there for quite some time. *Too posh to clean!* I could hear my mother say.

'MiWadi or 7up?' Mrs Tobin asked, opening their small fridge in the corner.

Now, 7up was strictly a birthday treat in our house, so we both said straightaway, '7up, please!'

She smiled as we greedily drank it down. She went to the window then. 'Franny, come here. Make sure your little sister gets a drink too.' And she handed out the bottle and three glasses to her. I remember feeling envious. Our mother would never trust us to be in charge of a whole bottle of pop.

When we were finished drinking, I took Declan's glass and my own and went to wash them in the sink. I must have looked a bit perplexed as to how to tackle it given the big pile already there because Mrs Tobin laughed and said, 'Don't worry, just leave it. I'll get around to it eventually. Maybe tomorrow if the sun isn't out!'

I put them down, a bit embarrassed, and said, 'Thanks. Well, I suppose we'd better get going.'

'So, tell me again where you're off to?'

'Just up to the barley field to look for some stones.'

'Ahh,' she said, looking thoughtful. I noticed she had a splattering of dark freckles across her nose and her face had a sheen to it. She wore lip gloss and it showed off her even white teeth. *American teeth*, my mother would have said, as though having nice teeth was indecent. I remember thinking she looked young, not at all like my own mother, whom I always regarded as being of an indeterminable yet mother-appropriate age.

'Do you know, I've never considered how rocks and stones are formed. I wonder would anyone be able to enlighten me?'

She didn't look at Declan when she said this, but I think she intuitively knew that he would be the one with the answer.

He looked unsure, as if surprised to be asked such a question from a grown-up. But I gave him a nod, and though self-conscious at first, he soon warmed up and gave Mrs Tobin an in-depth explanation of the formation of igneous, metamorphic and sedimentary rocks. Mrs Tobin listened with rapt attention, her eyes shining, and seemed to drink in every word. Not the usual way adults listen, kind of distractedly, but as though she was giving weight to each and every word that came from his mouth.

When he had finished she bent down, put her hand on his shoulder and looked him in the eye. 'Thank you. You have a beautiful and curious mind, young man. Curiosity is the wick in the candle of learning, as my daddy used to say.' Then she stood up straight and raised her hand in a salute. 'Now go forth and find a most splendid specimen!'

Declan looked equal parts embarrassed and delighted. We turned to leave. Mrs Tobin didn't shepherd us out like most grown-ups do, but sat down at the cluttered table and left us to find our own way out. As we were walking down the hallway I heard her mutter something to herself. It sounded a bit like *Isn't he a little wonder, Daddy?* But I couldn't be sure, it seemed such a weird thing to say. At first, I thought that maybe Mr Tobin had been in the kitchen too, that maybe we hadn't seen him.

But Mrs Tobin didn't seem to me to be the kind of woman who called her own husband 'Daddy' in front of the children, the way I'd heard other mothers do.

I told Declan not to tell Mammy about going into Mrs Tobin's house. Not that she would have been angry or anything. Mostly because I didn't want her asking loads of questions, trying to get information in that wheedling way parents had, pretending to be all casual. I knew she'd be judgemental about the mess and the fizzy drink. She'd be dying to tell her cronies over a cup of tea and a cigarette in the kitchen. I felt protective of Mrs Tobin. In the same way I felt protective of Declan sometimes; as though they could easily be misunderstood. And I think Declan understood why I asked him to say nothing. I know he would have loved to have visited her again, regaled her with more of his knowledge. I think Mrs Tobin would have loved that too. I think they would have become good friends in time. Kindred spirits, both a little out of step with their peers. But that wasn't to be.

That Indian summer–like August gave way to September, and soon we were back in the routine days of school. When I think back to that month it seems, in my memory at least, to have been particularly wet and dreary, even for Ireland. Mammy insisted on us wearing our neon yellow raincoats every day. I hated mine, felt I looked like the lollipop lady who stood outside our school to help us across the road. I was always envious of Conor Tobin, who appeared to be allowed walk to and from school in whatever he pleased. Sometimes a raincoat on, sometimes not. Obviously Mrs Tobin did not share my mother's dread of *catching your death* if we stepped outside without something waterproof on.

The day it happened was wet again. It's funny, but details from that day, even the early part, are etched in my brain, even though it started out like any other. I think it's because I've thought about it so much, going over every moment, thinking of all the things I could have done different. Should have done different.

I remember the damp smell in the classroom from our outerwear and soaked shoes that we had to take off and leave in the cloakroom, a tiled area at the back of the room. The smell of food mixed with the damp, as we had to eat indoors that day, exacerbating the sense of claustrophobia. There was a feral restlessness in the class. Thirty frenetic little bodies unable to release any pent-up energy outside. The older kids who came to supervise us during break times made things worse, with their attempts to lord it over us. I was in a foul mood. I'm no good indoors, I've discovered. As the afternoon dripped on I could feel the frustration grow, so by the time the bell rang at three I was fizzing.

I grabbed my belongings and made my way to Declan's classroom. He was still putting on his shoes when I got there, sitting on the tiles, lunch box and schoolbooks scattered around him. I felt impatient with him and stuffed his belongings into his schoolbag without doing it up. He could sense my annoyance and that made him fumble with his shoelaces. He'd only just learnt how to do them. Mammy had sat down with him one afternoon, reciting the rhyme over and over, *in through the rabbit hole, round the big tree* . . . until finally he'd got it. He was so proud of himself, and spent the rest of the day perfecting his new skill. For all his brains and talent, coordination had never been his strong suit. *Two left feet*, Daddy would say, tousling his hair affectionately. Even Declan's imperfections were regarded warmly in our house. But now my scowling presence loomed large and his little hands struggled to finish the job. *Leave them*, I said, already turning to go, *I can't wait all day*. So he stood up, clumsily gripping his over-spilling bag, and tripped after me as fast as he could.

It's that interaction between us that day that bothers me the most. Well, maybe not the most but . . . I could have been gentle and patient, just like he would have been. I could have helped him with his shoelaces or encouraged him to finish the job himself. I could have said, *Don't worry little mate, take your time*. I could have packed his bag carefully while he did so and buckled the straps while I waited. I could have taken his hand when he'd finished, asked him how his day had been as we walked along the tiled school corridor, watched over by the ghostly photos of past pupils that lined the walls.

I never told Mammy about these last interactions though she grilled me hundreds of times, desperate for any titbits that might have indicated that his last moments, at least, were happy ones. I just shrugged, said he seemed grand, same as always, too ashamed of myself to tell her and not wanting to make her feel worse than she already did. I know she blamed herself as it was. Played the *What if* game over and over in her head the way we all did. *What if I'd gone to pick him up from school that day? What if I'd left the bloody baking till he got home, sure he loved to help anyways? What if, what if, what if . . .* Over and over in your head till you're driven half-mad.

I wondered if, like me, she sometimes fervently wished he'd never been born, just so she would have been spared the pain of his death.

I wondered if, like me, she sometimes wished *she'd* never been born.

They say losing a child is the greatest grief of all. If it is, then I can't begin to fathom its depths, because I can't imagine a grief greater than losing a sibling, someone you were supposed to have in your life longer than any other, someone to reminisce with, to grow old with, someone who'd understand you more than anyone. Someone who just *got* you.

As we walked out the double swinging doors that opened out to the teachers' carpark then on to the general carpark at the front of the school, I saw a group of my classmates standing over to one side, gathered around a boy called Gary Prendergast. Now, I could never stand that fella. He was a show-off, and a liar to boot. Always boasting about one thing or another, true or imagined. His family's foreign holidays to France; the fact that he got a can of Coke in his lunch box while the rest of us had to make do with generic home-brand juice boxes; his new Atari game console. The list was endless. Normally I'd have kept on walking, not wanting to show any interest in his latest brag-fest, but as I said, I was in a hyped-up mood that day. Maybe I wanted to cause trouble, let off some steam by denigrating whatever it was he was showing off about. Maybe I just wanted to annoy Declan by taking a detour when I'd only a few minutes earlier been complaining about our delayed exit from the school. Anyway, I went over to see what was happening.

Gary was proudly showing a piece of rock to his audience. In fairness it was a beauty. The Pet Rock craze, whilst dying out, still had a grip on some of us and this one was perfect. Flat, smooth and almost symmetrical, it looked like milky quartz. 'Found it on the beach in Arcachon,' he was saying, delighted to have yet another opportunity to boast that he'd been to the south of France in the summer holidays. I couldn't stand it. 'Declan's got two of those in his collection at home,' I said. 'Found them in Termonfeckin last year. They were all over the place, common as pig shit.' I could feel Declan looking at me, wondering why I was lying to Gary and probably shocked at my cursing, but he said nothing. My comment had the desired effect though; a few of my classmates laughed and moved away from Gary, no longer impressed with his find. Gary scowled at me, then headed off himself in the direction of home.

I stood there for a few moments, weighed down by a sudden feeling of the unfairness of the world, which seemed just then to be encapsulated in my lack of possession of a milky quartz stone.

We carried on through the gates to the general carpark. A familiar blue Hillman Hunter was parked in front of us, the engine running, wipers sashaying noisily across the windscreen. The windows were a bit fogged up but you could see Mrs Tobin sitting in the driver's seat. Declan raised his hand in a wave, a smile spreading across his face. I didn't bother to wave but I'm not sure if she saw us anyway, she seemed to be scanning all around for her own kids.

We walked past her car and as we did something glinted in the corner of my eye: Gary's stone, discarded between the rear tyres.

I figured he must have thrown it away in deference to my bogus Termonfeckin claim. I felt smug, having been able to outwit him so easily. I carried on walking for a couple of yards, not wanting to be too obvious, in case Gary was still in the vicinity. There were still lots of kids around and with the rain, which by now was almost torrential, it was hard to tell one umbrella-covered, plastic-sheathed figure from the next.

Declan stopped beside me, his face upturned to mine, wondering why I had come to a halt.

'Do you see Gary's stone under Mrs Tobin's car?' I said.

He turned back and looked. 'I think so.'

'Go back and grab it. I'll just stand here to make sure Gary isn't looking.' There was no way I wanted to be seen retrieving the very item I had just belittled.

'Okay,' he said.

For a long time afterwards, when I thought back to this moment, I could picture the rear of the car clearly. The black and white number plate with the registration *AZN 707* burnt into my brain; the position of the belching exhaust; the large scratch running along the left side of the bumper; Sinead Tobin's curls poking above the back seat. But something about the image always bothered me, as though a detail was missing from my memory. Years later, in Australia, my father came with me to buy my first car. I had put off learning to drive till my twenties, even though all of my friends there had learnt as teenagers. I think they thought it was just a weird Irish thing, but the truth is, even to this day, there's something about cars that gives me a sick feeling in the pit of my stomach. Anyway, we stopped to fill up at a petrol station on the way home from the car yard. We were standing by the pumps and Dad was giving me tips on how to make sure my car was safe to drive. Told me that filling up the tank was a good opportunity to check on safety features in the car. He was a practical man but also, like me, probably carried some semblance of dread related to cars. He sat back in the front seat and started putting on the indicators and brake lights and calling back to me to check they were in good order. I was growing impatient with him. We'd only just picked the car up from the dealer, who had tested everything with us anyway. Dad put the car into reverse. And it was then that a bolt of a memory made my heart seize up. For a moment I couldn't find my breath. The yellow reverse lights. They had been on when I had sent Declan back to get the stone. I must have seen them at the time. But my desire to get that stone, and more importantly, to get one up on Gary Prendergast, had created some disconnect in my head. Or maybe I'm being kind to myself by calling it a disconnect. Maybe I fully understood the danger but sent my little brother there anyway. After the horror of this realisation, I spent many years full of self-loathing. Eventually a girlfriend of mine convinced me to see a counsellor, who taught me to stop judging my action from the perspective of a grown man fully cognisant of the outcome, and instead forgive the impetuous eight-year-old I had been. And to some extent it worked.

But while I may have partly forgiven myself for what happened to Declan, I can't let go of my guilt about Joy Tobin.

In the school carpark, I knelt down on the wet tarmac and held his hand, told him he'd be okay. But I knew he was gone.

Adults crowded around us, tried to hustle me away, as though to protect me, but I refused to let go of his hand. I had seen both grandfathers laid out in their coffins, and on the instruction of adults – but against every instinct in me – had placed my warm hand on top of their cold ones.

So, I didn't want to let go of Declan's just yet, because I knew that soon it would be cold.

It was a garda who got me away in the end, the same one I saw drive Mrs Tobin and her children home later. He asked me, if I was able, to tell him what happened. I told him I was looking the other way and that was the story I stuck to. *No, I didn't see it. No, I don't know why he was at the back of the car.* To be honest, no-one pestered me that much about it. It was like they'd all decided that Mrs Tobin had been grossly negligent and that was that. After all, the rumours about her drinking and perceived general fecklessness meant that people were only too willing to cast her as the villain. I know the guards investigated, called it a tragic accident. But that didn't change anyone's mind about her guilt.

I only saw her once again before the family moved away. It was a couple of months after the accident. I was sitting in the back of our car, waiting for my mother to come out of the post office in town. She had gone in there to post a pile of acknowledgements, thanking people for their cards, flowers and condolences. It must have been around early December, because I remember there were coloured lights strung across the street in the centre of town and a large Christmas tree erected in the town square, which was not yet decorated.

I was staring at the lights, wondering if we'd put up a tree in our own house. I didn't feel like I could ask. I believed my role then was to be a good, undemanding son. To not question anything, and certainly not to rebel. I was to acquiesce, to be obedient. Most importantly, though, I was simply to stay alive. It's almost like overnight I grew up. Eight going on thirty-eight. I became a bit like Declan in fact, an old head on young shoulders. Some children become angry and act out when they grieve. I became more dutiful.

It was then that I saw her. She was walking along the street and had her head down against the wind. She had a scarf tied around her hair and knotted under her chin. It was such an old-fashioned sort of look, the way only old women those days wore scarves, or the way you'd see in old movies from the forties or fifties. It was so at odds with her previous demeanour – the woman who only a few weeks ago had been sitting sunbathing in her front garden – that I wasn't completely sure it was her at first. She stopped though just as she drew alongside our car. Our green Volkswagen Beetle was pretty distinctive. She glanced first into the front then, seeing no-one there, looked at me in the back. There was a moment when our eyes locked and I swear, even at eight years old, I felt I could read the depths of pain in her eyes. I was so ashamed, I put my head down and squeezed my eyes shut and thankfully, when I opened them again, she was gone. I wondered if I'd dreamt it. I hoped I had.

I think about that brief encounter a lot and how my shame must have been interpreted as hatred. And I'm so sorry for it.

Time moved on. The Tobins left and another family moved into their house, which took on a much smarter appearance. It was freshly painted, the rickety fence was fixed, the weeds were pulled from the garden, and you'd never see the curtains still pulled at lunchtime. I avoided walking past it as much as I could, but when I had to I was always filled with a profound sadness. Our street football games resumed but they were missing a certain Georgie Best flair with Conor Tobin gone. Life in our house resumed a new kind of normal. Routines returned, but I always felt we became a bit like ghosts, shrunken into ourselves, each of us enveloped in our own shroud of grief, existing in a kind of joyless afterlife. Not exactly hell. Purgatory, maybe.

I thought about Joy Tobin almost constantly. More, even, than I thought about Declan. I'd lie in bed at night wishing I could somehow telecommunicate an exoneration to her, let her know it wasn't her fault. I had chickened out of telling her that day when she passed the car, but I figured writing to her would be easier. I had no way of knowing her address of course, and no-one to ask without raising suspicion.

One day, probably a couple of years after the accident, I watched as my mother sat down at our kitchen table, a letter in her hand. I couldn't see what the letter was, but I knew from her demeanour that it was something significant. I was making myself a sandwich at the time, and she told me to bring it into the sitting room to eat it. This was enough to pique my interest as she never let us eat in 'the good room', as she called it. I went into the hallway and peered in through the doorframe crack. She turned the letter over in her hands several times. I could see her hands were shaking. Eventually she opened it, but instead of reading it she ripped it with some violence into little pieces and stuffed them back into the envelope, which she then resealed with Sellotape from the kitchen drawer. She walked quickly past me in the hallway, grabbed her coat from the hook by the door and left the house without as much as a word to me. Of course, I couldn't know what the letter contained or who it was from, but I had a strong feeling, based on my mother's reaction, that it was related to Declan, and therefore to Mrs Tobin.

I couldn't sleep that night thinking about what might have been in the letter. I imagined Mrs Tobin, writing feverishly in some far-flung place, desperately seeking forgiveness, unaware that she had nothing to seek forgiveness for. I got up, sat at the little desk in my room and wrote a letter of my own to my mother. I told her all about Gary Prendergast and the stupid stone, how everything was my fault and not Mrs Tobin's. I even told her about going into her house that day and how nice she'd been and how she'd taken a real shine to Declan. I thought this was important to add. As though if my mother knew this detail, she'd understand that Mrs Tobin never meant any harm towards him.

But things often appear different in the clinical light of day, and when I woke up the next morning I lost my nerve. The thought of her hating me was too much. Instead, I placed the letter between the pages of an Enid Blyton book on my shelf, *Five Get into Trouble,* in a kind of passive attempt at confession. I told myself that it could easily be found, although I knew my mother was as unlikely to open and read a children's storybook as I was to look through the pages of one of her recipe books.

I justified it to myself though, likening this quasi-confession to a sinner unloading to a priest, safe in the knowledge that they would only be accountable to God and not to, say, the law or their angry parents.

My parents separated a few years after Declan's death, the stress and grief causing them to turn increasingly away from each other. Once I had finished school I joined my father in Australia to work in his landscaping business. My mother gave me her blessing to go. I think she understood my father might need me more than she did.

She rang me regularly, though. Towards the end of one of our monthly chats, when I had assured her that I was doing well and she had given me all her updates from home, she said, 'I hope you don't mind, but I've finally got round to doing a bit of a clear-out on your old bedroom. I thought Tony and I could use it as office space.'

I assured her that was fine.

'I gave some of your old children's books to St Vincent de Paul, you know, all those Enid Blyton ones. I thought other kids might get some enjoyment from them.'

I laughed and told her that was fine with me too. I hadn't read them in years.

And then she said, seemingly apropos of nothing, 'Brendan, be kind to yourself over there, love. You've been through so much already in your life. Just remember you are not responsible for what happened. No-one was.'

After we'd hung up I thought about what she'd said, and at first assumed she had been referring to her and Dad's separation;

that she was worried I'd take it upon myself to somehow try to heal my father. I dismissed it as nothing more than maternal concern and forgot about it. But later that night the conversation replayed in my head, and the specific reference to Enid Blyton struck me as strange. And that's when I remembered. I hadn't thought about that confessional letter in years. But I knew then, beyond doubt, that my mother had read it, and was absolving me.

And I understood too that when she said no-one was to blame, she had also absolved Mrs Tobin.

I would never consider myself to be spiritual. I don't believe in an afterlife or anything like that, but I swear I can still see Declan on occasion. He comes to me sometimes. And it's not painful anymore. It's always a comfort to see those straight dark brows above his curious mossy-green eyes. And the times he chooses to come are usually those when I feel down or unsure of myself. And he's there, urging me to see something I haven't seen before, like the scientist or professor I'm sure he would have become.

And although it sounds crazy, I hope he's able to reach out to Mrs Tobin too, help her see the truth. Banish the other ghosts I know she must live with. If there was anyone capable of doing that, it would be my little brother, Declan.

JOY

I'm in a dark room. I can feel hands on me and for a moment I panic that they belong to Mr Reilly and I'm in the cellar out the back of the pub. But I realise the hands are gentle, and the voices I can hear around me are soft and non-threatening.

And then the voices all melt into one. And it's a woman and she's reading to me. She sounds like Miss Lally, and I allow the words to wash over me, lose myself in the musical cadence of her voice.

But suddenly I'm yanked back to that day. I don't want to be here, I struggle to get away, but I'm here and I'm driving the car and it's raining and the baby's crying. I'm sitting in the car, and I can't breathe now, and I don't want to see those little yellow-raincoated figures but here they come anyway. And they walk past the window and the little one waves at me.

But this time I remember to wave back because I know it's important. He stops outside my window and looks in. And for a moment we lock eyes, and he stretches out his hand, urging *me to look. And I do. He holds a milky-white stone there and he smiles at me.*

And now I'm out of the car and back at King Kong's Belly, the dip in the field behind my house. And I run exhilarated, free, drunk on the momentum, my eyes wide shut, until the dip, and this time I almost make it back up the other side without tripping.

Dejected, I sit down, and when I look up, there he is again, the little green-eyed boy. He is holding out his hand to me. I grasp it and he helps me up beside him. And we smile at each other.

FRANCES

When Livvy was twelve and displaying some of the mood swings Frances recognised as precursors to puberty, she had, in a mild state of panic, gone to her local bookshop to try to get some help.

Lauren, the lucky owner of three teenage girls herself, had scoffed and said, 'Girl, there's nothing that can help you now except a doctor who's willing to write you prescriptions for Valium.' Lauren was also the owner of a doctor husband and happily availed of some of the perks that offered. However, preferring to take a more virtuous route and feeling optimistic that she could successfully and soberly navigate the choppy waters to come, Frances picked up an authoritative-looking book with the pleasingly aspirational title, *Parenting Teens: How to Build a Positive, Respectful Yet Fun Relationship.*

Like any self-help book she'd tried before, she found it hard going. Hated the self-conscious metaphors and obvious, patronising advice. Despite her dismissal of it, one chapter, 'Leaving the Door Ajar', comes back to her now as she sits in the kitchen bathed in late-afternoon sun, a few hours after the removal of her mother's feeding tube. The sun is showing up some obvious marks on the large window over the Belfast sink. She might clean them tomorrow. Livvy is sitting opposite her, eating a sandwich. Unusually – as has been the case in recent weeks – she hasn't taken it to her room to eat.

She looks at her daughter, chewing deliberately, gaze fixed on some spot in mid-air, as though trying to solve a problem that hovers before her, one only she can see. She's always eaten like this, with care, even as a toddler, and it fills Frances now with a great rush of love, so much so that she has to take a deep breath and the exhalation sounds like a sigh.

Livvy's eyes move from the unseen problem to her mother. 'Are you okay, Mum?'

The book had dribbled on about metaphorical (and sometimes non-metaphorical) doors being slammed regularly in parents' metaphorical (and sometimes non-) faces, but occasionally, if the parent was open enough – had left their door ajar, if you will – their teenager might willingly enter. (Or was it the other way around? That the teenager beckoned the parent in through *their* open door?) It irritated Frances at the time, this notion of being in a constant state of hypervigilance so as not to miss an opportunity to bond with your teen. But whatever, she senses a crack in the door now.

'I'm fine, darling. Just, you know . . .'

Livvy nods. 'How was it today, at the hospital?'

'It wasn't as bad as I expected. In fact, it was kind of nice.'

Frances is surprised to realise the truth of this. After Sinead had read Brendan's story, a sense of peace descended on them all. No-one spoke. They may have wept a little, for the two little boys, for themselves. But mostly for Joy. And she liked it, sitting there with them all. Could have stayed all day. For the first time in her life, her mother's presence didn't make her feel like running away, leaving the room. She thinks of all the Saturday mornings she has spent in recent years, helping her mother clean or running errands for her. None of it done out of any sense of affection, but out of duty. And now, strangely, she feels a great rush of love for her little shrunken mother lying in a hospital bed. She realises she wants to go back there now. Spend as much time as she can with her.

She wants to sit next to her, take her hand. Lean forward and whisper in her ear. She wants to tell her that she understands. Understands that motherhood does not come easily to every woman. Understands how you can feel robbed when you're a wife and a mother, even when you love your family. How your world contracts, like you're being suffocated in shrink-wrap. How first your name and then your identity become tied to others. You're referenced in a list of contacts as so-and-so's wife, so-and-so's mother. How you can feel resentful. And how those resentments can look an awful lot like lack of love. How you can look forward to the release of alcohol because it's in those brief hazy anaesthetised moments that you still recognise yourself. She wants to whisper, *Thank you, I know it was hard. I understand.*

Her phone buzzes on the countertop. She picks it up, makes a face and types something, then puts it down again.

'What was that?' Livvy asks.

'Just Donna,' Frances says, 'wondering why I changed the name of the WhatsApp group from Swim Moms to Swim Bots.'

Livvy's eyes are wide with delight. 'Oh my God, you did not! What did you say?'

'I said, "Woops, my bad", then left the group.'

Livvy laughs. 'Love you, Mum.'

'Love you too.'

'Can I go with you tomorrow to the hospital? I thought I could read to her. Sinead left a book of poetry she found there.'

Frances feels almost about to burst with wonder at her lovely girl. She can hardly bear it. She does not want her to grow any older. To become jaded with life, to have her heart die in little increments, in the way it does as we become adults. She hates the idea of all the future careless boys, untrue friends, grief, loss, failure, infidelity, illness, old age. She is angry at the knowledge of her girl's certain death. She wants to cocoon her, preserve her just as she is, because really there is no better age. Her daughter will never be as optimistic, as idealistic, as true to herself as she is at this moment.

'Let's go there now,' she says.

CONOR

That same day, after the removal of their mother's feeding tube, Conor walks and finds a bench around the back of the hospital. It faces away from the building, out towards the tree-lined riverbank. He wonders how many people have sat here before him, the view a brief respite from whatever they've left inside. There is a plaque on it that reads:

In memory of Dr James Frederick Underwood. 1966–2015. May you live all the days of your life.

He sits down, closes his eyes and enjoys the sensation of the sun on his face. It's one of those perfect early autumn days, not a breath of wind. It's always been his favourite time of year. There's a stillness and a melancholy he appreciates, a pause between summer's brashness and winter's decay. He imagines himself lying on his back in the little garden of the house back in Ireland, just as Brendan described. A happy family scene. A sunbathing mother, naked kids in the paddling pool. 7up and cereal boxes. So normal. Except everything is tainted with what has happened since. Suddenly the warmth evaporates, and he opens his eyes expecting to see a cloud. Frances is standing over him.

'Jesus, you're like a ninja.'

'You looked so peaceful, I was debating whether or not to disturb you.'

'You're back.'

'Yeah, I brought Livvy. She's with Mum now, reading some poetry.'

'She's a good girl.'

'I know, I'm so lucky.'

'Aren't you going to sit?' He pats the space beside him.

'"May you live all the days of your life."' Frances reads the plaque on the bench before sitting down. 'Well, that's easier said than done.'

'Yeah, it's the kind of line you can only posthumously attribute to someone. He was probably a cantankerous prick when he was alive.'

'Promise me no inspirational epitaphs when I die.'

'You know you'll outlive us all, Franny.'

'No doubt. And I'll be left sorting all your shit out. Dealing with your paternity claims and Sinead's drug debts. Fuckers.'

He laughs and reaches over to take her hand. He can feel her tense up at first, then relax.

'Conor, there's been something on my mind. About the day of the accident. Since hearing Brendan's account, I've had this horrible feeling of dread and guilt. You know when he talked about being impatient with Declan and how he wished he'd behaved differently?'

'Yeah?'

'I was just remembering why we were so late coming out of school that day and I think, I'm sure, that it was my fault. I remember making such a fuss about going back to my classroom to get something I'd forgotten. Do you remember? And that delayed us. And I keep on thinking if only I hadn't been so uptight about everything, if only we'd just left on time, it could all have been avoided. We'd have left before the Smith boys and just driven home and well . . . we probably wouldn't be where we are now.'

Conor does remember. Frances had left her new lunch box behind the day of the accident. She'd loved that tin box covered in pictures of ponies. Conor remembers she had been begging their parents for months to get a horse and that lunch box was as close as she ever got. She realised it wasn't in her bag just before they walked out the school entrance. They went back to get it and she became almost hysterical when they discovered the classroom had been locked. It took him several minutes to convince her to leave. He thinks of her, mortified at the prospect of bringing her lunch the next day in a plastic bag.

But he says, 'I do remember that, Franny, but it was a different day. I'm sure of it. The reason we were late leaving was because of me. I stayed to talk to Mr Ward about the football team he was putting together from our year. I remember being annoyed and arguing with him because he made me fullback and I thought I should have been a striker. You know me, always seeking glory.'

'Oh. I was sure . . .' she trails off.

'It was just an accident, Franny. We were all just kids, doing normal kid stuff. No-one's to blame. Not me or you or Sinead or Brendan. Not even Mum.'

'Yes, you're right. But sorry anyway for being such a pain about it. I remember how patient you were. How kind.'

They sit for a while longer in silence, till the sun disappears behind the elm trees on the far bank of the river. Conor steals a glance at his sister's profile. She looks deep in thought, her brows knitted together as though trying to solve a problem. She looks so like their mother. Even the pattern of freckles on her nose is the same.

She turns to him and asks, 'What the hell are you looking at?'

'I don't know, but whatever the hell it is, it's looking back at me.'

She smiles, her teeth white and even just like Joy's, and punches his shoulder lightly. She nods towards the building. 'Shall we?' Then they stand, link arms and walk back into the hospital.

SINEAD

Her mother is getting smaller. She was never what you'd call robust, but still, it's like a layer of her has gone missing since they removed the feeding tube a week ago. Whatever it was that lay between epidermis and bone has disappeared so that her skin now rests in an unnerving way on the skeleton underneath.

Sinead thinks of herself as a teenager, longing to disappear. How happy she'd be if only she was thin.

Her mother's breathing changes to a pant, but just as Sinead wonders if she needs to call someone it slows again and resumes a regular pattern. Her lips are cracked and look painful. Sinead is unsure if she should wet them or not. She remembers the excruciating dehydration from the yellow pills and takes a tissue and water bottle from her bag. She wets the tissue and holds it against her mother's white mouth. There is no grateful pressing together of her lips and Sinead is relieved. A drop slides down her mother's chin and she dabs it away.

The heart rate monitor beeps on. It seems to Sinead that it has quickened its pace in the last couple of days, as though hastening towards death. Brendan caused her own heart to beat a little faster last night. He had asked her not to go back to Dublin. She said she would think about it, and she did, in a removed kind of a way. She imagined staying in New Zealand, moving in together, maybe working alongside him in his landscaping business by day, writing at night. There was merit in a life like that. She imagined being closer to her siblings. Funny how even a few months ago that idea would have been anathema to her. But now there was appeal in that too.

While she had been thinking about Brendan's proposal, she received an email from Maggie. She hadn't heard from her for two weeks, since her phone call confessing to the plagiarism. On that call Maggie had told Sinead she was done with her, then had hung up angrily. Sinead had tried to call her back, apologise, maybe come up with a plan to pay back the advance in instalments. But Maggie had ignored her. Sinead then sent the short story about Declan, told Maggie that she was writing more, would she be open to the idea of a collection? Because her story about Declan has sparked a love for writing again. She has already written another one. She had become so obsessed with the idea of a novel, so hung up on churning out another four-hundred-page masterpiece, so stressed about intricate plots and a cast of characters, that she had forgotten the simple satisfaction she used to get from a short story. Just shining a light on one moment or incident and leaving so much inferred.

The way you could get to the heart of things so quickly. The careful crafting of it, the succinct language, the immediacy.

But best of all, the way you could just *finish* it.

She'd opened Maggie's new email with trepidation.

Sinead,

I hope I won't come to regret this, but ok. A short story collection it is. I've somehow managed to smooth things over with the rest of the team. Pretend that short stories were always in the plan.

But Sinead, you can't let me down again. The book will be published next summer whether the stories are good or not. So it's in your best interest to make them as brilliant as you can. I need ten at least. And I need them November at the latest.

Maggie

She's been so lucky to have Maggie.

Rather than strangulating her, she finds the idea now of the hard deadline almost exhilarating. After she replied to Maggie, promising to stick to the agreement, she stayed up half the night, the bones of another story already taking shape in her head.

And this morning she had told Brendan she couldn't stay. That she will go back to Dublin. That enticing as staying here, escaping, with him would be, she has to grow up, return to her life there, take ownership of it. And she wants – needs, even – to be there. Because it's where she feels most herself. She needs to pick her way across Trinity's cobblestones on a crisp morning, steaming takeout coffee in her hand, soaking up the energy from the students, and then out to D'Olier Street to browse in her favourite bookshop. She needs to meander up Grafton Street, stopping awhile to listen to the buskers like a tourist; she'll never tire of it. She needs to wander the side streets off Grafton Street, stop in to her favourite little shop on Drury Street, full of curiosities that she picks up and puts down but rarely buys. Or eat a sandwich sitting on the grass in St Stephen's Green on a summer's day. She thinks of how the spring evenings in Dublin will be starting to lengthen now, so that soon she'll be able to wander home along the canal in the lingering twilight, the gloaming – a word that only made sense to her when she first experienced an Irish summer's dusk – maybe stopping awhile on a bench beside Patrick Kavanagh, and feeling momentarily in awe at the little city and its literary heritage, which she has made her home.

She thinks of her rented flat on Stamer Street just off the South Circular Road, with its red door and entrance hall shared with Seamus who owns the house and lives in the top half and sometimes leaves her grumpy notes admonishing her lack of attention to the cleanliness of that shared space. The thought of it fills her with longing.

Brendan had been disappointed, and she had toyed with the idea of asking him to come back with her to Ireland, but she knew that even though he might, he shouldn't. New Zealand had been healing for him in a way that it hadn't been for her mother. Joy had shrivelled here, become parched, whereas Brendan had weathered. He'd become tanned and strong and revelled in his outdoor life. He didn't drink but spent his weekends mountain biking in the forest or hunting or fishing with his friends. Bringing him back to Ireland now would be like bringing back a native puka tree and expecting it to thrive in the wet and the frost. She can't imagine him being with her circle of Irish friends, whom she loves dearly but has to admit are cynical and maybe a bit jaded. He would be a fish out of water. The single lifestyle she and her Irish friends share, which revolves around art-house films, theatre and comedy clubs, bars and Sunday-morning liquid brunches, may be wearing a bit thin now they are all approaching middle age. But that is her life, for better or worse, and she can't imagine a different one.

She let Brendan down about staying but hopes she has given him a kind of absolution from his brother's death. Like the gift he gave them too. Last night she told him about Joy's mother's letter that she found in the train case. How she thinks her mother would have ended up here regardless of what happened to Declan, how it was really to do with her mother's cruelty, her father's death, her stepfather's abuse. How maybe all the roads led to the same place anyway. How maybe it was even written from before she was born with whatever darkness lay in her father's head. Brendan was unsure. From experience, he mused, surely the pain that was most intolerable was the pain you believed was of your own doing. How the other things were beyond her control.

Sinead thought then about all the hangovers she had endured, the self-loathing after a big weekend, the come-downs that made you swear you'd never indulge again, or worse, caused you to pick up a bottle or do a line just to delay the inevitable. She thought of the little yellow pills and their raging side-effects. She thought about her mother unable to seize the opportunity of a fresh start in New Zealand the way Brendan had, and she said, 'She might have been able to cope with anything, but it was the booze that did her in. In the end.'

He'd looked at her gratefully, and she felt the need to confess something to him then. 'Brendan, I hope you won't mind, but I took a bit of poetic licence with your story that I read to Joy.'

'Well, I didn't expect a verbatim retelling.'

'No, I mean, I added a whole incident. That you wrote a confessional letter to your mother, which she found years later. That she rang you and told you that no-one was to blame for the accident. And how you took it to mean she had absolved Joy. I thought it was important for her to hear that. Important for Conor and Franny too.'

He furrowed his brow, and she was anxious that she'd made a big mistake, angered him. But then he said, 'I think that was a brilliant idea. I just wish it was true.' And he cried.

Her mother's breathing quickens again briefly, then resumes its normal pace. Death is close; she can feel it bearing down. The enormity of it strikes her. Her mother will be gone soon, along with every memory and thought and experience. Her mother, whose feelings and pain were so large they could suffocate you sometimes. Her whole world is in her own head and so soon that whole world will die too.

A notification comes through on her phone. There's a message from Tara, the publicist.

Maggie told me about your little faux pas! We all make mistakes, Sinead! Anyway, I've been thinking. What about penning a Mea Culpa piece about the whole episode to drum up some publicity for the story collection? People adore that sort of thing! Love hearing about other people's fallibilities! I think it would make a rather brilliant essay. Tara x

And Sinead smiles to herself and thinks how she is going to enjoy being back in the game.

JOY

I am sitting on the side of King Kong's Belly. Everything is bathed in a clear, bright glow. The little green-eyed boy is talking to me about rocks and geology and how the earth was formed. And I am so mesmerised by him that it takes me some time to realise that there are other people here too. Daddy, his arm around me, his face impossibly young. And beside him Conor, Frances and Sinead. They look careworn, older than Daddy. And I experience such a swell of tenderness for them I feel my heart quicken and my breathing follow.

Then Daddy stands up and reaches out his hand and says, We need to go now, my Pride and Joy. And I take his hand and walk with him. After a moment I stop and turn back to look at the children one last time. They are not looking back at us as we leave but talking animatedly amongst themselves.

Daddy says, Are you all right to keep going, Joy? And I say, I am, Daddy, I am.

FRANCES

They are kneeling side by side on the lawn. The soil is hard and dry after weeks without rain, so it takes some effort to pull the weeds from the edge of their long driveway. Frances has discarded the thick gardening gloves she wore earlier that hindered her progress and now her hands are starting to redden with the strain of removing some of the more deep-rooted interlopers. The dirt is impacted tightly under her fingernails, and she thinks how she will relish scraping it out later with a sharp file.

She steals a glance at Harry. She notices how there are some new greys appearing at his hairline, and for the first time, some peppered through his beard. How handsome he was. Still is. She remembers seeing him for that first time at a house party a few months after she'd broken up with Andy. He was standing at the kitchen island, surrounded by other women, making them cocktails, making them laugh. She thought he was way out of her league. And yet he went home with her. It still surprises her. She's never been able to shake the sense that she is not good enough. It's clung to her all these years.

The three creases that run from the outer corner of his eyes down across his cheeks are still evident, even though she hasn't seen the wide smile that etched them in the first place in some time. At least not directed at her.

She thinks of Andy's bleached grin, which somehow never travelled as far as his eyes. She squeezes her eyes tight for a moment to get rid of the image.

They had cremated her mother a few days ago. It was a simple, secular service, with just a handful of people, and presided over by a celebrant recommended by the funeral director. Not knowing Joy from Adam, he spoke of her in hushed, reverential tones that would have made her turn in her grave, had she been put in one.

Livvy had read a rather startling poem by Emily Dickinson, 'I felt a Funeral, in my Brain'. She and Sinead had chosen it together. It certainly wouldn't have been Frances's first choice. She had suggested that nice poem from *Four Weddings and a Funeral*, that 'Stop all the Clocks' one. Sinead had laughed and said she was pretty sure that referred to the death of Auden's male lover, and Livvy had said that her gran had an inexplicable aversion to Hugh Grant. His films were embargoed on their movie nights. So Frances had to defer to the more literary members of the family. Livvy read the poem starkly, with long pauses, and Frances found it a bit melodramatic, both in theme and in tone. She glanced at Harry at one stage, who looked as though he was trying to stifle a giggle. Sue Preston, their old neighbour, also looked taken aback when Livvy read the final bleak verse and trailed off as though in mid-sentence, taking a long, lingering look around the room as she did so.

Once the coffin had withdrawn back through the curtains and they had thanked the small number of attendees, Frances was happy to leave things there, but Sinead thought it fitting that they have some sort of a get-together back at Frances's house. 'You *Pakehas* don't know how to do death properly,' she said, as though she considered herself to be a different race entirely. Frances was afraid she would just use the occasion as a chance to get wasted, but to her surprise Sinead drank nothing stronger than tea. Brendan was good for her. She recognised, regretfully, the tender and attentive way he looked at her sister. Harry would never look at her that way again.

Conor had been quiet, willing to let his sisters take the lead with the funeral arrangements and reluctant to make any contribution at the service. He seemed less confident to Frances now than the older sibling who'd always overshadowed her; slightly deferential and unsure. He came into the kitchen while she was putting a platter together and sat at the bench nursing an obscenely expensive whiskey that Harry had received as a corporate gift and insisted on opening.

'You don't have to drink that, you know. I can pour it down the sink and not tell Harry.'

Conor laughed and said, 'He'd never forgive me.'

'Yes, I know how that feels.'

He walked over to her then, gave her a hug and said, 'He'll come round, Franny. He loves you still.'

Frances allowed herself to be hugged by him, said into his shoulder, 'Sometimes that's not enough. Anyway, you've been very quiet. Is everything okay?'

He let go. 'It's weird, but I actually feel this enormous sense of relief. Gratitude, even. I know that sounds crazy.'

'It's okay to feel like that, Conor. We've been existing on a cliff edge our entire lives. Maybe we're all a bit at peace now.'

'It's more than Mum being gone though. It's hard to explain without sounding deranged.'

'Try. It's not like we're not used to crazy in this family.'

'It's just that I feel *thankful* for what I've gone through recently. Thankful for the breakdown. For falling off that edge. Because it's as though before all this happened, I wasn't truly feeling stuff. Or feeling the right feelings but about the wrong stuff. I was comfortably numb. To quote the song. I feel a bit more alive now. Does that make sense?'

As Frances had looked at him, she thought that he was wearing his new vulnerability well, and it struck her that maybe he had gained more than he had lost. She wondered how to articulate this but didn't get a chance. Without warning, the door from the sitting room, where everyone was gathered, burst open. A dishevelled and flushed-looking Sinead lurched through them, pushed aside her siblings, and proceeded to produce copious amounts of vomit into Frances's sparkling sink.

They both watched on in disbelief, Frances feeling a sense of dread forming in her stomach. Eventually her sister lifted her head, wiped her mouth on her sleeve and said, to herself more than anyone, 'Sinead Tóibín, you fucking eejit.'

Frances is brought back to the present by a plane flying overhead. She wonders if it's Conor, who is due to take off for Auckland. Sinead is also in the skies, probably somewhere over Western Australia by now. She misses them both already. She feels a lump form in her throat thinking of her little sister heading back to the other side of the world. At least she's not entirely on her own this time. Frances smiles at the thought.

Harry kneels back and lets out a groan. He wipes some sweat from his forehead and as he does so, manages to smudge some dirt above his eye. Frances instinctively raises her hand to wipe it away, but Harry stops it before it reaches his face.

'Don't,' he says.

Livvy is sitting nearby on one of the Cape Cod chairs on the front veranda, reading a book. Donne is lying under her feet, and both are trying to soak up the last few slanted rays of the autumn sun. She glances intermittently at her parents, as though keeping guard. She has been watchful of late, as though afraid they will hurt each other if she is not around.

Wary of alarming her, Frances holds back the tears that are threatening and says instead, 'Will we ever get past this, Harry? Start over?'

He pushes the trowel into the earth and says, looking down at it, 'You don't get to start these things over, Franny. But I'm here and I'm staying. Can't that be enough for you? For now?'

She looks at him, then her daughter, who is now stroking the old dog's head. The edge of the lawn is looking better than it has done in weeks. The benign weather means there is washing drying on the line that she will fold and put away later. She will do that for her family. And this evening she will sit down at the table with them and eat the steak – currently marinating in the fridge – that Harry will cook on the barbecue. He will do that for his family too.

The *for now* gives her hope. She thinks of her mother, who wouldn't allow herself any hope, any happiness, felt she was undeserving of it.

And she says, 'Yes. I think it is.'

CONOR

He hasn't been back to his apartment since the sleeping pills. He opened the door with trepidation, worried he'd find the remnants of his misadventure; a toppled whiskey glass on the floor, a bottle of pills stuck in the corner of the couch. Maybe even the television still broadcasting a ghostly game of cricket to the empty room. But, of course, Sharon the cleaner has erased his embarrassment and the place looks as sterile as ever.

The apartment has never felt like a home to him. In truth, no place ever has. This morning he told Frances and Sinead that he would like to buy them out of their share of Joy's house in Tauranga. Partly – though he didn't say as much – it is to expedite the transfer of funds to Sinead. But partly it is because he wants to have somewhere that feels more real and grounded than a flashy penthouse in an ever-changing, inner-city landscape. Sinead laughed and said it didn't get more real than a three-bedroom, one-bathroom, weatherboard, ex-state bungalow in a Tauranga cul-de-sac with Sue Preston as your neighbour. Frances said she knew a great interior designer who could work wonders on the place. But Conor thinks he might leave it as is for a while. He told them he thought he could do with spending some time with the ghosts of their childhood.

'Ah,' Sinead had said. 'I think Proust talked about that. How we reach a stage in life where our ghosts can enrich us.'

'Well, that Proust guy sounds like he knows what he's talking about. Yes, I like the idea of that.'

After he relayed his plan and Sinead had left the room, Frances told him to pay her share of the value of the place to Sinead as well, but not to let her know what they had done. She'd never question the amount, wouldn't have the vaguest clue as to what it was worth anyway.

'But what about your inheritance, Franny? I know it's not much, but after all, you're the one who picked up the flack while we were MIA. And helped Mum out financially, too.'

Frances just shrugged and said, 'That's all good. Anyway, I got Donne.'

As if on cue, the old labrador, who had been asleep in his basket by the bench, raised his meaty head from his front paws and gave his new mistress a doleful look. Sinead came back into the room and Conor and Frances smiled conspiratorially at each other.

And a kernel of an idea has been forming the last few nights, reigniting something in him again. Doing for television what TheOneForAll did for charity. There were too many choices now when it came to streaming services. Everything was too fragmented. What about amalgamating all those services, Neon and Netflix, Amazon and Apple TV, into one, easy-to-manage platform? And if it didn't work out, there was always Law.

He opens the blinds and looks down on the street below; it is starting to rain. He walks over to the sliding door, pulls it back and steps out onto the balcony, sidestepping the expensive and rusting Weber grill that has languished out there, unused. It is early on a Saturday evening and the tempo outside is just starting to quicken. He can hear the thump of music and the pulse of conversation leaking from nearby bars, the caterwaul of a police siren in another suburb.

A group of giddy young women trip past on heels, pulling their jackets over their blow-dried hair as they feel the first drops begin to fall. One of them stops and throws her head back to look at the sky as though trying to gauge the forecast. She spots him looking down and waves. He waves back, embarrassed, and she runs, laughing, to catch up with her friends. She says something to them, and they all turn to have a look. He takes a step back out of sight.

Closing his eyes, he inhales the earthy smell of rain baptising dry city streets. He lifts his face to the sky, enjoying the sensation of the water even as it pools behind his neck and slips down the back of his sweatshirt. Rain always puts him in mind of Ireland. It's as though all his memories of the place are shrouded by an oppressive low-hanging sky casting a grey filter – the opposite to the kind people put on their holiday snaps to induce envy. Maybe it's time he went back to Ireland and made some new memories. Better ones. He'll have the perfect excuse to visit soon.

He stands there, even as the rain becomes a deluge, and his clothes cling to his skin. Along with the water he feels an easiness drench him. He accepts the rain and his wet clothes. He accepts what is to come and what has been.

He can't say he is excited exactly for the future – perhaps that's a luxury only the young have – but it is enough that there *will be* a future. It does not need to be a remarkable one. It is remarkable enough that he is here.

And it is good enough that right here in this moment, on this rain-soaked balcony, he can say that although he is not ecstatic to be alive, at least he is thankful not to be dead. It is enough.

SINEAD

The plane emerges from the grey mist so that the clouds form a pillowy white blanket underneath, and she can no longer see New Zealand.

She settles back in her seat, willing the seatbelt sign to go off. It feels uncomfortable across her stomach, and she wonders if the discomfort is just a psychological trick. Some mysterious evolutionary mechanism that induces care and protectiveness for what lies within. Certainly, there is no bulge there yet, but she runs her hand over and realises she is looking forward to her belly getting rounded. The thought makes her smile.

She thinks of the large suitcase below in the hold, a far cry from the little backpack she arrived with. Frances had dragged out a large box from the attic, filled with expensive baby clothes, all folded neatly and beautifully preserved between sheets of delicate tissue paper.

'Why did you keep them all, Franny?' Sinead asked, then held her sister as she wept and said she wasn't quite sure.

She hasn't told Brendan yet. She thought to keep it from him, knowing that he will insist on following her. Worried about transplanting him somewhere he wouldn't thrive. But Frances said to her, 'You've got to relinquish control to him, let him make his own choices.' Which seemed a very un-Frances-like sentiment and surprised them both when she said it.

So, she will tell him. Soon. But for now she just wants to get used to the idea, so that when he does come, she will be ready.

She reaches under the seat in front and carefully pulls out her backpack. She places it on the empty seat beside her. When she'd boarded, one of the crew, an expensive-smelling man her own age, had said, as though she were a halfwit, 'Ma'am, you are required to place your bag in the overhead locker.'

She was prepared to overlook the condescending tone but could not forgive the *Ma'am*.

She beckoned to him to lean down, showed him the wooden box contained within. '*Sir*, it's all that remains of my dear Mammy. I'm taking her back to the old country to put her at rest. Please let me keep her close.' Frances and Conor would have been mortified at the brogue.

He recoiled slightly and said, 'Well, just make sure it's – I beg your pardon, *she's* – stowed properly for take-off and landing.' Then he wafted away on a cloud of Tom Ford.

Conor and Frances had argued over what to do with the ashes. Conor suggested that as the most settled of them all, Frances should perhaps keep them at her house, maybe make a little shrine in the ample back garden. Frances, horrified, said she couldn't bear the idea of her mother's permanent presence.

It would be like she was being watched over and criticised *all the time*. Frances suggested Conor keep them. After all, he'd soon be living back in their mother's old house. Conor countered that Joy had mostly been miserable there, so that would be like subjecting her to an eternity of unhappiness.

Then he'd asked, 'By the way, does anyone see little signs of her? You know, the way people talk about seeing birds come up to the window and they take it as a sign, like an embodiment of their loved one's spirit?'

Frances said, 'Now that you mention it, I did see a malevolent-looking hawk circling the garden the other day.'

'Jesus, Franny,' Conor said, shaking his head.

Sinead, who had stayed quiet during their argument, thought about the photographs stowed in the little train case under the bed, her grandfather's kind face, Joy sitting proudly on his knee, the inscription on the book – *My Pride and Joy* – and said, 'I think I know what to do with her.' She knows he was from somewhere in Mayo. It'll be easy enough to find out exactly where. And to find a suitable place there to scatter her ashes.

Sinead feels oddly at peace. She'd expected a torrent of suppressed grief after the funeral. But she realises that the yearning she has carried her whole life for her mother is diminished now with her death. She can finally let go.

She leans over to look out the small oval window. The sun explodes like flames off the wing of this giant steel bird, a phoenix heading for rebirth. She thinks of her mother's cremation and Livvy's recital. The line of another one of Emily

Dickinson's poems comes into her head about hope being the thing with feathers.

The clouds have cleared and below is the vast expanse of the Pacific Ocean. It is a homogenous grey, churned through with frothy white patches. She is not defeated by its size, though. She feels larger than she did on the journey here. And soon she will be larger, literally, and she welcomes that. The ocean is far enough below to look if not exactly benign, then at least not menacing. Still, she squeezes her eyes shut and says a little prayer – to no deity in particular – for the plane to carry on defying gravity and stay safely in the air. She has much to live for.

ACKNOWLEDGEMENTS

I am indebted to the book *Inside Coma* by Pierre Morin and Gary Reiss (Praeger, 2010) which inspired the idea of portraying Joy as experiencing an altered state of consciousness.

Thank you to my very first reader, my sister Niamh. Your completely biased praise of the first twenty pages gave me the confidence to continue. Thank you to my brother Tom, my second reader, for encouraging me to write in the first place. Thank you to my brother Brian for the entertaining phone calls that distract me from writing. And thank you to my sister-in-law Yvonne, for your support and championing of this book.

Thanks to my dad, Kevin Tiernan, for always making me believe I could be anything I wanted to be.

Thanks to my surrogate NZ parents, Jill and Terry, for everything you do for us.

Thank you Nuala O'Connor, for taking the time to read an early draft and for the very kind words of encouragement and invaluable practical advice.

Thank you Emma Walsh at The Literary Professionals. Your assessment of my manuscript and your encouragement and advice are what gave me the confidence to submit to publishers.

Thank you Patricia Bell for your copyediting. You've added so much polish. Thank you Cathal O'Gara for both stunning cover designs. And thank you to Aonghus Meaney for the proofread.

Thank you Kate Stephenson, Ciara Doorley and Sherise Hobbs for believing in this book. You've changed my life. And thanks also for your editorial insights and instincts and for being generally lovely people. Four heads are better than one. You've made the book so much better.

Thanks to everyone at Hachette NZ, Hachette Ireland and Headline UK for all the work that goes into getting a novel out into the world: Mel Winder, Emma Dorph, Suzy Maddox, Tania Mackenzie-Cooke, Sacha Beguely, Sam Barge, Sharon Galey, Chrysoula Aiello, Cyanne Alwanger, Elaine Egan, Ruth Shern, Joanna Smyth, Breda Purdue, to name but a few. Book people are the best people.

To Molly, Oscar and Jack. I love you. And sorry I've been a bit distracted lately.

Thank you, Matt, for your endless love and support and for never even once suggesting I get a proper job.

And finally, thank you, Mum. I know it was hard.

Anne Tiernan was born in Zambia and grew up in Navan, Ireland, a small town about thirty miles from Dublin. She studied English Literature and Psychology at Trinity College, and worked in banking before leaving to travel the world with her Kiwi husband. They arrived in NZ in 2005, and have lived there ever since, raising three children, and settling in Tauranga.